A WAR
AGAINST THE
COWBIRD

A War Against the Cowbird

Cover Design: Tracey Arvidson

Editors: Anna Ottosen, Dr. Bruce Lewis, Michelle Pugh, Stephanie Norton, and
Robin Sartain

Layout: Anna Ottosen

ISBN-13: 978-1522720218

ISBN-10: 1522720219

For my husband, Tommy, and our children, Grace, Benjamin, Jack, and Isabelle. Where they are, I find home.

PART I

Chapter 1

We live more than ten miles from the Pulse, the center of Colony 215. There's life out here, but it's not much. I wake to the sound of my mother scrambling eggs that she probably collected before the sun was up. I know even before I see her that she will be fully dressed in her work uniform, hair parted to the right, and smelling like earth and citrus.

My mattress springs complain as I lean on my elbow and pull back the sheer curtains to see our backyard. The chickens look like sentries on the eastern fence, moving in step to some arrhythmic and eccentric marching orders, jealous of our neighbor who is feeding his own chickens. "I hate you," I tell them before falling back on my pillow.

My right cuff beeps. I hold my arm above my face and close my eyes. "Please be Radius, please be Radius."

I touch a button on the inside of the cuff near my elbow to unlock the message. It's Lex. The words appear one at a time, with the first vowel centered and in red, the New Colony method for rapid-reading six hundred words per minute. I was trained on the Old method for reading, and it takes two repetitions of the message before I understand it: "I think he's going to give it to you today!"

Fully awake, I'm out of bed and dressing quickly. I've been saving a new outfit for my Panel interview, but decide it'd be better for me to wear it today. It's an iridescent dress, studded with gold along the neckline. Of course, I must wear something over it that my mom will approve of—a conservative blouse and skirt.

I open my backpack and throw in a box with the word "Splendor" written across it in shimmering, curly letters. Lex promised she'd do my hair and makeup since I'm still so awkward with it. I press a couple of buttons on my right cuff and respond to Lex: "Meet me before? Need help!"

My stomach burns as I enter the kitchen. "Hey, got to go early today," I tell my mom, who is putting my eggs and some sort of boiled green vegetable on the table. She smiles weakly and sits in the wooden chair next to the one I should be sitting in.

1

"Of course," she says and waves me toward the door. I finger the lunch bag she's placed on the counter. "Ok, so . . ." I shift. I hate myself, or I hate her. I take turns with it. "Then I'm off." My right cuff beeps again and the left one lights up with different announcements and images for the day. My mother smiles and blows a kiss as I let the screen door slam behind me. I go out of my way to kick at a chicken. The Splendor box keeps the beat as it hits my back and rattles with each staccato step.

"Hey! Rebecca!" I walk faster as Grayson pants behind me. I don't have to turn around to know he is dressed sloppily in Old-style clothes and has a puppy dog grin on his face.

"It's Lark," I say, irritated.

"Ok, Lark." He raises his hands in surrender as he jogs to keep up. "I could take your bag," he says, but I shrug him off. "Are you ready for the Panel?"

I give him a fake smile. "Getting there."

"Yeah, well, you've got nothing to worry about. I mean—"

"Who says I'm worried?"

"I just mean that I think you—"

"Ok, look, Gray." I stop on the road and round on him. "Don't need your advice. Nor do I need your help carrying my bag. And I don't need you to walk me to school. It's not like I'm eight years old anymore. Got a plan, ok? I'm getting out of *here*." I motion at the cracked road and swaying pines.

Gray cocks his head and bites his lip to repress the start of a slight smile, but doesn't look away.

"What, Grayson?" I ask, rolling my eyes.

"Nothing," he whispers and kicks at the dirt, the smile becoming broader on his face.

I roll my eyes again and shake my head. Like my mother, Gray will always see me as a little girl from the Old Colony.

"I'm going to be in the Pulse next year. No pep talk necessary," I tell him coolly.

Gray crosses his arms and takes a step back. "Got it," he says as I turn and walk away determinedly, my head up.

I saw the hurt in Grayson's dark eyes, which softens me. I want to turn around and tell him I'm sorry. I understand his loneliness out here in the forgotten part of the Ancillary. But the difference between Gray and me is that I'm adapting and he's not.

I scroll on my cuff and tap my "Current VL" icon. It reads 342. Up fourteen points since yesterday. It's only a matter of time.

2

The ballooners are out. At first, I can see them only as dots on a cloudless sky. But, after twenty minutes at a quick pace I can see their advertisements as they shift in the sun—hundred-foot women, dynamic in their flirtation, float above the Pulse. Lavender eyes on one of the balloons blink and look from side to side— "Splendor Eyes," the ad says. I take a mental note on how the lashes curl. Maybe I should have also opted for the lavender contacts.

Another ballooner has an image of a girl with the wind blowing around her. She's wearing sheer white and is covered in skin jewels, which probably cost more than my mother has made working at Cherish since she moved from the Old Colony. Below her are the words "VL: 1,000, Luminstones."

Far beyond the celestial creatures who undulate alluringly above our colony, zeppelins with high-definition images display the work of demons. Pictures of destruction flash and replays of natural disasters that have ravaged the world over the past century throb above our colony—houses and buildings convulsing under a moving earth, conflagrations, sink holes in slow motion devouring brick homes with white fences, deluges consuming bridges. Below the images flash the letters of scientific updates for certain hotspots that are being monitored or discovered: "Movement in plates in Colony 2220 detected. Seismologists predict significant damage." National Council President Leviathon Drake appears with an intense expression, his eyes as piercing as a dragon's, and issues a preparation warning to Colony 2220. More words flash on the side of the blimp: "130 ft asteroid identified. Misses earth by a near 1,700 miles."

My cuff beeps again. Radius's picture floats across the metal around my inner arm. I tap his symbol on my cuff for his message: "Hi, just thinking about you." Warmth spreads from my chest to my cheeks. I kiss the cuff with his image on it and swing my arms so that I'm practically skipping. Guys like that go for VL-600 girls at least. But Radius is different. He says he *sees* me and soon everyone else will see what he sees too.

About six months ago, Lex, a girl in my tech class, and I were paired for a project. She's very Pulse—wears her hair different colors every day, never wears the same dress twice. From her diamond-studded eyelashes down to the matching, perfectly placed studs on her pedicure, she looks like the type of girl who takes great pleasure in tormenting us Ancillary kids. But Lex is different. She invited me to a party in her friend's apartment—the first time I'd ever been invited anywhere in the Pulse. "No, thanks," I told her. Surely I was being set up for some epic prank.

But Lex just scrunched her dainty nose. "Oh, come on," she said in her ever-cheerful, bubbly voice. "I'm just being friendly. Honest."

Curiosity won.

My first step across the threshold sent a ripple of color that pulsated across the floor.

"I'm going to make you my little darling, Rebecca." She laughed as she tilted my head from the floor to see everything else.

I took in the boldly dressed, beautiful people who made up the kaleidoscope of a Pulse party. My wide eyes made me stand out just as much as my Ancillary clothes—skirt to knees, plain cotton top. I was a moth caught up in a collection of glimmering butterflies.

"Come on," she said as she dragged me into the bathroom. She turned off the black light so she could apply some of her own off-brand Luminstones to my face. They were the kind the younger girls wore, the kind that just stick to your skin instead of being embedded, but you could hardly tell. She pulled my hair back into a tight clasp. I looked in the mirror at how the stones outlined my eyebrows. Lex tossed me a shimmering black dress with part of the torso cut out and some metallic shoes with a curl instead of a heel, which I reluctantly put on.

"You look incredible," she said, stepping back to admire her work.

No one, and I mean *no one* from the New Colony had ever given me a compliment that I could remember, maybe with the exception of teachers remarking on my schoolwork. Her words collided with years of rejection. I looked into the mirror at the awkward Ancillary girl staring back sheepishly and tried to see what was so "incredible" about her. I shook my head and covered my abdomen modestly.

Lex threw her head back for a deep laugh. "Stop it, Rebecca! You're just not used to it. But trust me, the Pulse won't know what hit them."

Lex was my first New Colony friend, and her friendship sparked a very small hope for citizenship. She held my hand up as she escorted me through the group of Pulse citizens, the least of whose VL scores doubled mine. Lex kissed an incurious guy with a shiny cerulean and silver jacket that just brushed the floor.

"Hey, Jamison," she purred.

I took a step back. The guy looked very Pulse too, but there was also something dangerous about him. Lex didn't seem intimidated, though. She petted him like a kitten until he reached inside his pocket without seeming to notice her and removed a small, silver patch. Lex grabbed it in one swift motion.

She smiled, kissed him again quickly and said, "Hey, this is my friend." She motioned back to me as I averted my eyes and tapped my curl heels nervously, leaving ripples on the floor.

The guy reached back into his pocket and handed her another patch. "Thank you," she cooed, and winked at me. Lex shuffled me to the balcony and tossed my ponytail to one side.

"Turn around," she commanded, holding up a patch and starting to undo the packaging.

"Oh, umm. No, it's ok, Lex. I mean, those things are expensive," I protested.

And illegal.

"Stop it," she said playfully, sticking a patch on the back of my neck. "Trust me, Old Colony. First party ought to be done right."

It was cool on the balcony, but whatever laced the patch emanated warmth. Everything Old about me faded, and I became one of the butterflies. No longer was I an awkward foreign girl who lived in the Ancillary. I wasn't a Valueless with a VL of 258 pulsing on my cuff. I, Rebecca Flora, was above Value Level, graceful, strong, sexy. *Captivating*. That night I didn't hate myself. I didn't even hate my mother. I felt boundless. I was bold. I was the beauty shimmering on the ballooners' ads, floating above the city.

Lex leaned over the balcony and howled into the wind. "I'm going to be out there one day, you know." Lex looked longingly to the sky. "Floating above everyone."

I looked at Lex as she struck a pose and batted heavy lashes. "You mean on a ballooner ad? You're pretty enough for it."

Lex blew me a kiss playfully. "And I know the right people to make it happen. It's a matter of time. I pay my dues," she said seriously, "and one day, my time will come."

"Well you're lucky—you were born into the Pulse. You're already at the top."

Lex giggled. "Then there's only one place to go next." She wiped her hand across the sky. "Come on. Patch won't last," she said, taking my hand.

Inside the apartment, people drifted from room to room, smearing the floor with new patterns of glowing lights. A girl, covered in gems, was holding a fox kit in her arms, and other sparkling girls were gathering around to get a turn holding it. The animals that were once feral, pre-colony system, have now become domesticated and are the ultimate status symbol. Men were leaning against counters, whispering low and eyeing some of the girls who had just come in that looked like they might be as young as thirteen or fourteen, just two or three years younger than me.

Colors were more vibrant; I detected the sweet smell of anise that was coming from the drink a couple was spilling as they went in for a long kiss. A caged owl painted gold turned his head mechanically and laid his large, knowing eyes on me as though he had identified an intruder.

"Hey," a guy whispered in my ear. He appeared out of nowhere. His eyes were piercing blue, intensified by whatever the patch was doing to my color perception. I guessed he might be twenty-four or twenty-five by the way he carried himself, sure and refined—unlike the coarse boys in school. Even with my new boldness, I staggered.

Lex appeared at my side, but the guy didn't react to her presence. He was taller than me by at least four inches, even with my added height in those shoes. His very gaze made my skin oversensitive, like I was coming alive under his energy.

"Hey, Radius," Lex said.

The guy didn't even seem to notice her.

"Oh, ok," she said, rolling her eyes at the guy. "Her name's Rebecca."

Lex pushed her brows up and down and smiled at me. Even if I could fool him with the renovations Lex had made to my appearance, my name revealed me to be Old Colony.

Radius held out his hand to shake mine and smiled. I had instinctively put my arm behind my back before he had a chance to glance at my cuff. In a moment, with a simple handshake, it would all be over. That look, which was suspending me, would fall as soon as he realized my Level. Reluctantly, I placed my hand in his, turning away shamefully from the VL that was giving me away with glowing numbers on my cuff: 285.

No use trying to hide it. He could easily look it up two seconds later on my Contour Sheet. He'd know I'd never had a boyfriend. He'd see that I'd never had more than a handful of people voting for me on my Sheet, that my mom worked as an assistant director at Cherish, that I was from the Old Colony eight years ago, and that you literally couldn't live any farther from the Pulse and still be considered part of Colony 215. He'd be embarrassed later that he had even wasted a handshake on me.

He held my hand longer than was necessary, or maybe it was the patch playing with time. Touching him was like taking hold of an electric wire that sent a shock through my arm that ended with a piercing in my chest. My sense of smell was so heightened that I could pick up on a hint of saffron and wood even from where I stood.

The boldness of the patch took over. "How about some fresh air?" I heard myself ask. Once again I was the girl from the ballooners' ad, flying high above the city.

Lex winked at me, her long eyelashes batting in slow motion.

"I'll take good care of her," Radius whispered in a deep voice.

On the balcony, the air carried voltage from the center of the city. The rhythm of music from the apartment below throbbed through my body. I turned to see Radius aglow with the lights of the Pulse. I took in his snakeskin bowler jacket, black-laced boots, the LED tattoo that was pulsing on his neck. I bit my lip imagining where that glowing ink led.

He had a coolness about him, as though he had stepped from a thirty-foot projected ad on one of the buildings, but he held an intense warmth too. His light eyes watched me attentively and drew out secrets unloosed by the coaxing of the patch. I told him about my father and my neighbor Grayson. I confided that Lex was my first friend here, and that all I wanted was citizenship. He listened sympathetically and rubbed the small of my back as I confessed my issues with my mother.

"She just doesn't get it," he said, shaking his head. "A girl like you is going to blossom." His hands wiped across the fake Luminstones that Lex had used to outline my brows. "You've been through a lot, huh?"

I nodded.

Radius looked out across the city. "You've been out of here. Most of us can't say that. We'll live within these walls all our lives. But to leave it all behind . . ." Radius turned to me. I saw compassion and gentleness in his eyes. "That must have been very hard."

Tears began to well up. It had been hard, yes, but the tears came because of the tenderness in someone recognizing my struggle.

"Hey," Radius said, brushing his fingers under my eyes. "You're brave. My little girl from two worlds." He bent to look me in the eyes and smiled.

I looked away.

"No tears, ok? I couldn't have tears," he said in the same voice my mother used with the younger children at Cherish. I gave him a small smile. "And you look nothing like a 'Rebecca,'" he said.

I blushed.

"I'm going to call you Lark."

"Lark," I repeated.

"It's more New Colony, more Pulse . . .more *you*."

"I like it."

I was addicted to Radius. He'd never zap me; that is, I'd never get a message or a vote on my Contour Sheet. Still, I was swimming in each moment of his held attention. By the end of the night, I knew very little about him in comparison to all that I had told him about myself. He lived in the Pulse, of course. He had graduated from the Business Design track a few years back. His VL was 758. And my mother would hate him.

The patch was starting to disintegrate, and I felt myself slowly deflating back to reality.

Radius let out a short laugh. "Hey, I know that look." He smiled as he put his hand under my chin. His eyes still held their power even though the patch was running out. "I'm taking you home, Lark."

"No," I protested, the shame of being Ancillary suddenly coming back in full force. No way I wanted him to see my house.

"It's ok. It's no big deal. I know you live in the Ancillary, and I'm taking you home."

In the past eight years I have ridden in a car exactly twice: once because I was competing in a history competition across the colony—another parent offered to let me ride with her when a snotty-nosed Pulse student had dropped out because of nerves—and once because I had broken my arm during free time and a sympathetic school official drove me to meet my mother at the hospital. Ancillary don't have cars. We take the Convoy line.

Inside Radius's car was another world. It smelled like him and reflected his sleekness and intensity. I'd have to enjoy it while it lasted. My fingers blanched on the seat as he flew through the city. I couldn't make up my mind whether I wanted him to go faster for the thrill of it or to slow down so it would all last a little longer.

"Thank you," I said softly while fingering my cuffs to zap Lex to let her know where I was.

Radius turned to me with his head tilted down and eyebrows up. "You're welcome," he said.

There wasn't enough air in the car if he kept looking at me that way.

The lights were off at my house, except for one in my mom's room. I'd have to face her, but it was all worth it as far as I was concerned. Radius pulled up in front of my house, the dirt swirling in the headlights. He put his hand on my knee and smiled—it was as though he were a lightning rod for the current of the city, and his touch sent a spark through my chest. "So, Lark."

I swallowed hard.

"There's this thing at my place again next week—"

"Wh—?" I slapped both hands to my face. "You mean that was *your* apartment?"

Radius laughed. "Yeah, I thought you knew that."

"You said you lived in the Pulse. *That*," I motioned out the window, "was the pulse of the Pulse."

Radius crossed his arms in front of his chest and smiled like he was amused.

"Look," I said. "You're going to go home tonight and regret all of this—driving me, talking to me, *looking* at me. This is Lex's, you know? I've never in my life owned something like it." I looked down at the dress. "My VL is not exactly six hundred. So you should—"

Radius moved in swiftly and kissed me before I could tell him how quickly he should run. Run for his life.

The Pulse is the heart of the colony. I throb with its energy as I remember my first meeting with Radius and make my way to see Lex. Ancillary residents emerge from the roads that all lead to the epicenter. We, the faded but hopeful, come alive as we approach the Pulse. The Convoy slows on the rails to release more of us students, who pour out eagerly as though we've been holding our

9

collective breath and must gasp for the oxygen that only the center of the colony provides.

I am no longer alone on the road. We ride invisible energy waves from the city and allow them to vibrate through us, become us. It's alive in its grasp as it pushes out our numbness with an almost tangible flow of vibrations and warmth. We crave it.

More ballooners enter the sky, raising our heads involuntarily and filling our minds with the city's dreams that become our own. Motorcycles with black and shiny riders weave unseen patterns. Hundred-foot, 1,000-VL women, with pouty lips and breasts covered in gems, dance on glass buildings in flowing golden skirts for men whose skin is alive with glowing and moving art. I pull my Ancillary shirt over my head as I walk, pausing to cast off my skirt and shove it into my pack so that I've shed my Ancillary cocoon. In the iridescent dress I'd saved for the Panel, I am new. The bass from stores beats under my feet, and I start to run.

I press a button on my cuff and speak into it: "Hi, Ray. Be at your place in thirty minutes."

I slide into a side door off the main strip and climb the stairs to the second floor. Lex is already waiting at her table, which is strewn with products like an alchemist's shop. She squeals and pulls me into a chair when she sees me. I pull off my pack and toss the Splendor box on the table along with the other contraptions and jars of color already on it. After only twenty minutes with Lex, my transformation is complete.

Radius has left the door cracked for me. I catch a glimpse of myself in his floor-length mirror; I have reason to be confident. Lex let me borrow her glitter extensions that flow down my back. I am covered in different shades of blue Luminstones, and she's brushed me with gold dust. My eyes are darkened exotically and my lashes are so thick I can see them when I blink. I'm used to the heels now and practically float in them.

I find Radius in the bedroom. "Hey," I say, closing the door behind me.

Chapter 2

I have few memories of the Old Colony. They've faded now, like they've fallen in some murky pool. Sometimes I allow myself to reach into the depths and retrieve fragments—old faces, colors from the bedspread my grandmother made, my legs dappled in the shade of the tree I used to sit under in our yard.

But every now and then the memories come without my permission. Certain smells unleash an insurrection of images in my mind's eye, and I am at their mercy. They are always there—the rebellious pieces of my past that are never discouraged no matter how hard I try to suppress them.

The first earthquake hit Colony 108 at 11:13 p.m. Three more followed throughout the night and into the morning. At first I thought I had been having a nightmare. I screamed my mother's name as contents from my shelves rattled free onto the floor around me. My father was there in a moment, lifting me from my bed as I cried out in horror upon realizing that the earth was moving below me.

I knew well what was happening. We had seen footage and heard scientific explanations numerous times at school. The world might have been shaking loose from its axis, but it could have come down around us with me safe in my father's strong arms. He whispered in my ear that it would end soon. My mother huddled next to him in the doorframe of my room. And in my naivety, I believed the three of us were safe simply because we were together.

The first quake didn't last long. The three others were equal in intensity. The damage was minimal to the community buildings that had been designed to withstand it.

My father was the president of our colony, and he was the steady force in the midst of the aftermath, holding down the below-surface panic that I perceived plainly in spite of my young age. Colony 108 was only too familiar with the fate of its neighboring colonies that sat on the quake line. Their destruction had begun like this. The earth might have stilled, but what it unloosed was reaching higher magnitudes inside of us all.

11

I got the full story only after starting school in the New Colony. My teacher explained how the world had shuffled off us mortals as we sat tensely in our desks. The earth seemed to have reached a new era of natural disasters. Tsunamis and massive earthquakes had forced an already dwindling human population to move to safe zones—or, at least, where they believed they were safe. It took science almost a century to catch up with the destruction.

Melissa A. Hubert was the first scientist to determine that the earth was actually changing axial rotation; our planet was becoming unhinged, off balance. Diminishing ice mass on the poles was changing the gravitational pull on the earth as it turned around the sun. In other words, it had gotten thrown off—shifted on its axis.

The result was that the plates below ground started shifting, letting free a string of cataclysmic earthquakes and tsunamis that ravaged coastlines. Our landmass shrunk. According to my Cataclysmic Preparation teacher, that's when we humans moved inland. Scientists scrambled to determine what land was balanced above the break lines several miles below ground, silently waiting to buck the infrastructure.

Countries scrambled to rebuild. And the United States, as it was then called before becoming the American Colonies, directed by the National Council, scrambled for resources. The earth swallowed whole communities, and survivors packed their cars with whatever belongings they could and drove to the next state rumored to be free of sinkholes. More often than not, they met more earthquakes and fires there. Panic was rampant, as though the earth was unleashing demons from its enraged depths. Looters took over cities.

However, the District of Columbia was spared. Survivors came in droves, looking to the elected, but equally panicked, leadership for protection. My father told me how my great-great-grandparents had walked there from our family's home that was once Fauquier, Virginia. They and their two young children had camped on Pennsylvania Avenue and had become a part of the masses of survivors, waiting desperately for words of hope. Those words never came, and so they returned to their newly ravaged land as pioneers.

Soon after my great-great-grandparents and the third of their hometown that had survived returned to rebuild, the superpowers of Asia and Europe took the opportunity to eliminate the United

12

States as a threat. Missiles struck Pennsylvania Avenue at midnight on April 11, 2189, and the next day the city of Atlanta was completely eliminated through biological warfare. The US Army launched counterattacks, but not before the White House and Congress were taken out. The world was at a standstill as our wounded allies, weakened by the natural disasters, rallied.

Our government collapsed, and what was left of our military defense held off the Asian and European conglomerate until we were able to negotiate trade terms regarding access to the well-preserved Middle Eastern oil supplies. Scientists worked tirelessly to determine safe zones and hordes of survivors moved, setting up primitive camps and seeking some semblance of order. Though once the most prosperous nation in the world, America scrambled simply to find means of preservation.

We looked to science for answers. Our government was replaced with the National Council, made up of the most distinguished military scientists, neuroscientists, evolutionary theorists, NASA professionals, and genetic experts. They orchestrated the structure that exists as it is today: humanity was preserved in bubbles of representative samples of genetic diversity.

The head of the National Council, Dr. Elizabeth Allen, was elected for her cool demeanor and natural leadership. Biographies would later reveal her social avoidance and her struggle with severe obsessive-compulsive disorder. They would also expose eccentricities such as her radical avoidance of red foods and her unnatural propensity for pulling out her own hair. She was never seen in public without a hat, a widely copied style during that era. Though acutely neurotic in her private life, she was known for her genius in the field of conservationism, especially for her work in preserving many aquatic endangered species. And since we were becoming endangered species ourselves, we looked to her for preservation—an unlikely hero in desperate times.

Geologists determined areas of the earth that were less likely to consume us, and then zoologists took over. Dr. Allen saw us as rare fish to be shipped off to certain aquariums to meet their genetic needs. Our DNA determined our fate. So, the American population was scooped up from the muddy pockets of the dwindling earth and plopped into shiny new bowls. Each bowl was a colorful genetic representation of the country as a whole.

Flyers fell from the sky like seed pods to populated regions, announcing the country's newest tactic for safeguarding the race.

13

My great-great-grandmother plucked a bright flyer from in between the purple rows of cabbage that she and my great-great-grandfather had been working along with the other Fauquier pioneers.

Some protested and fought as they were dragged away from loved ones. My great-great-grandfather had three fingers blown off as he and fifty other re-settlers stormed the soldiers that forced the evacuation. But most, near starvation from unsuccessful efforts on their own, or exhausted from spending each moment in anticipation of the next natural disaster, went willingly; they greeted the soldiers as rescuers.

The National Council had done well in creating their microcosms. Colonies rebuilt quickly and populations increased. No one went hungry, and the panic that had once ruled the hearts of a broken and divided country was replaced by a peace in knowing that citizens were being taken care of.

Unfortunately, this peace was short-lived as the population grew and new assimilations became necessary to redistribute new genes. Communities were forced to evacuate based on scientists' predictions that they sat on hotspots or were in immediate danger of future earthquakes. Thus began a century of civil unrest as several northwestern colony leaders refused admittance of certain genes that would "contaminate" their established population and cultures. The National Council finally resorted to military strength when resistance continued.

Communities deemed to be in safe zones were forced to allow admittance of evacuees, but after just one generation these foreigners had become slaves. A new war ensued when one colony stood in opposition to enslavement. That one colony was my colony. We were a proud, though small, world. And we led and won the war for gene equality and the abolishment of slavery. Every child in our colony had been taught our honorable history and knew it by heart. Two generations later my father was elected president of 108. He spoke daily of the sacrifices our grandparents had made in upholding freedom.

It was against that backdrop that my father had had to make the most difficult decision of his life. I entered his study cautiously. I had often played under his desk during meetings as he passed me lemon candies to keep me quiet. The day following the earthquake, I found him there in his study, kneeling with one hand over his face and the other hand bracing him on the floor. His shoulders heaved.

My mother was eerily calm, handling the influx of calls and visitors with a steady grace. From the pale lavender cushion of the window seat in my bedroom, I sat looking at the visitors that had gathered on the pristine lawn where I had spent my summers in play. I watched them until lightning bugs silently illuminated the somber faces of the citizens who had become statues waiting for word and hope from my father.

"Rebecca," my father said from behind me. He was wearing his best suit. Though taller than most men, he seemed even larger that night. But where warmth and joy had once filled him, a new sedateness took over. "Rebecca," he said again gently, bending down and touching my cheek before he closed my curtains. "I have made a choice. And I know what is coming."

I nodded.

"We will be away from each other for some time."

I put my small hand in his. "It won't be long, will it?" I asked.

My father smiled. "I don't know, sweetheart. But I will never stop fighting for you. Not for a moment."

I leaned into his chest and allowed the peace that emanated from him to become my own.

The next morning, my father stood in front of our home facing a swarm of cameras and silent, tense gatherers. "Friends," he said, holding up a hand to address the crowd. "I have received the official results from the Department of Colony Geological Safety. The data indicate that our homes are at imminent risk of destruction."

I noticed a man in the crowd stand taller and his lips become a straight line as his wife knelt to the ground and covered her mouth. Several people began to sob.

"Evacuation must begin immediately. According to National Council law, you will be given your New Colony assignments based on the genetic needs of that community. Also according to law, the Council will place other high-ranking colony leaders and me separately so that we will we pose no risk to the existing governments."

My mother took my father's hand as it began to shake.

"My faith is that our citizenship to Colony 108 runs spirit deep. We will be entering new worlds, and it will be our daily choices that determine our attachment to them. We are a people who originally battled for freedom. We look to our grandfathers and grandmothers who fought so courageously to ensure that those

15

injustices would never threaten their own children. And now, we stand protected here because of their sacrifices. Let us carry that truth with us, no matter where we are placed, no matter how we will be divided." My father's voice broke on his last word. My mother's knuckles blanched as she squeezed my father's hand, bringing him to life again. "They will know us for the Truth we have fought for and the integrity by which we live. We stand upon a foundation that *cannot* be shaken. So let us go boldly." The crowd stomped its feet in rhythm. Those who had been brought to their knees pounded their fists on the ground.

The carriers arrived on an icy day in January. Glass boxes filled with armed men and women were flown high above our colony. My father kept his hand on my shoulder as they landed. These were the first people I had ever seen from another colony, and I stared openly. Government workers in gray uniforms stepped out of the boxes and set up shiny tables to initiate the process of evacuation. We were given a small bag for our worldly belongings, which were later searched. Material possessions in our New Colony were to be comparable to those in our Old Colony— everything would be provided. Because we were assimilating, we would not be allowed citizenship into the New Colony initially, and thus would not be granted full New Colony rights until we were established and accepted. Along with the bags, we were issued jumpsuits: children were given white, adults light blue.

A second shipment of hundreds of glass boxes arrived the next day by drone. Thousands of us were escorted by gunpoint in a thick line to the awaiting glass boxes. My father and mother kept their hands on my shoulders and stared ahead as the glass doors closed. I held onto the pole to steady myself and touched hands with a younger child who was swinging back and forth on it. Her mother stood above her, tears streaming down her face as she stared at her dark-haired little girl, ignorant and unburdened.

We watched as our home became the Old Colony. An older woman beside me sank to the ground. My mother and father kept their hands tight on my shoulder. I thought I heard my mother whisper, "Steady," but I couldn't tell if it was directed to my father or to me. Perhaps it was to herself.

The home I had always known, arranged neatly in concentric circles, became smaller and smaller until we glided silently above a

16

dark green sea of volatile land that stretched out beyond our small bubble of safety.

"We will reach our destination in twenty-four minutes," the speaker announced. "Please hold on while we approach the Decontamination Center, a district of the Executive Colony."

We were ushered into white towering buildings that stood tall against the backdrop of gently rolling plains. Children who were too big to be carried were still held tightly in their parents' protective arms. A series of perhaps fifty identical, severe white buildings with glass tops rose to the sky upon the ocean of gold.

Our glass pod was lowered expertly upon the top of a building on the northwest extreme of the starkly geometrical structures. A small portal opened in the floor of our pod. My mother nudged me gently. I paused on the top step and looked down the spiraling metal stairs that descended into a different world.

"It's ok, Rebecca," my father whispered.

I shifted my gaze to the people of the Old Colony who stood frozen, looking wide-eyed at me, expectantly.

My first step echoed. The others followed behind robotically as we were led into a building and down a set of steep steps lit with fluorescence.

The stairs led to an open, white room staffed by a dozen or so fully-covered Decontamination workers who gave us instructions as we lined up and told our names and ID numbers. Adults aged sixty-five or older were combined sexes and sent to the base floors. My mother and I were escorted to the sixteenth floor, while my father was directed to the seventeenth floor along with the other men. I grabbed his hand before he turned to leave and shook my head. My mother pulled me close, but I wouldn't let go of my father's hand.

"I'll be back," he said convincingly.

I started to shake as terror set in. He pulled away and became lost in the crowd of men.

Thick doors were locked behind us in an ominous metallic thundering after more workers entered to perform a decontamination of potential deadly viruses, unleashed in our breath, that might threaten our New World's existence. We were prodded and palpated and pored over with lights and metal instruments. Scarlet vials were taken by sharp pricks directed by thickly gloved, expert hands. Full body scans were issued for cancer detection. Then, more needles appeared to administer high levels of vitamins and calming agents to combat the deleterious emotional effects of the ordeal.

We remained at the Decontamination Zone, divided in our towers, for four days while doctors and specialists assessed whether or not we would be exposing new colonists to any potential diseases, or would burden them by strange genetic variations that would necessitate more care, thus draining their resources.

I held my mother's hand as we were led into a large room full of bunks where the men were already waiting. My father sat with his head in his hands but immediately straightened when he saw me. I ran to his arms. We sat in our bunks on the all-glass floor of the facility. It had been designed to calm, with soft music and pumped-in air thick with smells of home—baking bread at some times and fresh grass at others.

We waited anxiously for our names to be called over the loudspeaker in a computerized voice. "Barry, Raphael. ID number 01412, please report to floor thirteen. ID number 01412, floor thirteen," the speaker called coldly. We watched as our old neighbor walked slowly across the room and exited into the elevators. My mother sat with Raphael's wife as she slowly rocked herself on her bunk until his return almost an hour later.

Colonists gathered around to hear his report that they had found unusual cell growth in his pancreas and he would be denied assimilation until he could receive treatment. He would remain at the Center until he could be deemed fully recovered and allowed assimilation later. I pretended to tie my shoe as I strained to hear the woman behind me speaking in hushed tones to another woman. "I don't understand why they won't do the treatment after assimilation," the woman said anxiously.

The other woman leaned in closer. "Assimilating him would mean that he would take a healthy person's space in a colony. It would be too risky if he didn't fully recover from the treatment and had to take a less-skilled job. And, then of course he could die."

He and perhaps three dozen others silently walked across the floor to the elevators as their names were called. Each returned with sobering news of more cancer, imminent heart attacks from clogged arteries, or borderline diabetes that would need to be stabilized before they were allowed assimilation. I had watched intently as a little girl from my school, one year younger, had been called. "Robison, Olive. ID number 02104, please report to floor thirteen. ID number 02104, floor thirteen."

Olive cowered as she heard her name called from the speakers in the ceiling, as though a hand might reach down and grab her. Her mother clutched the little girl against her chest instinctively. Fully suited workers entered to escort Olive through sliding doors for further prodding. She walked behind them bravely as her mother covered her face with her hands and other women, including my mom, came to sit with her in silence.

Two hours later, the doors opened to reveal a pale Olive, clutching a printout of her fate. She too would remain at the facility for treatment of a rare blood cancer. Her parents would be forced to assimilate as their child, for whom they had tended every sore throat and skinned knee, was left alone to be cared for by strangers.

My father made his rounds to visit other families. In soft whispers they exchanged their fears and provided comforts to one another as we counted down the moments to assimilation. My father remained stoic as families embraced each other and sobbed openly, mothers occasionally letting out soft moans as they rocked sleeping babies that would soon be taken from them. Often, Dad stood by the window and looked out at the seemingly endless expanse of earth beyond the Decontamination Center as though he were searching for something beyond it.

"Rebecca," he called in his deep and soothing voice.

I stood beside my father and looked out to see what he was seeing. I took his large rough hand and held it tight in my own small one.

"Our choices are not always easy," he had said. I thought perhaps he was speaking to himself and not me. "Sometimes they don't even feel like a choice."

I nodded as though I understood and searched the rippling golden grass that swelled the earth on the horizon.

"I have a secret," he whispered, still looking out the window.

I looked at him eagerly.

"Something that will help me to find you. Something that *they* don't know about."

"Good," I whispered back. "I don't like them."

"They don't know what they're doing. I'm going to inject something right here." He rubbed the back of my neck. "Behind your hair. It will help me find you when the time is right." His thick hand was warm on my skin.

19

I nodded and turned slightly to see the rest of our people who were engaged in quiet conversations. I pulled my long brown hair to one shoulder and leaned on my father's arm.

"Good girl," he said. He reached into his pocket with his right hand. Within a few seconds I felt the burn of a needle in the back of my neck. I didn't make a sound.

I looked up to my father and smiled. "You'll find me, won't you, Daddy?"

My father bent down to pick me up and for one last time I was held in his arms, safe from the world in spite of the growing fear all around me. He kissed me softly on the forehead. Sometimes, even now, I can feel the warmth of his lips on my head.

We spent our days blindly watching shows the Center provided on TV, eating without tasting, and taking in our last moments together as families. Husbands and wives held onto each other and mothers drank in the words and caresses of their children. On the fourth day, names and ID numbers were called in groups, and we were asked to report to the main room. Parents exchanged panicked glances as their children were called to a group and held onto one another for what they believed might be the last time.

"Just another exam," an older woman repeated reassuringly to her husband as he was called. We watched as they exited the room and stared intently at the door as though we could will their return with our intense gazes. More groups were called and the alarm increased. Children began to cry as they absorbed the horror without understanding its meaning.

My mother was the third to be called in the twentieth group. She reached her hand to my arm and held it tightly. I started to cry. "What's happening? What's happening?" I asked.

My mother turned to me. "We're going to be together, Rebecca. I promise. You must be a brave girl, darling. You know what we've taught—"

Suddenly, after a string of other names, the loudspeaker announced, "Flora, Rebecca. ID number 02134. Flora, Rebecca."

I saw my father drop to his knees. "You're together," he whispered to my mother in a shaking voice. "Thank God," he said over and over. He grabbed my mother and held us close as more names were called.

My mother held her hand to his cheek for one last time and took my hand. "It's time to go, Rebecca," she said soothingly.

I strained to hear my father's name, but the voice was instructing us to gather our things and exit the room.

"No," I protested. "I won't! I won't go!" I pulled away from her and threw my arms around my father's neck.

"You must," my father said calmly. "Rebecca. Go, darling." Slowly he removed my arms and held them firmly by the wrists.

"I won't!" I screamed over and over. "Please, Daddy! Don't let them take me!"

My mother wrapped my own arms around me to subdue me. "It's going to be ok," she soothed. "I'm coming with you."

"I don't want to go with you," I seethed. "Daddy!" I begged as I struggled against my mother's grasp.

"Take her now," my father commanded, his voice steady. He slowly walked to the windows and stood looking out, the sun illuminating him. He put his hands on either side of the window to brace himself.

I called his name over and over. "Daddy! Look at me!" I wailed.

Two suited Decontamination workers came to assist my mother. I fought them wildly, bloodying my own lip in the process. The few colony members that still remained in the room looked on helplessly until one older woman who had taught me in preschool came over to help my mother. "We can handle this," she told the suited workers in her frail but authoritative voice.

I continued my wild kicking and hysterics, pushing my old teacher's gentle touch away with the hand that I had broken from my mother's grasp.

"Daddy, look at me!" I yelled to deaf ears.

More colony members came to reason with the suited workers who were reaching for me as my legs cut wild circles in the air. I broke free for a moment and lunged across a cot to reach my father. The workers grabbed me roughly when I was only a few feet away. Then I felt the sharp pain of the needle being injected into my leg.

The last memory of my Old Colony life was the sight of my father's back, his hands in his pockets. I blinked with heavy lids in the glare from the sun.

Chapter 3

I woke as our glass pods flew over the New Colony. Through the floor I could see our new home—from the distance it appeared as a crumbling nest holding a nascent egg, shimmering with life. We passed the tops of dozens of floating orbs that were alive with images of beautiful people welcoming us and announcing our arrival. Our pod slowly descended into the gray fragments that surrounded the luminous and bustling center that I later learned was the Pulse. I was still quite groggy from the sedative that the workers had given me. I had surrendered the fight, but not the anger. My mother supported my arms to help me walk from our glass box to the industrial building.

New Colony members were dressed in such vibrant colors that it appeared they were powered by some energy that incited their glow and ran through to their faces and unnaturally white smiles. I stared with hate at the citizens who were to be our hosts in this foreign world.

In my mind, I saw my father, every detail of him—the fullness of his bottom lip, the pinch between his eyebrows, the curve of his jawline, the intensity of his dark eyes. I wanted my father. I wanted his strong arms that were my home to shield me against the strangeness of this place.

My mother guided me through the line for us to receive our lunch. "This won't be so bad," she said gently as she looked around at the other members of our Old life who had been transferred with us.

I scanned the crowd for familiar faces. My best friend, Liza, must have gone somewhere else. Somewhere, she too would be standing in line in a strange cafeteria looking for me, maybe. I recognized a few adult men who had worked with my father. They shuffled in line with their heads down as though sleepwalking.

A little blond girl with bright blue eyes, Grace, who had been just a couple of years ahead of me in school, sat holding a toddler girl. The girl, a small replica of her pretty older sister, was reaching for her food with chubby hands. She had been transferred with her sister, I thought with relief. I smiled to think that they would have each other. "Sit down, Isabelle," Grace whispered gently. I guess she would be her mother now.

Other adults were comforting younger children, who had not been so lucky as to assimilate with family members, and helping them with their plates. There was the father of a boy that I had known, weeping openly at his table. A few others had also broken into tears. The rest of us were too numb.

My mother put her arm around me. "We can make this work, Rebecca," she said. "We are some of the lucky few. We're together," she whispered as she extended her plate to a smiling man with a thin mustache.

"Welcome!" he said enthusiastically. "What else can I get for you?" he asked, placing his hands behind his back and bending slightly at the waist.

"This will do," my mother said flatly.

"All righty! This way then, ma'am." He motioned to a row of empty metal seats.

My mother and I paused tentatively next to another woman who held her fork with a shaking hand.

"Eleanor," she nodded to my mother.

My mother returned the nod and squeezed her arm. "It's going to be all right," my mother assured her.

I watched as a large screen was lowered down one wall and brightly colored women with short skirts busied themselves in escorting people to empty chairs. "You'll want to be sure to position yourselves to see this," they said, indicating the screen with grand gestures.

I followed Mom to a table where a dark-looking man with an intense look sat. He was lean and muscular—maybe a professional athlete in the Old Colony.

"Will Skycap," my mother nodded to him. I had no idea how she would have known him.

But he immediately turned his gaze to her and nodded seriously. "Ms. Flora."

"Colony 215 got a swift one," she smiled.

Before I could ask my mother what she meant, a boy a couple of years older than me whom I'd seen many times at school sat down next to me. He was with a young woman who had dark curly hair. My mother gave the woman a fragile smile and extended her hand. "Marissa," my mother exhaled.

The woman beamed. "My baby cousin is here." She warmly put her arm around the pale boy, who didn't look up.

My mother smiled down at the child and patted his shoulder. "Very good to see you," she said sincerely.

"What's your name?" I asked the boy.

"Grayson," he whispered without looking up.

"Rebecca," I returned.

I startled as a tray clattered next to me. A small man with a kind face sat down next to Marissa and nodded to my mother.

"Bruce." Mom extended her hand, which he shook unceremoniously. I thought I saw the man wink at my mother before ceremonially arranging the food on his plate in neat little rows.

My mother put her elbows on the table and leaned closer to Marissa. "It's quite a team," she whispered.

Marissa giggled and rubbed Grayson on the head. "It is. We got Stephanie and Robin as well." Marissa's eyes darted to a petite, serious but peaceful-looking woman sitting across from another woman who had a broad smile in spite of the grieving people around her. "Quite a team," Marissa said, raising her eyebrows.

Just then, a woman walked slowly and dramatically to a podium that had been placed in front of the screen. She wore a skintight black dress outlined in small metal spikes. Her white-blond hair was pulled back into a tight ponytail that flowed down her back.

"Welcome!" she said, her deep voice magnified without any visible microphone. "You are most, most welcome to Colony 215. On behalf of the Colony citizens I want to tell you how thrilled we are to have you assimilate." She paused to look around at the crowd as we stared back at her blandly. "We understand that without this assimilation your very lives would be in extreme peril." She paused again, seemingly to allow the weight of her statement to sink in. We continued our blank stares. "*But*, I hope that you will look at Colony 215 as much more than a haven. I hope this will become your home and that you will come to love your New Colony as we do." She put a hand on one hip and posed as though she were expecting someone to take her picture.

"First, it is my great privilege to introduce to you the president of Colony 215—Mr. Stewart Kayne!" The woman clapped dramatically above her head and smiled so severely that I thought it must be hurting her face.

We all cast glances at each other as a man with dark sunglasses, a shaved head, and dark pants tucked into high boots took the podium. This was our new president? I had seen him on one of the balloons as we floated over the colony, but I had thought it was an advertisement of some sort—to sell watches or toothpaste or something. A few people clapped robotically.

"Welcome," the man said without smiling. "Colony 215 welcomes you. I believe 215 to be the greatest colony there is, and now you get a chance to be a part of it."

I looked to my mother, who was biting her lip. "So," the president continued, "I hope you will embrace the colony as it embraces you."

He turned abruptly and left through the door to the right as the woman, still smiling idiotically, returned to the podium.

"Our president," she said, clapping until he left. "Finally, we have prepared a short clip to introduce you to your new home, and I think you will find that it answers most questions that I'm certain you have at the present." She looked serious momentarily and then her face suddenly transformed once again to the ebullient expression. "Following the clip, we will exit through these doors." She gestured with both hands to a set of doors on the right.

"There you will be greeted by our staff to help you find your new houses," she said, leaning forward and raising her eyebrows up alluringly, "and to receive assignments for your placements for schools for your children."

The woman closed one eye and made soft clicking sounds as she pointed out several of the children in the room. "You adults will receive employment assignments and further instructions."

A few hands rose into the air for questions, but they were ignored. "Now," she said, rubbing her palms together, "Please enjoy the film!"

The woman's spiked pumps clicked loudly as she returned to her seat. She waved her hands dramatically for the lights to be dimmed. The film opened with aerial images of lush land and flourishing cities. A woman's voice narrated: "Our country was once a prosperous world. Our population reached over 5.2 million." The video moved to more images of children playing on the sidewalks of bustling cities and couples holding hands on the beach. "We thrived as a country." Rapid images appeared of Olympians holding gold medals, large houses, architectural feats—bridges, massive buildings—and then space travel.

"But in the year 2189, our world was struck by a series of devastating events." The film changed to clips of natural disasters—whole houses being consumed by immense tidal waves, and people running to safety during massive earthquakes on the east coast that measured 11.0 on the Richter scale.

More images of fires and pandemics appeared. Soft, melancholy music played as we watched a beautiful world being destroyed—a world of prosperity that our great-great-grandparents had helped build. We watched with dulled expressions. Inside each of us, unseen catastrophic forces raged just as strong.

"But, in the spirit that has always predominated our country, we rebuilt. Where other countries perished, we found ways to grow. Our population had dwindled to numbers that resembled the size of our country in its infancy: 1.5 million." The camera panned to vacant buildings and a mass exodus of people. Next, it showed scientists and professional men and women, reviewing maps and heavily engaged in discussion.

"Our surviving scientists acted quickly to determine which areas remained at considerable risk and which were safe. They, along with the military, determined a solution to protect and grow our population so that we could once again thrive: the colony system."

"Colonies make up cells," continued the narrator. A map of our current country was shown from space: the east and west coasts had dissolved into the blue. In the midst of barren terrain, small sectors of light appeared as glittering orbs making up the gestalt of larger glittering orbs. "Each colony is selected to reflect the genetic diversity and skill diversity needed to promote healthy growth of our population. In the last century we have become adept at determining when, and if, new colonies are at risk of catastrophe. When they are, that colony's population is dispersed and individuals are assimilated to safer colonies."

I looked at the modish woman who had introduced the film. She was nodding seriously, sometimes looking out into the crowd and smiling. She clasped her hands together and put them to her mouth pensively as the narrator said, "Your colony, Colony 108, was at serious risk for annihilation by earthquake."

A digital animation of our colony was displayed with images of it being shaken from the earth. We watched as familiar buildings and homes were felled. "If this had been the case, survival would not have been possible. We welcome you to Colony 215."

I leaned forward slightly as images of our new homes were presented: beautiful buildings, alive with advertisements, the Convoy opening to happy children who ran to a new school that was several stories tall, and smiling doctors in a state-of-the-art hospital building.

"You will find that all of your needs are anticipated and cared for. As new assimilants, you will receive housing in the section we call the Ancillary."

I stared at the tidy houses with small manicured yards and iron porches that flashed on the screen.

"Current adults, that is over the age of sixteen, may apply for full citizenship in the Pulse after living here for one year. However, application does not necessarily guarantee citizenship. If citizenship is granted, you will receive the benefits allowed to all colony citizens. You will also not be eligible for any future assimilation unless, of course, the entire colony is assimilated because of risk of imminent catastrophe. Children under the age of sixteen are considered minors and may apply after coming of age."

I did the math quickly. My heart pounded as I realized I would have to stay in the New Colony for eight years. "Your individual compatibility with Colony 215's goals and culture will be assessed using our Value Level (VL) system."

On the screen appeared a smiling young woman who stood looking at flashing numbers on pliable, metal bands she wore around each wrist.

"Both Ancillary and Pulse members are given numbers for a variety of things: school and employment compliance, social compatibility, and general contribution to the community, including financial investment through the purchase of colony products. This tool is used as feedback to help motivate colonists to contribute to our community and ultimately to help determine citizenship."

The images on screen flashed to a young boy meeting before a table of brightly colored people who were asking him questions seriously. Then they all smiled and the boy approached the table.

"Citizens are identified with a data chip."

The boy on the screen smiled as one of the people from the table leaned over to him and injected something into his bicep with a shiny syringe, just as my father had injected me in the back of my neck.

"Children who did not transfer with a family member will be cared for by Cherish."

The film showed images of happy children playing tag outside a white building staffed by what looked like happy medical professionals. I scanned the room for children sitting by themselves. One little boy was crying. Babies had been lined up in a row in prams along the back wall. Their fists waved in the air as a few had begun to cry. The little blond girl I had noticed from my old school was staring stoically at the screen, holding her sister.

"Adults will find that we have matched you with jobs that best fit your skill level and meet the needs of the community," the narrator continued. More images appeared of happy men and women sitting before a large monitor with the skeleton of a building design. The people made grand hand gestures to suggest that their artistic ideas for construction were being considered.

"Let us also not underestimate the importance of finding compatibility," the narrator said, as a young man and woman slow-danced on screen and laughed playfully with one another. "And each year the colony hosts the 'Catastrophe Challenge,' which simulates various destructive forces by which our ancestors either survived or perished. It is meant to be entertainment, *but* contestants who compete and do well will also receive a bolstered VL score! Only the fittest will succeed!"

We looked on listlessly.

"The Pulse has a staff dedicated to assuring that your assimilation goes as smoothly as possible." The video cut to a blank screen.

We blinked against the lights that flickered on and turned our attention to the woman who clicked her way over to the front of the room. She directed us by dramatic gestures to the next room. Slowly, each of us returned full plates of food to the staff and robotically made our way through the automatic doors, where we were to be introduced to our New lives.

I wondered about my father, if he too was being handed a set of keys to a new, empty house. "Mom, I want to go home," I said with an upturned face.

She put her arm around my shoulders and squeezed hard. "We're together," she said.

Overly friendly staff ushered us into lines in which we received our cuffs—the flexible metal bands that fit around our wrists—with a thick pamphlet to explain how the VL system was used for motivational purposes. It also detailed how to increase our number and track it using our assigned Contour Sheet. I thumbed through pictures of happy young boys and girls. A girl with flawless skin and bright teeth was looking at her smiling friends with the caption, "I'm up thirty points!"

At another table I was registered for school and given detailed instructions on where and when to go. I would begin on Thursday, after the two days we had been given to "acclimate" to our new home—two days to allow the shock to wear off. The workers winked, and I rolled my eyes.

My mother would be working for Cherish, the home for orphaned children. She knitted her brow in concentration as she read the assignment. "Good," she whispered seriously. "That's good."

Marissa, the young woman who had sat with us in the cafeteria, was leaning on a table next to us to address the staff worker in harsh tones. She was pointing to the little boy, Grayson, who was looking at the ground as though trying not to cry. "He's staying with me," she said through clenched teeth.

"Don't move," my mother instructed me. Mom put her hand on Grayson's shoulder and spoke softly to Marissa, who continued to stare coldly at the smiling staff worker.

I ignored my instructions and stood beside the little boy. His face was dark and panicked as he watched his only family member fight for him to stay with her rather than strangers. My mother turned to me abruptly as Marissa pounded a fist on the table and continued to argue her position at an increased volume.

"Rebecca, take Grayson over there." Mom's voice was authoritative.

I reached for his hand and walked him to a corner of the room as my mother and Marissa continued to plead.

Grayson avoided eye contact and searched the room wildly.

"Hey," I said. "Cherish wouldn't be so bad."

He began to sob. I watched him helplessly, and then gently put my small arms around him. He in turn wrapped his wiry arms around me. I barely came up to his shoulder. We stood there, two lost children in a strange New world.

"Don't worry, Grayson," I said. "My mother will take care of it."

A few moments later Marissa pulled Grayson from me and swung him back and forth. "You're with me!" she sobbed. "We're together. You're not at Cherish." Marissa kissed every inch of his wet cheeks and then ushered him over to an empty bench.

My mother put a hand out to me.

"You could have taken care of him at Cherish," I said.

"Yes, but now I'll still take care of him right next door. Gray and Marissa are our neighbors. We just had to"—my mother paused and looked at Marissa—"make some compromises on where we would live."

Several hours later, after more registrations, more information packets, confusing Convoy instructions, and signing of papers, I realized exactly what my mother meant when she said "compromises" were to be made on where we would live. We walked together with Marissa and Grayson for almost a mile down a dirt road to what must have been the farthest extremity of the Ancillary. So much for pristine yards and curving wrought-iron porches on double-story homes.

"Maybe we took a wrong turn," Marissa said lightly, tussling Grayson's hair.

I held my mother's hand. The woods on either side of the road seemed looming and portentous. I jumped as an unseen animal rustled dry leaves. Grayson pointed high into the air at the small cargo drones that carried goods between the colonies like spreading viruses. Maybe our family and friends would be purchasing those goods in stores at their New Colonies. Grayson and I looked at them longingly. How desperately we both wanted to float out of this foreign world.

After we had walked for so long that I began to wonder if we would simply walk right out of the colony, two dilapidated houses standing in isolation came into view.

"Ok," Marissa said slowly as she checked the house number on the paperwork. "One hundred three Patmos Road. We have our *own* colony, then." She rubbed her hands together enthusiastically. "Come on, Grayson." Marissa took her cousin by the hand and led him to the brown house on the right.

I thought of how I had waited for my father on our old steps that led to what I would ever after think of as a castle. I shuffled my feet on the hewn stairs that led to the small paneled house with dirty, blinking windows. An intricate abstract of curls and spirals adorned the wood where insects had fed in meandering paths.

"These were the scientists' homes," my mother sighed.

The door creaked as I opened it for my mother to enter first.

"What scientists?" I asked, scanning the open rooms, empty with the exception of some furniture all pushed to the side. I jumped as a small creature scurried to a corner.

"The scientists who first set up field surveillance to determine the safety of the area—probably just data collectors, not the lead scientists. These houses are maybe one hundred years old."

My mother investigated the kitchen first, opening cabinets and turning on the faucet. "They assured me that we would have heat and plumbing." She clucked her tongue in concentration. "We'll need a lot of things," she observed. "The basics are supposed to arrive by drone this evening."

I ran my finger along the edge of the counter, making a long white trail in the thick layer of dust. "We're too far out to carry much of anything, anyway," I said.

My mother let out a low laugh. "It was part of the negotiation with those idiots," she mumbled, more to herself than to me. I had never heard her be condescending about anyone before.

"What do you mean?"

"They were going to send Gray to Cherish. Strangers would have cared for him even though Marissa was more than willing to take him on."

"I don't understand why they wouldn't have let them just stay together in the first place." I looked tentatively into the fireplace for any more small scurrying animals.

"Marissa was most likely recruited for her medical skills. Plus, she has a strong background in research and will probably be involved with that as well. The colony staff reasoned that she wouldn't be able to take care of a child by herself given her young age and the fact that she will be working long hours at the hospital. I explained that I would be able to step in as necessary and bring him along with me to Cherish on days that Marissa wouldn't be home. The exchange," my mother sighed as she supported her head in her hand, "was that we took the last choice for housing."

"Oh," I said dejectedly.

"The nice part, though, is that I think I can actually cut through the woods to get to work." My mother walked toward the back door, which opened to a yard overgrown with tall grass and climbing vines on the trees. She stood on tiptoe to see beyond our yard to a clearing made by massive power lines that rose and fell over the undulating terrain. "I think I'll just go through that way," she said, absentmindedly fingering her cuff. "They said there's a directions device on this thing."

"Mom," I pleaded. "We could get out of here. We could go find Dad."

My mother put her hands on my shoulders and drew me in. "No, sweetie. We can't."

I clung to my mother's rough jumpsuit as I buried my face into her. "Mommy, please," I begged, the tears beginning to come. "We're not supposed to be here. Daddy needs us."

"Yes, he does," my mother whispered. "He needs us very much. More than you know."

That night and many more nights after, I cried beside my mother as we lay in her bed. It was only after my tears had run dry, and she thought that I was asleep that my mother took her turn, her body shuddering with restrained sobbing.

Chapter 4

My mother took her homesickness out on our house each weekend. The shed in the back contained a menagerie of vials and whirling instruments, which became the only toys Grayson and I had, as well as shovels, clippers, and even a solar-powered lawn mower. We played "scientist," filling up the glass bottles with soil and small rocks and then broadcasting reports from a tree stump that our colony was safe in our hands. Meanwhile, Marissa and my mother attacked weeds that reached the top of our porch with awkward thrusts from too-small shovels.

We shared our part of the colony with a host of new and exciting creatures. Grayson spent almost an hour trying to lure a small green lizard into one of the vials. He nearly dropped the glass when the little beast bobbed its head and spread its neck into a thin scarlet fan.

I lined bits of saved toast in neat rows to entice one of the many birds that nested in our trees. Marissa screamed as she accidentally touched a small brown snake that had wound around a fallen tree branch. She fell back gasping for breath as the snake slithered away. Grayson and I ran to investigate in spite of my mother's harsh warnings. I reached out a curious hand only to have Grayson grab me by both shoulders, pull me backward, and leap in front of me.

Marissa laughed her deep laugh. "It's ok, Eleanor," she said, out of breath. "It's harmless."

"See?" I said to Grayson's back. "Harmless."

We were soon put to work to keep us out of trouble—cleaning windows, finding rocks to line the paths to our porches and whatever other chore Marissa and my mother could come up with. Slowly, our little matching houses went from dilapidated to habitable. And each night we sat with Marissa and Grayson, huddled around one of our small tables searching for anything to talk about besides the Old Colony or what our families might be doing without us.

Often, we discussed Marissa's work at the hospital. She had been trained on hospital procedures the first few weeks and then moved to working more than eighty hours a week. "Their science is behind," she said as she blew on the steam from the soup my mother had made.

"Not surprising," my mother grunted.

"I'm catching them up already." Marissa winked at Grayson and nudged him with her arm. "Ok for Grayson to stay with you again this week, Eleanor?" she asked. "I've just been approved for a new research study. I'll be burning the midnight oil."

"Of course," my mother smiled. "Always welcome."

Grayson and I tapped hands beneath the table. I relished the times Gray stayed with us. The house was less quiet, and I was less lonely, but I missed my best friend Liza terribly. She would be the last little girl to be my friend.

Liza and I spent hours making creations from the simplest of things—string webs to decorate our tree, small rocks that became rock families, or sticks and pieces of paper to make fairy houses in which my father, when we weren't looking, would hide cinnamon candy that he insisted were from the fairies. We created magical worlds, Liza and I, and we lived in that magic. I wondered if in some other colony there were small stones in circles with little leaf beds in hopes of fairies. No, I decided. Those would be memories of the Old Colony for us both.

Grayson was more than two years older than me and his games were so different than the little girl games I had played in the Old Colony. He and I gathered stones from the yard at Marissa's instruction and then took turns seeing who could throw them the farthest. We ran races in the open clearing beneath the old power lines and played "rescue," a game in which we used sticks to pull out lost colony members from collapsed salt mines and sinkholes. Gone were the days I held hands with a little girl or braided her hair while we told soft secrets. But he was my only option as we were too far away from everyone else in the Ancillary, and he was kind and playful. Grayson became a brother.

School was much worse. I had only two other Ancillary kids— Jack and Benjamin—both from the Old Colony, in my class. The two hadn't known each other before assimilation, but now they were inseparable, like twins. Though their presence was a comfort, I was a third wheel. Likewise, the Pulse children stuck to themselves, and I definitely wasn't a Pulse kid.

For one thing, I was completely clueless in discussions of Pulse music, films, or fashion—and what else was there? And, thanks to my mother, I wore only Old clothes. A stranger could have walked into our room and picked us Ancillaries out in an instant. Citizen girls wore their hair in all different colors and their clothes were miniature replicas of the adults'. Some of the kids even had miniature cuffs in their parents' style even though those models weren't typically issued until children turned ten.

Once I added a bright green streak to my ponytail with some stolen art paint. When I emerged from the school bathroom, I smiled coyly at one of the girls my age. She walked over to me and tilted her head to the side. "Nice try, Ancillary," she smirked, flicking my ponytail and then regrouping with her friends, who began pointing in my direction.

I returned to my corner with the two other Ancillary boys and sank into my chair. "It looks weirder on her," Benjamin said, and Jack shot the girl a look.

I shrugged my shoulders and gave them a half smile.

Grayson and I walked home from school together every day, no exceptions, at Marissa's and my mother's insistence in spite of the fact that all the colonies reported very low levels of crime. Anyone who did commit certain crimes was simply exiled. Cataclysmic events had given rise to a philosophical sect that believed the earth itself was responsible for decisions against human civilization, and that the destruction was in some way a judgment of individuals.

A National Council member, openly influenced by this belief, proposed that the humane reaction to criminality was to allow the earth to decide their fate. Thus, individuals were exiled and the earth "decided" whether or not they would live or die. Though most thought it to be preposterous, it was cheaper; exiles began in 2197. Crime plummeted. So, we felt safe taking the Convoy home and walking down our dirt road to Our Colony, as Marisa called it.

When Gray saw my hair he couldn't contain his laughter. I looked at him indignantly. "Shut up," I said as I kicked at his shoe. Gray was unusually quiet. I knew he was having his own problems with some of the other boys in his grade. That day two older Pulse boys had shoved him into a wall as everyone watched, or snickered. I had made eye contact with him from across the room and started to walk over, but he shook his head at me to stay where I was.

"I hate it here so much," I said as we walked back. "Nothing fits here—no, *I* don't fit here."

"We," Grayson sighed, picking up a stone from the road to throw. "*We* don't fit here. We were made for the Old Colony.

Grayson took my hand and pulled me from the road to a clearing in the woods.

"What are you doing?"

"Exploring. Come on." His eyes shone. "Sometimes when it rains I can hear something rushing. I think it's a big river, and I for one want to check it out."

I pulled my hand away. "What if we get out of the New Colony? I mean, what if we go across the boundary?"

"Suit yourself," he called, shoving tree branches out of the way to go deeper into the woods.

I watched Grayson until the leaves closed in around him and he was consumed by the woods. For a moment, I considered turning around to go home to tattle on him as soon as Marissa or my mother returned from work—but only for a moment.

"Grayson!" I called. "Wait up!" I wiped spider webs from my face as I followed. A squirrel made a daring leap above my head. The woods were so different than anything I'd experienced in the Old Colony, where any wooded areas had been thin enough in the winter to see to the other side.

My father and mother had often taken me to parks, which were plentiful in the Old Colony. Each neighborhood had one, and new trees had been planted when the Old Colony had been in its nascence. The magnolia in front of our house had become a summer home for Liza and me. The wide leaves and oversized blossoms made us feel that we were miniature in the protection of its umbrella. We took turns picking my mother's blackberries from her bush and handing them up to whichever one of us had already made it up to her branch. It was a small kingdom of bugs and nesting warblers, inchworms, and roly-polies, all ruled over by Liza and me.

But never before had I been embraced in the great expanse of woods. It was both frightening and comforting, as though the forest was wrapping itself around me. It was cozy and alive but full of mysterious new sounds and an unfamiliar earthen smell.

I yelled for Grayson several times, but he didn't respond. I recalled stories of the outer boundary and hoped that he had not gone too far. My mother had said that each colony was enclosed with some sort of fencing to prevent animals from entering. In the collapse of so many cities, many of the zoos had been destroyed along with much of the human population. In others, however, compassionate or perhaps foolhardy zookeepers couldn't bear to

38

allow the species that they had dedicated their lives to protecting to be trapped in their cages as they awaited certain death. So, many animals—orangutans, boa constrictors, giraffes, elephants—were given the chance to prolong their lives and roam the abandoned cities, for as many hours or days as the enraged earth would show mercy.

My father told me stories that had been passed down, perhaps more myth than truth at that point. He told of a zebra walking through the halls of the public library and survivors who went to battle with lions or gorillas, as much for sport as for subsistence. In a few of these cities, some of the more fit survivors were able to escape the city and finally become free—wolves and tigers feasted on abandoned cats and dogs and then retreated into the wild to try their skills at hunting for the first time without human assistance. Many of them, spoiled and tamed, survived only a few more days or weeks at best. Only the strongest endured.

For the cities deemed viable for the colony system, existing zoos were put into question. They were a drain on resources, and in the end those gentle souls who advocated sharing resources with the animals lost their fight. A compromise was struck and any animals that did not serve an immediate purpose as a food source or research test subjects were to be disposed of. Protesters lined the streets of the new capital in Old Richmond, Virginia (when Virginia existed), demanding justice for the innocent. Signs reading "Freedom for All!" showed pictures of sad, caged animals, denied their rights. Other signs read "Extinction!" and showed pictures of small, fluffy puppies or kittens.

The National Council decided that the animals would not be euthanized, but that they would instead be exiled. Our species' survival couldn't afford to share resources, but our humanity couldn't stand a mass euthanization of house cats or nearly extinct giraffes. Nor, realistically, could we provide the medication needed to euthanize on such a large scale. So, they were rounded up and shipped out to the more questionably habitable land, and fences were erected to separate the human species from the beasts.

In the world around our small colonies, evolution was on like it had never been before. Bears and mountain lions, gorillas and tigers duked it out to win the right for their genes to be passed along. Only the most savage or most elusive would survive. Other smaller creatures such as foxes, chipmunks, or raccoons that made it over or under the walls were tamed, bred, and sold to wealthy citizens who claimed them as status symbols.

I imagined glinting eyes of the most evolved predators blinking in the bushes as they waited to pounce.

"Grayson!" I called again when I heard the rush of the river. The forest opened up to a clearing surrounded by towering pines, draped in richly purple wisteria vines. I was in awe.

Gray sat upon a bark-less tree that had fallen across the river, his feet dangling. "Right here," he said.

I exhaled the breath I didn't know I had been holding. "I thought you had gotten over the boundary and been strangled by a boa constrictor," I told him irritably.

"Nah, I fought him off."

I thrust my shoes onto the bank and allowed the cool water to soothe my feet that had been rubbed raw from walking so far in shoes that had been sent a half size too small by the New Colony provisions.

Gray pointed to a red bird that had just alighted on a tree across the river. "That guy right there can go from colony to colony if he wants to."

I studied the red bird as he hopped upon the branch before taking flight. "For all we know, he just came back from wherever your parents are. Or my dad," I whispered, scanning the trees for more birds.

"Exactly," Grayson said. "He can sail way above it all, back and forth between us. And he's too quick to even worry about what's lurking on the ground. Up in the tree all day long. That's the life."

"The Old Colony didn't have as many birds," I realized. "Look at that one." I pointed to a small yellow-breasted fellow with a black head, immersed in song.

"No, it didn't. But have you ever seen this many trees either? Not as many places to nest in the Old Colony."

"They're ours now too, aren't they, Gray?" I asked.

"They are. All of this is Our Colony." He stepped into the water up to his knees. "This belongs to us," he declared in a deep voice with his hands on his hips.

I giggled.

"Come on, Rebecca," he said as he walked to the bank and looked around. "Here." He pointed to the roots that were sticking up in a tangled wall from a downed tree. "This will be our fort."

Gray started picking up sticks and lined them along the root wall at an incline until it made the skeleton of a small shelter. "Go get some branches with leaves," he instructed in his adult voice that always annoyed me. I found a small sapling and struggled to remove a branch that was still sinuous with life. Gray covered the stick he had laid with my leafed ones until a small hovel we could crawl into emerged. We stepped back to admire our work.

"You can't ever tell anyone from school about this. Not even other Ancillaries," Gray said solemnly.

"Ok," I agreed.

And I didn't. It was our secret and our hiding place from a world in which we feared we would never fit. For hours each day after school until my mom returned from work, we built our small kingdom.

Grayson found a hollow in one of the trees, where we kept jars of candy and special rocks we had collected. We discovered one majestically tall tree, clothed in wisteria, which was perfect for climbing. Grayson named it the Messenger Tree, and we'd take turns one at a time climbing to the top as high as we could to whisper messages to the birds to bring to Liza and Grayson's parents, and, of course, my dad. When they chirped back we interpreted.

"My mother says it won't be long now," Gray shouted down to me from the branches as he studied a bright blue bird with a Titian breast. Grayson always insisted that those birds were from his mother. Liza's messenger birds were the small brown and white ones that whistled "Re-bec-ca, Re-bec-ca, Re-bec-ca." But my father's were the large gray and white feathered with speckled undersides and large yellow talons. I waited anxiously to see one alight on the very top of the tree, looking down below with its seemingly mechanical head.

"Tell him where we are," I whispered to the regal bird. He spread his wings wide and rose above the forest to fly directly to where my father was awaiting news.

Liza sent me ladybugs that I captured in a jar or butterflies on days when she knew I needed some cheering. Lying on our backs, Grayson and I watched billowing clouds with symbolic pictures meant just for us.

"Look!" Grayson would say. "That one there looks like my old bicycle. Father's reminding me of our rides together."

And I would agree and point out the outline of a face that was sent by my dad to remind me that he wished with all his heart that he had only turned around to say goodbye.

We returned gifts and messages by the river—Grayson made small boats from curved bark on which we would put flowers or pretty stones to drift back to them. As is the gift of childhood, our fantasy felt so real that it became our reality.

In Our Colony, we didn't have to be a part of the New. There was no New as long as we were here. There was no VL system or exhausted caretaker. Homesickness was met with hope, and our imaginations took us beyond the borders to a hidden world that didn't believe in them. All creatures were subject to our rule, and they carried word from the ones we loved so that we were no longer completely separated.

But then, as the sun began to disappear behind the trees, we knew we'd have to leave our reign as king and queen of our kingdom and return as unwanted aliens to the New Colony. We agreed not to mention our afternoons to Marissa or my mother.

"They wouldn't understand," I told Grayson. "And, it wouldn't be right to allow them in. They'd say it wasn't real, and then maybe the birds and the river would stop believing too."

Gray took my hand as we walked home that night. "You're right," he said. "It's better left a secret." Marissa and my mother never found out about our kingdom, although once, from the Messenger Tree, Grayson insisted he saw my mother walking along the other side of the river with Will Skycap. I didn't believe him but hid all the same. Perhaps they too had found comfort by the waters.

Marissa's hours were long. Often, Gray would not see her for days at a time. The New Colony was right. She couldn't have taken care of him without my mother's help. On nights when Gray stayed with us, my mother made a small cot out of extra blankets and pillows on the floor in the living room. She tucked him in as she had me when I was a little girl in the Old Colony. "Good night, sweetheart," she would tell him softly.

Many times I would watch Grayson between the crack in my door as his cheeks glistened in the oblique moonlight that streamed from the adjacent window. One night I tiptoed to his pallet and stood as he knelt by the windowpane. His back was to me, but I knew he was crying.

"Gray," I whispered.

He startled at my voice but did not turn around.

"Are you all right?" I asked in a hushed voice.

He put his head on the window. "No." He lightly tapped the glass with his finger.

I knelt behind him and looked at the outline of the swaying trees. "It's hardest knowing they're out there somewhere, but not knowing where they are or what they're doing. Or if they're ok. It's the not knowing that's the hardest, isn't it?" I asked.

Grayson turned to me. "Yes," he said. "It won't always be like this, though. They'll come for us." He was resolute. "I know my mother and father. They'll find us."

I rubbed the small lump on the back of my neck where my father had said he was giving me something that would help find me one day. And then I pictured my father as I screamed for him to turn around. He wasn't coming back.

"Somehow," Grayson said, "they'll find us. It'll just be like a bad dream, and then one day it will all be as it was before, only we'll be older."

"You'll have a beard," I told him seriously.

Gray nudged me as he wiped his face with his other hand. I leaned my small head on Gray's bony shoulder.

"Some things even earthquakes can't shake," he said. "They'll come back."

Chapter 5

For the first Sundays of our new life, my mother hosted gatherings in our house for the Old Colony transfers. They would come from all over the Ancillary—some emerging from the woods like ghosts, others taking the Convoy and making the trek down the dirt road to our front steps. But the homesick poured in throughout the week as well, if they knew my mother was home. It seemed as if, for months after assimilating, we'd have someone over from the Old Colony at any given time. My mother was always ready with clean mugs and coffee on the stove, and a thick potato soup that had been a staple in the Old Colony. They'd sit in the living room and talk softly, the visitors often crying and my mother, in spite of her own homesickness, stoically reassuring them.

Many times gifts were left—baked pies, homemade clothing in the Old Colony style, extra seeds for the garden, and to my mother's delight, matched by my horror, several cages of chickens. Sometimes the presents were left on the porch with cryptic notes that I didn't understand, including numbers and names. I once opened a carton of eggs with the shells covered in numbers. My mother simply shrugged when I showed her. "Homesickness does something to a person," she had said blandly.

Each time I heard footsteps on our front porch I thought it was my father, like he'd escaped to save us. Maybe my mother did too, the way she'd run to answer the door. But always there were the same distraught faces of people there to lean on my mother, like she was still our first lady with solutions and not someone just as misplaced as they were.

They came more frequently as we approached the anniversary of our transfer. Some of the adults were eligible for transfer after a year and I could hear them discuss their hopes as well as their distrust of the system in hushed tones.

That first year, not one of the transfer applicants was accepted to leave the colony. Not one left. We did receive new transfers in, but always these were from other colonies that had been assimilated. To no one's surprise, transfer applicants' second, third, and fourth attempts were also denied. We were stuck. Even ever-optimistic Grayson began to doubt that his parents would come. Even still, New Colony officials assuaged our frustration with the assurance that the National Council always had our species', and the colonies', best interest at heart.

Many years ago, transfers were much more prevalent. Oftentimes, though, they went terribly awry. Rumors spread that our Automation teacher's husband had put in a transfer to Colony 215 only to find that his wife was on year two of a three-year union contract. It's the risk you take, I guess.

Union contracts were one of the New Colony idiosyncrasies that my mother abhorred the most. The Old Colony had upheld marriages and recognized nothing else. The New Colony, on the other hand, insisted that more short-term commitments were more likely to be successful as well as increase the likelihood of gene dispersion, as more people were likely to have multiple offspring with more partners. More gene dispersion, more diversity of the gene pool. It also decreased the likelihood that people would seek transfer.

Six years ago was the darkest time since the assimilation. Marissa died unexpectedly, and our world went darker. We knew she was sick, but none of us were prepared for her death, and the shock of it shook us in a way that the assimilation could not; even after our separation from the Old, we had found new comfort in our togetherness. But then the ultimate separation, death, had found us. Visitors poured in to share their condolences, which we received numbly.

Gray was so deep in his grief that he hadn't even considered what would happen to him once Marissa was gone. Though my mother was prepared to go to war with the colony in order to gain guardianship of Grayson, the colony hadn't put up much of a fight. Cherish was becoming overrun with children from other colonies transferring in, and they didn't want to add to their numbers. As long as my mother would take responsibility for him, he could stay. Mom prepared his old cot for him by the window.

One night I lay awake, staring at the ceiling and thinking of Marissa. At midnight, I slipped out of my room to check on Gray, half expecting him to be looking out the window at the moon as he did when he was a little boy during our first nights living in the New Colony. But his bed was empty.

I took the quilt from his cot and wrapped it around myself. The door moaned as I opened it, but my mother didn't stir. Quietly, I put on my rain boots that had been left on the porch. I knew exactly where Grayson would be.

The woods were quiet, inviting me with their peace. I found Gray sitting on a log next to the river. He glowed in the moonlight, shaking and rocking back and forth. Silently, I sat next to him and wrapped the quilt around us both. He grabbed onto me and sobbed into my hair. I took Grayson's hand in mine and kissed it gently. The river rushed on in spite of our grief.

Gray clung to me until the sun came up. We were familiar with the searing pain of separation. But this was a new, deeper ache. I figured that even Grayson couldn't hope beyond her death. But as the sun illuminated the woods and the frost gleamed, Grayson turned to me and whispered, "One day."

"One day what, Gray?"

"There's just got to be more."

I looked at him incredulously. No, there wasn't more for us. Beyond this river there was a wall that we would never overcome. There might be more, but it was far beyond our reach. Gray was a fool, but I was jealous of his hope. "Sure there is," I lied as I stroked his head.

I left Grayson in Our Colony and returned to my house in case my mother woke and worried where we had gone. I had only been lying in my bed for about an hour when she called for me to start the coffee.

There had been a knock on the door the second day after Marissa's death. A man and a woman came in, all smiles. "Well, hello there," the woman said cheerfully, bending down to eye level with me. I was fascinated by her jewelry that was made to look like flowing water droplets. It must have used LED technology to make it appear fluid. She wore a flowing shirt that ruffled at her knee and also looked like rushing water. Perhaps it was meant to calm those around her. It wasn't working on me.

The man's hair was slicked against his head in greasy, flat curls. "We just need to talk to Mom for a minute, honey, ok?" he said, thickly sweet.

I swallowed the words "She's not *your* mom, buddy" and turned to hide behind the corner where I could still hear. "Ms. Flora—"

"Mrs. Flora actually," my mother interrupted. "But you may call me Eleanor."

The man cleared his throat. "Ok, Eleanor. We're from the New Colony Assimilation Committee. Our job is to assist with the assimilation of new colonists. We're here to serve and aid in this transition process as best we can, as we understand this is a difficult time."

"I see," Mom said flatly.

"Yes, aid in the difficult transition, as it were," the woman said in a high, singsong voice.

"Very well, I'd like my husband back." My mother's voice was unwavering. I could hear the woman tap her pen nervously.

"Ms. . . . umm, Eleanor," the woman said gently. "As I'm sure you understand, that is not a possibility. It is the National Council's value that we preserve healthy genetic diversity within each colony. That decision is very much out of our hands, I'm afr—"

"And, it's a Colony 108 value that marriages cannot be separated."

I imagined the man and the woman exchanging uncomfortable glances. "Colony 108 no longer exists, and therefore its values are not recognized in the current crisis."

I held my breath, wanting to scream at the woman. What were they doing here, anyway?

The man attempted a firmer tone. "Ma'am, your ex-union partner—"

"My *husband*," my mother interrupted coolly. "My husband, the ex-president of Colony 108, made a very difficult decision, one that I stand by."

A large tear rolled down my cheek when I blinked.

"For the family members who still have the knowledge that their loved ones were denied assimilation with them, it makes for a difficult transition, as you say," my mother continued.

"I'm sure you are aware from inter-colony reports that ex-president Flora is serving in the Executive Colony," the man said caustically. "I'm certain he has found his new life there to be comfortable, and I'm sure he would hope the same for you."

I froze. Up until that moment I had assumed that my father had been assimilated to another colony like us. I imagined him waking up to an empty house like ours and going about whatever assigned task his New Colony had given him—agriculture support, perhaps, or maybe a desk job doing accounting. But no. He was working with the group that upheld the colony system. While we were thrust to the outskirts of 215, he was enjoying the luxury of an executive position in the headquarters that supported our inferior, non-citizen status.

I felt my insides twist as I tried to accommodate this information. It was at that moment as I stood with my back against the wall that I determined I would become a citizen—throw myself full force into creating a new life that had nothing to do with 108.

I heard the leather from my mother's favorite chair strain under her weight as she sat down. "Look," she said softly. "I understand why you're here. Two fifteen has an unusually large number of 108 colonists. I'm sure the 215 president has asked your due diligence in keeping an eye on so large a group as it could . . . *disrupt* order."

The woman cleared her throat. "Given your background," she said in a sickly sweet voice, "I would imagine you have a certain propensity for understanding the delicacies of politics."

"Indeed," my mother agreed. "And you're worried by the number of people gathering at the residence of an ex-first lady's home. It is noted, and I can assure you that I am comforting the homesick and the grieving for one of Colony 108's finest citizens who recently passed."

Without even seeing her, I knew the superior expression she was giving them.

"Eleanor." The man's voice was sympathetic. Now they were on a comfortable topic for the Assimilation committee. "Homesickness is a normal response, but it is also a temporary unpleasantness. I hope that you will visit some of our services. Here, let me see—"

I risked looking around the corner at the man handing my mother a small pamphlet. "Feel free to have any of your friends contact one of our representatives as we are happy to arrange several options including Virtual Desensitization, Memory Therapy, or medicinal patches."

"It is our pleasure to help New become Home," the woman interjected with the committee's mantra.

The first lady smiled politely. "This isn't my home."

Chapter 6

Radius sits on the edge of the bed and stares at the small birds that dart inside the glass aviary that has been built into his bedroom wall. Their flapping creates quick eruptions of blues, greens, and reds. I brush my fingertips from his shoulders to his lower back. His LED tattoo comes alive under the pressure of my touch—glowing flowers bloom and unfurl around two horns of a lamb in an electric display. His shadow on the wall beside the aviary moves slowly as the detectors pick up his movement and display it as throbbing art.

Music from the floor below overflows into our room, its vibrations making ripples of color on the pressure-sensitive floor. Radius does something on his cuffs with his head tilted to the side. He is the most beautiful thing I have ever known in my gray world.

"I've got something I want to give you," he says absentmindedly, without looking around. "This little one looks lonely." His voice seems far away as he has suddenly become distracted by a flutter of green wings. He stands and walks to the aviary.

I attempt a casual sprucing of my hair and hope that he doesn't notice.

"They're beautiful, aren't they?" he says as he places his hand on the glass. Slowly, he opens the side door and reaches his hand in so gently that a small green bird allows him to take hold of her. He clutches the bird to his chest and smiles as he speaks sweetly to her. "Shhh," he coos, and strokes her head with a finger. He looks up to me like a little boy showing his mother a new treasure, just discovered.

I giggle.

"This one's my favorite. Aww, aren't you sweet, darling." He speaks to her in a singsong voice like the Cherish workers use when fawning over a new baby.

"I'm going to take a video," I laugh. I hold up my cuff and am poised to hit record when suddenly Ray freezes and his face instantly turns dark.

"No," he snaps.

I drop my cuff.

For a moment more he stares at my cuff as though remembering something. "I don't do videos," he says with some irritation.

I detect the slightest hint of fear in his voice, but perhaps I am imagining it.

"Oh, I'm sorry, Ray. I just thought you looked so sweet with your—"

"Never video me, Lark. It makes me . . ." Ray turns his back to me to restore the bird to her glass house. "When I was a boy, there was this guy. . ." he murmurs like he's hypnotized as he recalls some memory. "No video, ok?" I notice his hands are shaking as he latches the door. When he turns back around he is smiling and fully himself again, confident and in charge.

He reaches for a small box on the bedside table. I stop breathing. I open it to find a constellation of Luminstones, the largest one with his symbol, an R inside a circle, printed on it. I forget to breathe. "Want me to take you to get them put on today?" he asks.

I cover my smile with my hand. "Yes," I say, holding one up to my neck.

"Good." Radius kisses me just below my ear before turning to the bathroom.

If we were in the Old Colony, I would hope to marry Radius. I hope it even now, though I know the concept is foreign to Radius, who was born in the Pulse. Colony 215 is different than most colonies—no, more practical than most colonies. It appealed to have union contracts for as short as twelve months. The Council granted it. Today I am one step closer. He could belong to me, if only for a year.

My mother still wears her wedding band. Once I mentioned that she should get a boyfriend. It was like I had slapped her. "Rebecca, I am married to your father," she said, dumbfounded.

"You *were*," I insisted. "Not now. Dad might have new kids for all you know. He could have a string of unions." The words were meant to hurt my mother, but the thought of my dad having a new family pained me just as much.

Even though I'm sure Radius has had the opportunity before, he's never had a union contract. I could be his first, and if I am, then I might be eligible for citizenship-level VL and residency in the Pulse. I've never mentioned it to him before, but he's got to be thinking it.

I roll onto my side and arrange the covers so that my curves are accentuated, tossing my hair so that it splays on the pillow. I can hear Radius talking on his cuff to someone in the bathroom. His tone is harsh and biting. I strain to hear but can't decipher any words. Like my father, Radius emanates power. It draws me in. And like the Pulse, there is mystery about him. It's difficult to imagine Radius as a little boy, although I have sometimes caught glimpses of him, like when he watches his birds, when I think I see a hint of who he once was. But then the glimpse is gone in a flash, and he is the confident and powerful Pulse man again.

Like the colonies, his freedom and his strength come from his autonomy. He is a man without past—or at least he has rejected his past. He just *is*. And I have learned not to ask about the peripheral details of his life. Being with him is to be in the center of it all—everything may spin around us so quickly that it seems it ceases to exist.

"Hi, sweetheart," he says gently when he returns. "You're just captivating, you know that?" He traces the curve of my hip with his finger, and I blush. "But you *don't* know that, do you?"

I shrug as he moves his hand to sweep the hair from my neck and rubs my shoulders. He gently strokes the back of my neck and then stops suddenly. "What's this?" he asks, tapping a bump on the back of my neck.

I reach my hand to caress the tracking device that my father inserted. Suddenly it feels like it is radiating searing heat. "Nothing." I cringe. "I thought it would—no, it's nothing."

Radius pulls me up onto his lap and cradles me in his arms after tenderly wrapping me in the sheet. I press my head onto his chest like a child. "Captivating," he whispers, "but so much hurt."

I close my eyes tight.

"You're safe now, Lark. I'll keep you safe, my beautiful little girl." He kisses my forehead over and over, slowly and gently, bringing my skin to hyperawareness where his warm mouth has touched. And then he strokes my hair with strong hands.

I have never been with another boy before. I know that I am not Radius's first, of course. But to be with him is to become a part of him, a part of his world, a part of something bigger. It is peace and I crave it. I find home.

Lex messages me while I'm having the stones embedded. I ignore the buzz on my wrist and shift in the reclined chair. Radius indicates a constellation of places on my neck and whispers specific instructions over me to the technician—start behind my ear, run them down my neck. Ray points to my skin as he gives orders and the woman nods as she takes note. His face becomes intense as he repeats the instructions. I shift uncomfortably as they talk above me, gathering my courage for the procedure. Radius looks down at me warmly.

"But be gentle with her," he says firmly. "She's delicate." Ray squeezes my hand and kisses my neck gently.

The tech nods and winks at me. "Take this," she says and hands me a small pill.

I watch her as the pill takes effect almost immediately after I swallow it. Her tattoos seem to come to life and extend off her arms into the space around her. Even with the pill I can feel the intense pressure as the stones are placed in my skin.

It takes almost an hour to have the stones embedded.

"So sexy," Radius says, kissing the other side of my neck as I admire them in the mirror. I kiss him back.

"Thank you again, Ray," I say as his cuff beeps. I don't like how serious Radius becomes suddenly. "You ok?" I mouth as he presses the speaker on his cuff and stands up.

He has an implant in his ear that allows him to get reception. There's another implant on his throat so that he can speak. I'm still fascinated by it since everyone in the Ancillary just has the receivers in the cheapest cuffs they make, the only ones we can afford. Radius ignores me and stands to take the call, where I only pick up a few words. He paces by the wall and points his hand emphatically like he's lecturing someone.

"No," I hear him say. "No deal, man." Radius gestures for me to leave. "Taking you home now," he says. "I've got something to take care of."

"Everything ok, babe?" I put my hand on his shoulder and lean my head to the side so that my stones catch the light.

"Sure, fine. Let's go."

I stumble behind him, bracing myself on the tables and chairs to walk out as clearly the pill has not left my system.

I was hoping to get the chance today to ask him to serve on the Panel for me. I get to choose a sponsor. Radius's VL is so high that his scoring of me will carry more weight. But now's not the time.

Radius looks perturbed. "Call Jamison," he tells his cuff once we get in the car. "Take care of this guy," he says a moment later and hangs up.

I run my hand along his leg and turn my chin upward to show off my stones. Radius does not turn.

"Just stop here," I tell him before we pull too close to the house. I can see my mother watering plants in the back garden.

"Ok, so, thanks again." I lean in for a kiss before my mom comes to the front.

He kisses me briefly and looks out the window. "Sure, no problem, you know," he says distractedly.

"I love you so much." The words just slip from my mouth without my permission. Radius turns to me with a blank expression at first that quickly softens.

"You too, Lark," he says, smiling. "My little girl from two worlds."

My heart throbs up into my temples. "K, bye." I practically float as I close the car door and take the steps to our front porch. I wave like a five-year-old as he pulls away.

He loves me. The gaping hole that opened inside me when we moved here starts to close a little. My eyes ache with how quickly they fill with tears. He loves me. I said it first, but he didn't hesitate to say "me too." Maybe he'd just been waiting for the right time to tell me. I want to hear him say it over and over again. He loves me. I inhale sharply so I don't break into a full-out hideous cry. The healing of knowing he loves me is almost painful, like the throbbing relief of salve on a burn.

Grayson calls from his front yard, "Hey, Rebecca!" He's pulling weeds and is covered in dirt.

I didn't even notice him there. I blink lightly so that tears don't fall. Normally I'd just roll my eyes and go inside, but I'm dying to show off my new stones to someone, anyone. He'll have to do.

"What's new?" I say, turning my head to the side and smiling. Gray stops in mid-pull of a knee-high weed and does a double take.

That's right, Grayson—I told you I had a plan.

Gray stands up without brushing himself off and walks over to me. I jerk my chin when he tries to reach out to touch the stones. For a moment we stand looking at each other. Gray's face turns from compassion to anger. I leave before he can come up with anything pathetic to say. He stands there dumbfounded and mad.

I look around my house differently this time, like I'm seeing everything as it will be when I leave and come back to visit, if I ever do. The disdain I usually have for this house, which is intensified after returning from an extended time in the Pulse, has dissipated. It's only a matter of time now.

The back screen door whines and slams shut. I hear my mother stomping dirt off her boots. "Rebecca?"

"Nope," I say bitterly. "It's Lark."

"Where have you been?" she demands. "I've sent you about a dozen messages. I thought you were going to be at Cherish this afternoon."

"I was out with friends."

Mom sits in the chair slowly, with her back straight and ankles crossed like she's sitting for a press conference and not like she's just been feeding chickens after a shift taking care of discarded kids in the Ancillary. I want to scream at her—for her fake nobility and for holding me back. Today I hate her because a boy—a Pulse man, a VL-758 citizen—loves me, and she won't think he's worth it.

"Rebecca," she says softly. "Please sit down with me."

I cross my arms over my chest and lean against the wall.

"You're hurting." She says it in a way that I find particularly irritating. It's like she's talking to one of the Cherish kids.

I shake my head in frustration. Not anymore. A man just said he loves me, and I can't tell her about it. What does she expect me to do? Live in her 1,000-square-foot fragment of Old Colony that is our house? Accept rejection without even trying?

"I'm figuring out how to make it here. And I'm doing it pretty well," I smirk.

"With that man?"

"Yes, that man!"

"Sweetheart, you have to understand—you have to be *careful*. Promise me. You're different. You're above this and there are dangers here—this isn't our home."

"It's not *your* home! I can't live in this place and choose to just not be a part of it like you can. I'm not going to be in the Ancillary for the rest of my life, ok? *I'm* going to actually have some value!" Tears are hot on my face.

"What are you talking about? You're not a *score* someone gives you. Your father—"

"Don't!" I say, putting my hands out in front of me to shield myself from her words. "Don't you dare say his name! He doesn't exist!"

My mom remains unfazed and stands to put her arms out to me. For a moment, I almost want to collapse into them like a child, risk telling her that a boy loves me on the chance that she might be a little happy for me. Instead I beat the back of my head against the wall and take in a ragged breath.

My mother gasps and turns my head to the side with both hands. She lets out a moan and shakes her head in disbelief as she studies my stones. I wrench myself away from her and look her right in the eyes, which are wide with panic. She covers her mouth with a trembling hand. For the first time in my life I see that the first lady is shaken.

"He branded you," she says.

Chapter 7

My dad often brought me flowers from the bushes outside our home and put them in little places where I'd find them as a surprise—in my paint box, under my hand when I woke up in the morning, on my doll like she was holding them herself. He'd feign surprise when I found them.

We had a spindly little azalea bush growing in a corner of our yard here in the New Colony. Each year I'd snip off the buds before they had a chance to blossom in the spring. Finally, I poured my mother's container of salt onto its roots and watched with satisfaction as it shriveled over the course of a week.

Last night I dreamed that my father was holding a bouquet of brilliantly white azaleas. He smiled and held them up like he wanted me to take them from him. As I reached out, he dropped them to the ground and they shattered like glass. He turned slowly and started walking away.

"Wait!" I screamed. "Daddy! Take me with you!"

He was walking faster to a ballooner's basket. "Daddy, wait!" I yelled as I tripped again and again. He got into the basket and started floating away.

I think I can still feel the ground shaking, but it's just my sobbing as I wake up. The earth is still. I put the palm of my hand on my neck and it calms me.

My head pounds as I remember the night before. My mother is wrong, jealous even. She says that Radius is claiming me.

"Yes," I told her sarcastically. "I'm his *girlfriend*." I threw the words at her like knives. "And, he's my boyfriend."

"No," my mom pleaded. She shook her head and almost laughed, like she was getting hysterical over it. "Not your boyfriend. Your *hawker*." Her face showed pity, which outraged me all the more.

I locked myself in my room and screamed at her from the other side that she was jealous. It was ridiculous to think that Radius would sell me. Hawkers work in the section of the Pulse known as the Pound. The bottom floors of the tall buildings that line the streets are shops that sell everything from body art and lingerie to patch enhancers. There are dance halls on the bottom floor and pleasure theaters. They were all illegal in Colony 108, as far as I know, but here it is a thriving business district. On the upper floors at the Pound, girls and boys entertain and service clients. Hawkers recruit and manage the girls. Radius isn't one of them. Those guys don't love their girls; they *sell* their girls.

My VL went up overnight. Radius's Contour Sheet posted images of me, which directed traffic to my Contour Sheet. Sixteen people—sixteen *from the Pulse*, had voted for me. Two of them had even zapped me to say they'd like to meet sometime. I spent the night messaging back and forth with Radius but couldn't talk to him out of fear that my mom would hear me from the other side of the door. I hesitated to tell him my mother's crazy theory that he was a hawker, but I wanted him to see just how far off the deep end she had gone this time.

He was clearly offended, hurt even. I wished I hadn't mentioned it.

"I'm coming to get you," he said, and for a brief moment I considered what I could throw into a bag to take with me.

I talked him out of it, though. It would only make things worse.

"Hang in there, Lark," he said at about midnight. "I love you," he typed. The words flashed quickly, the I and O's in red in the New Colony rapid reading style. I repeated it over and over again.

"Then nothing else matters," I wrote back. "Love you too." I must have fallen asleep in a matter of minutes.

My mom knocks on the door just as the sun is illuminating my curtains. "Rebecca, are you awake?" Her voice sounds thin.

"Yeah," I say. "I guess I am." I know for a fact that she slept in front of my door last night. I got up to go to the bathroom around midnight and had to step over her.

"How about you come to work with me today?" She looks pitiful. For a moment I forget that she seems determined to make me miserable. She looks so worn. I feel a little softened toward her.

"I've got school, remember?"

"No, you had school yesterday. You skipped yesterday. Today is Saturday; you're legitimately off."

I give her a look to tell her I don't think she's funny in spite of the fact that she's smiling like she's said something hilarious.

"Fine," I mumble.

60

Maybe I'm in a good mood from my VL shooting up last night. Or maybe I'm just too tired to argue with her anymore. I'd like to go hang out with Lex, but if the woman is willing to sleep outside my door, she'll be willing to follow me and make an embarrassing scene.

"I'll go get dressed."

I meet my mother at the kitchen table. She hands me a hot mug of coffee and a hard boiled egg, sliced on toast, the breakfast she has eaten every morning for as long as I have known her, one of the few threads she says runs through her Old and New lives.

We take a shortcut through the Ancillary to the easternmost part of the colony to Cherish. If my mother were to ride the Convoy, it would take almost an hour and a half to get there one way with all the stops. Instead she walks along the clearing of the power lines, no matter the weather. She has walked this path twice a day, six days a week, for the past eight years. I struggle to keep up with her over the three or four miles that she walks each day. We cut through a thicket in which my mother has cleared a narrow path that opens to a small neighborhood of older homes.

I don't know many of the people in the houses we pass. Most of them came from other colonies before we arrived. Some of them were born in the Pulse, but didn't have high enough VL scores to retain citizenship.

The houses all look the same—brick and whitewashed but chipping and grayed from the pollution of the neighboring factories. The short side of their rectangular shape faces the road. In front are two rock steps smoothed by the rainwater that drips from a metal roof, sloping at a steep angle. The differences between houses are subtle as they are worn in varying degrees—one's balusters are broken or missing in the railings, giving the appearance of a grin full of chipped teeth. Some yards have been maintained and even have small pots of blue or yellow flowers lining their steps, as though their owners are making the best of it. Others have allowed vines and weeds to overtake them, like they've given up.

For several years I looked for the pristine homes that the New Colony had shown in the film. I had been furious that Grayson and I had been so slighted while the rest of our transferred colony citizens were enjoying their meticulous gardens from their balconies.

It was Grayson who pointed out the row of houses in one of the neighborhoods that had been used in the film. We stared at a line of two-story houses with boarded windows and rusted railings. "Look at that one," he said. "In the film it was blue. It's the one I was hoping Marissa and I would get. I was going to put a swing in that tree," he said, pointing to a dying oak that he insisted had been verdant and thriving in the film.

"That was a different house," I said indignantly.

"Nope, same one."

"But this is the old section of the Ancillary," I returned.

Gray shrugged.

We had spent the day riding the Convoy line that picked up Ancillary residents around the perimeter of the Colony. We passed the south side with its factories billowing smoke from tall towers and the large agricultural center in the north and all the broken-down remains in between. We got off several times in search of the luxurious section of the Ancillary, following young passengers with shiny watches or leather purses as we reasoned that maybe the nicer section was reserved for the well-dressed kind of Ancillaries. But, each section turned out to be the same—weather-beaten and crumbling as though the Pulse had pushed them out to be forgotten.

My mother waves to an old woman who rocks herself to a hunched, standing position from her chair. Her back is so curved that she looks to be in the process of sitting. Her gnarled hands grip the railing that is chipped to show its gray undercoat, not unlike her own skin. "Eleanor," she calls, motioning to my mother with a stiff hand. "Come on now. Come on," she beckons.

Mom smiles and nods for me to follow. She couldn't be from the Old Colony, I think. How does my mother even know these people? I shake my head and step over the roots in the sidewalk as a cat flees from the porch—house pets had been exiled, but some of the cats were able to make it over the wall to beg a meal. They proliferated quickly. I hate cats.

The woman's accent is thick, probably residual from another colony, where she once lived. "Ha!" her voice is deep and abrupt. "Ha!"

My mother is all smiles as the woman grasps her face with both hands and plants a kiss right on her lips. Oh, wow. "It's a goods day," she says, and I instinctively take a step down before she can grab and kiss me too. "Ellies, she's a sugarbean," the old woman says, eye to eye with me even though I'm two steps down.

My mom is still beaming. "Yes, she's something," she says brashly.

I shoot her a look.

"Wells, girl. You's Hope walking down the street, I'd reckons. Takings care of them babies. Bless yous."

My mother bows slightly at the waist. I give the woman a small wave and turn to catch up with my mother, who has already taken off and is nodding hello to other people whom I also don't understand how she could possibly know. I keep my head down as the rejected people wave pathetically to my mother as though she is their queen. This Ancillary road to Cherish is enough to motivate anyone to gain citizenship.

In the film clip, Cherish was a handsome white house, stately in its expanse and surrounded by smaller care centers, concrete buildings in pastels. I imagined children running around it in a game of catch and reading or painting on one of its balconies. And from a distance it could have been that, perhaps. But as we get closer it's clear that the house is in much need of repair—new paint, patched boards. Broken toys are left in the yard that has long since been weeded. What was meant to be a haven for children has experienced years of abuse from its inhabitants' small hands. My mother has tried for many years to get more colony funds for improvements; all requests have been denied.

In spite of the differences with my mother, I have always been grateful not to have been raised here. I think of how close Grayson was to being sent to live in this place. No wonder Marissa fought so hard to keep him. She never trusted the New Colony. When we saw the film introducing the New Colony, her mind was already translating the images into what they truly were.

A small, balding man opens the front door and a dark, muscular man walks out.

"Hi, Will," my mother addresses him, which he returns with a nod and then walks off quickly.

"Mr. Skycap was just helping with some instructions for the Seventeen years," the balding man, Mr. Porter, explains.

"I see," my mom returns as she puts her arm around me.

"Morning, morning!" Mr. Porter crows cheerfully as he notices me. "Hi, Rebecca," he says in the same singsong voice he would use to greet a six-year-old. His accent is thickly Old; even after all this time I still cringe to hear it.

"Hello, Mr. Porter," I say politely.

Nicholas Porter worked with my father as the Education Director. Many times he came to our house to discuss colony business with my parents in our front room. I occasionally played on the floor as Mr. Porter enthusiastically presented data sent between colonies regarding best practices in teaching and findings on children's cognitive development.

My mother had taught in the same school where he had formerly been the principal. "He's a brilliant man," she told me once.

I wondered why he had not been given a position working for the Pulse school system, but my mother told me that the position was reserved for colony citizens only. So, he governed the small village of technical orphans and threw himself into his work. Perhaps his obsession with work was because he himself had left five children to be transferred to other colonies, where they were now likely in another colony's version of Cherish.

"Eleanor, we need to discuss test scores for our Ten and Eleven years," he said. "Will you join me in my office? Rebecca, I think you could best help if you would serve breakfast to the Threes and Fours."

I sighed and headed down the long hallway.

The main building of Cherish includes educational rooms for children that Pulse classrooms could not accommodate. Dyslexic, hyperactive, and unfocused children that the Pulse teachers could not tolerate as distractions from their other Pulse-bred pupils were relegated to the confines of Cherish. And for children who had been separated from parents and siblings and thrust into a new world, the "unteachable" constituted the majority of them.

Under the patient care of Mr. Porter and the gentleness of workers such as my mother, children began to emerge from the counterpane of depression and homesickness; Cherish, as decrepit as it was, became home. But, as test scores improved, proving them to be "teachable," these children were thrust into Pulse schools.

Of course, it would only be a matter of time, thanks to the *warm* welcoming of Pulse children, that the Cherish children would once again regain "unteachable" status as they retreated inward after being removed from a world where they had only just begun to find stability. After several of the children had bounced from

Cherish-outcast to Pulse-outcast, back to Cherish-outcast again, my mother found ways to coach students to either not score as high, or, for the younger children who were less easily persuaded to answer questions incorrectly, she simply changed the scores herself.

I walk down the long corridor past busy rooms of students engaged in a variety of projects. Mr. Porter has re-written Colony curriculum to project-based learning based on the empirical findings of educational studies. I pass by a classroom in which young children are laying out a variety of vegetables they have grown in the garden on the table. One is measuring a small pumpkin. A little boy is counting seeds in a squash and recording the number on a data sheet.

One room down, a teacher is drawing bubbles around different words to describe "dolls." In a room across the hall, two little girls are engaged in discussion over a book while occasionally giving instructions to a little boy who sits in the middle of a large and intricate construction of blocks. He is consulting hand-drawn instructions for whatever architectural plan they have concocted.

Even though I am grateful I don't live here, I wish my own school could be more like this. I envy how oblivious these kids are to the pressures of Pulse life. They are content and engaged in their little rejected egg of the Ancillary. I asked my mother if I could go to school at Cherish when I was a little girl. My mother had smiled warmly. "No," she had said. "Not allowed."

In my fourth year here, the annual exams began. For verbal skills I ranked high—two standard deviations above average. But for visual-spatial and quantitative science, I ranked embarrassingly low. My scores were turned in to the Panel and almost overnight my VL went down by about a hundred points. "Forget about it, Rebecca," Lex had said. "The Colony is looking for future scientists, not poets."

I worked for hours each night on my math and science assignments. Meanwhile, my language arts and social scores plummeted. But, it didn't seem to matter. I was pegged. My brain wasn't designed to promote colony prosperity as a catastrophist or microbiologist. But, I wasn't going to let my brain's wiring hold back my citizenship. There are other ways to get ahead here.

Cherish kids are different. They don't stand a chance without any links to the Pulse. Who would vote on their Contour Sheets? No one, except each other, and what good would that do? Their VL's are so low, there's no point in even trying, and yet here they are, their little chins on their fists as they lean forward to hear their teachers read them silly stories and send them outside with a basket and a ruler. They've been cast so far out from society that they've ceased to care. I pity and envy them for that.

Mr. Porter calls for me from down the hall. "Examination Day, Rebecca. Think you could help us with something?"

"Sure," I return. Once a week, all the students at Cherish are required by law to take part in a series of experiments. Their data is collected as part of the research the Pulse behavioral scientists will later use to improve upon the education system of the colony in general. My mother hates Examination Day, partly because it is never announced until the morning it is to be administered. There is no preparing the children and that, of course, is intentional.

But then, nothing is predictable at Cherish. Each morning the Education Committee sends over a new schedule—for rising, meal times, free time, and lessons. Children are traded to different lodgings at random so that they are never quite sure if the bunk mate they were becoming friends with will suddenly be asked to move across campus. It is all part of the plan, my mother told me—to keep Cherish on its toes. But more, she assumes, to give the children the sense that they have no control over their environment. It makes the teachers' jobs nearly impossible.

Mr. Porter and my mother knock mildly on a blue painted door. "Excuse me, Ms. Salomini," Mr. Porter asks. "May I have your class for data collection, please?"

A young woman with dark hair and equally dark eyes drops her book to her hip. "Sure," she says. The woman marshals a broad smile for the sake of the class. "Ok," she says, standing up. "Let's get this over with." She taps a small bell and motions for them to line up at the door, which they do reluctantly.

Mr. Porter and my mother lead them to one of the buildings in the back. We pass by a small garden outlined in rocks with small gourds hanging from poles.

The class enters a pastel blue cement building that is hidden from the front entrance. My mother holds the door as the children file in silently and sit obediently on small benches on the back side of a narrow room that faces five wide doors.

Mr. Porter stands at the front of the building, holding a device in his hands, and reads robotically: "Good morning. Today is again Examination Day, a day when you, the student, provide the colony with data for the educational research scientists to better understand the developing minds of children. All research will be privately held and used for the advancement of colony academic policy."

As Mr. Porter reads the instructions, he sporadically glances from the children to the corner of the room. I follow his gaze to a camera that is adhered to the ceiling in the corner. "Please follow the specific instructions as they are given in your examination rooms." Mr. Porter smiles warmly at the children, almost apologetically before continuing. "So, we'll go by fives," he says, counting off the first five children on the benches and jutting his thumb toward the five doors where they are to line up.

The children must be no more than seven. I watch their little faces drop as they stand in front of the doors. A petite girl with rosy cheeks and her hair in pigtails is the first to turn the handle of the door, after holding her small cuff up to a monitor to be scanned. As she opens the door I catch a glimpse of a table with a set of headphones and a built-in lever facing a screen that is alive with the words "Welcome, Mai Selig." I strain to hear what might be happening in there, but the rooms are soundproof.

The children waiting patiently on the benches keep their heads down. A few minutes later the doors open again and the testing subjects emerge, their faces downcast.

"All right," Mr. Porter calls. "Well done. You all may return to your classes."

The little girl with the pigtails walks somberly to the exit.

"Next five, please," Mr. Porter says.

"Ok, Rebecca," my mother whispers. "Your job now—walk them back."

I get up quickly to follow the five children to their classroom. I jog ahead to be able to open the door for them and smile at each of them as they make their way back into the building. The children spread out to play in different areas of the class.

I reach for the pencil basket. "Anyone want to draw?" I ask. The girl with the pigtails shrugs her shoulders and sits down at the table in a small chair. "What's your favorite color?" I ask, rummaging through the basket.

She shrugs again.

"Yellow, maybe? Wait, here's a blue—I'll bet blue's your favorite since it matches your shirt." I cringe when I realize that all Cherish kids wear the same uniform. She's never picked her own shirt to wear. She probably hates the color, but she picks up the pencil anyway and taps it.

"Examination Day is not your favorite, huh?" I ask.

She shakes her head.

"You're what, seven? Eight?"

"Seven," she says.

"You've got lots of time before you're up for citizenship. Nine years. One test won't change anything,"

The little girl looks up at me with soft green eyes. "I've failed all of them." Her bottom lip begins to quiver.

I put my hand on her bony shoulder. "Your teacher could help you prep for them a bit more."

The room is strung with pictures of planes from different periods of history—from the first dragonfly-like craft with the words "Wright Brothers" below it, to large army carriers, to the sleek drones of today. A red replica with black trim dangles from the ceiling from a thin wire.

"Maybe the Colony is testing you on things you haven't been taught yet," I reason. "I bet there isn't a single kid in the Pulse who could pass a test on airplanes at age seven."

The little girl picks up her pencil and begins to trace a circle over and over again on her page. "It's not like that," she says. "I can't make the sound stop. You win by making the sound stop." She breathes in deeply and lets it out in a shredded exhalation as she continues to trace the increasingly dark circle.

"I don't understand what you mean," I say, looking around the room at the other children who have settled in to reading books or working on their model planes.

"The sounds are awful. People screaming, things falling apart. Crashing. They're scary noises."

I turn to look at the little girl, who is making new circles now.

"Then sometimes there's buzzing and these whistling sounds. I hate having to put the headset on."

"That doesn't sound like a test to me."

"But it is because you can make the sound stop. That's the test. Make the sounds stop."

"Well, how do you do that?" I ask.

"You have to figure out the lever."

I remember the device I saw on the table when Mai opened the door. "So, you push the lever and the sounds stop."

"Sometimes," Mai shrugs. "Your job is to help the dog jump over the wall before the earthquake." Mai makes jumping motions with her hand.

"What dog?"

"The one on the screen," Mai says animatedly. "There's this little dog that comes out, wags his tail. It's your job to get him over the fence. You make him jump when the earthquake happens. If you get him over, the sounds stop too. You've got to use your brain, move the lever every which way and in different patterns to figure it out," she says, tapping her temple. "I couldn't get my dog over today."

"Maybe it wasn't working?" I offer.

"Well, it did for Suzanne." She gestures toward a little girl painting a propeller white. "She told me on the way over here that her dog got over."

"Seems like a dumb test."

"Yeah," Mai agrees. "Either that, or I'm dumb."

"Dumb test," I say definitively.

Moments after the last few children come back from the Examination House, a series of bells ring to indicate it's time for lunch. Then after a short break, it is classroom time, then outside, then classroom time again—a totally different schedule than the day before, or the day before that. I am exhausted.

"That place is nutty," I tell my mother as we leave.

"That's the point, Rebecca," my mother says, looking straight ahead and walking briskly. "It's Pulse-run. Not much we can do."

I hurry my pace to keep up. "I don't understand how that test is supposed to be able to be used for data collection. I mean, how can identifying a pattern to press a lever really show them how smart they are or not?"

"Nicholas Porter was the first to figure that out," my mother says. "They're just trying to determine one thing: when will they give up."

I stop walking. "I don't get it. They *want* them to give up?"

"Exactly. There's nothing they can do to pass that test. It's completely out of their control."

"So, then why don't you tell them that? Why do they care so much?" I want to run back and hug little Mai.

"Believe me, we tell them, but their VL scores go down every time. It's just the power's way of keeping their thumb on them—and doing it legally."

My mother walks home much more slowly than she did as she raced to Cherish. The old woman we met earlier has gone inside. I look around at the Ancillary houses. There's no way those kids will ever be able to gain citizenship. They'll move into the houses on this row, maybe moving just a few blocks from the only home many of them will ever be able to remember. And, without the right education and training, it will be difficult for them to be eligible for transfer since other colonies won't be anxious to admit new colonists who aren't able to contribute more than basic labor to the work force.

"It's not fair," I tell my mother as we turn down the path through the wooded area.

"Sure isn't," my mother agrees. "We're doing our best. Nicholas combats it with everything he can. Teachers help the kids understand that it has nothing to do with them and everything to do with the test. We give them as many choices as we can—basically let them set the curriculum according to their interests to help counteract the colony's lesson that they have no control.

It's brilliant. Pulse leaders come in and see the children studying something like dolls for three months and assume that we are self-destructing under our own ignorance. Nicholas always stays one step ahead of them. The kids aren't supposed to take off the cuffs, for emergency tracking purposes, but we cover them with tape. We have a saying at Cherish: *You're beyond a number.* Some of them get it; others can't stop looking under the tape." My mother raises her eyebrows at me. "It's all nonsense, Rebecca. You know that, right?"

I shrug. I hate school in the Pulse too. I figure whatever clowns are calling the shots for Cherish are the same ones making the decisions for all the schools. But, that doesn't mean that citizenship isn't worth it.

My cuff buzzes. My mother shoots me a look that dares me to check it.

"Mom," I say, "when I get citizenship, maybe I'll become the Education Council President or something. I'll change it."

We walk the rest of the way home in silence.

Chapter 8

Lex taps me on the shoulder in the hallway at school. I turn to find her posing behind me. "Oh, my gosh! I love it!" I say. Lex flips her hair, which is a solid lavender to match her eyes.

"It's perfect," I smile, touching it.

"Well, got to keep it up, you know," she says coyly.

Every time I see her, Lex has a different look. She's an artistic genius with make-up and transforms herself so drastically sometimes, it's as though she's another person. Today she is all eyes. I asked her once what her original hair color was. She laughed and said she couldn't remember.

Lex links arms with me and leads me to our next class. "So, there's this thing tonight." Lex is extra bubbly today, even for her. "Radius told me you have to come."

"Tonight?" I shift uncomfortably. "My mom is really on me right now."

Lex sticks out her bottom lip, which I notice is fuller than it was the last time I saw her. "Of course you can. I can't go alone. And besides, Radius really wants you to come."

I shake my head slowly. "My mother will definitely not let that happen. I promise you—"

Lex holds one finger to her mouth. "Shh," she says. "Wait and then make up your mind."

Lex reaches into her translucent purse and takes out a small plastic bag that she pushes into my hands.

"Lex, you shouldn't have gotten me anything."

"*I* didn't," she says. "This is from your *boyfriend.*"

I bite my lip to keep from smiling. "I don't know if he's my boyfriend."

I take out a shimmering white dress with a high neck and thick bands around the waist. "Oh, my gosh. Seriously?" I couldn't even tell how to put it on with all the strings. "No," I say reluctantly. "No way. I saw one like this on one of the ballooner ads."

"Yep." Lex poses like the girl in the ad, batting her eyes and pouting her lips out. "Same one. Come on, Lark. He must have spent a fortune on this."

"I can't believe he did this for me."

"And, shoes." Lex takes out a second bag with a pair of diamond-studded heels.

I fight back tears. "It's too much."

"Plus, he gave me strict instructions to take you out. We're skipping right after this class, by the way." Lex grabs the dress and shoves it back into her purse before the teacher can see it.

I cross my arms over my chest. "It looks too small."

"That's kind of the point. Right after this class we have an appointment and then it's time to go. You are not going to say no after all that."

"What kind of an appointment?" I look at her suspiciously.

"To take you to another level, my dear. Radius made that appointment himself."

I look up to the ceiling as I blow a long, slow breath. "Ok, fine," I concede.

Lex squeals and gives me a big hug.

The entire class I think about what lengths my mother will take to make sure I never do this again. She's probably ordered Gray to spy on me and report every step I take. It occurs to me that she might be waiting after school for me. Thank goodness Lex already has plans to leave early. Hopefully that will prevent my mother from completely losing her mind on school property. Or maybe she'll do that anyway, but at least I won't be there to see it.

I picture Radius in one of his sleek suits, searching for the perfect dress for me in the shopping district. I imagine the woman taking the white dress and folding it into the bag. "For someone special?" she might have asked.

"My girlfriend," Radius would have said.

I send Radius a message as soon as the teacher turns her back. "Love you. See you soon," I write.

He responds almost immediately with the same message as he did last night. "Love you, Lark," he types.

I cover my mouth with my hand to conceal my smile. Whatever my mother does to me after this will be worth it.

Lex takes me to the Crave section of the Pulse. This is my second time coming here, the first being when Radius had my stones embedded. There's electricity in the air, a sensual energy that makes me come alive. Between tall buildings I can see drones carving low-hanging clouds as they pass. A ballooner floats overhead, the bottom of the basket visible and surrounded by the bulbous, living sphere that suspends it.

Boldly dressed men and women in glimmering shirts and suits line the streets. "Hey," Lex elbows me. "See that one?" She motions to a girl who looks like she can't be much older than I am. "She's a VL-1,000."

My chest aches with how badly I want to be that woman and how very different she and I are from one another. One of her arms has been completely jeweled in swirling, glittering art. Her hair is a deep mahogany with a rich blend of different colors that bring out the brilliance of the multi-colored gems in her skin. Her eyes are bright blue and slightly slanted. Below high cheekbones, her full lips part slightly to reveal the whiteness of her teeth.

"Honestly, if I tried to wear that skirt . . ." Lex looks down at her own petite figure. "I've never seen legs that long."

The woman crosses the street to greet an equally superior-looking man.

"Come, on" Lex sighs. "We're in here." Lex pulls open the door to a ground-level building. Images flash in the windows of alluring women posing to show their newly bejeweled nails and thick, glowing hair. The store is smaller than I would have expected from seeing the front.

"Hey, Dylan," Lex waves to a young, apathetic looking girl at the counter. She has an LED tattoo of a tiger on her shoulder that comes alive as she taps her cuff absentmindedly. Her eyebrows are outlined in emeralds that bring out the green of her eyes.

She smiles brightly when she sees Lex. "So, this is Radius's new girl?" She looks me up and down and gives me a sideways smile.

Not that I mind being Radius's girl, but something about the way she says it makes me blush.

"Forget her," Lex says to me.

I hold out my hand to Dylan. "Nice to meet you. I'm Lark."

Dylan takes my hand in hers and holds my nails up to her face. "Going to need some work on these," she leers. "And this." She flips my hair the way the girls at school had done when I painted it with a green streak.

Suddenly I want to run. I can see myself through her eyes—the Ancillary stereotype, pathetic and Valueless. No wonder Radius is sending me here to be improved upon before taking me out to meet his friends. He doesn't want to be embarrassed.

I follow Dylan to a chair facing a mirror and sit down. "So, I know I'm going to need a little work."

The girl raises her emerald eyebrows in feigned surprise. "Little, hon?"

"Ok, a lot. I need a lot of work, but the problem is that I don't know if I can actually afford everything that should probably be done just to get me to look decent."

Dylan and Lex look at each other. "Boss is paying for it," Dylan says flatly. "I've got strict instructions to do whatever I think is necessary."

"I don't understand." I look to Lex, who is smiling mysteriously, and then back to Dylan. "Who is your boss?" I ask her.

Dylan leans down to my ear as she pulls my hair back. "Your boy is my boss."

I look at her in disbelief. "You mean Radius owns the salon?" I see Lex beaming in the mirror.

"Radius owns a lot of things, honey," Dylan laughs.

For several agonizing hours, Dylan fusses over the state of my nails, skin, and hair. Between her muttering curse words under her breath and rough handling, not to mention the constant buzzing on my cuff from my mother, I have had just about enough. A few more customers come in and Dylan knocks on a door to the back. Two girls emerge—a small mousy one and an overweight girl with more tattoos than Dylan. She motions to the door for the customers to be taken care of.

My whole body has been sprayed with something that makes me look golden. My hair is thick with extensions of different colors, some glowing. I tap my new French-manicured nails together to make a pleasant clinking sound. Dylan has injected my lips to plump them and cinched my waist. I blink against the discomfort of the contacts with small diamonds surrounding my iris. I avoid eye contact as she leans in close to my face with dozens of small brushes and different shades of pencils. Dylan furrows her brow as she works. She continues muttering and cursing under her breath any time she makes a slip.

Lex comes over to check on my progress. She studies me with a furrowed brow. "Little fuller lip," she tells Dylan, who immediately reaches for a red pencil.

"What do you think about the stones around her eyes?" Dylan asks.

"No, those are perfect." Lex grabs my hand to admire my nails.

"I don't deserve this," I whisper.

"Of course you do," Lex mumbles absentmindedly as she rummages through her bag. "Come put this on when she lets you go." She hands me the dress and shoes.

"Ok," I cough as Dylan surrounds me in a cloud of hairspray.

I don't recognize myself in the mirror. With my dress on, there is no hint of Ancillary about me. I turn around in the mirror, wobbling in my shoes.

"Whoa," Dylan says as she enters the changing room without knocking. She holds my hand to spin me around and look at the miracle she has created with an arsenal of sprays and paints.

"Do you think I could pass for someone in the Pulse?" I ask shyly.

"Not with that attitude, honey," she scoffs. "You look it, but you don't act it." Dylan stands behind me and pulls my shoulders back forcefully. "Stop walking like an Ancillary. Chin up."

I try to make the aloof expression as the VL-1,000 girl we had seen on the street.

"Better," Dylan laughs.

When I come out, Lex is applying gems under her eyes. "Oh, my gosh," she whispers when she sees my reflection in the mirror. "That's unbelievable." She turns to look me up and down. "I mean, this is exactly what Radius is looking for. You're perfect."

"So, you think he'll like it?" I ask.

"I think he's going to pretty much die," Lex laughs.

The two customers who are getting their hair done in adjacent chairs strain to look at me. I can feel their gazes floating up and down my golden body. It is energizing. So this is what it feels like to be Pulse. There is power in it.

Lex rummages in her bag and pulls out a small patch. "We just have to make sure she doesn't act so damn Ancillary," Dylan says irritably.

"That's what I'm doing," Lex says, taking the patch out of the package.

Dylan helps hold my hair up so that Lex can apply it. She stands for a moment with her hand behind the back of my neck. "How many girls would kill to be in your position?" she whispers.

The patch emanates warmth almost immediately. I look at myself in the mirror and am even more transformed—the colors in the gems and in my hair become vibrant, my skin more rich and my eyes more piercing.

"He'll be here in less than five minutes," Lex announces.

I pace as I wait, catching glimpses of the transformed girl in the mirror. I see his black car pull up in front of the shop. When he opens the door I am standing there, a Pulse girl.

Radius extends his hand, and I take it. "Wow," he mouths.

"I missed you," I pout like Lex does.

"I've missed you too, Lark," he says. "Turn for me, sweetheart."

I do a slow, sensual turn, holding his eye contact on the way around. "You didn't tell me this was your place," I say casually.

Radius lets out a small laugh and smiles mysteriously. "Ok, so you ready?" He leans toward the door to open it for me. "Thanks, girls," he says, waving to Dylan and the other two stylists who are still with their customers.

"See you soon," Lex calls, not pausing her focused efforts in applying mascara.

Radius walks me around his car to open the door for me. I push it closed again and pull him close. "Thank you for this," I tell him.

Radius kisses me softly and puts his hand behind the small of my back. "No, thank *you*," he whispers in my ear. A couple of passers-by clap as Radius kisses me again. I run my hand along his neck, making his LED tattoos come alive.

My cuff buzzes again. I check the message as Radius closes my door and walks to his side of the car. My mother has sent me about two dozen messages so far—threats and pleading for me to get home.

"Your mom?" Radius asks when he gets in and notices me fingering my cuff.

"I'm not worried about her," I smile reassuringly. "I have never been better in my life."

It seems that Radius knows every person in the restaurant. I am introduced to well-dressed men who stand as I approach. I look down at the girls they are with and let them take me in. I hope desperately that I will see one of the girls from school, but I don't recognize anyone. The restaurant is dimly lit; our seats pound out the rhythm of the song that is playing from the speaker under our table. Radius leans in close. "How do you feel?" he asks.

"Like one thousand," I smile.

"Well, you look it tonight."

"I feel like I belong here, you know?" I scan the room of smiling couples. One of the men is nodding at whatever the girl sitting across from him is saying, but keeps shooting me a glance. I pull my shoulders back like Dylan instructed.

"You do belong here," Radius says.

"That's what I think too. I'll be before the Citizenship Panel soon. You know who I want as my sponsor?" I ask, emboldened by the patch.

Radius shifts in his chair. "It might not matter, Lark. The interviews are tricky, you know?" He takes my hand and presses it to his lips. "And, you know it doesn't matter to me what your number is."

"So, is that a yes or a no?"

Radius holds my hand against his cheek and looks down at the table. "Lark, you look gorgeous." He smiles and looks up at me. "You know everyone keeps turning this way to see you."

I raise my eyebrows as though I don't know.

"When we go to the party tonight, there's a photographer friend I'd like you to meet."

"You want a picture of me?"

"I was thinking that lots of people would like a picture of you, actually," he says. "It would be kind of a favor."

I study him quizzically. "Who, exactly?"

Radius leans in closer and kisses my lips softly. "I was going to sell them. You'd be a professional."

"Like a model?"

"Like a model."

I pause for a long time. Even with the euphoria and confidence lent by the patch, I know I am not model material. I drop my head and look at my hands. Radius pushes my chin up with his finger so that I'm looking into his eyes.

"My clients will love you. They'll beg for you."

"You have clients?"

"Yes, I own the salon as well as a modeling agency of sorts. Lex has modeled for me before."

I bite my lip and look away. "Lex?" This shouldn't come as a surprise. I shouldn't be jealous, but I am, and it shows.

"It's just business, Lark," Radius soothes. "You know, I owe her so much for introducing us."

Begrudgingly, I agree. "Me too."

The party is on the fourth story above the club that attracts glittering men and women. The floor throbs with the rhythm of the music below. Like Radius's apartment, each step makes the floor come alive with glowing ripples.

Lex must have gotten ready in half the time that it took me, but she is utterly transformed in an emerald green dress that is similar to mine but with a higher split on her right leg. I wonder if Radius has asked her for pictures tonight too. I wave to her as she kisses a man on the cheek and winks at me.

The patch Lex gave me is starting to wear off, but the energy of the party takes over where the patch leaves off. I smile confidently in the knowledge that Radius has asked me to model for him. And, the men that Radius introduces me to raise their eyebrows at Radius as if to say, nicely done. He isn't embarrassed by me. Tonight I belong. I am a Pulse girl, and all the pain since moving here is worth it. My only nervousness is that I won't photograph well. I'm desperate to talk to Lex to get some pointers.

I try to catch her eye, but she is sitting on a man's lap, throwing her head back as she laughs. That's what I need to be more like, I decide. Dylan was right. I look Pulse, but I don't act it. I lean into Radius as he talks to one of the men about his drone business, holding my hands on his shoulder and leaning my chin on him seductively like I've seen in some of the ads. I can do this, I think—just be Pulse. Radius slides a hand behind my back and continues to talk.

Lex taps my shoulder from behind. "Hey there," she whispers.

I kiss Radius on the cheek and turn slowly to leave with her. "Hi! This is unbelievable!" I stage whisper once we are out of sight of Radius.

Lex takes my hands and pulls me behind a large fish aquarium of exotic, glowing fish. "So, did he tell you?" Lex asks.

"You mean about the photographer? Yes. I have no idea what I'm doing. You're going to have to help me."

"Of course I will." Lex studies my makeup and reaches into her purse to retrieve her lipstick, which she uses to touch me up. "I'll go first and you just watch me. Nothing to it."

"Sure, nothing to it." I roll my eyes.

"Just don't be shy, you know? Pretend that the camera is Radius."

I nod anxiously. And wonder who she pretends the camera is.

"Want another patch?" she asks.

"Yes, please. It will help keep down the nerves."

"Coming right up." Lex takes another patch from the packaging and rubs it on the back of my neck.

I feel its effects within moments, just in time for Radius to come and get me.

"Showtime!" he says.

The photographer is a young woman dressed in dark red. She appraises me as I enter a back room with Lex.

Radius kisses me as I go in. "Have fun!" he winks. "I can't wait to see them."

The woman closes the door behind me and Lex beckons me over to a gold sofa that has been lit up with more than a dozen lights.

Chapter 9

Radius and I are silent on the ride home. I ask him to drop me off at the end of the road so that I can avoid the embarrassment of my mother unleashing her wrath on me in front of him.

"Thank you," Radius says before he opens the door for me. I sit momentarily and open my mouth to beg the question I'm desperate to ask: do you have to sell the pictures? My lips part to form the words.

"Your dress is just stunning," he says abruptly. "I like getting you nice things. It makes me feel good."

And my words are gone.

Why can't I just do this for him? Selling those pictures probably won't make up even a fraction of what it cost for the dress and the gems. I owe him. Besides, he was doing it for me.

"Love you," I hear myself say instead. And, then there's that: I love him. Small rocks crackle under my shoes as I step into the night.

"I'll send you a message," he says.

I nod and wave as he turns his car around in the road, Ancillary dust swirling in his headlight beams. As soon as he pulls away from sight, I double over and vomit by the side of the road until my stomach is emptied.

My house is completely dark except for the flicker of the porch light. I take my shoes off before stepping on the first stair.

"Rebecca?" I jump backward onto the ground and clutch my chest as Grayson catches my eye from his front porch. "What happened to you? Are you ok?" he calls. I can see his figure in the shadows, and I know he is looking me up and down.

"Well, with the exception of the heart attack you just gave me, I'm fine," I snap. And then I remember the dead patches still on my neck. With a casual move, I rub them off like I'm scratching an itch.

Gray is standing beside me, running his fingers through his hair. "I've been—Your mother is sick over you," he says in annoyance.

"No need to be. I'm fine, see?" I say, holding my hands out to either side.

"It's only, what? Four a.m.?"

I roll my eyes at him in the dark. "Listen, Gray, I also have to take this from my mom when I get in, so you can just—"

"Your mom's not here," Grayson says, softening a bit. "She wanted me to wait for you."

"Well, then, where is she?"

"Looking for you, of course. Where else would she be?"

I look down at my cuff. Thirty-seven messages, all from Mom. The last two read: "Please come home," and, "Let me know where you are. If you get home before me, just stay. Everything's going to be ok. I'll come to you."

I want to scream at her or run into her arms to shield me against my own shame. I desperately want to tell her about those pictures and how disgusted I am with myself. At the same time I want to bury the truth so deep that she will never know about them. Besides, she couldn't make them go away. As heartbroken as she is, Radius has never been more proud of me. I can't have both worlds. If I am going to make it in the Pulse, this will have to be part of it. I just have to get harder, tougher, even if that means becoming numb.

Grayson busily taps his cuff. "Ok," he says. "She's relieved. She says for you to just stay here, you guys can talk in the morning." Grayson looks up with his gentle eyes. "Rebecca, I was so worried. Please, whatever you need . . . I mean, look, Rebecca"—Grayson runs his fingers through his hair again—"I'm here, you know? I don't want you to get hurt. So if there's ever a time when you need me, just tell me, ok? I'm *always* going to be—"

"Fine." I burst into tears as soon as the door slams behind me.

Lex didn't demand that I take my dress off. The photographer didn't either. No one forced anything. It was my choice, and I seized an opportunity. It was for Radius. It was for the New. How many other Ancillary girls would do anything to be a model?

The bath water is almost scalding when I step in. The water draws the humiliation from me and replaces it with the soothe of burning pain. I scrub every inch of my arms and legs, my chest and face until I'm a deep pink all over. I pinch the contacts out of my eyes and watch them collapse in on themselves in the water. I want to rip out the multicolored extensions that are tied into my hair, mostly for the steadying pain of it. I lean back into the water until only the top of my head is above surface. I wait until my lungs burn before I am purified enough from the water to live with myself again.

From under the water, I can hear my cuff buzzing on the counter. I push myself to standing to get it, leaving puddles of water on the floor. Surely Gray has spoken to Mom already. I expect a biting message from her and prepare a glib remark. But it's Radius. "My little girl from two worlds—you were all Pulse tonight."

I open the attachment he has sent and look at the daring girl in the picture. The photographer has the lighting perfect so that it brings out my eyes. I'm looking at the camera just the way that Lex told me. And I do look stunning. Bold. Beautiful. *Captivating*. Why would I be so embarrassed about this? I look at myself in the mirror, dripping with water, my makeup and contacts gone. I am Ancillary again, invisible. Nothing. It comes down to this choice, and I know what I have to do.

My mother comes in at 5:00 a.m. She puts her hand on my chest softly as though trying to make sure I'm still breathing. I pretend to be asleep. She stifles sobs as she leaves. I want to get up and comfort her, or at least make her understand. I want to show her the picture where I am beautiful. I want her to be proud. Instead, I pretend to be asleep. Moments later she slumps in front of my door.

I awake three hours later to the strong smell of coffee. My mother is in the kitchen and I know I cannot avoid her.

"Good morning," she says as I sit down at the table. "How about some breakfast?"

I look at her suspiciously, waiting for the explosion that is surely coming. "I can make it," I say stubbornly.

"No need. Got something right here." She puts down some eggs and boiled greens with my coffee and sits down beside me. "I'm scared for you."

"Don't be. I'm doing fine," I say curtly.

"You know what he is, Rebecca."

I look hard at my mother, who returns my glare with her staid, compassionate expression.

"Yeah—my boyfriend," I spit.

My mother looks horrified but then takes a deep breath. "You know you don't have to do anything you aren't comfortable with."

"Mom, please," I say, putting my hands up.

"And, that if you ever need me—"

"Got it, Mom." I stab my eggs with my fork.

"You call me," she says. I notice her hands are shaking.

We are both too tired to continue fighting. But it's her own fault that she's so tired, after all. It's not like I asked her to come looking for me. I certainly didn't need her to. But I don't want to have to face anyone at school, and besides, my mother will never allow me to stay here by myself, so I agree to help her at Cherish today.

My mother has me cutting out pictures of different kinds of vehicles for the youngest children. I almost nod off as I trace around the edges of an old-fashioned train. Then, I fold identical, light blue uniforms in the laundry room as well as complete another list of tasks that my mother comes up with—weeding the garden, assisting the cafeteria crew with washing plates, sanitizing bottles. Whatever mindless chore Cherish needs completed becomes my task.

It gives me time to consider last night. I decide I'm glad I did it, but that I'm not ready to do it again for some time. Radius will understand, and he'll help me with citizenship. Everything's working out just fine.

My mother has insisted that I remove my cuff while I'm here. I'm worried that Radius will try to contact me and wonder if I'm ignoring him, but he'll probably assume my mother has taken my cuff. Besides, I'll get back to him as soon as I'm finished here.

At 1:00 Mr. Porter asks me if I'd like to join some of the classes for lunch. I abandon a large pile of cloth diapers that need folding and walk to the dining hall.

"Hey," pipes a little girl with short hair in front of me.

"Hey yourself," I say, nudging her. "You look like this little girl I know named Mai. But, you can't be because she had long pigtails." I tussle her hair.

"Haircut day," she says quietly.

"Well, I like it."

Mai shrugs. "Not what I'd pick." She blows a loose strand from her face and huffs dramatically.

"Maybe not, but you look good. Very Pulse." I wink.

Mai rolls her eyes. "Great," she says sarcastically. At least my mother has gotten through to someone.

I almost nod off eating lunch with Mr. Porter and my mother. "Go home," my mother says wearily. "Take a nap."

I shuffle back to the kitchen to return my tray and then make the long trek through the woods at record-breaking slowness.

Grayson is wearing his work clothes, heavy boots and ash-colored shirt still covered in sawdust, and is sitting on my front step when I get home.

"So, let me guess. You're supposed to confirm that I made it back."

"Hey," he says, standing up but looking down.

I raise my eyebrows at him.

"Here are your cuffs." He holds out my cuffs like they could bite him. "They've been buzzing like crazy." He taps some buttons on his own cuff, I assume to report that I made it.

"Nice. So she gave *you* my cuff. You've been assigned to be my protector, then. Touching."

"Look, Rebecca," he says. "That guy's dangerous."

"No, Gray. He's not."

"He's going to take advantage of you— "

"Stop. Just stop." I put my hands up. "If anyone is getting taken advantage of, then it's him, ok? You should see what he's gotten for me," I hurl the words as I step around him, but he is at the door first and holds it shut with a strong hand as he looks down at me.

"Snap out of it, Rebecca. You're more than this." Grayson looks pleadingly with his eyes. "Come on, Bec. I miss you." He is close enough that I can detect the faint smell of sweat and wood. "Rebecca, I can help you get out of this. I'll do whatever—"

"It's Lark," I tell him coldly. "Let me in the house, Gray."

Grayson sighs and steps to the side. "I'm always here, *Rebecca*."

Yes, he'll always be here, forever Ancillary. "Whatever you say," I huff.

I take my cuff to my room and check my messages. Radius has sent me no fewer than thirty messages, all wanting to know where I am, the last few increasingly intense: "Call me, now!"

I push his icon to call him. "Where the hell are you, Lark?" he asks coldly.

"Hi, it's ok. I'm fine. My mother just insisted that I go with her to work today and leave my cuffs here."

I can hear him breathing on the other end. "When I call you, you need to call me back."

"Ok, I'm sorry. I just couldn't today. My mother—"

"Lark, when I call you, call me back. Got it?" he repeats slowly.

"Ok," I say. "I'm sorry, Ray. I get it. You were worried."

Radius clears his throat. "I was initially calling because I missed you and wanted to invite you to this thing tonight."

I swallow hard. "I missed you too, of course. But, tonight—Radius, my mother is really not going to allow that."

"I'll even pick you up."

I pause for a long time. "I'm going to have to climb out my window, I guess. My mom slept in front of my door last night."

Radius laughs. "I'll call you when I'm there. Have you back before sun-up. Ok?"

"Ok," I say hesitantly. "Yeah, sounds good."

"Some more people would like to meet you. By the way, check your VL."

I quickly scroll to my Contour Sheet as soon as Radius hangs up and cover my open mouth. *Fifty points*? I went up fifty points overnight? At this rate, citizenship is a certainty. I lay back on my bed. In spite of the excitement, I am exhausted.

My mother wakes me several hours later by knocking on my door. "Rebecca, you hungry?"

I prop myself up on an elbow and cover my mouth as a wave of nausea sweeps over me. "No, definitely not," I say, collapsing back on the bed.

My mother cracks open the door and smiles. "What can I get for you, honey?" she asks.

"Nothing, Mom. Seriously, my stomach hurts."

Mom sits down on my bed and puts her hand on my forehead. "You have any chilling?"

"I'm fine." I swat her hand. "I just need more sleep. Probably something I ate at Cherish today."

Mom laughs. "That's definitely a possibility, actually. Ok, rest up." She looks relieved. I guess she figures having me too sick to get out of bed means she won't have to guard me as much.

I type out a message to Radius, pausing as the waves of nausea crash in on me. "I feel so sick. Any way we could go out another night?" And, then I promptly erase it. Toughen up, Lark, I tell myself. I sit up and feel my heart beating wildly. I run to the bathroom in just enough time to vomit into the toilet. I rinse my mouth in the sink and look in the mirror. Great, I think. I look like I feel.

I lay back on my bed. The rich food smells coming from the kitchen are making my stomach turn again. I decide to sleep until Radius sends me a message.

At 11:00 my cuff buzzes. The nausea is worse and now my head is pounding. "Coming," I type slowly. I can see my mother asleep in her bed across the hall. She must have assumed that I was too sick to worry about leaving. And after sleeping in the hallway last night and then a full day's work, she's probably more tired than I am.

I slip on the white dress Radius bought me and slowly make my way out of the house, tiptoeing over the floorboards that I know will give me away. Radius is waiting outside with his lights off. I wave at him halfheartedly and get into the car. He laughs when he sees me.

"What's so funny?" I ask irritably.

"Oh, nothing. Here you go, sweetheart," he says gently, opening a compartment in his console. I take the patch he hands me and put it behind my neck. "Hey, I'll get you some to take home in case you need them, ok?"

I groan but within minutes the nausea is subsiding. "Sweet little thing," he says, tucking a loose strand of my hair behind my ear.

Lex and Dylan both are at the party. Lex pulls me into a back room with her toolkit, and she and Dylan both work diligently to get me in order. Within minutes I am transformed. "You're going to be a hit again," Lex squeals.

"What do you mean?" I ask.

"Few more pictures tonight."

"No," I insist. "I'm not interested. Radius didn't mention anything about more pictures."

"Well, of course more pictures. You're a model now. So, what, now you quit?"

"I said I'm not interested. Just not tonight anyway," I say with less confidence.

Lex shrugs her shoulders. "Look at yourself, Lark. Panel's what, a matter of weeks now?" Lex stands behind me in the mirror and pulls my hair gently to tilt my head. "Besides, the pictures are already out. What are you worried about now?"

I look down at my shoes. "Fine," I say. "But, I get to decide how far I go."

"Of course," Lex smiles. "It's always your decision."

Chapter 10

I can barely keep my eyes open in class. Almost every night now I get the call for a modeling job. I leave my bedroom window and meet my ride just past the bend in the dirt road. Always, I'm taken to different condos, luxurious with vibrant and affluent Pulse citizens. So far, my mother hasn't caught on, but I worry how long my luck will last.

"You look tired, sweetie," she says, and puts a hand on my forehead but doesn't ask any questions. In fact, our relationship hasn't been this good in quite some time. I'm too tired to argue and too close to becoming Pulse to be discouraged.

My pictures are in high demand. In one month's time I am outselling any model Radius has ever represented. The gifts pour in— new dresses and shoes, purses, trips to Dylan's, and stones that cover my neck and collarbone. Thank goodness it's almost winter now. Concealing my stones from my mother is much easier with thick scarves. And luckily, my mother is so consumed with work that she is too distracted to push anything.

Radius asked Lex to take me under her wing. "I don't need her to help me out," I told him irritably. "Aren't I doing just fine?"

Radius kissed my forehead but said nothing. He hasn't even been at the parties. I ran to his car one night only to find her driving instead. I slammed the door and turned with the intention of going back into the house but thought better of it after only a few steps. I huffed loudly as I slid into the seat next to Lex.

Although she's as cheerful as usual, Lex has to know how annoyed I am with her, but it doesn't seem to bother her, which annoys me all the more. And I'm growing tired of her endless chatter about how close she is to being on a ballooner's ad. Even after all that she's done, I've grown resentful of her, and I don't hide it well.

"Relax," Lex says happily, batting her new turquoise eyelashes after I snap at her for brushing my hair too hard tonight. "Radius is tied up with business right now."

And then as she does each night that she picks me up, she hands me a small gift that he has sent along. New emerald earrings, designer handbag, something sparkly for my hair—I am dripping in gifts now.

"Ray suggested you wear your hair up," she smiles.

I roll my eyes.

"And this," she says, handing me a piece of stretchy material.

"What is this thing?" I pull the fabric between my hands.

"Goes around your waist." Lex winks at me.

I blush and toss it around the room. Now every time I see him, Radius scans me up and down for ways to improve upon my body, hair, eyes, lips, even the way I walk. At first Radius was subtle. His compliments guided me—he just loved my hair a certain way or the work Dylan had done to make my lips fuller. And if I ventured from his preferences, he gave a look of disapproval, which might as well have been a cow prod. I have learned what he likes and have never steered from where he has led. I want to hold his gaze, captivate him. So if a certain dress or lipstick will do it, so be it.

But lately I feel his eyes always upon me, no longer taking me in for his own pleasure but to change me for the benefit of the camera. A few times he has casually mentioned that Lex's waist seems slimmer. I didn't eat for two days. Always now I see myself through his eyes. It is exhausting. And maddening.

Jamison, a burly man with hard features, meets us at the door. He is at every condo I am taken to now. I met him at my first party in the Pulse—the guy who supplied Lex with our patches.

Jamison looks me up and down and then slowly nods a reticent approval to Lex, who kisses him on the cheek, before he hands her a patch. Jamison makes me uncomfortable. I kind of hate him, but somehow I crave that nod of approval almost as much as Radius's.

"I'll let the photographer know you're here," he says gruffly.

Lex shows me how to mingle with the men who have come to the party, how to flirt, how to mix their drinks. The pretense of it all is enervating. I'm not in the least bit interested in the rambling conversations about the latest in colony politics or business. Or worse, they're familiar with my modeling and want to ask me all about it. But it's networking—the more prominent Pulse citizens who like me, the higher my VL. This whole nonsense is an investment.

Occasionally some of the men, liberated from their self-restraint by the coaxing of a patch, become bold. When I attempt to shove one off who has moved in for a kiss, Jamison jumps on him. He flashes metal from his coat pocket and the man leaves quickly. I

90

only realize later that Jamison has showed him a gun, a rarity in the colony. Lex is by Jamison's side, whispering softly to him as he paces with anger until she is able to help cool him down.

But it isn't the men, or even Jamison's quick temper, that I hate most about the parties now. It's the other girls. I've met more than a dozen girls that work for Radius—most of them my age, maybe a couple of years older, a few of them younger. One of them, Pearl—a tall girl with white blond hair and a prominent overbite who called me "Ancillary" in front of all the men—won't so much as make eye contact with me. I am hurt, angry even, when I discover that all the girls have his symbol: the "R" enclosed in a circle on a stone.

"Oh," Jamison said mockingly one night when he noticed me flushing at a young redhead with the symbol on her neck. "You thought that you were—what is that Old Colony notion you grew up with again? Did you think you were married?"

I could feel his hot breath in my ear. At Lex's warning I knew better than to provoke Jamison's temper with a smart comment. I avoid him now as best I can, but he seems to always be there, watching. Most times he is my ride home.

Tonight, after Jamison drops me off at my house, I call Radius repeatedly until he takes my call. "I'm done!" I yell into the speaker when he finally picks up. "I don't need to be just another of your many, *many* girls."

"Lark, don't be jealous," he says derisively.

"I thought you were *my* boyfriend, but there seems to be quite a few other girls who think the same about themselves."

"Who bought you everything you're wearing right now? Who helped bring your VL up to a miraculous four hundred points?"

"You did," I seethe. "So you can take me to some Pulse condo and have my picture made. How much money am I bringing in every night, anyway?"

I can hear him exhaling slowly. "After everything I've done, you're going to say that? Tell me, Lark, where exactly would you be without me?"

I want him to stroke my hair like he used to, pull me onto his lap, and tell me he still sees more than a number. My hands shake. I know what I could be throwing away. He's right, after all. I'd be where I started—no chance of citizenship, no status, and a VL score that makes me invisible. But I am wearing down. I can't do this every single night. I'm not tough enough for this. "I'm out," I repeat. My whole body shakes as I hang up the call.

The next day is spent alternating between relief and panic at what I have done. I expect Radius to call that night. But he doesn't. At midnight I try calling him, but he doesn't pick up. I pace my room and pound my pillow as I check my VL score. It has gone down significantly overnight. What have I done? Radius was my only way out and he loved me. No one has ever showed any interest in me and won't again. There's only one option if I'm going to make it here.

I crawl out my window in one of the dresses that he bought and make my way to the Pulse. I don't even know where to find him, but fortunately Lex is sympathetic. "It's just a spat. Apologize. You're tired is all," she says brightly.

I open the door to the address she had given me and see Radius across the room. He doesn't get out of his chair. A small brunette sits on the armrest as he sips some blue drink.

I walk over to him, shaking and nauseated. "Hi," I interrupt.

He raises an eyebrow at me. The girl looks me up and down. I resist the strong urge to pull her off his lap by her hair.

"Hi, Ray, can I talk to you for a minute?" I ask while glaring at the girl.

Radius puts his hand on her leg to stand up. "Excuse me, fellows," he says to the men sitting next to him. "This will only take a minute." He escorts me to a back room and closes the door. "I can't imagine what that was about," he says.

"I'm sorry—"

"I trust that it won't happen again."

"No. I was out of line." "

"Good," he smiles, his piercing blue eyes melting me under his gaze. "Forgiven."

I exhale deeply. "I feel terrible. Just tired—that's all. I want to make it up to you after all you've done for me."

"Certainly understandable," he says, tilting my head back to kiss me. "And, I mean it, Lark. That has to be the absolute last time you ever talk back to me again. Get it?" he asks, pulling my hair back.

"I get it."

"Excellent. There's a special guest here tonight. He'd like to watch a photo shoot."

I want to run, but I smile back instead.

"What's the difference, Lark?" Radius says, noticing my underlying panic. "He'd be seeing the pictures anyway. Shouldn't make a difference if he's in the room when they're being taken, now, should it?"

"No, of course not."

My skin is now chapped I've taken so many scalding baths. It's the only thing that helps wash away their gaze that I can feel even after I leave. Now the calls I get are for more than pictures, more than movies. Lex has been teaching me how to dance.

Radius is just full of surprises. He owns two clubs at Crave, I'm officially a dancer at Deep Secrets Lounge, and my VL is hovering right at five hundred. Radius says he wants to make sure that I'm still going to school and getting enough rest, so he has now restricted my hours to only three a night. But he has set me up with Syncopate, a virtual experience, so that I can take calls at home. Now the Pulse is able to reach into my own bedroom. I sit in my closet and tell whoever calls exactly what they want to hear. I'm only on call once a week or so, but it's my least favorite night. I'd rather not say anything to those guys, or girls, as is sometimes the case. I'd rather Radius pick me up and take me anywhere. That car ride from Ancillary to Pulse in the little world inside his car is my favorite time of day, when I have him all to myself.

He wants to take care of me. If any of the guys at the club get out of line, he's on it, or he arranges for Jamison to fix it. I feel safe with him.

"You're going to be on that balloon before you know it, Lark," he says, squeezing my hand in the car.

I squeeze him back. "Almost there," I breathe out.

Maybe I can live with Lex when I get citizenship. I mentioned it to her once and she winked and giggled at all the trouble she said we'd get into.

But what I'm really hoping is that Radius will invite me to stay with him, and I think there's a good chance that he will. He's been so busy lately that I haven't brought it up. It really makes sense, though. He's always picking me up. I could make the case that I'd really be saving him time. Plus, he used to pick me up to stay over with him, and he says he regrets now that I'm so in demand that we can't spend as much time together—but the way my VL is skyrocketing, he'd be holding me back to take me away from my modeling. Living with him would solve both problems. If he doesn't bring it up after I'm offered citizenship, I will.

School is less dull now. My new game is to look around the room and imagine the expressions on their stupid faces when they realize that I'm one of them. I haven't let my grades slip in spite of my long hours. For one thing, they are an easy way to get VL points. For another, it's a useful thing to bring up with my mom when she seems the slightest bit suspicious. Holding up an essay with "Excellent" written across it completely eliminates any doubts she's having.

"You look tired," she says.

"I am," I admit. "Big test coming up, Mom." And she's pacified.

I'm only days away from citizenship. My VL is hovering at 504. I've successfully broken five hundred, which is more than most any Ancillary kid my age has ever done. Radius has agreed to represent me and has even bought me a new dress—turquoise with one sleeve missing to show off my stones. Dylan has agreed to make me look better than I ever have.

"You're so in." Lex bumps me with her shoulder on the way to class.

"Hey, Ancillary," one of the Pulse kids yells across the classroom as I take my seat.

I roll my eyes. "Not for long," I mutter under my breath and turn away.

"I'm talking to you, Ancillary," the boy smirks. He is slight with greased hair, his LED tattoos revealing intricate patterns on his temples as he runs his hands through his hair.

"Yeah, I've seen you around." He raises his eyebrows at his friend, who makes a face like he's lost in pleasure and starts to laugh.

I turn to my desk. My heart is racing at the thought of where he could have seen me before.

"Got a few of your pictures," he says.

I freeze. With just a few taps of his cuff he activates Radius's site and shows it to the class. A couple of the girls lean in closer to look.

My legs are trembling visibly, but I force myself to stand. "Shut up."

94

"Oh, ok," says the boy sarcastically. He pushes a couple of buttons and then the image is displayed on the screen in the front of the classroom.

I cringe at the sight of myself looking back at the class defiantly. I lunge at the boy. "Turn it off!" I scream.

"What's the matter, Ancillary? You know, I was thinking of talking to your hawker about a private viewing." He brushes my hair away from my neck and leans in like he's going to kiss me.

I shove him as hard as I can and run out of the room into the hallway. Laughter is roaring from the classroom behind me.

"Forget them, Lark," Lex says. She is out of breath behind me as she struggles to keep up in her high heels.

I push her away and make my way toward the bathroom.

"Look, he took it down before the teacher saw anything!" she shouts from behind me.

I ignore her and push open the door. I slam the bathroom stall door shut and type out a message to Radius, asking him to come get me.

"Lark," Lex knocks on the door. "Forget about that guy. It just goes to show how well known you're becoming. What did you expect?"

"There are Ancillary kids in there, Lex." I start to cry. "Don't you get it? *Ancillary*. And if word gets back to my mother, I'm done."

"No, it won't. Relax."

"Yeah, it will, Lex. Actually, it will," I say flatly. "If my mother finds out, she will pretty much board up my windows and padlock my room. If Radius calls me, forget it—it's over. I can't come. He'll be furious and I really need him to represent me for the Panel."

"It's not going to get out, ok?"

I sit back on the toilet to cry and wait for Radius to return my message. I stare at my cuff until I hear two more bells announcing the beginning and end of the next class.

"Sorry, can't right now. Love you," he writes back just as I stand to leave.

For a moment, I am numb with the shock. He's not coming. But it's going to be just fine, I tell myself. Get tougher. Not even everyone was in class when he showed the picture. It's not a big deal, just like Lex said. And, what's more, I look amazing in that picture. The girls are probably jealous. Plus it just proves what that guy is up to. It looks worse for him, maybe. Just hold your head up like you're Pulse. Be Pulse and walk down the hallway like you don't care.

I can feel eyes following me as I pass, or maybe it's my imagination. Just one foot in front of the other. I make a face at a girl who is whispering something to a friend, and that's when I see him. Grayson is leaning against my locker. I immediately turn to go the opposite direction with plans of skipping school. "Forget it," I say aloud, putting my hands up.

"I'm walking with you," he says.

I round on him. "No, you aren't. Go back to class, Gray. Just leave me alone," I practically growl through clenched teeth. I can tell with one look at Gray's determined face that he's not going to be deterred that easily.

"Fine." I throw my bag over my shoulder and take long strides toward the door.

A boy from my class stands in the threshold, blocking my way. "Hey, Ancillary," he says. "Where you headed so fast?"

"Excuse us," Grayson says. The boy turns to Gray as though just noticing him and smirks.

"Who can I call for a private showing, hmm?" the boy whispers to me, ignoring Grayson.

"Just move—"

Before I can finish, Grayson has his hand on the boy's throat and has pushed him into the door. The surprise on the guy's face quickly turns to anger, but he's coughing so hard he can't do anything.

"I said, excuse me," Grayson tells him calmly as he opens the door for me. I exit before the boy can go find some more Pulse kids to help take on Grayson. I walk resolutely toward the station with Grayson following.

"Convoy won't be here for another three minutes, Rebecca."

"Well, at least I have some company." My sarcasm is weakened by my voice cracking.

"It's not too late."

I bite my lip hard as a final defense against the tears. The ballooners are out. I raise my head to take them in and allow the energy of the heart of the city to sweep over me. You're so close, I tell myself. Just let it blow over, and then everything is going to be ok. I reach in the front pouch of my bag to find a patch. Ugh. All out.

"So, you saw the pictures, I take it? Did they turn you on?" I look him square in the eye.

Grayson doesn't look away as I expect he will, though he does blush. "Those aren't you, Rebecca," he says with an irritating amount of sympathy.

"Want to know what else I've been up to, hmm?" The tears come freely now.

Grayson shakes his head. "It doesn't matter, Rebecca. It's not too late."

"You are so naïve. They aren't coming back, Gray—not my dad, not your parents, not Marissa. This is it." I thrust my arm out at the kaleidoscope world around us. "*This*. Our choice: either stay where you are and crumble into dust, or make it here. That's it—the only two options. And I'm making it work."

Grayson takes a step toward me, but I turn my shoulder to him. "No," I say.

"Ok. Let me walk you home, then," he says dejectedly.

I study the boy with whom I used to collect ladybugs. That boy, who used to look at the night sky hopefully, never gave up that his mother and father were out there and would bring him home one day. The child who would throw his hand out in protection to save me from the things that crept in our magical world, my king in our own little kingdom, had become a young man. But his eyes still showed the vulnerability of that child. I know I hurt him and already regret it. The part of Our Colony that we had created to buffer us from the reality of the New is still very much alive in him even now.

I want to tell him that I miss him. I want to tell him that I'd do anything to run away again to Our Colony in the woods where hope flowed like the river.

The Convoy squeals on the rail as it turns the bend, a serpentine machine charging toward us. I turn to my deposed king. "It's too late, Gray," I tell him.

Chapter 11

It was springtime in Our Colony. The air was warmer everywhere in the New Colony, but only our kingdom in the woods could truly claim spring. In the afternoons after school, Gray and I would walk through the cement and flashing lights of the Pulse and step into the grayness of the Ancillary that was brightened by the occasional sprout of grass or struggling sapling. But down the dirt road that led to our childhood kingdom, spring reigned in the woods as it became dense with foliage and alive with the sinfonietta of birds. Our trail was becoming overrun in the thick enthusiasm of reaching branches. Even the river flowed with a renewed vigor from the thaw, and somehow it sounded more awake and cheerful than it had before.

In the mornings I would find a daffodil on my windowsill or on my front step and I would know: it was Gray's secret way to ask me to meet him in our little kingdom. I'd run through the woods clutching my flower and two biscuits, stolen from our pantry, to meet him as he waited for me expectantly on the log by the river.

Gray and I savored the delicate beads of nectar from honeysuckle and puckered at the bitter juice of what we thought were raspberries, but were actually blackberries, still unripe and beyond our naivety. From the Messenger Tree we nibbled the bitter fruit and whispered our secrets to be carried by the wind to my father and Gray's parents. The gifts the woods gave us were treasured up in our hole in the tree, which overflowed with new blossoms, smooth pebbles, translucent cicada shells found clinging to bark, and richly colored feathers.

Grayson and I spent two days collecting large stones to dam off a small outlet of water that pooled and stagnated away from the river. We floated flowers and made boats from richly verdant magnolia leaves and silken blossoms. Gray was able to catch some small minnows from the edge of the river, and these too were added to our pond. I discovered a small creature underneath rocks that escaped by unexpectedly swimming backward at lightning speed. It took us both, squealing at its waving claws, to round him into the bucket.

One day I found a small egg lying on the ground. "Look," I told Gray sadly. "It fell out of the nest."

Grayson and I knelt beside the small blue egg, unbroken in the cushion of the grass. I gingerly took it in my hand to examine. "Let's keep it," I suggested, but Gray was already looking for the nest.

"No, Rebecca. We can't just keep it."

"Sure we can," I said, blowing hot breath on it. "We'll rig something up, like a light, and make our own little warm nest. It can stay in my room."

"No," Gray said authoritatively. "If it fell out of its nest, then we'll put it back."

We found the nest in the "Y" of two branches, not far from the base of the tree. "It's going back," Gray said resolutely.

"I could raise it," I pouted.

Gray cupped his hand over the small egg and peered into the nest on tiptoe, ducking quickly in anticipation of the mother bird flying out, and then peering in again. "Mother's gone," he said, moving his arm slowly to return the egg. But he froze midair and looked at the egg and back in the nest.

"What is it?" I jumped up and down to catch a glimpse.

"It's so strange. There are three other eggs that look like the one that fell out, but there's another egg too."

"Let me see." I dragged over a small log we used as a chair. I held onto the trunk to balance myself. "It's so much bigger." I reached a thin finger out to feel the smoothness of it.

"Don't touch it, Rebecca," Gray said, giving me a sharp look.

"Aren't you going to put it back in?"

"How can I? There's no room. Why is that egg in the middle so much different?"

"It's just a really big brother one," I surmised. "The mother just laid a big one, that's all."

Gray shook his head. "That egg didn't come from the same mother. It couldn't have."

"Well, I don't know about that, but can I keep it now?"

Gray knit his eyebrows. "*We'll* keep it."

"Fine."

He clutched the egg gingerly to his chest as he walked it home. "How do you think it fell out?" Gray asked.

"How would I know? Maybe the wind? Or a snake? Maybe the mom accidentally knocked it out."

Gray and I used one of my mother's coffee mugs, filled with a shredded cotton sock that had long since lost its match. I added some honeysuckle blossoms for decoration and placed it under a light on my bedside table after thorough instructions from Gray about making sure I didn't accidentally knock it, and to have a spare bulb just in case the light were to go out.

"I have to turn the light out to sleep, though," I insisted.

Gray gave me an irritated and stern look.

"You can take it during the day, but I'll keep it at night," he said. I agreed.

The next morning, Gray knocked on my door as I was eating breakfast. I answered it hurriedly. "Did it hatch?" I whispered excitedly.

Gray shook his head and grabbed my backpack. "We have to go back to Our Colony. Now."

"I'm going to school, Mom!" I yelled to the back room where my mother was still getting dressed.

"Ok," she yawned loudly.

Grayson took my hand and pulled me out the door. "I read all about it," he said excitedly.

I picked up my pace to keep up.

"It was a cowbird."

"What are you talking about?"

"The egg didn't fall out. It got *pushed* out by a cowbird."

"Cowbird," I repeated. "That's a weird name."

"I looked it up. A long time ago they made their way over from the west coast by riding on the backs of cows and eating the bugs that were buzzing around them. Their great-great-great-grandparents flew around the land that's now under the ocean."

"So, why push out other birds' eggs?"

"It's how they survive. They push out an egg from another bird's nest and lay their own in its place."

"So, that big egg was a cowbird egg?"

"Exactly." Gray pushed aside the branches in the path to our kingdom.

"Are we going to pull the big egg out?"

Grayson shook his head. "The mother bird thinks it's hers. I say we just wait until it hatches and then take it out."

"Well, why do that? Won't she miss her baby?"

"Maybe she'll think it just flew out or something. I looked it up. Once it hatches, it will take all the food from the others, and they'll starve." Grayson ran his fingers through his hair nervously.

"Come on," I said gently. "We saved the one that fell out. That's the best we can do."

Gray looked into the other branches of adjacent trees. He paused at a small birch by the river. "I'm going to stay here today."

"We have school. Let's go, Grayson. Come on," I said impatiently.

"You go. I just need to stay here."

I looked at him incredulously. "Mom's going to kill you."

Gray shrugged. "I've got things to do."

I put my small hands on my hips and shook my head. "Mom is going to be—"

"I get it," Gray said, taking a seat on a log and looking up into the trees.

I kicked at a tree trunk before heading back toward the path.

"I guess I'll see you after school then." I looked back, hoping he'd change his mind, but he was still sitting there with his backpack on, intent on watching the sky.

That was the first time I had walked to school by myself, and I was irritated to be on my own.

"Where's your boyfriend?" a dark haired girl from my class asked as I walked in from the Convoy. I ignored her and made my way to the lockers.

Another girl who typically followed the lead of the head bully pushed me from behind. "Excuse me, Ancillary," she said nastily. "Didn't see you there." I kept my head down and continued walking.

Grayson had always walked me through the hall before class, and because he was a head taller than most of the kids in my class, it was one of the few times during the day that I wasn't berated with insults. Without him there I was fair game for any of the kids looking for someone to take a bite out of before school started.

The bullies knew no limits. Once Grayson and I had returned to our houses after school and found them trashed. Someone had come in, opened drawers and cabinets, and thrown our things on the floor, probably trying to find something to steal, or just to scare us. We had called the police to report an attempted robbery, but they did little to follow up. Being bullied was a way of life if you were Ancillary, and without Gray there, I spent my day dodging rolled-up balls of paper, launched at my head, and ignoring insults.

I counted down the minutes until the last bell rang and ran most of the way back to the woods. I found Gray where I had left him, cradling something in his hands.

"Well, you didn't miss much," I announced from the path. "Hope you at least stopped to get some lunch for whatever important business you had."

Gray didn't turn around. "I killed it," he said with his back to me.

I swung my bag onto the ground. "Killed what?"

"I killed the cowbird." Gray uncupped his hand and held out the still brown and gray bird. "I got her," he said. Tears streamed down Gray's face.

I looked at the mother bird, so delicate and harmless in death. How could that small creature have pushed out another's child for her own to live? Grayson was defeated. My heart broke thinking of him here by himself, taking on the responsibility of upholding justice for the innocent of his little kingdom. To me, that day, he was a king. A broken little king.

I put my small arm around him. "You did good," I said, putting my head on his shoulder and taking the dead bird with my other hand. "You had to, Gray. You did good."

Chapter 12

My mother is waiting for me on the porch as Grayson and I walk silently down the dirt road. I'm still fighting back tears after the boy plastered pictures of me for the class to enjoy—that they're still probably enjoying as I walk. I know she's upset even from the distance of the bend in the road by the way she's standing like she's been hit in the stomach.

"Did you tell her?" I ask Grayson accusingly. He shakes his head.

"You *sure*?" I ask him.

Gray attempts to reach for my hand, but I snatch it back menacingly.

My mother rubs her neck when we get closer. I haven't seen the expression on her face since Marissa's death. I consider running back toward the Pulse, but the Convoy won't pick up for another hour. There's nothing left to do but face her.

I don't recall my mother crying in front of me when we left the Old Colony. At night, when she thought I was asleep, she sobbed, but never in front of me otherwise. When she sees me now, she squeezes her eyes hard, and two large tears roll down her face. "Rebecca, I'm so glad you're home," her voice breaks.

I want to run into her arms and tell her that I'm back and not going away again. I want to scream that I want my father.

"Gray must have told you," I hear myself say.

My mother looks behind me at Grayson, who is still lingering on the steps. "No," she says slowly.

"Likely." I turn away so I don't have to see her hands shaking.

"No, it was Nicholas, actually. One of the Cherish kids is in school with you. He thought I should know."

"So, then everyone knows." My eyes ache from holding back hot tears.

"Rebecca, it's ok. We can fix this."

I laugh. "How can *we* fix this?" I mock. "There's nothing to fix!"

"I just mean that he's taking advantage of you, sweetheart. We can figure out a way to keep him away for a while."

"Taking advantage of me? Are you kidding?" I spit the words at her. "You're the one who's been taking advantage of me. I stay here with you, but I don't want to. I want to be Pulse, but you've done everything you can to make sure that doesn't happen. You've done all you can to hold onto everything Old, and that just happens to include me."

"That's not true," my mother says, shaking her head. "I want to keep you safe. I want to be a family. I want you to go home one day—"

"This *is* my home!" I scream. "Only I don't belong yet. But, I will as long as you don't stop me."

My mother puts her hands on either side of her face and her face contorts as the tears come steadily.

"You might be all right being stuck here on the outskirts," I tell her, "but I'm not going to be Ancillary all my life. Someone loves me. Why can't you be happy for that? People are paying money just for my image. There are some people who actually think I'm beautiful."

"Of course . . ." My mother looks completely stunned. "Well, of course you're beautiful, darling. There are people *here* who think you're beauti— "

"Doesn't mean anything," I huff. "It's what *they* think." I point my finger toward the Pulse. "I've finally got some worth and you want to tear me down to zero again. But I won't let you." I push past her and slam the door.

I pace in my room, waiting for my mother to come back in. When she doesn't, I scream into my pillow until my throat is rough and the fury has subsided. It's a matter of hours before I get the call from Radius for a job. I wipe my eyes and type out the message: "I'm really sick tonight. Can't make it." Maybe he'll be able to let me do one of the phone calls, although I did one two nights ago, so I doubt it.

He writes back almost immediately. "What's going on?"

"I'm just sick. I need a little break."

"No problem. I have a patch that will help."

I swallow hard. "Tonight is just not good," I type and wait.

Nothing.

Maybe he's just busy and doesn't have time to respond. But I know the truth.

I wrap my arms around myself and rock on the bed. I've seen Radius angry before. And if he sends Jamison, things might get really bad. This could ruin everything. I cannot afford to upset him right before the Panel interview.

I write a note to Lex: "My mother isn't going to let me out tonight. Don't know what to do. Think Radius is upset."

"Sorry, hon. I've got nothing," Lex writes back.

I stand up and pace my room as the anxiety rises. I've got to get out. If Radius comes here tonight, I don't know what my mom will do. For all I know she's already called the authorities. If that's happened, there will be an automatic punitive decrease of my VL score if they can prove that my provocative image is being sold when I am underage. I cringe thinking of what that will do to Radius.

There's only one thing that can be done. I have to pacify my mother. I take a deep breath and open the door to my bedroom. The door to her room is open, revealing her neatly made bed. I expect to find her in the front room, but she isn't there. Instead she's sitting on the porch step. She appears so much smaller from the back, slumped over in defeat, her head in her hands. It's the first time I've ever thought of my mother as old.

"Mom," I say, opening the door.

She doesn't turn around. "Yes, sweetie." Her voice breaks. I clear my throat.

"I want to try to get along," I cross my arms over my chest.

My mother nods her head weakly. I want to put my head on her shoulder. I want to be a little girl again, crawl into her lap and wait together until Dad gets home.

"I want to get along too," she says, turning around to me. "Where did I go wrong? I've always wanted so much more. I haven't been here enough," she says softly.

"Mom, stop. Nothing went wrong. This is just—it's just how things work here."

My mother covers her mouth with her hand as her eyes begin to well with tears again. "You're right that that's how things work here," she says, shaking her head. "But this isn't our home, Rebecca." She implores, begs me with her eyes to never accept the New. "Don't you remember where you're from? You've forgotten who you are. This isn't the end of your story, but you're settling—"

"What? Having a man who loves me and wants to help make this my home isn't good enough? I'm getting the best that I can—"

"You were made for more, Rebecca," my mother says firmly and brushes a loose strand of hair from my face. "You were made for so much more than this. We all know that. It's the truth, but they've put something in you that has pushed that truth out. That's what they do. It's how they survive. You have to push back."

I let my mother stroke my hair and cheek and allow her to believe that her words can change me. It's too late. I'm too far in now.

"Let me help you make dinner," I smile.

I know my mother loves me. But I've outgrown her. We both had our Own Colonies that helped us survive when we moved here. Gray and I found our refuge in the woods; for my mother, she found a haven at Cherish. She'll be ok. She has Nicholas and the children and her hope, always her hope. It's enough for her.

My cuff buzzes a few minutes after midnight. I was expecting it. "I've got a client who is requesting you. A big client. I'm on my way."

I breathe out slowly. "Ok," I respond, drained.

Mom has been quiet for hours now and is most likely sound asleep. I toss my shoes out the window first and slide down so slowly that I barely make a sound. I wait on the side of the house until his car lights turn the bend in the road. I wave with my shoes and tiptoe to the front walk.

"Rebecca," my mother says. "Get back in the house."

I let out a small scream and jump backward. "Mom, no," I plead. "I *have* to go tonight. It will be completely fine."

My mother is leaning against the post of the porch. "Rebecca, get back in the house," she repeats coolly.

I freeze as Radius opens his car door. "Let's go, Lark," he says with matched calmness.

My mother steps off the porch and into the headlights of Radius's car. "She's staying here," my mother says, like she's talking to one of the Cherish kids who is being unreasonable.

The other car door opens. I squint through the light to see Jamison. My stomach turns. Not Jamison.

"Mom, it's ok. These are my friends." I begin to walk toward the car, but my mother steps in front of me.

"Get back in the house, Rebecca," she whispers.

Radius seems so calm, too calm, and it scares me. But it is Jamison's presence that makes me panic.

"I'll be back tonight, Mom. I promise."

Radius and Jamison are both staring at my mother with a steely look. I turn to Mom. She is standing with her arms outstretched; her fingers blanche on the gun she is gripping, pointing it directly at Radius.

"Mom!" I scream. "What are you doing?"

"Get in the house, Rebecca."

I step in front of Radius, blocking my mother's aim.

"C'mon, lady," Jamison says. "We're friends here. Your daughter's boyfriend just wants to see his girl is all. Let's all calm down." Jamison has a wild look in his eye. Without Lex here to help keep him calm, I'm worried.

My mother glances at Radius, who is smiling with his palms out. Suddenly Jamison raises his hand in the air. In the light I can see the metal flash from his gun, which he points at me. I inhale sharply, and my mother turns her gaze to Jamison. She's at a distinct disadvantage with the car lights in front of her.

"James, come on. We're cool here." Radius's voice is smooth.

My mother doesn't take her eyes off Jamison. "Rebecca, just get in the house."

I swallow hard as Jamison keeps his gun trained on my head.

"Jamison." Radius draws his name out slowly, trying to calm him down.

"I will shoot you," my mother says sedately.

"Mom, *please*," I beg.

Jamison continues to walk around the car in front of my mother to get to me. I take a step back.

"Oh, I'll shoot too," Jamison smiles. "See, she wants to come with us," he says sweetly as he steps in front of my mother and places the gun only inches away from my head.

I look at Radius, whose hands are still up. His face is placid.

"Ok, Jamison," I say. "You're scaring me." He pulls back the hammer of the gun. I start to cry when I hear the metallic click.

My mother remains still, like she has been turned to stone. The headlights show her face, hard and resolute. Ancillary dust swirls in the headlight beam around her legs.

"These aren't the best Old Colony manners," Jamison says, turning to my mother. "You know, I could shoot her and no one would even notice."

I turn behind me to see Radius, who remains as he was.

"It's so tempting," Jamison taunts.

Radius won't let him, though. But then again, it is Lex who is more skilled at bringing him down when he gets like this. I swallow hard and close my eyes as hot tears stream down my face.

"Radius," I whisper pleadingly.

The loud crack pierces the night. I drop to the ground and grab my head, expecting to feel warm blood flowing from my temple where the gun was aimed. I frantically wipe the side of my head and look to my mother who is still standing as she was with her gun now pointed directly at Radius. Jamison is lying in a pool of something dark and creeping at my feet.

When I register what has just happened, I reel backward in the dirt. I hear Gray's door slam shut and him running across the yard. Radius curses loudly and pulls himself back into the car. I crawl on my hands and knees to get out of his way as he pulls onto the road.

"Come back!" I scream as he tears around the bend in the road.

Gray is now holding the gun away from my mother, who is shaking violently, but her voice is steady. "Get into the house, Rebecca."

"What if he's still alive?" I yell hysterically to Gray, whose eyes are wide and panicked. I stumble trying to get up and end up crawling up the steps.

My mother walks behind me. "Into the house, Rebecca," she says again.

"What did you do?" I scream. "He's dead!"

Gray lifts me to my feet. "Rebecca, he was going to shoot you."

"Radius wouldn't have let him," I sob.

My mother opens the door and sits down at the table. "They'll be here soon," she says in a faraway voice, like she's remembering something. "We'll tell them the truth. These men were going to hurt my daughter. I had to," she says, more to herself than to us.

Gray stands behind my mother and steadies himself by gripping the back of her chair.

"This can't be happening." I slide down the wall and sit on the floor. "He's out there, Mom!" I yell hysterically. "*Dead.* You killed him!"

My mother runs her hands along the table. "I didn't have a choice." She slides to the ground from her chair and crawls toward me. "Whatever happens after this, please don't go back to him," my mother pleads. "I will be ok. Do you understand?" She shakes me by my shoulders.

"Why couldn't you just let me go? If you had let me go, then none of this would have happened." I am crying uncontrollably.

She takes my head in her hands and then pulls me onto her lap. "Shh," she says. "It's going to be ok. Rebecca, there's more than this. You have to see beyond this and know what is com— "

The door bursts open, and two uniformed policemen come in and point their guns at us. My mother stands with her hands up. "I shot the man outside," she says and offers her hands in surrender with the quiet dignity she has carried since she was first lady of the Old Colony.

The second policeman holds out her hand and motions for me to come with her. Her gun remains trained on me. I follow her obediently and walk toward the drone that has landed in the dirt road outside our yard. I stumble as I pass Jamison's body lying awkwardly in the grass. Another carrier craft lands in Gray's yard and more police officers rush out.

"Meets description, we got 'em all," the officer leading me says to two uniformed men who get out of the craft.

My mother is being placed in a separate drone by herself. Her hands have been bound. "It's going to be ok!" she yells to me. "There's a plan. We'll get you," she says as the officer pushes her head into the carrier.

Chapter 13

Gray and I are led to separate rooms for questioning. A blond woman with glasses and black pants follows behind me and points to a dark gray chair with large cushions. I glance behind her shoulder as I sit down and see that Grayson is being escorted into a room across the hall.

"Do I need some sort of a lawyer or anything?" I ask her apprehensively.

"Well, did you shoot anyone?"

"No."

"Then you won't need a lawyer now, will you? Just answer some questions. Be a good girl and then we'll see you on your way. How does that sound?"

"Ok," I say slowly.

The woman has already taken my cuff. No doubt there is a small team reading my messages and piecing together my connection to Radius and Jamison. I close my eyes and swallow hard when I realize that they will also uncover a host of pictures and videos. I'll have to be extremely careful not to get Radius into trouble with careless answers. Nor do I want my mother to go to prison. The room is suddenly stifling.

"So tell me about tonight, umm ..." the woman looks at the printout on her lap, "Rebecca."

"Well, I was just going out with some friends tonight. They were picking me up." I glance to a camera on the wall.

"Friends. Uh-huh. So you wanted to go?"

"Yes."

"And your mother? She didn't seem to want you to. Is that correct?"

I pause. "Yep."

"We got a call tonight from a young man, Jonah Treadway."

I bite my lip in concentration, trying to figure out if I've ever met someone by that name. Programming class, maybe? "Never heard of him."

"Also goes by the name Radius." She smiles and takes off her glasses.

I want the floor to consume me. "Oh, yes. I know him." I attempt to sound casual. "He's my boyfriend."

The woman stifles a small laugh. I feel the blood rushing to my face.

"All right. Boyfriend. Jonah—Radius has indicated that your mother was abusing you. Do you agree?"

I stare at the woman. "Radius didn't say that," I challenge.

She looks down at her notes. "He would often pick you up at your residence so that you could get away from your mom. Is that correct?"

"No," I shake my head. "I mean, well—yes, that's part of the reason that Radius picked me up—to get away from my mother, I guess. But she wasn't beating me or anything."

The woman looks at her notes again. I rub my sweating hands together. This is going to be more difficult than I thought. I would do anything to know what Radius has already told her.

"It's true," I continue, slumping a bit in my seat to sound more casual. "I was trying to get away from her. Radius is right. He was really helping me." My stomach turns. "But she wasn't *abusing* me. It's just complicated."

"Complicated," the woman repeats. "And the gun? Where did your mother get a gun?"

"I don't know. I didn't even know she owned a gun. I've never seen it before."

"And she shot the victim, Jamison Salt, at close range."

I clear my throat as I fight the panic incited by the image of Jamison lying bleeding on the ground that has just flashed in my mind. "Yes, that's right. But he also had a gun and he was aiming it at me," I say irritably, tapping my temple where he had aimed it.

"We were able to collect his gun off his body. It wasn't loaded."

For a moment, my mind holds onto her words, heavy and difficult to process. "What do you mean, it wasn't loaded? He had it up to my head and—"

"There were no bullets in the weapon that Mr. Salt was holding." The corner of the woman's mouth turns up slightly.

I look up to the ceiling to fight back the tears that are coming at the thought of Jamison holding the gun to my temple. "We didn't know he was bluffing. I thought—she thought—he was going to kill me."

"But these were your friends, were they not? You were worried that your friend who was picking you up to get away from your mother would shoot you in the head?"

"No! I mean, yes—they were my friends. Radius was more my friend than Jamison."

"Your boyfriend?" She knits her brow in feigned confusion.

"Yes, my boyfriend. Jamison was just coming with him. But he was a little off, you know? I never quite knew what he was going to do. My mother shot him because she was trying to protect me—from Jamison, *not* Radius."

"I see." the woman leans back in her chair "And this Radius saw someone pointing a gun at your head—his girlfriend's head—and he wasn't concerned by that? He didn't do anything?"

"He was trying to calm him down. I don't know. He must have known it wasn't loaded," I say, looking down with this sudden realization.

The woman sits up straighter in her chair and puts her glasses back on. She leans forward and is all business now. "If you'd be willing, I'd like to have you sign a statement to that effect."

"All right," I agree. "I'll sign something that says that Jamison was getting out of hand, and my mother thought he was going to shoot me."

The woman opens the door and motions for me to exit into the hall.

"So, is that it then?" I ask.

"That's it," she says in a singsong voice and smiles at me.

The door to Gray's room is still closed.

"Can I go home now?" I cringe to think of walking past where Jamison had lain on the ground.

"Not yet. Couple of things to sign and then you can go."

"What about my mom?" I ask.

"She'll be staying here with us for a little while."

It will be her first night away from our house since we moved here. "Ok," I say, trying not to cry.

"Just wait right here." She indicates a wooden chair down the hall. "We'll get right back to you."

I walk robotically down the corridor. I can't stop the deluge of images that overtake my mind—Radius standing expressionless, the look in Jamison's eye as he pointed his gun at my head, my mother resolute and fierce.

115

I am torn between hating myself for Radius getting into trouble and worrying over my mother facing exile for murder. But both emotions are so overwhelming on their own that I feel like I might explode. Steady, Rebecca. Steady.

I should call someone. Someone should know to be here for my mother. Nicholas Porter, maybe, but that would mean having to tell him everything. He probably already knows about Radius, and if he steps in here, he'll tell the police. Although Gray's probably handling telling every detail he knows about Radius and me to his interviewer as I stand here. Maybe I should just tell them myself.

But if I go back in right now and tell that woman that Radius was picking me up to service clients, then he'll probably go to jail because they'll assume he's a hawker. But will it matter anyway? My mother could still go to jail even if I do tell them. It won't help anyone. No. Keeping my mouth shut is the best strategy.

The man who was interviewing Gray walks out first and points to where I'm fidgeting on the bench. Gray looks worn. He makes brief eye contact with me and smiles like he is either exhausted or simply trying not to cry. He sits and stares at the wall in front of us.

"Please tell me you told them," Gray whispers without looking at me.

I look down at my hands.

"Tell me you told them," he whispers again, giving a sharp look.

"Tell them what, exactly? I told them the truth," I say, avoiding his eyes.

"So you told them why Radius was picking you up?"

I shrug. "I told them the truth, Gray. I told them that Radius is my boyfriend."

Gray runs his hands through his hair and grips the bench tensely like he's waiting for a wave of pain to pass.

"It's going to be fine, Gray. I explained to them that my mother was only trying to protect me. Jamison was unpredictable."

Gray turns to me. I suddenly feel like I'm on fire. I return his look defiantly.

"Go back in there and tell them the truth, Rebecca. Your mother—"

"It's not like you didn't already tell them. They already know, so what does it matter now what I say?" My heart races at the thought that Radius will be brought in after the testimony Grayson gave. At the very least, I don't want to be responsible for that.

"They hardly asked me anything important. And the guy interrupted me every time I tried to explain. He told me, just answer the questions he asked, which were about *nothing*: how long did I know your mom? What time does she get home from work normally? Does she usually stay up late?" Grayson's voice is shaking with anger. He stares at the wall again and rubs his pant legs with balled fists. "This isn't good, Rebecca. Your mother shot him," he says, lowering his voice. "You admitted that and so did I. Your mom will tell them she did. The only way she's going to get off is if we can prove she was trying to protect you, and that you were being forced. She had to do it."

"But, I wasn't being forced."

Gray turns to me and for a moment he looks like he wants to hit me. "Go back in there and tell them the *truth*, Rebecca." His eyes bulge with anger.

I glance at the police officers at the desk as they talk in low voices to one another. The woman keeps casting glances at me.

"He was going to kill you. He wouldn't have blinked an eye," Grayson says, almost sympathetically now.

I continue to look past Gray at the woman who is gathering some papers. "He wouldn't have killed me."

"His gun was aimed at your head. I saw it," Gray whispers with clenched teeth.

"It wasn't loaded."

Gray looks at me incredulously and then puts his head in his hands and cries like he did when he was a boy waiting for his parents to come back for him.

We say nothing on our way back to the Convoy. The sun is coming up just as we round the bend to our homes. The authorities made quick work of Jamison. There is nothing to indicate that a dead man had been lying in my front yard just a few hours earlier, with the exception of some white powder that I'm assuming was to help absorb some of the blood. Gray pauses at my porch as though he isn't sure what to say. He raises a hand to point to his house, but I interrupt him.

"I'm ok," I say. "Go home. I'm going to get some rest."

Gray nods and makes his way to his own steps, which he trudges up like they're the last of a mountain he has just climbed.

Immediately, I go into my room and send Radius a message: "I didn't tell them anything." I wait, fighting back tears.

Finally, a message appears: "I knew you wouldn't."

Hot tears stream down my cheeks with relief. Radius calls within moments.

"Hey," I say into my cuff. "I'm so sorry." I can barely get the words out. "I'm so, so sorry about Jamison."

Radius says nothing.

"I had no idea she had a gun, I swear," I whisper.

"Lark, I think we had better lay low until after the trial."

"But I want to be with you right now. I need you," my voice cracks.

"I know. There's nothing you could have done. I just think I need a little time, ok?"

"I'm so sorry, Radius. This is hard for you. I just thought I could help."

Radius breathes out slowly. "Few days until things blow over. That's all. I need some time."

I fall back onto my bed. "Of course. It's what you need." I cover my mouth and will myself to stop crying.

"I'll see you in a couple of days."

"You mean, at the Panel interview?" I hold my breath.

"Yeah, sure. I'll see you then. This isn't completely your fault, you know."

"I would have done anything to make things different. Jamsion was your best friend."

"Let's just say you owe me."

The patches helped me get through the first day. But I'm out now, so I call Lex to come to my rescue. I watch her walk up the path and pause at the section of disturbed dirt sprinkled with white powder. Her face drops as she tiptoes around as though Jamison is still lying there dead. But when I open the door, she is all smiles and hugs as usual.

"Radius is ok," she assures me. "He doesn't blame you." But by the way she says it, I have my doubts.

I try to give Radius the space he needs. Too many times I have typed a message and deleted it before getting the courage to send it.

Lex assures me that Radius is doing all right and that I shouldn't worry about the Panel interview. "He'll be there, Lark," she says, shaking me playfully by the shoulders. "And I'll be there to make you look gorgeous."

My VL score has gone down two dozen points so that now I am below five hundred. Between worrying about the Panel, Radius, and my mother, I have developed such stomach pains that I can hardly eat.

My mother is everywhere in the house. I close the door to her room and collect the teacups she had out on the counter the night she shot Jamison. The police have done a thorough search of the house, for more weapons I expect, and I spend several hours putting the emptied contents of closets—towels, books, gardening tools, dishes—back in order. I cringe when I enter my room to find gifts from Radius, which I had hidden under my bed, now splayed upon the floor.

"Any news?" Grayson writes me the night before the Panel interview.

"No," I write back. The police officers had promised to let us know something the day after Mom was arrested, but more than a day later we still have heard nothing. A few minutes after the message comes in, Grayson knocks on my front door.

"I'm going to see her. You coming?" he asks. He looks like he hasn't slept for days. But then I guess he hasn't.

"Is that a good idea?" My stomach turns and I start to perspire. I could use another patch. "I mean, we were supposed to wait until we got a call. They're not going to let us see her."

"You coming or not?"

There is no place I want to be farther from. They might remember they have more questions for me. "I just don't think it's a good idea, Gray," I say delicately as he turns and walks down the steps with his hands shoved into his pockets. "Wait, Grayson. She's coming back. We just don't want to make things worse by being too pushy."

"Wake up, Rebecca!" Gray yells, wheeling around to face me. "Your mother is *Ancillary*. She just shot and killed a *Pulse* man with an illegal weapon." Gray points to where Jamison died. "Her job is working with rejected kids. You think they're going to just let her out to go back to business as usual?"

"It was an accident, Gray." My stomach is cramping so severely now that I can hardly stand. "She didn't want to kill him. She was just trying—"

"To *protect* you!" Gray storms back up onto the steps so that we are eye to eye. "She doesn't want you to be *sold* anymore, and you did nothing to help her."

I stare at Grayson. I feel the hate rising from my chest, and I want to hit him with all of my strength.

"You're coming with me," Grayson says calmly now. "You're going to go see your mother. Hell, you might even try telling the police the truth."

"It's not my fault Jamison is dead. And I can't fix this now." I turn back into the house, slam the door, and walk straight to my room. Frantically, I unwrap patches and slap them on the back of my neck until they spread their beautiful numbness throughout my body and suffocate the fire that Gray's words have set within me.

Grayson still hasn't returned. My guess is that he's waiting on the same bench where we sat the day of our interview. I keep up the naïve optimism of a child as well—she doesn't deserve exile, and any moment Grayson will be walking with her around the bend in the road. But the patches quiet the fight inside me so that only the truth is able to surface: she's not coming home. Ever. And I'm able to know the truth without its full pain.

My cuff buzzes and I look to it slowly. "I'm coming to get you in five minutes," Radius writes.

One more day until the Panel. I have to harden to make it here. I walk robotically to my closet and slip on a new gold dress that Radius bought for me several weeks ago. A pale girl looks back at me from the mirror. "I'm ready," I type.

I use the railing to help lower myself down the steps. I shake my head to get the world into focus. Radius is rounding the bend. I fall to the first step and wait for him to get out. I am weak from not eating but bold from the patches.

"Let's try this again," Radius says, opening the passenger side of the door.

My head hurts so intensely when I wake that I think I might vomit. I can still smell the men from last night. I wrap the covers around me tightly and sob.

"Hey," Lex says from the doorway. "You're up."

"Yeah, I'm up."

"Whoa, here, take this," Lex says, handing me a trashcan, which I dry heave into.

"I'm running you a bath, ok?" I nod slowly. "Radius left you something," she calls from the bathroom.

I look at the chair in the corner with an emerald green dress and matching shoes.

"It's stunning," she says.

"Where is Radius?"

"He'll be in soon."

"Last night—" I say hoarsely.

"I'm taking you shopping today to celebrate after your Panel interview is over." Lex says. "And before, we're making a little stop at the salon."

"Last night—" I say again. Lex carries a towel and a robe to the bed and sits down.

"What's the big deal, Lark? You were already doing it."

"No—Lex," I cry. "Not like that. Last night was awful. I did it for Radius. There were four men. One right after the other. Before, I had never—"

Lex throws her arms around me. "You are a good girl," she says soothingly. "You did good."

I shiver in the hallway of the Panel building. After a hot bath and Dylan's work in the salon, I look better. Last night was just a nightmare. It didn't really happen, I tell myself. Lex gives my hand a squeeze. "It'll be just fine," she says. I tap my high heels nervously. I've got to calm down before I get in there. There are at least thirty young girls and boys lined up on the bench in the marble hallway looking as nervous as I am.

"Where is he?"

"Sponsors wait in a different room. Relax." Lex primps my hair and gives me a squeeze. "We'll celebrate after."

A bored-looking woman with a ruffled collar and black skirt opens the door, and the sound echoes in the marble hallway. "Rebecca Flora," she calls, looking down the long row.

When I raise my hand she looks me up and down and breaks into a broad smile. "Ah-ha," she says. "We've found you. Right this way, Ms. Flora."

I straighten my shoulders before following her into the well-lit room.

"You got it," Lex whispers.

The key is to act as though I already have citizenship. Be Pulse. This may be the last room I enter as Ancillary. I give the judges a forced smile and hope they can't tell how nervous I am.

Six judges. A man in the middle is tapping on a device on the raised table in front of him. "Have a seat," he says casually.

The woman who escorted me indicates an oversized leather chair with a high back that sits directly in front of the Panel. The Panel is elevated, and I become so small once I take the chair that I hope the floor will open up and swallow me all together. There is a side table to my right with two empty chairs. That must be for the sponsors, I think. Maybe they'll bring Radius in after they ask me questions individually.

"I'm having trouble loading the Flora documents," a young woman with long, unnaturally red hair on the end of the table says.

The lady who escorted me in walks over to her and starts pushing buttons on her device.

"All the same, I believe we can get started," says the man in the center, who must be the leader.

I shift uncomfortably. An older man on the end smiles at me warmly. I smile back and then look to the head man, who is staring at me intently.

"Tell us a little about yourself, Ms. Flora," he says.

"Certainly." I expected this question and am ready for it. "I have lived in the colony for half my life. I can say with all confidence that this is the best place for me to have citizenship."

A woman with a tight red dress and severe haircut leans forward. "The best for *you,* perhaps. Our job is to decide what is best for the colony."

I clear my throat and look to the man on the end, who is still smiling. "Absolutely," I say seriously. "I would be an asset to the colony as well."

"Could you elaborate?" the woman in the red dress says.

"You can see by my grades that I have always done well academically."

Several of the Panel members press buttons on their devices. A man on one side of the leader nods slowly.

"You can also see that my VL score is almost five hundred," I say, trying to sound confident.

"It is 515," the leader says.

It must have gone up last night.

"This is where I belong. It is my home now," I say. "And I want to serve my home."

"And how will you do that?" the woman on the end asks pompously.

"When I graduate, I plan on becoming a model." When no one looks up, I add, "I enjoy business as well and would like to attend the business school."

A man on the other side of the leader continues on his device without raising his head. "We don't have a need for that, Ms. Flora. And although you do appear to be quite," he pauses to look at me, "*decorated*, the modeling business is quite a reach." He crosses his arms and leans back in his chair.

The metal taste of blood fills my mouth from where I have bitten my lip in an attempt to not reveal how much his words sting. I look to the other Panel members for some indication that they might disagree with his assessment.

I swallow hard when no one appears to show any signs that they will speak against him. "That may be so. But I do believe that I could make it in that field." I look at them indignantly. I have already been bringing in thousands of dollars.

"Actually, it appears that you already have," the woman in the red dress says, smiling. I feel my face becoming warm. What had she retrieved on her device? She slides it slowly to the leader, who clears his throat when he sees it.

"Perhaps you would be sustainable in the modeling industry after all," he says.

I can't tell if he is being sarcastic or not, but I want to run out the door as fast as I can. I re-cross my legs and sit up straighter. "I could make it," I say, feigning confidence.

"We understand that your mother is now facing exile, correct?" a man on the end who has not spoken yet asks in a quavering voice. The man next to him continues to smile warmly, as though I had only been asked to give an account of my favorite colors.

"My mother, not me," I whisper.

"Ahh," says the man.

"Yet another reason she would want citizenship without her mother here anymore," the woman reasons.

"Perhaps." The leader rubs his chin pensively. "Nancy." He motions for the woman who brought me in. "I think that will be all for now. Please escort Ms. Flora to the door."

Nancy walks towards me.

I blink as I process his words. "No, there must be more," I protest.

"That is all that is required, Ms. Flora," he says. "Not to worry. We will also take into consideration your DNA profile. The colony may need you yet."

"But my sponsor wasn't called in." I grip the armrest of the chair.

"Was there a sponsor?" The man at the end leans forward and looks down the Panel.

"No indeed." The woman in red gives a half smile.

"Yes, there is. It's a mistake." My eyes dart to the door as though he'll walk through it any second. "Radius is here to speak on my behalf." I begin to feel lightheaded.

"He declined." The woman indicates something on her device to the leader. My heart stops beating, and there is a ringing in my ears.

"That is all that is required, Ms. Flora," the leader says again.

Nancy stands beside my chair and takes my arm to lead me out. I snatch my arm back. "He wouldn't have declined. Is there some way that I could call him, maybe? Please?" I look to the smiling man for some sign of sympathy, but he continues to smile back stupidly. "This is supposed to be my home," I say pathetically.

"Thank you for your time." The woman is curt and sharp. I hate her.

I look pleadingly to the Panel members who are busily typing away on devices as my life ends. Just like that, it is over. Eight years. All of it.

The woman with the ruffled neckline and black skirt stands beside my chair and holds out a hand to indicate that I should exit. I walk torpidly to the door. There is no fight left. The door closes mercilessly behind me.

Lex smiles when she sees me, but I shake my head. "Next year!" she says cheerfully. I want to slap her.

As quickly as I can, I walk down the hall with Lex trailing behind. "Hey, slow down," she says.

I pick up my pace under the gaze of all the hopefuls waiting on the bench. I straighten my shoulders and walk resolutely, hips swinging and heels clicking authoritatively. For all they know I'm a citizen now.

My toe catches on something and I stumble. I breathe in deeply from the pain in my knee. A girl about my age is sitting on the bench. She doesn't turn her head when she sees me but shifts her eyes to look down on me. "Ancillary," she mouths.

"Come on," Lex says, helping me up.

"What did you just say?" I ask the girl, but she doesn't turn around. I can feel my cheeks flushing. "You're Ancillary too," I say, more loudly this time.

The girl raises an eyebrow and pushes some buttons on her cuff. "Not like you."

"No, exactly like me."

The girl laughs sarcastically. I want to punch out every single one of her overly white teeth. Lex takes my hand to lead me outside before I can.

"You're Ancillary too. *Just* like me!" I yell to her as Lex jerks my arm.

Lex turns around to give me a sharp look. "Don't make a scene."

My hands are shaking. "He didn't show," I remonstrate, my voice shaking.

Passers-by on the street are beginning to stare. I grab Lex's purse to rummage in it for some patches "Why wasn't he there?" I groan.

"Let's go celebrate." Lex smiles nervously as she notices a few people who have stopped to stare.

"Celebrate *what*?!" I yell maniacally. "There's nothing—I have *nothing* now." I can't find a patch and throw her purse back in frustration.

Lex reaches out to put her arm around me, but I swat her away.

"Everything just fell apart. Why wouldn't he show?"

"It's over now," Lex says tepidly as I pace back and forth in my feverish state.

"What's left?" I stop abruptly as I realize. "You knew." I point an accusing finger at her. "You knew he wasn't going to come!"

Lex hesitates and shakes her head, but her hesitation confirms it.

"Get away from me." I look her directly in the eye.

"I'm your family, Lark."

I shake my head.

"You still belong here. Where are you going to go?" she yells after me as I push a gawker out of the way and run. "You'll come back home!"

Chapter 14

I call the only person I can think to call. "I want to visit her," I say.

Gray meets me at the police station. "Didn't go well?" he asks. "Don't look so happy."

I note that Gray is wearing the same clothes he wore the day before. "So have you seen her?"

"Rebecca," Gray's face drops. "They let me see her, but there's not good news."

"They delayed the trial?" I guess.

"Your mom confessed."

"But she isn't guilty."

Gray shakes his head. "At this point, your mother doesn't even want to contest it. We know how it will turn out. It will be easier on everyone to expedite it, but at least they are saying it was unintentional. She's pled guilty to third-degree murder."

"*No*, it was self-defense. Or she was defending me. Doesn't that count?"

"She had a contraband gun, Rebecca."

My cuff buzzes, but I decline. "This can't be happening," I say under my breath. "So what you're telling me is that my mother is going to be exiled?"

"Unless the court grants clemency. Your mother has done a lot for the colony working with Cherish."

"The colony hates Cherish. You should see how they treat them. They don't exactly consider her an asset, and my mom has always been a squeaky wheel there."

"Rebecca, what do you have to lose now? Just tell them everything."

I put my head in my hands. What does it matter now that Radius has abandoned me? I nod my head slowly.

"Where is she?" I ask.

Gray puts his arms around me. For a moment I feel a safety and a calm, as though nothing can hurt me anymore. I am neither Ancillary nor Pulse, just a hurting girl with a friend giving temporary shelter from a messed-up life. I fight against the images of the night before. If Grayson knew, he would push me away with disgust.

Gray leads me to the desk in the hallway. My cuff buzzes again. It is Radius. While Gray gives our names to the woman at the desk I read the message Radius has sent: "I'm so sorry, Lark. They came by yesterday to ask me more questions. I was afraid that if I went to the interview today, it would hurt you more than help. I had to stay here. I love you."

"It couldn't have hurt any more, trust me," I write back and remove my cuff to hand to the woman.

But almost immediately I want to take it back to read that Radius said he loved me.

The woman pushes a piece of paper for me to sign, showing that I understand the regulations for visiting a prisoner. Gray and I are led down a long corridor and take an elevator to the sixth floor.

"Think she'll be mad that I took so long to see her?"

"Your mom has this peace that's come over her. I think she'll be ok."

"Always the first lady."

We have to wait for almost an hour until my name is called. I follow a large man in uniform into a room with a metal door and dark gray walls. I sit in the wooden chair that faces another one. A few minutes later the door opens and my mother is escorted in. She is wearing an all-white jumpsuit and her hair has been neatly pulled back. She smiles serenely when she enters.

Gray was right, there's a peace about her. She shuffles to the wooden chair across from me. Her feet as well as her wrists are shackled together. When the guard has her seated, he takes a small metallic chip and places it over her wrists, which releases them. He puts her hands on a metal plate on each armrest so that she is then anchored to the chair by some sort of magnetic device. He does the same with her feet. I watch in horror as my mother is completely immobilized. I want to scream at the guard to let her go—she isn't dangerous.

"Mom," my voice breaks. "I'm so sorry."

"Shh, shh. Everything's going to be ok." My mother glances at the corner behind my head. "We're being recorded," she observes and smiles.

"Gray told me that you decided not to fight it."

"Yes, I thought it best. You need to get on with your life. An extended trial would be everywhere. You couldn't escape it."

"But, Mom. If it meant a better chance at not being exiled—"

"It won't," she says plainly. "Rebecca, there are a lot of Ancillary people who want to take care of you."

I roll my eyes and look away. "I know what that means," I say.

"Mr. Porter has said that they would give you the very best of everything at Cherish. You could live there. It would only be until you're of age."

"Mom, no—"

"The kids love you. Think how valuable to them you would be."

I stare at my mother blankly. It will never happen, but I nod that I understand. "Sure, sounds like a plan," I say. "If you get exiled, which you won't."

"Rebecca, your father and I love you so much."

My eyes fill up with tears. Dad would be broken to know what has become of his family.

"There's more than this, Rebecca. I promise you." She jerks against the chair as though trying to get up. "Rebecca, look at me," she whispers. "There's more to this. You know your father's heart," she says emphatically, lowering her head. "You know his heart, Rebecca."

A sound buzzes and the guard comes to take her back. "Can I hug her?" I plead. The guard lets out a heavy sigh and jerks his chin at my mom. I lean over to hug her. She no longer smells like earth and citrus. I breathe in the heavy soap and metal smell in her hair. "I'm sorry, Mom," I say. And I am.

She jerks against the chair again. "My sweet girl," she smiles. "My sweet girl."

I lean down for her to kiss my forehead.

"That's enough," the guard says, pushing me back.

The door from which I entered opens, and a woman on the other side motions for me to come back in the hall.

"I have to talk to someone about something," I tell the guard.

"Sure, hon," the guard says apathetically.

"Mom, I'm sorry," I tell her again with tears in my eyes before the woman takes my arm and leads me back to Gray. My mother continues to stare at me serenely until the door closes with a heavy, metallic finality.

Gray is leaning forward with his elbows on his knees.

"I need to talk to someone," I tell the guard again.

Gray stands up and puts his arm around me. We take the elevator back down to the first floor. I walk quickly to the desk in the hallway.

"Excuse me." I clear my throat and wipe the moisture from my cheeks. "I'd like to talk to the person who first interviewed me after my mother was arrested."

The woman looks up lazily.

"I have something to add to my testimony."

She looks at me with weepy eyes and blows her nose. "Darn allergies," she sniffs. "So you've already been interviewed?"

"Yes." I lean forward onto the desk.

"Last name, please."

"Flora. My mother is Eleanor Flora."

She presses a series of buttons on her screen.

I bite my bottom lip while I wait.

"Well, now, the detective assigned to that case isn't here today," she says irritably and blows her nose again.

"All right, then how about another detective?" I ask.

The woman shakes her head no and tosses her tissue into the trash bin.

I look desperately to Gray. "Let me leave a note for her?"

"Suit yourself." The woman pushes forward a piece of paper and hands me a pen.

Gray knocks on the door to my room. "I brought you a cup of coffee. Can I come in?"

I wipe my eyes with the back of my hands. "Yeah, come on in."

The door creaks open. Gray hands me the steaming mug and sits down on the rug by my bed.

"I hate waiting." My voice is shaky.

"It's going to be ok." He gives up on forcing a smile and looks out the window instead. "She's been my mom too, you know."

"I know," I whisper. He has dark circles under his eyes and needs to shave. "You're a better son than I am a daughter, that's for sure."

"Nah," he says. "Have you talked to him?" Gray's tone becomes steely.

"No." It's an unconvincing lie. I take a long sip of the coffee. I have been trying to ignore Radius's calls, but I've been desperate to hear his voice. My mother killed his best friend, after all. He's just messed up right now.

Gray rolls his eyes. "Rebecca, come on. After all this. Please just tell me you won't go back to that creep."

"I'm here, aren't I?"

Grayson rises up on his knees so that he's eye level with me on the bed. He takes my head in his hands. "I'm serious, Rebecca. I just can't take losing both of you."

I turn my head away and feel the sharp pang of guilt in my chest. Gray has had so many losses. Now that Marissa is gone, my mother and I are all he has left.

"You're not going to lose Mom," I tell him reassuringly. "She'll be walking through that door any minute." I say it to comfort us both. I can't allow my mind to rest even momentarily on the alternative without the defense of the patch, which will steady the wrecking balls that the truth will unleash.

"I'm going to make some dinner." Gray pushes off the floor to stand.

"I'm not hungry."

"I'm not either, but I've got to do something."

I lean back on my pillow. Radius has sent me another message: "Just need to see you."

I look to the door to where Gray just left. He is loudly banging pots on the counter in the kitchen.

"I need to see you too," I write back. "I'm losing my mind waiting."

I cross the hall to the bathroom and look in the mirror. "What are you doing, Rebecca?" I run water in my hands and splash my face. My hands are shaking.

I hear Gray's quick footsteps in the hall.

"Rebecca, someone's here," he says on the other side of the door.

"Who?" I ask impatiently.

Gray looks worried when I open the door.

"Why are you so pale?" I am suddenly alarmed.

We both jump at a loud knock at the door.

Gray stops in the kitchen first to turn off a pot that is boiling over. A silver car is parked in our front drive with the Colony symbol on it.

"It's the police," I call toward the kitchen.

131

Gray has suddenly become very busy. I turn the knob slowly. A man and a woman in uniform are standing on the porch.

I swing open the door. "Can I help you?" I ask abruptly.

"Are you Rebecca Flora?" The man's words are drawn out like he's about to yawn.

"Yes."

"We are here to escort you to Cherish."

I take a defensive step back. "My mother is coming home. You can't take me."

Gray comes out from the kitchen holding a small towel and a spoon. "Does this mean she's been exiled?" he asks anxiously.

"No, it means that currently there is no one to care for Miss Flora, and because she is a minor, it is Colony policy that she stay at Cherish."

"I'm going to be eighteen in *two years*," I protest. "I can take care of myself, and there's no way I'm going to spend two years at Cherish."

Gray looks panicked. "I can take care of her," he says in the most authoritative voice he can muster.

The man shakes his head. "No, son. Not allowed."

The woman looks at me kindly. "Can I help you pack?"

"No, because I'm not going anywhere." I cross my arms. "And how come he doesn't have to go anywhere?" I ask, pointing at Gray.

"He's losing his guardian."

"Correct," returns the man. "An evaluation was done for Grayson. Because he currently has a job and is set to graduate soon, Grayson will be permitted to stay here with regular supervised visits from Colony Child Services until he graduates next spring."

Gray shakes his head. "Rebecca," he whispers. "Don't fight this. Just do what they ask you to."

I can feel my hands trembling. "No, Gray," I hiss between clenched teeth. "You get to stay here. Who knows how long I'll be staying at Cherish."

"Just until your mother is released," he reassures me.

"Come on, honey." The woman looks irritatingly sympathetic. "You can bring two bags."

If I go to Cherish, then my chances for colony citizenship are completely gone for next year. I run to my room and slam the door while Gray continues to plead my case. There is only one thing to do.

"Need help." I write to Radius. "Police are here to take me to Cherish." I open a bag and start throwing clothes in from my drawers. "This can't be happening," I say aloud.

"Hold on," Radius writes. "They're there right now?"

"Yes!" I write. "You have to come get me." I throw a pair of shoes and hairbrush in while I wait.

"Ok," he writes back after what seems like several minutes. "But you need to go with them for right now."

I burst into tears. I'm too angry to write anything back. If I try to run now, there's no way I can get away with the police in my living room.

Someone knocks on my door.

"You doing all right in here?" the woman asks.

I hate her.

"Just fine," I snap. I open the door roughly and throw the bag over my shoulder. "Got everything," I shoot her a sarcastic smile. "Let's get this over with."

"It won't be so bad," the woman smiles. I follow her and the man out the door to the car.

"I'll visit," Gray yells from the porch, still holding the dishtowel and spoon. "Rebecca, I'll visit. When your mom gets out—"

I wave my hand at him dismissingly. I don't turn back to look at Grayson as we pull away, but I know he is still standing on the porch. We pass the woods where I spent the remainder of my childhood. I put my head on the window as I watch them disappear.

Chapter 15

Children are playing in the yard when we pull up to Cherish. I recognize a few of them. A couple of kids run back into the house or around the side when they see the police car, but a few peek from behind trees to get a better view. The boldest of the lot get closer and run off as the car door opens. I keep my head down when I step out.

A little girl who has been watching from the window runs to me. "Rebecca!" she squeals.

"Hi, Luce," I say.

"Where's your mom?" She looks into the car eagerly.

"She's not here yet," I tell her gently.

"I have something I want to show her." She bats her big eyes.

"Maybe you can show me," I say wearily. "I'm going to hang out for a little while."

Lucy takes my hand and pulls me after casting a suspicious glance to the man carrying my bag.

Mr. Porter opens the front door and nods to me seriously. I've never seen Mr. Porter without a tie. Today his hair is disheveled and it looks like he hasn't shaved in several days. He barely makes eye contact as he takes my bag. It never occurred to me before now that Mr. Porter might blame me for this and be angry. In losing my mother, he is losing the only other person who kept Cherish running. Surely he knows everything. And now I am under his care.

A few of the children shadow us down the hall. Lucy takes my hand. "When's Ms. Ellie coming back?" she asks softly.

"I don't know, sweetie," I tell her. "I wish I knew. But I'm here now." I cringe as soon as I say it. No, I'm not staying.

"Can I show you what I made?"

"Of course. Just as soon as I get settled in, all right?"

Lucy smiles, and I let go of her hand when the bell sounds. Mr. Porter opens the door for me to follow him through the courtyard.

"Thank you both. We'll take it from here," he says to the police officers, who look at first as though they might protest leaving. Mr. Porter gives them a hard look and they turn to go. When we are alone, he slows down for me to catch up with him.

"What did your mom tell you, Rebecca?" he asks in a low voice.

"What do you mean? I talked to her for a few minutes yesterday. She didn't say much."

Mr. Porter turns to face me and appears to be searching me for answers that I am hiding.

I look aside. "I'm sorry," I whisper. "For all of this, I'm sorry. I know how important my mother is to Cherish."

Mr. Porter sucks on his teeth and clears his throat. "I should have known something like this could happen. It's my fault that I wasn't more proactive about it."

I start to ask what he means but decide that not saying anything is probably the best strategy.

I follow him into one of the vacant dormitory cabins.

"One empty bed in here," he says, pointing to a top bunk in the corner. "I'll get you sheets and your uniform."

I look around the elongated cement room with its neat rows of bunks for my future Cherish-mates as Mr. Porter busies himself in an adjacent room. He returns with his arms full of linens and a light blue jumper, which he puts on my bed.

"Rebecca, I need you to listen to me," he says in a hushed tone. "It's going to be all right here. This is a new chance. A new beginning."

So he does know everything.

"Think of it as that, will you? Your mother . . ." He looks away and clears his throat. "Your mother would be so proud if—you have a chance now to make such a difference with these children. You have so much of your mother in you, you know."

"This isn't my home."

"That's not either," he says abruptly, pointing emphatically toward the Pulse. "Don't think you can try going back there. You understand how dangerous that would be for you. And to bring anyone in here . . ." he raises his voice before tapering off. His face flushes a bright pink. "Think of how dangerous that could be for the children."

I nod that I understand.

"And I'm going to need to know right now if you have brought anything with you that could possibly be harmful to you," Mr. Porter says decisively.

"No. Nothing."

"That's good," he says softening a bit. "I'm going to have to do a search of your bag anyway."

I had expected that. "Of course."

Mr. Porter looks apologetic. "It's only that we must take every precaution, you understand. Protocol."

"I understand."

I look around the room, which will be full by tonight. Stuffed pigs, rabbits, turtles, and small dolls wait patiently on smooth pillows. "So, there will be all girls my age here?" I ask, sitting down on the bed below mine and twirling the curls of a stuffed fairy.

"No, actually. Just you and two other girls your age—Miranda and Rachelle. Our oldest help care for the youngest. You all have girls between the ages of five and seven. Miranda and Rachelle will show you the ropes." Mr. Porter unscrews the cap to my shampoo and smells it before putting the cap back on. "Very good." He empties the contents of my bag onto my bunk and examines each item methodically. "Rebecca, you can be happy here. It's not so very long. You might find that this is a place of belonging for you."

I think of Mr. Porter and his five children from whom he is now separated. Could he ever belong here after that? Could he ever truly belong anywhere? Could any of us?

"But my mother will be out soon, and I'll return to live with her."

Mr. Porter clears his throat again. "You're right, Rebecca," he says. "The decision hasn't been made yet. Forgive me. It's a lot for me to take in."

"She's coming back."

"I know," he smiles. "I really do. I have so much faith in your mother. And your father."

I feel a pain in my chest when he says the words. "Your father is a great man."

"Well, I guess you knew him better than I did."

"Your father didn't have easy decisions to make."

"I know that."

"Neither did your mother." Mr. Porter puts his hand on my shoulder. "Enough of this. How about you get changed and then we'll see you in the dining hall? Oh, one last thing," he says as he turns to go. "I'll need your cuffs."

I put my hands behind my back protectively. "Why?" I ask. "How am I supposed to—"

"You won't need to," Mr. Porter says blandly. "It's the rule here."

Reluctantly, I un-strap and hand him the cuffs. I can feel my heart racing. My face is getting warmer. So much for messaging Radius to come get me.

137

"Wait."

Mr. Porter pauses with his hand still on the door.

"How will I get updates about my mother?" I ask.

"We'll keep you as informed as possible," Mr. Porter promises. "If there's any word at all."

I wait for the door to close all the way before kicking the metal frame of the bed as hard as I can.

Hundreds of children turn their attention to me in the dining hall. My jumpsuit is loose in the hips and pools around my ankles. Heads turn as I pass. I cross my arms in front of my chest and stare a hole into the head in front of me. Someone taps me on the shoulder from behind. I startle and turn around irritably. A girl shorter than me with tightly curled dark hair and high eyebrows is smiling cheerfully.

"I'm Miranda," she says.

"Oh, right. Bunkmates."

"For a little while anyway. Until there's a move."

"Yeah, I won't be here long. I'm going back pretty soon. This is only temporary."

"How's your mom?" Miranda asks, furrowing her brow.

"She's fine. That's temporary. What's good to eat here?" I change the subject as quickly as possible.

"Nothing," she smiles. "Want to sit with us when you eat? I can tell you about the girls."

"Sure," I say, grateful to not be left completely by myself to eat.

"Good. We're right over here." Miranda points to a table of several girls our age. A couple of them have younger children on their laps or sitting so close to them that they're almost in their laps.

I take my tray over to the table and awkwardly sit next to Miranda, who is immersed in conversation with a fish-lipped girl to her right. I smile at the little girl across from me, who is chewing her food slowly as she examines me. "You're Ms. Ellie's kid, aren't you?" she asks with a mouthful of food. "I've seen you here before."

"I used to come help out sometimes."

"Well, you look pretty different with that suit," she says, pointing her fork at me. "You look *better*."

"Excuse me—"

"Hey, Miranda, isn't this your new friend?" She waves her forked green beans to get her attention.

"Oh, hi!" Miranda turns toward me. "Let me introduce you around. You already met Annsleigh."

I nod to the girl across from me, who is examining every inch of my face as she eats. "This is Bobbi." She points to the girl next to Annsleigh.

"Hi, Bobbi," I say.

She smiles and takes the hand of the little girl in her lap to make her wave. "Say 'hi,' Sarah," she tells the girl.

"Hi, Sarah," the little girl giggles.

Miranda rolls her eyes. "This is Rachelle." She leans back so I can see the bright blonde girl next to her. "She's also in our unit."

"Welcome." Rachelle holds her hand out for me to shake. "I'm glad we have some extra help." Rachelle leans forward on her elbows. "Piper's having nightmares again. Hey Piper," she says gently to the little girl across from her with a shock of red hair and bright blue eyes. "Go easier on that pudding tonight. I think it didn't sit well yesterday."

The little girl smiles mischievously and takes an extra big spoonful of the chocolate pudding. She looks side to side as though it's making her nervous.

"It wasn't the pudding, Roshie," she says, looking suddenly serious. "It was Miranda's snoring that gave me the dreams. I thought she was a monster."

Rachelle cocks her head to the side and gives Piper a look. "You've got to sleep tonight," she says, reaching across the table and wiping some chocolate from her chin with her napkin. Piper giggles with delight and looks at me with a big smile. I smile back and wink at her in spite of myself.

I help Rachelle and Miranda walk the younger girls back to our dorm cabin. The evening is cool, and I can hear the crickets like at my own house. It's almost as if the Pulse doesn't exist. This little community of parentless children is all that there is. Gray, my mother, and Radius might as well be on another planet. Jamison isn't dead. He might not have even existed.

There is a calm here that contrasts the Pulse chaos I have grown accustomed to. It is a different kind of energy and chaos. Kids are running and laughing or crying, but it's less intense—

unlike the Pulse energy that can either bury you, or bring you high enough to soar above it all. It draws people in and consumes them, but it makes you feel real. Here, it shakes you in just the right way until you feel alive in a different sense. Even still, I can't stay here.

Miranda and Rachelle talk quietly together as we walk back. The two girls laugh and tussle small heads as they run past. Their hair is thrown carelessly into messy buns—Miranda's is almost white and thin, Rachelle's thick with tight curls. I imagine how Dylan could transform them if they would let her. I wonder if they know they aren't pretty.

And yet, there is still something of beauty about them that I can't quite put my finger on. Maybe they're too dumb to know. Either way I hate them a little for it. And I hate myself for how much I wish I could be like that—content. Content anywhere, really. But the Pulse has me. Radius has me. I can play the games here just long enough for me to catch my breath, but I know where I belong.

As soon as we enter the cabin, Miranda and Rachelle become all business. "You all have ten minutes to dress, brush teeth, and put *everything* away," Miranda instructs in a deeper voice than I would have thought possible for her.

The girls move more quickly as she walks down the aisle between the beds. Rachelle bends between two little girls whose legs are sticking out underneath their bed.

"It dropped under here somewhere," comes a small, high voice.

"Ok, ok," Rachelle says, putting her face to the floor. "I'll find it. You girls get those teeth brushed."

A third little girl crawls on the floor under the head of the bed. "Found it!" she squeals, holding up a stuffed turtle triumphantly. "It was wedged between the bed and the wall."

Girls in various stages of getting dressed scurry about, giggling and crawling from one top bunk to another.

"You handle teeth," Miranda says, pointing to me.

"Oh, ok," I mumble, almost tripping over two little brunettes who are rushing to get in line. A row of five sinks has two girls each taking turns spitting into them.

"Sing the song! Sing the song!" pipes a little one covered in freckles.

"What song?" I ask.

Her mouth drops open. "You don't know the toothbrush song?"

"Afraid not."

She slaps her forehead and shakes it dramatically. "How are they going to know when they can stop brushing?" she asks incredulously, indicating her lost friends at the sink.

"Could you do it for me tonight so I can learn how?" She puts her hand on her hip. "Rebecca, I'm going to sing it for you tonight, but tomorrow you do your job, ok?"

I nod seriously, trying not to smile as Freckles sings a tune twice through about a crocodile and a chicken brushing their teeth. When she stops singing, the girls at the sink stop brushing, and the line moves up for the next girl. The song begins again.

When Freckles steps up, she is delighted that I have learned the song and can now competently do my job. I hand out paper towels to white frothy mouths in front of speckled mirrors.

"You did good," Freckles says when she's finished. "You're going to be ok here." She throws her arms around my waist and squeezes me before running off to Miranda, who is yelling, "Arabella! Your things are everywhere."

When I return from the bathroom, the girls are all in their beds, and the room is as tidy as it was before we came in. Rachelle is visiting each girl in her bed and kissing each head. One little girl wraps her arms around Rachelle's neck and kisses her squarely on the cheek. "I love you!" she says, throwing her arms out wide.

Miranda flashes the lights. "Almost time, ladies," she says sweetly. "You all did an excellent job of getting in bed tonight."

"Book!" says a little girl with dark braids, clapping her hands and jumping up on her knees in the bed.

"Yes, book," Miranda sighs.

Piper motions from her bunk for me to sit. I smile and walk over to her quietly. When I sit down she holds my hand and gives me a big, toothless grin.

"I think you and that chicken might have the same number of teeth," I whisper and squeeze her hand back.

The girls listen attentively while Miranda reads a chapter from a book about a young girl who takes a voyage with her father across the ocean. It's a mythical story now. No one has crossed the ocean in decades. My mother read it to me in the Old Colony. I watch the girls as they take in the part where they spot a whale. Piper slowly squeezes my hand. I put my arm around her.

"No whales around here," I assure her. But I remember being her age and being terrified of the largest animal on earth. I had snuggled closer to my mother during the same part. Suddenly, I am overcome with missing her.

When Miranda closes the book, I notice that a few of the smallest girls are already asleep. I help Piper settle into her bed and pull thick blankets up tight like Mom used to do. Then I crawl into my bunk and pull the covers over my head. I wait until I think the other girls are asleep before I allow myself to cry.

I wake in the middle of the night, covered in sweat and groaning. I make it to the bathroom just in time to vomit. I would do anything for a patch, but there's no chance of that. I consider asking some of the older girls or boys who went to school in the Pulse. There has to be someone here who has one. Or maybe not. I look at each of the little blue jumpsuits and rosy-cheeked girls and boys who have lived in the outskirts of the colony their entire lives. There is one teenager who looks more Pulse than Cherish, with her hair streaked different colors and pulled back in the Pulse fashion. But when I get closer she looks me up and down critically and turns away as she takes a big bite from her bagel. I walk back to my seat self-consciously. Even if she does have a patch, she won't give me one, most likely out of spite. Plus, it would be two minutes before Mr. Porter was alerted, and then what?

I try to eat some dry cereal to settle my stomach.

"You don't look so great," Rachelle says.

"Just not used to the food is all," I spit back. The motion of the children running around is making me sick again, so I excuse myself to return to our dorm cabin.

One of the children has drawn a picture of a butterfly on the ceiling above my bunk. I stare at it so hard that it seems likes its wings are beating. Someone knocks at the door and even the soft sound makes my head hurt worse.

"Come in," I yell, covering my ears.

Mr. Porter walks to my bed and stands at eye level with me. "Miranda tells me you're sick," he says, louder than necessary.

"I'm ok," I whisper, trying to give him a hint to keep it down.

"You look it. How about a visit to the nurse? Just to check you out?" Still just as loud.

"I'm fine," I tell him. "I just need to sleep it off."

"Rebecca," Mr. Porter looks down at his feet and clears his throat.

142

I sit up quickly, my head pounding when I do. I can hear in his voice that something is wrong.

"Could we take a walk?"

"No," I say. "What's going on?"

Mr. Porter smiles softly but his eyes still look troubled. "You have a visitor, Rebecca. Grayson is here to see you. I thought the three of us could take a walk."

"No, we can't take a walk. Tell me what it is." I jump from my bunk. "If it's my mother, tell me now." I clench my teeth as my head pounds uncontrollably.

"She was exiled, sweetheart."

I shake my head, which is now filled with rushing water. I hear his words, but they don't make sense. My headache clears and all I feel is numb.

"No. She wasn't," I protest.

Mr. Porter places a hand on my shoulder that I immediately shrug off.

"No. She was innocent."

"The decision was made yesterday."

"So they had a sentencing that quickly?" I ask in disbelief. There has been a mistake.

Mr. Porter's eyes fill with tears. "No trial," he whispers.

"What the hell do you mean no trial? They can't do that."

"But they did," he says.

Guilt floods in like a dam has broken inside me. "I have to go talk to them. There's more they don't know!" My voice rises as I become close to hysterical. Mr. Porter takes me by the shoulders.

"No!" I scream and sink to the floor crying.

Mr. Porter sits down on the lower bunk and puts his head in his hands. "Rebecca, your mother knows what she's doing. As soon as I can, I'll explain everything."

The street is silent and dark, motionless with the exception of a stray cat lurking between fences. There is just enough moonlight for me to see where I'm going as I walk from Cherish to the Convoy line.

I keep my head down as I walk, my heart pounding with the fear that they might discover I'm missing. I detect motion from the corner of my eye and freeze in a shadow.

"Hey, sugar bean," a rickety voice calls out.

I cover my mouth to stop from screaming.

"Darlins, your mama didn'ts belong here anyways," she says. "Neithers do you."

I pick up my pace as I pass by the older woman who had stopped my mother and me what seems like a lifetime ago on our way to Cherish.

"You's are making a mistake, sugar bean," she says again as she pushes herself to a hunched standing.

I start to jog. Crazy old woman.

"It's nevers too late, darlin'!" she calls behind me. "It's hows you finish it."

I break into a full sprint. The Convoy line is empty this time of night. I slump into a seat as I ride it into the Pulse.

It will be another three hours or so before someone alerts Mr. Porter that I am gone. By then it will be too late. I will be hidden in the kaleidoscope of the Pulse. Lights dance upon the window as I approach the center of the colony. I can feel myself coming back alive as we enter the Pulse. I get off at the stop closest to the Crave section and step into the street. This part of the colony is just waking up.

I walk to the door of Radius's apartment and nod to the man at the front desk, who recognizes me. "He should be up there," he says and eyes my light blue Cherish jumpsuit, which I thought was better than the pajamas, my only other option.

I cross my arms over my chest self-consciously as I wait for the elevator. I can hear a steady bass beat coming from inside Radius's condo.

"Great," I say aloud.

He's hosting tonight, and I'm showing up here like this. I ring the doorbell and a tall, lanky girl with ebony skin opens the door. "I'm here to see Radius," I say.

"Who are you?" she asks, her gaze lingering on my jumpsuit.

"I'm his—" I stop myself. What am I now? Radius might be horrified that I show up like this in front of his friends. Maybe I should have gone to Lex's first. "I'm no one, ok? Just go get Radius, please." She leaves the door open just enough that I can see him. His back is turned to me. The girl whispers in his ear, and he pauses. I breathe deeply while I wait. My heart pounds as I stare at the door. A shock runs through me. He might not turn around. I consider bolting.

Suddenly the door swings wide open. Radius looks up and down at my outfit with an expression of both confusion and amusement. As always, he looks so cool, like he's floating above it all. Every fiber of him is under his impassive control. I cry with relief. "Hey," I sob.

"Lark. Hey, no, no, no," he says, taking me into his arms.

I can't stop crying now, and I grab onto him in desperation.

"It's all right, Lark," he says softly. "You're home now."

PART II

Chapter 16

The wind blows it in. I can feel it. And, I can smell it—this Darkness that the wind blows cold and grasping. It's our part of the world's turn I guess. Somewhere across the vastness, which humans no longer traverse, I know the world is bathed in sunlight and warmth while we wait anxiously for our turn at summer. But now I can't even conjure up the envy that also brought me some hope—our turn would come back around. Our azaleas will bloom and the melancholy of the winter will be remembered like a bad dream. But I don't want the Light anymore. I don't want the warmth. I crave Numbness.

I walk the path I followed every day to go to the Pulse, when I was drawn there like a moth. Now, dressed in my heels and leather, studded in gems, having burned my wings, I withdraw. Trees shuffle off their leaves, making invisible helixes as they float to the ground. They are like me. At first the trees glow red and orange, the last passionate bursts of protest. And now they reach gray, contorted fingers to tear at a gloomy, uncaring sky.

It was in winter that we came to the New Colony. And it was winter one year ago that my mother was exiled and Radius abandoned me and then took me back so I could repay all that I owed. Winter is now woven into me. I can smell the Darkness, and I know what it wants.

I've spent the last year servicing clients that Radius arranged—men, women, all colors and ages, all levels of prestige in the colony—whom I obliged with the body that no longer belonged to me, but to Ray. They have ripped into a deep part of my soul and taken it, no matter how much I told myself they were only taking my body. They tore spirit deep and hollowed me out.

Once I believed the lie that I could have had some value in the Pulse. The Pulse became my home and, finally, I became Pulse. Now I am pushed out of myself, and all that remains is the reverberations of the city that fills the space where I once existed. I'm just an echo now.

And so, the Numbness has set in. Not the numbness from the patches that Radius always makes sure I have to get through my work—a different numbness. I don't rally against it anymore, and my mind's screams are now replaced with a silence that answers the Darkness. I want what the Darkness wants too—what it has always wanted. There will be no spring this year.

I finger the patches in my pocket that I have been saving up. I know I have just twenty minutes or so before Radius will send someone to check on me. I'm supposed to be going back to my covey, Radius's group of other girls and now a few boys that work for him. And if a new job comes in, I'll be expected to meet the new mug. When I don't show, he'll go ballistic. I pick up my pace, not out of fear of Radius anymore, but toward the Darkness that has whispered and promised relief, and I know I have only a short time.

I stop and savagely unhook my boots. My fingers are so cold that I fumble with the metal and hurl them with obscenities as far as I can. I start running, barefoot, the pain from rocks on the path keeping me calm.

"I'm home," I tell the house that knows me as Rebecca from the time when I once had a name.

I haven't been back here since my mother was exiled. I stand on the stoop like I did the first day she and I were assigned here. It became my home without my permission, and now it invites me to find permanent refuge. The door is unlocked, to my surprise, but of course there would have been no one to lock it in the first place.

It smells like her. Earth and citrus. The Numbness is overwhelmed with how much I miss her. And hate myself.

"I'm sorry," I sob over and over as I slide to the floor, holding myself and rocking. I can't even bear to touch the floor where my mother once walked. I cry until I can't breathe.

My cuff beeps shrilly.

"Stop it!" I scream and claw at my arm with shaking hands to get it off me. I remember the key I stole from Lex and fumble with it as the beeping continues. "Just stop it!" I yell, throwing it across the room. I will not die shackled.

The patches bulge in my pocket and I lay them in front of me. Forty. It should be enough to go quickly. The sight of them calms me. I can't do it in front of the door—I'll block it so they can't get in as easily. I take a step toward my old room. No—the kitchen. I can't bear to pass my mother's room in the hall. I sit in my old chair, but my mother's chair is empty next to it. "You are everywhere!" I fall to my knees and crawl under the table to unwrap the first patch.

"Rebecca?"

I scream in terror. He's found me. Or he had me followed by his new man, who is even more volatile than Jamison was. I prepare to fight back, pushing the chair in front of me. "Get away from me!" I yell.

"Rebecca," the man whispers. "Rebecca, hey. It's me." Grayson kneels in front of me with his hands out.

My panic turns to dread. "No," I groan. "Please, Gray, please," I beg.

"It's ok, Rebecca," he says, slowly crawling under the table beside me.

Hearing my name, my real name, is both searing and soothing. I sob as I scramble to gather my patches before Grayson can take them from me. But he just sits there.

Gray says nothing but takes off his sweatshirt and wraps it around my feet. I cringe at the first kindness anyone has shown me in so many months.

"You're bleeding," he says.

"So what?" I spit. "So the hell what?"

In spite of the cold of the house, he's not shivering, but slowly and tenderly pats my feet.

"You know what I did, Gray. You know who I *am*. I deserve this," I say, holding up a handful of patches.

"I love you, Rebecca," Gray meets my eyes. Shame overwhelms and crushes me from the inside out.

"I—don't—deserve—it," I sob. "If you only knew."

"I do know, and I've done everything I could think of to get you back for the past year. And, I said I love you," Gray says confidently in spite of my growing hysteria.

"I can't afford for you to love me," I say, leaning my head against the wall and rolling it back and forth as the tears fall.

Grayson lets out a small laugh. "You don't deserve it. Yeah, you got it. None of us do. Deserving isn't a part of it."

"Well, then it's complete and utter nonsense."

Gray leans his head back on the wall next to mine and smiles that sweet little boy smile that delivers me to our kingdom. "Yep. Nonsense. Luxurious nonsense and it's the only thing that's true."

It sounds like something my mother would say. I collapse into sobbing and don't stop him when he puts his arms around me and rocks me. "It's the truth, Rebecca. It's the truth. Shh. Give it up. It's true." His voice is steady and certain. His arms hold me tight. Each time I protest, he stops me. "Lies," he interrupts each time my cuff beeps. "I'm telling you truth."

I cling to Grayson's words. "He'll be coming for me," I tell him as my cuff begins to beep continually. Gray nods and clenches his jaw. He sits back on his heels and runs his hands through his hair. "Right." He breathes out slowly. "Just keep quiet."

Grayson pulls me from under the table and carries me down the hall in the dark, past my old room where I can see my bed unmade, and then out the back door. He steps quietly through the gate and across his yard.

"Stay here," he says sternly.

I shiver in the cold as he enters the chicken coop. I can hear the rustle of chickens as they stir in their small house.

"You have to come in."

"No way."

"You know he's coming, Rebecca," he says. "Come in now."

It is true, of course, that Radius will be coming. It's either Radius or chickens.

"Fine," I concede. "I hate you," I tell the panic-stricken birds. "Just shut up."

It's surprisingly warm in the coop. I stop shivering but cover my mouth and nose to block the sickeningly sweet smell of chicken poop.

Gray is now running back and forth between the coop and his house bringing towels and sheets and an array of different things. "Put these on," he says, throwing me some of his clothes and thick socks. I put them over my tight dress as I shiver uncontrollably while he frantically hammers a thick canvas into a makeshift hammock between the front and back beams of the coop. "Get in," he instructs.

I might be uncomfortable, but I'm not on feces-ridden floorboards with my cut feet. I swing between two rows of pissed-off chickens.

He covers me gently with a thick blanket that smells like him. He hands me a small bucket with feed. "Sprinkle some of the grain beside you if they make much noise."

"Thank you, Gray," I say, my voice faltering.

"Don't get out until I come and get you."

I nod. "Gray, he's coming." It will be easy enough for him to trace my cuff.

"I know it," Gray pulls something from his back pocket. "Rebecca, sorry I have to do this," he says, sounding totally deflated. "I need some of your stones."

Reluctantly, I pull my shirt down to expose a shoulder as he cuts out four stones. I don't care why he wants them. I welcome the steadying pain and being free of them, and it is over quickly. "I'm sorry," he says sincerely. "Just stay here". Grayson takes my stones and I wait, swaying, and praying for a miracle.

It isn't long before I hear Radius's car pulling into my driveway. I hold my breath. If he really comes looking, there'll be no way for me to get out. Will he beat me like he did Pearl when she tried the same thing? I see her in my mind's eye, bleeding on the bathroom floor. Her quota had been doubled and Lex had followed her to every job. I'll never get out if he finds me. I squeeze my fist full of chicken feed until my hand shakes.

Get in your car and leave, I think over and over, willing it to happen. Why isn't he driving away? I strain my ears but can't hear anything past the chickens rustling. I don't know where Gray is, or what he has planned to do with the evidence that I have been there. If he got rid of my cuff, then why did Radius go to the house? And, I must have left some blood on the floor from my feet, though it was much less than it could have been, thanks to Gray's quick thinking in carrying me out. And then the patches. Had Gray remembered to take the patches?

I listen for a gunshot. If I hear a gunshot, I'll know Gray is in there. Or maybe Gray will panic and let Radius know where I'm hiding. Should I run? Maybe I should go back in and plead with Radius not to hurt Gray. I sit up, rocking my makeshift hammock and disturbing chickens. After what seems like an hour, I hear Radius's tires tearing the gravel road. I lay back, my whole body throbbing with relief.

A few minutes later Gray unlatches the door and stands beside me. "He's gone," he whispers. He runs his hands through his hair and blows out slowly. "Rebecca, he's not coming back. Lark died tonight," he says dully.

"How?" I ask.

"She drowned."

Grayson had thought fast, and it saved both of our lives. As soon as he had stashed me, he took off his own cuff in case Radius had gotten paranoid and checked on him too, which it seems he had.

Gray slowly tends my feet as he recounts the story. His voice is steady, but his hands are still trembling.

Immediately after leaving me in the coop, Gray went back into my house, grabbed the patches and my cuff, and left the stones by the front door, where my blood was already on the ground from my cut feet. He tipped a chair and emptied three patches, leaving the wrappers by the front door. Before leaving, he sent a message from my cuff to Lex, who had been trying frantically to get messages to me.

Grayson typed back on my cuff: "I'm sorry, Lex. I couldn't do it anymore. You were a good friend. Goodbye." Then he ran the three quarters of a mile to the river and threw my cuff into the middle of it. He sprinted back to his house. Sending the message to Lex instead of Radius had saved a few moments as Lex then had to relay the information to Radius.

Radius had immediately left a mug who was probably furious to be stood up. By the time he traced my cuff, it was heading away from my house to the river with Gray. Lex probably never told Radius that I had stolen the key to get the cuff off. It would have only gotten her into trouble, and when Radius had gone back to the house, he had seen what looked like evidence that I had gotten high from three patches, cut out some of my Luminstones, and left them and my blood on the floor. Radius probably had only spent a few moments at the river before piecing it together.

My cuff was tracking quickly downriver and stopped in the middle as it got stuck on some debris. Gray returned just in time for Radius to pull up to my house. He snuck in the back of his house so quietly that I didn't hear him even yards away in the coop. To my horror, I learned that he had had just enough time to stab himself in the arm, bandage it, and put his cuff back on, so that it appeared he hadn't left the house. He waited by the window to see what Radius would do.

I imagined Gray's heart must have dropped when Radius banged on his door. Gray kept cool, but he knew why he had come over. Radius had been paranoid enough to pull up Gray's tracking record. Earlier in the evening, before I got there, Grayson had been sleeping at my house and wearing his cuff. He had been waiting for me, as he had been doing for a year. Radius would find this out easily, and it would make him suspicious.

154

Gray ran to the door to open it for Radius. "What the hell happened?" Gray demanded. It was a bold move, and it confused and outraged Radius.

Radius had stepped in his house and started looking around immediately. "You tell me, Grayson." He looked in every room as Gray followed. "You were staying in her house, so you tell me."

"How did you know that?" Gray feigned surprise and perturbation at being tracked.

"I have my ways. Tell me where she is," he said, pushing Gray against the wall.

"Listen, buddy. She was crazy. I promised her mom I'd look out for her. I've been staying at her house at night in case she comes home. And tonight, she did. Man, she was crazy."

Radius loosened his grip on him.

"At first she just sat there quietly in the living room putting on patches. She was crying like mad. She didn't know I was there, and when I came into the front room I tried to calm her down, but it freaked her out and then she really lost it. I told her, 'Hey, we can work this out. Just calm down,' but it made things worse. She started walking up and down the floor and her cuff kept beeping, and the more it beeped the crazier she got. She started talking about how she'd had enough. It would have killed her mom and she just needed out. She grabbed a knife from the kitchen and started popping out those jewel things from her skin. I lunged at her to try to stop her, and then she stabbed me." Grayson had looked down at his arm.

Radius withdrew in disgust as he realized that where he had been holding Gray was now seeping with blood, and he was getting it on his hands.

"She ran out before I could grab her. So you tell *me* where she is." Gray had looked panicked.

Radius wiped his hands on his pants, leaving a smear of Gray's blood. "Accidently drowned," he said and turned on his heel.

Gray tells me the story as I sit on his kitchen counter while he bandages my feet and gingerly cleans the holes where the three stones had been. I can barely look at his arm, which is turning his bandage a dark red where he stabbed himself.

"He was convinced, Rebecca," he says reassuringly. "You're not his anymore. You're free."

"Free," I say, leaning my head back as silent tears fall.

But I'm not free only because I am out of Radius's grasp, for now at least. Even if he could have dragged me back, I'd still have this new freedom that Grayson has offered—to be loved in spite of all that I have done.

"What was your plan, Grayson? You were really waiting for me all this time?"

"I was," he says simply, looking up into my face.

"But, why? What were you going to do?"

Gray rubs his brow in concentration, inadvertently smearing some of my blood on his forehead. "Sit with you under your table," he smiles wryly.

I laugh and cry and shiver.

It is nonsense whispered against the world.

Chapter 17

Grayson has never recommended that I move back to my house. It still feels too dangerous—maybe Radius will come back on a whim. Selling me was better than selling patches, which eventually run out. I was the drug that could be sold over and over and over again. When I think of all the money I made for Radius, it makes me crazy. I stayed awake for hours calculating the total. Thousands. In a year, almost a hundred thousand. I made him rich. And powerful. All that money kept him in the center of the Pulse, in a fancy penthouse, with a fancy car and other fancy friends who thought he was worth something. My consolation is that he won't be able to afford all of that without me bringing in my quota each night.

But then with horror I realize that he'll stop at nothing to make up the difference. I don't know if he'll increase the other girls' quotas, or if he's now looking for a new girl to train, maybe another girl from the Ancillary. Still, it will cost him, at least temporarily. It took months for him to get me ready to be a dancer at Deep Secrets and even more time and investment for me to service a mug—all those masterfully woven lies and pretty gifts. Someone will pick up the slack, and I can only allow my mind to think who that new girl might be for a moment or two before it overwhelms me, and I become physically sick.

Grayson let me take his room. When I insisted that he have it and let me sleep on the floor in the living room, he said it made more sense for me to stay closest to the back door, just in case. If we hear a car pull up, I'll go back to the chicken coop.

In all the years I've known Gray, I had never been in his room. I'd only been in his house a handful of times. It is plain, like Grayson—simple wooden furniture and the smell of sawdust, no doubt brought home from Gray's construction job. It is the same as our house's layout—kitchen and living space in the front, with a small hallway that leads to a broken back door. Grayson uses the second bedroom for gardening supplies and construction tools. Simple and utilitarian.

The last time I was in his house, Marissa had just died. My mother and Marissa's friendship had become more like a sisterhood, and Marissa was often at our kitchen counter when I came home from school, throwing her head back and laughing a deep guttural laugh that seemed strange coming from such a small body. She worked the night shift at the medical facility in the Pulse. She was young and pretty but with lighter features than Gray. She was youthful, rosy cheeked, and witty.

"Well, hey, girlie," she'd say, winking at me when I came home from school. She must have left parents and siblings too, but I never saw her downcast, especially not in front of Gray. She'd often sit with an arm around him and brag on him to other people in his presence. "Hey, little man!" she'd beam as though he were the light in her gray world. Even after night shifts, even when she got sick, she'd glow when she saw Grayson. Any homesickness she might have had was transformed and poured out as love for Gray. Marissa became his mother, even though she was only twenty-eight when we moved here, and he was nine.

She died quickly, or at least it seemed so to us. It haunts me still to think that her family from other colonies never knew she passed. Maybe they had felt it. I wonder about my own father. Would I somehow feel his death? I no longer feel his life. Maybe he has passed too.

Marissa must have known for months and suffered more than she showed. It was a rare form of cancer in her brain. My mother had tended to her in Gray's room during her final days. His room had more light and a lower bed for her to get into. Each evening after her shift, my mother would walk the short distance across our yard to her house.

Mom had promised the colony officials she would care for Gray. He lived with us for a short time, sleeping on a cot in our living room. No one moved into his house, so he'd go back and forth between the two—showering, doing his homework, or even doing laundry in his old house. When he was fourteen, my mother said it would be ok for him to move back; after all, our houses were so close that they felt like one house anyway. I don't know how he could bear to be there by himself without Marissa.

It is strange now to stay in the room where Marissa died. It still seems like a death room to me. But maybe it is fitting. After all, I just drowned. I feel like I am still in the process of drowning. I may be free, but there is so much mess to clean up in the wake of my freedom.

Radius had made sure I was hooked on patches, and this is the first time in months I have been without. By the second day, the nausea came in crashing waves and the headaches came like lightning strikes. By that night I had vomited so much I was dry heaving.

"Please," I begged Gray. "Just one patch," I pleaded. "I can't take this," I said over and over.

He looked heartbroken but resolute. "No, Rebecca, I can't," he said gently.

I search frantically each time he leaves to check on the chickens or go to the bathroom. Did he throw the patches in the river too?

I consider walking back to the Pulse. I know where I can get patches and what I'll have to do to pay for them, and I no longer care. I pace in Marissa's room, willing myself to stay put and focus on Gray's sacrifice for me. When I start shaking violently, Gray's eyes get wide and he too starts pacing and running his fingers through his hair. Finally he reaches quietly into his pocket and pulls out one patch that he gingerly opens and applies to the back of my neck.

"Thank you, Gray," I sob pathetically.

I sit on the edge of the bed and rock while the patch begins to relax each muscle, and warmth flows from my neck up through my head, pushing away the ache that has consumed my whole body. Gray is tapping on his cuff outside my door. I lie back on the bed and turn to face the wall, but there is Marissa lying next to me, eyes smiling. I am shocked, but the patch won't let my body react to it. I lie still and blink.

Marissa strokes my hair. "You look rough," she laughs.

"Yeah." I blink hard. "I drowned."

"In that case, you look great."

"So you're one of those funny ghosts, then."

"Something like that. Tell me, princess. What's this about?" Marissa runs a cold finger over the Luminstones on my neck.

I pull back, but it feels like moving in slow motion. I moan.

Marissa props herself up on one elbow. "You're going to have to take care of him now." She nods toward the door.

"Ok," I whisper. "Because I'm in good shape for that." I give her a weak thumbs up. She bumps my fist with a cold one.

"Soon enough," she said.

"Marissa, my mom—"

"This wasn't her home, kid," she says, smiling. Suddenly Marissa gets up, wearing her white coat. She bounces to the window and throws open the curtains. "You need sunlight," she says, laughing her deep laugh that's too big for her. I raise my hand to block the blinding light that consumes Marissa.

Gray is hovering over me and shakes my arm gently. "Rebecca?" he whispers.

The nausea is setting in again.

"Yeah," I return. The word leaving my mouth seems to un-dam some bile that has risen in my throat. I groan. Between the lightning strikes in my head, I squint at Gray against the deep headache that seems to extend even beyond my body.

"Rebecca, this is Asa." Gray gestures to a dark-featured, small-boned man behind him.

"Hey, there." The man smiles as he moves, clinking bottles and metal things on the dresser.

"Asa works at the hospital."

I nod, not understanding. Maybe it's another ghost. I push back my soaked sheets and shake my head as Asa reaches for my wrist.

"Rebecca," he says. "Just bear with me. Brought some things to make this easier."

I relax a little as he takes my pulse and then pulls back the sheets to check my legs and arms. He runs a finger along each of the Luminstones like Marissa had done and then pauses at the bandages.

"Those were the ones I removed," Gray explains. Asa knits his eyebrows. I flinch when he flashes a light in my eyes, back and forth. The lightning bolts in my head start again and I want to scream.

"Rebecca," he says calmly. "How many did he give you each day?"

I shrug my shoulders, still not wanting to open my mouth as the nausea grows.

"It's important that I know, Rebecca."

I hold up a hand with four, then five fingers.

"Ok," he says.

I pause and then hold up a few more fingers. Finally I hold up all ten.

Asa lets out a sigh. "I see. Always the same person give them to you?"

I nod a slow yes.

"This is the fifth day," I hear Gray murmur behind him.

The fifth? Not possible. I open my mouth to protest and dry heave instead. In an instant, Grayson is beside the bed holding a bucket. He looks unnerved but not disgusted. I notice he needs a shave badly and his hands are trembling.

"She's severely dehydrated," Asa says as he rearranges bottles.

"I thought the withdrawal would eventually get easier." Gray sounds totally dejected.

"It's a hawker trick." Asa's eyes narrow. "Those *rocks*," he says the word with contempt and gestures with a small vial in his hand at the stones in my neck, "those precious gems, little girl, are slowly dissolving into a poison that is now in your system and making you very sick. Old hawker trick."

I turn my head toward him.

"Whoever put those stones in you was also giving you patches that were laced with something to keep you high—and compliant, I might add. But the patches were laced with a chemical that was counteracting the poison from the stones." Asa makes clucking sounds with his tongue as he inserts a needle into the vial and extracts a clear liquid. "Hawkers do it so that if you do get out, or let's say another hawker takes you on—you die without the anti-chemical to neutralize the stones' poison."

Grayson shakes his head as I dart my eyes between the two of them. "So, that's his chain on them. They leave for too long and they have to go back for patches."

"Right," Asa says, inserting the needle into the muscle of my arm. "And, if she were to go to another hawker, he'd have to either take all the stones out, marring his property, or she'd just die."

I don't even feel the needle being inserted into my arm. He was going to kill me. No wonder he didn't look too hard for me. Radius believes that if there were any chance I was still alive, I would have crawled back by now. I raise a hand to my throat and claw at it weakly.

"Yes, Rebecca. They've all got to come out," Asa says.

Suddenly I feel like every diamond embedded in my skin is on fire, burning me with their toxins as though they have suddenly come alive. I feel Radius's hands caressing them as he had so many times. Never before had I guessed that they were part of his black magic to keep me chained or to kill me if I left. Either way, he'd win.

Gray wipes his hair down from back to front in the nervous way he does. He blows out a long breath and clears his throat.

Asa puts a hand on his shoulder. "She's going to be just fine now."

"Yeah," Gray's voice cracks in acknowledgement. He rises quickly to stand with Asa, who is busily scratching out instructions on a piece of paper and holding up bottles and vials between his frantic writing.

Asa points quickly to the different medications as he gives rapid instructions to an attentive Grayson. "She's going to need anti-nausea medication every six hours. I already injected her with some. Let this dissolve under her tongue. And this. Inject thirty milliliters every twelve hours into her arm. It will lessen some of the symptoms—binds with the chemical residue from the stones and helps excrete it. Antibiotic, here—twice a day. Three of these every four hours. Really important to keep the swelling down. This one's the pain med. They keep a pretty close watch on this stuff in the hospital, so I could only get four pills—as needed. I might be able to skim some more later. Getting this?"

"Right," Gray says seriously.

"I'm going to bring back IV fluids after my shift. In the meantime, stay on top of the anti-nausea and do your best to keep her drinking."

I hear the distinctive clinical sound of rubber gloves being put on, paper tearing and the clink of metal. Asa sighs. "This was the best I could steal. I know we have a hooked tool that makes this sort of thing easier, but too many people were in the supplies room today. I grabbed it quickly. Should work, though."

The anti-nausea is working already. "Thank you," I whisper hoarsely.

"No problem, kiddo." Asa hands Gray a package of gloves that he quickly puts on while Asa wipes my neck with a cold, wet cloth. "I had a lot of respect for Marissa's work. Good woman," he says gently.

Grayson nods somberly.

"Ok, this will numb it up," Asa says, holding up a small needle. I jump as he injects small amounts of liquid around each stone. I turn my head to the wall as the pricks from the needle turn from

162

searing hot to icy cold. It feels as though the jewels have come together to make my neck and shoulder one hard mass, one large stone.

I feel the pressure of Asa pushing and tugging where my skin had been and now where he is harvesting precious stones from marble. He sucks his teeth and knits his brow in concentration, removing each stone, one by bloody one, and tossing them in the bucket that Gray had held out for me to vomit in. Each stone makes a pitiful plink against the metal. Gray dabs my skin with gauze and applies pressure where Asa points with a bloody rubber finger.

"Good night, there are a lot of them," Asa says, pulling back the collar of my shirt with a rubber pinky. "We won't have enough numbing agent."

Gray's eyes dart to mine. "It's ok," I say. "Please just take them out."

"Yeah, I've got to take them out. But it's going to hurt like hell."

I shrug my good shoulder at him.

"Give her a pill and a half, there, Gray—the pain med."

Gray gets up quickly to go to the dresser. Asa's face becomes more intense as he works. A few minutes later Grayson comes back with a cup and the pills. Asa stops his work long enough for me to swallow them. The nausea is completely gone now, but the lightning bolt headache is still very much there.

It takes Asa almost two hours to remove two hundred and seventeen stones that had been placed in a flowing pattern. The pain medication sends a shock through my body each time I turn my head. In spite of it, I can feel the burn and sharp pain as my marble neck loses its numbness and becomes flesh again. Removing the stones on my shoulder and arm is even more excruciating, like Asa has embedded needles where the stones had been and then lit them on fire.

"Last one," Asa says, tossing a red stone into the bucket. He tapes gauze over my neck and arm and gives Gray further instructions on how to clean and re-dress the areas.

"It's going to take some time to get all the toxins out, Gray," Asa adds.

Gray nods.

"She needs water. And food. And rest. I'll check on her after my shift today, ok?"

The panic has drained out of Gray, and now he just looks exhausted and worn.

"You too, Gray. Same for you. Water. Food. Rest."

Gray smiles.

"Thank you," I murmur again. "Thank you so much."

I didn't realize how hard this has been on Gray. I hate myself for how much I have put him through. He must have been missing school and work to take care of me.

I can hear Gray walking Asa to the door. "That was really close, Gray. But she's going to make it," I overhear Asa say. "She's going to make it." His voice rises reassuringly as Gray lets out a short sob.

"Yeah, yeah, I know," Gray says. "Thanks so much, Asa. I owe you—"

"It's not a problem, man. After everything your cousin did—no, problem. Hey," he says his voice rising again. "I was serious about you taking it easy too." Through slit eyes I can see Asa slap Gray on the shoulder.

I close my eyes hard. My neck is throbbing faster as my heart quickens with the growing realization of my debts: first my mother and now Gray—sweet and patient Gray, who had been waiting on me for a year. He'd risked his life for me, even stabbed himself, and then agonized over whether or not I'd live. My room smells like vomit and sweat. He's been the one cleaning up my mess. I want to love him for it, but I am so full of guilt and self-loathing that I can't yet, not until I've made it up to him.

Gray leans on the doorway. His eyes are red and his lip is trembling. If he cries, I won't be able to take it. I picture myself as he must see me—bandages oozing, hair plastered to my head from sweat, skin pale. I pull the covers over myself self-consciously and look to the floor. I am still wearing his clothes. He should have just left me. I'll spend the rest of my life trying to make it up to him if it takes that long.

"Rebecca," he whispers before I can get out a word.

I roll over to the wall.

"Rebecca," he says again.

I turn my head to him reluctantly.

"The worst is over. You look good." He is smiling.

I stare back.

Gray sits down beside my bed and his eyes linger on my bandages. "I would do anything to trade places with you right now, you know."

I look at him in disbelief. He should run away and not look back. "You are out of your mind," I say definitively.

164

Gray smiles bigger. "I am."

"I'm not sure I can make this up in one lifetime, Grayson. I'm going to try, though."

Gray pulls back the covers gently to look at my feet. "Whatever. That's not what this is about."

"Well, what is it about? I'm not worth this." I pull my feet back as he starts to replace some of the bandages. "Gray, seriously. Stop." Gray looks up at me.

"I'm not—I mean, look. You shouldn't spend any more time on—What I'm saying is this, Gray." He looks at me in a puzzled sort of way as I stumble over trying to tell him that he is an idiot for wasting time on me. He should get back to his life, or at least find someone else who has the capacity to care for him in return.

"I can't help it." Gray says simply. "I love you, Rebecca."

"I'm not your girlfriend, Gray."

He gives a sideways smile. "Slow down, Rebecca. I didn't ask you to be." He takes my foot in his hand and I, too confused to do anything else, let him slowly remove the bandages. This guy is a lunatic. But I feel something move inside my chest. The ache is still there, but something foreign stirs.

Once the pain medicine has begun to wear off, I get out of bed that night for the first time. Gray draws me a bath and helps me walk across the hallway. My legs look so thin. My skin is sensitive to the touch, but the water is warm and soothing. I sit up straight so that the bandages on my neck and shoulder won't get wet. Grayson knocks on the door every couple of minutes. "Everything ok?" he asks from the other side.

"I'm fine, Gray."

"Not dizzy?"

"No, I'm ok." And for those few minutes, I am.

I scrub my legs and arms until they turn an even brighter pink than the hot water has already caused them to turn. I rub my forearms where the cuffs had been. It feels so strange not to have them on. Without much pain medication in my system, my bandaged neck and shoulder feel like they're on fire. I realize that I'll have scars from the stones, but I don't care. No, I'm glad.

Gray knocks again on the door. "Do not wash your hair, Rebecca. Don't get those bandages wet," he commands. He already told me twice before I got in here.

"Oops," I call back.

"Rebecca—"

"Kidding, kidding."

I hear him mumble something from the other side of the door.

"I'm getting out now, ok?"

"Ok, easy does it."

I pull the drain and stand up carefully.

Gray had gone back to my house to retrieve some of my old clothes. He's laid out a long navy strapless summer dress on the towel rack. I run my finger down the soft material. The last time I wore it was when I was still at home with my mother.

"You look pretty, Rebecca," she had said.

But I had huffed and rolled my eyes at my mother's thinking I could be pretty. "You mean boring," I said as I left for the day. Would she still think I looked pretty? I would do anything to hear my mother say so.

The girl in the fogged mirror looks back at me. For so long I had looked at that girl with just one lens of analysis: what would Radius see? Were my lips supple enough? Face thin enough? Eyes alluring enough? Could I hold his gaze? What could I improve?

Now, I look at that girl as the condensation rolls down in streaks, and I realize that there is only brokenness. And that was all he had ever been looking for anyway. He was looking for a broken girl whom he could paint up for his own gain. And, he had seen that brokenness no matter how much makeup Lex had put on me. No matter the lavender or turquoise contacts, the lashes, the stones, or the injections. He wanted me for the broken places because that's where he could get in.

I run my fingers through my hair and sob because the truth is that even still, after everything, *everything*, there is a part of me that would do anything for him to come back right now and say, "You look pretty, Rebecca." I hate myself for that torturous hope that won't let me go. It's just a habit, maybe. My brain has thought that way for so long that I can't stop overnight.

And now there is this lunatic of a boy, sitting outside my door, who is worried about me getting my bandages wet. Thinking of everything he has sacrificed for me, the depth of it overwhelms me and I feel numb. I look in the mirror at the insolent girl who can't love properly and promise her that I'll pay him back. And as soon as I do, I'll get out.

"Ok, Rebecca." Gray knocks again. "You decent?"

No, I am inhuman. "Give me two minutes." I step into the dress and pull it up. Gray has hung a grocery bag on the bathroom door. I peek in to find a wad of bras and underwear and unmatched socks. He has meticulously selected a dress and stuffed every undergarment from my drawer into a bag.

"What's up with this bag?"

"Oh," he clears his throat. "I mean, I thought you might need those—I just, you know."

Good grief.

"I just thought it might be better for you to handle that issue yourself."

I grin from ear to ear and try not laugh loud enough for him to hear. "What's the matter, Gray?"

"So, if you're good, I'm starting dinner then," he says as he walks away.

He had lied coolly to an armed hawker but is completely unnerved when it comes to women's underwear. I picture him pacing in front of my dresser, rubbing his hands over his hair nervously and then finally deciding to just dump the entire drawer in the bag.

I pause as I rifle through the cotton prints. It's a choice. Even something as intimate as selecting my underwear had become a decision that was made for me—they were bought for me, and I was told which ones to wear. I search through until I find a pair of underwear with little rosebuds that I had always liked, a white strapless bra, and a pair of thick navy woolen socks. "I choose you," I tell them. Picking those items feels like stretching muscles that have grown stiff from sitting for too long.

I open the bathroom door and watch the steam swivel up to the light in the hallway. "All done," I announce, stepping out.

Gray is clinking some pots in the kitchen. "You hungry at all?" he asks. He pours thick soup into two bowls.

"Potato soup?"

"Yeah, Marissa taught me. All those nights she worked so late, I'd be in charge of dinner. This was one of her favorites."

"Mine too," I say. "We used to eat it all the time." It was an Old Colony dish. My mom had made it here most every weekend when we had so many guests stopping by.

Gray pulls out a chair for me. "Here you go," he nods to it.

I sit down quietly, shivering a little.

"Oh, hey." Gray gets up quickly for a blanket from the sofa in the living room. He wraps it around my shoulders carefully to avoid the bandages. "I thought that dress would be nice for the bandages," he says, gesturing to it, "since it doesn't have the sleeve things and all. But, it's too cold." He looks apologetic and gets up again to move toward the dying fire. "I'll throw on another log."

"No," I say. "It's perfect. Very thoughtful. I'm warm now with the blanket, thank you."

He sits back down awkwardly.

"And this is delicious," I say, taking a bite. "Besides, this dress reminds me of summer," I add as an afterthought.

"Me too." Grayson smiles. "You wore it on the last day of school last year. But you had a white sweater and your hair down."

I take another spoonful and look away, blushing.

"Your hair stinks."

I drop my spoon and look at him irritably.

His smile widens and he shrugs his shoulders. "After you take these guys," he says, pushing a cup with several pills toward me, "we need to get that taken care of."

A full meal gives me a temporary boost of energy, long enough for me to allow Grayson to lean my head back in the kitchen sink and wash my hair. I close my eyes tight and spit out water as he eases my head under the faucet. I try to assist with my left hand, but it's awkward, and I am getting soap everywhere.

"Just stop," Gray commands. So I give in and let him start at my scalp and work his way down my long hair. I use the counter to steady myself, and try to avoid bumping into his body, but he is so close to me that it's nearly impossible.

"Ok, that's *much* better," he says. Gray smiles at his handiwork in wrapping my hair in a loose and inept turban. He takes a breath in through his nose and lets it out dramatically. "So much better."

I roll my eyes. "Thanks," I say flatly, shivering.

Gray smiles and walks to the living space where he prods at the fire and adds a log. He has been sleeping on the sofa, his bed linens neatly folded beside it so that he can be in the front room in case a car pulls up. I drag a chair in with my good arm and sit next to him. The logs shift and hiss as he works, bringing the new flames to life. I wonder how often he has done this by himself, living alone for so long. Gray is only eighteen, but he has grown up fast.

168

I unwrap my hair and lay the towel over my shoulders so the warmth of the fire will help my hair dry. Gray stands and wipes his hands roughly on his pants. He looks at me sideways and then leaves to return with a large brush. "Here you go," he says. "Got it from your house."

It had been my mother's. I hold it gingerly and finger a long dark hair that was woven between the bristles. "That's great, thank you," I say, not looking up. I don't want him to see the tears welling up in my eyes. I clear my throat and quickly try to use my left hand to brush my hair, but my left side is so clumsy that I mostly just flail and keep hitting myself in the head. The more I try to hold back the tears, the harder I work. "Tangled," I say with clenched teeth.

Gray looks at me with his eyebrows up. "Tangled," he echoes.

And then, all at once, the dam breaks, and I cry convulsively, my shoulders heaving, the tears falling unashamedly.

I drop the brush and cover my eyes. Gray pauses and, not saying a word, picks up the brush and sits behind me. Gently, he brings the loose strands from my face and in a litany of strokes begins brushing the matted ends. I don't stiffen as he works, and I don't hold back. I cry for my mother—for the shame of what I have done to her. I cry because there is a weak part of me that misses Radius. I cry in anger, hating that weak part.

Gray works diligently as I wail and gasp for breath. His short, faltering brush strokes become long and smooth—long and smooth, long past it needing it. My hair begins to dry. I do too, my breaths becoming ragged and long, the tears falling silently and then not at all.

Gray stands again and leaves for my room. I sit quietly and stare into the fire blindly as it hisses and crackles in miniature percussions. I am too tired to do anything else. A few minutes later Gray returns and sits down without looking at me. "I'm too tired to sleep," I tell him.

He smiles and holds out the last of my medicine with a cup of water. I take it obediently. Then he extends a hand and leads me to my room, where he has replaced my sweat-soaked linens with new ones from my house. He's also put a couple of stuffed animals from my room on my pillow—a yellow rabbit with a pale blue bow around its neck and a white owl.

"I only took the friendly looking ones," he says, standing in the doorway. "The frog had to stay back. He had this wily look in his eye."

I give him a sideways smile. "I didn't trust him either."

"Asa will be here tonight after his shift," he says as I stand awkwardly, looking at my old comforter with the tulips blooming on it. "But you need to go to bed now."

I run my hand along the bed that Grayson has meticulously made up.

"He'll drop off some pills. So if you hear him come in, don't worry or anything."

"Thank you."

"No problem," Grayson smiles and closes the door.

In spite of my over-exhaustion and the throbbing that has returned in my neck and shoulder, I feel peaceful. I turn my head to look out the window and a shock wave runs through my body. It must just be from the pain pill. Or maybe it is because Gray is sitting a wall away. He is there and I realize he is what I need more than anything. And, I remind myself, he is what I deserve the least. There is so much that I can't fix right now—can never fix maybe. But somehow knowing that Gray is sitting a wall away makes it bearable.

Chapter 18

Each night now I dream of my mother. And always, it is the same dream. She and I are standing in a ballooner's basket. Below us is a desert with gems as big as large rocks. She is trying to say something to me, but it's muffled and I strain to hear. Suddenly, as if my hands have their own will, I push her so that she falls backward, toward the endless expanse of sand and the brightly colored stones. The balloon rises higher and higher as she falls. I get closer to the sun as I ascend and lose sight of her in the blinding light. "I'm sorry, Mom! I'm so sorry!" I yell. Then I wake.

The first time it happened, Gray rushed in, completely panicked. Now, after the third night, he just stands by the door and knocks. "Just a dream, Rebecca," he says sleepily.

I am quiet and nervous, but I have been getting stronger, physically at least. Asa visited daily for the first week and then declared that the toxins were mostly gone, but it might be another few weeks before they are out of my system completely. Grayson and Asa insisted that I stay at the house, partly because of the risk of being seen by Radius, which I believed by that time was no longer a concern. In spite of my protests Asa and Gray could not be deterred, though they do allow me to bundle and sit outside in the backyard for as long as I can endure the cold and the small herd of chickens bobbing around me. It is only a few minutes before I huff with impatience and go back inside.

"Food. Water. Rest," Asa reiterates each time he leaves. Grayson takes the food part especially seriously—at first mostly lightly salted noodles, potato soup, or toasted bread, and then as my appetite increases, eggs and roasted vegetables, thick hearty stews, and beans with spices and sausage. "Marissa used to love to cook," he told me as he chopped carrots and added them to a pot. "After really stressful days she'd come home and make a feast." He seems to be enjoying cooking for me and watches intently as I take my first bites of new meals. If I smile, he throws his hands up in victory to make me laugh.

Strangely, we didn't talk about much of anything for the first few days—never mentioned that night or my mother. It's almost as if it hadn't happened. For fleeting moments, I think maybe it had been a dream.

Often, we just sat in silence watching the fire, or Grayson would tell me about school after I had left, or we'd talk about news in the Ancillary. The latter topic seemed to make Grayson uncomfortable. Last night, we sat by the fire, eating our stew in the living room. Grayson took small bites and looked nervous.

"Strange things are happening, Bec." Grayson shifted. "Feels different since your mom left."

"It is different. *Because* she left."

"Fourteen other people were exiled within a month of your mom."

I allowed this to set in. "Coincidence. You're just focused on it after Mom. Colony probably has that number every month anyway in the news. They've got to report something."

Gray shook his head. "Wasn't in the news. Heard it from some of the guys at the last house we were working on."

"Then maybe it was rumor."

"Maybe." Grayson poked the fire with another stick, making it crack and pop under his prodding. "William Skycap's house was set on fire," he said bluntly.

My hands became clammy and my head began to swim. "How do you know it was *set* on fire?"

"Ok," Grayson conceded. "It burned down. You could smell the smoke from here."

"Doesn't mean someone did it. Could have been a number of things." I searched for possibilities. "Left his coffee maker on," I offered.

Gray shrugged. Pulse officials said a drone crashed into it after a malfunction. I don't buy it. He was badly burned. Lasted a few days in the hospital, I hear. He would have recovered from the burns, but he had too much smoke inhalation."

Will Skycap had visited my mother often during the days of the worst homesickness. I was reminded of the first time I met Will when we sat together on our first day in the New Colony for our orientation. He was handsome and lean but also had a severity that intimidated me. It was difficult to picture someone so vigorous, now dead.

"Strange things. Something just feels—" but he stopped abruptly when he noticed I was becoming uncomfortable. "Sorry, Rebecca. Not good timing," he said before launching into a story about how one of his friends had been dared to caulk his nose shut on the construction site. He switched easily into his usual lighthearted self, and any hint of concern was gone.

The next day I learned more bad news from the Ancillary and why Nicholas Porter had not pursued me more when I retreated into the Pulse. Initially he and Grayson both had been looking for me. Of course, Radius had changed my cuff so that I couldn't be tracked, and I was well hidden. But it had never surprised me that the colony hadn't done more to find me. If I had been absorbed into the Pulse, then I was one less child to worry about. They had followed protocol in sending me to Cherish, but they would leave it to Cherish to find me, and Cherish didn't have the resources to do so. I had seen it before. But for love of my mother, I thought Mr. Porter would have done more to find me.

Then Gray told me gently that Mr. Porter had died unexpectedly. I stared at the fire as I pictured his kind face. Like my mother, Cherish was his lifeline. He was so full of hope as he fought tirelessly against the system. My only consolation was that my mother would not know he had passed. Grayson watched me carefully for my reaction, but I was all out of tears.

After Gray has missed an entire week of school to tend to my every need, I insist that he go back. "You have to, Grayson," I reason. "It might look suspicious."

Gray looks pensive, but he can't argue.

I am left alone with a clear set of instructions—do not leave the house, do not take a bath without someone here in case I slip, take this pill at noon, just rest, don't forget to eat. Grayson nervously wipes his hair flat before he leaves.

"Go," I say, pushing him out the door and closing it behind me. I lean back on it with my full weight and sigh deeply.

I am now trusted to stay by myself—just me, my torturous thoughts, and the guilt that fills and corrodes me from the inside. I immediately ignore the rest of his instructions. By noon I have the house cleaner than it has ever been. Gray's domestic abilities are clearly limited to his culinary skills. I spend an hour and a half on the bathroom alone. Small as it is, scrubbing and bleaching grout that is host to a prospering mildew problem takes a while. And, I am fairly certain that the baseboards have literally never been wiped down. I even feed the chickens, those little beasts.

I get winded easily and my shoulder and neck begin to throb, but the blood flowing through me feels good, and it pushes out the heavy ache. I can forget the collapsing and mad world around me so long as I focus entirely, with a yoking obsession, on a single stain. Stain by stain I subdue the memories that threaten to surface. As the sun gets lower I start to worry that he isn't coming back. Maybe someone started asking questions at school and he said too much. My mind reels with the possibilities of what could have happened if Lex went to school that day. Of course, she is probably only looking for another girl to fill my shoes so that she can one day fulfill her dream of Radius putting her on a ballooner ad. I pace in front of the fireplace and poke it menacingly with the iron.

"Nothing happened," I tell myself and walk resolutely to the kitchen. I open cabinets, searching for something, anything to keep my hands busy. I begin pulling out bowls and spoons and flour and oil and small containers of salt and powders. "He's fine," I tell myself aloud as I work, flour going everywhere. I knead the dough as my eyes remain fixed on the window. The sun is getting lower and my heart begins to quicken. I slop globs of dough in uneven rows on a baking sheet and slam it into the oven before returning to take out my anxiety on the logs with the iron. It's too late. Something has to be wrong.

The latch on the door turns slowly. I stiffen and clutch the iron tightly, ready to stand my ground if it's Radius.

The door swings open. "Mmm, smells good," Gray says cheerfully.

I grip the mantle to keep from falling over. Gray swings his backpack onto the floor and stomps his feet on the rug. "Hey, you ok?" he asks, taking the iron. "Rebecca, you're shaking."

Relief rushes through me. "I missed you," I hear myself whisper.

Gray looks at me softly and smiles. "I missed you too," he says, bending down slightly to be at eye level with me. "I know it's later than I wanted—I'm sorry, Bec—" He reaches a hand out reassuringly toward my shoulder, but I turn away with embarrassment.

"Biscuits," I mutter as I return to the kitchen.

"You're incredibly bad at following instructions, you know," he calls from the other room.

"What do you mean? No bath. Ate all my lunch. Took that pink pill after lunch."

"And *rest.*"

174

"Oh, yeah. Well, got most of them," I say, taking the pan from the oven and letting it clatter loudly on the stove.

"Uh-huh," he says, sitting down at the table. "Rebecca, I saw Lex today."

I freeze. "And?"

"And, she didn't look good."

I know exactly what that means. "She was supposed to be keeping an eye on me. I guess he had to blame someone."

"I guess so," Gray says softly. "I could kill him, and all of the trash like him."

I study Gray, the boy who stabbed *himself* to outsmart Radius instead of fighting him. The little boy who took up a war against the cowbird and then cried over its broken wing. He couldn't grow into a killer. It has never occurred to me that Gray would really fight Radius, but I have never seen him this angry.

"You wouldn't ever do that, Gray. You wouldn't really hurt him if you had the chance."

Gray is worn. "If it came down to having to, I mean, if he tried to hurt you again—yeah, I would. And I wouldn't hesitate."

"But it was my fault."

Gray sits up straighter. "What are you talking about?" he asks slowly.

All of it. I *chose* it. None of this would have happened if I hadn't made certain choices. If you were to kill him because of me, it would be no different than if I killed him myself. My choice," I say, pointing a finger to my chest. "My fault."

Gray looks at me with an austerity I have not seen before. "Rebecca," he says. "That *man* took a young girl. He was looking for someone who had a chink, just enough space for him to invade with some beautiful lies."

I purse my lips tensely.

"And then those lies would grow into a demon."

I open my mouth to protest, but Gray interrupts. "He was very, *very* smart in doing it, Rebecca. I will give him that. He is damn smart." Gray taps the table emphatically. "Don't you get it, Rebecca? He wrapped himself up in so much light and glitter that you didn't even know he *is* the Lie—he's just looking for a girl with a chink, some sort of a wound that he can get in to infect. And then he can whisper from the *inside* that it's her fault and not his."

I shake my head slowly.

"That's how his kind survives, Rebecca. So, yeah. I'd like to kill him and all the damn hawkers and mugs like him. Today when I saw how bruised up Lex was, I wanted to track him down and tear him apart with my own hands until I could feel him take his last breath."

Grayson pounds a fist on the table, but I don't flinch.

"I spent every single night for a year praying you'd figure it out. I did everything I could to get messages to you. I begged the police, I walked the streets looking for you. I begged, I mean I *begged* Lex to tell me where you were, or to at least give you a message."

Of course Lex had never mentioned any of that, had never even let it slip that Gray was looking for me.

"I tried so hard to find some way in—I even posed as a mug and tried to pay for a meeting with you—but he had outsmarted every move I made with a counter-move. I lay awake at night thinking about how much hate I had for that man. I even spent some nights sleeping outside his apartment and waiting for the chance to try to grab you if you came out. When you finally did come home, I sat by your bed watching you breathe, praying you'd make it past the poison he put in your body just in case you stopped buying the Lie and wanted out. Of course, he'd already poisoned you so much that you were willing to kill yourself—the stones were just an added precaution. I thought constantly about how I could kill him. In some bad moments I made plans to actually do it if you died." The hardness in Grayson's eyes returns to his familiar gentleness.

"But I know that even if I did, even if I rounded up all the liars and erased them from existence in whatever gruesome and satisfying way I could come up with, if you're sitting here saying it's *your* fault, it wouldn't matter at all. Not at all." Gray runs his fingers through his hair and exhales slowly. "I could kill all those liars. But, it wouldn't kill the Lie."

I meet his eyes, those dark, warm eyes belonging to a boy who had drowned me so I could be free.

He searches me imploringly. "Don't you get it, Rebecca? The Lie would live."

Gray and I have fallen into a rhythm over the last few weeks. I wake each morning to his stirring in the front room, breaking the morning silence with the quiet thudding of logs and snapping of twigs as he starts a fire. As soon as I hear the back door swing shut, I get myself dressed while Gray tends the chickens.

It's strange to open the curtains to see my old house. I realize that this is what Gray would have seen each morning when he woke.

Once I hear the shower start across the hall, I go to the kitchen to wash the eggs Grayson has collected and placed on the counter in a basket. Grayson and I sit silently at breakfast eating our fried egg on top of toast and boiled greens, the breakfast my mother always made, and I make now. I know that Grayson likes his tea steaming hot and with a spoon of honey. He thanks me groggily as he clears the table to wash dishes while I leave to begin laundry. Then Gray gives strict instructions that he knows I will ignore, but it makes him feel better to give them all the same: just *rest* and eat everything he's left on a plate in the fridge. I agree in spite of the fact that my whole day will be spent in constant motion. If I become too still, the memories will gather in my mind like a flock of crows on a tree.

And that is the worst part about being in hiding—my pain hides with me. As I do my work, suddenly the walls begin to close in, and I struggle for breath. The first time it happened I thought it was the residual effects of toxins attacking my heart as it pounded out of my chest. I fell back from scrubbing the tub and gasped on the tile floor until slowly my chest loosened and my heart rate returned to normal.

While Grayson gets his backpack ready, I make a list for the day. One: baseboards. Two: ironing. Three: baking. Four: sweeping, and other such chores that aren't necessary for their own sake but for mine. Boredom is pushing me over the edge of my already dwindling sanity.

In some small way I am paying down my debt to Gray. But I know that polished baseboards and cookies aren't paying it down by much. I am barely earning my keep. Colony 215 gives Gray a stipend since he's still in school, but that will end soon, though he hasn't said so. He's probably dipping into Marissa's savings and whatever else he earned last summer at his construction job.

Grayson puts his shoes on. "I've got an errand after school—grocery. And, I'm going to pick you up some lotion. We're out, right?"

I deflate at the idea of his being late. I add more chores to my list as he talks.

"Oh, and vitamins. Asa said vitamins would be good," he mutters to himself. "I'm going to have to wait for the 6:00 Convoy, so I'll be later than usual. Do we need anything?"

Normally we just order things by drone, but orders for Ancillary need to be made at least forty-eight hours in advance. I'm slightly annoyed that he hasn't done this earlier so that he doesn't have to leave.

"Could you get chocolate chips? And some bleach if it's not too much to carry?"

"Definitely on the chocolate, maybe on the bleach. I feel like I'm enabling your manic cleaning thing," he says, rolling his eyes and heading toward the door.

"Wait! Lunch." I grab his nylon bag from the counter and meet him at the door.

Gray stands smiling at me with his hand on the doorknob. I pause for a moment, but instead of giving him the lunch bag, I throw my arms around his middle in an awkward hug. Gray wraps his strong arms around my shoulders and holds me tight. I look up sheepishly into his gentle face as he looks down at me warmly. He moves a hand to my cheek and kisses my forehead. I haven't been touched like that for so long. For a moment I feel the warmth of his lips and Gray's peace seep into me. But only for a moment. I break free of him and take a step back to hold out his lunch with a stiff arm. Grayson is still smiling as he takes it and closes the door behind him.

I have spent days trying to figure out where it is exactly that I will go when I am able to. I'm officially dead as far the colony is concerned. Only Grayson and Asa know the truth. My school records and genetic profile that the colony kept have been erased.

The Colony will now have to recalculate diversity and find my replacement. I picture another blue-eyed, brown-haired girl receiving word that she will be eligible for Colony 215. My house remains empty and otherwise available for another family, but new colonists won't be moving to the Ancillary until spring, when the Genetic Diversity Administration makes its final decisions based on the year's analysis. Other Ancillary colonists who have applied for new housing will be unlikely to request my house anyway. It isn't exactly prime property this far out, and so Grayson and I feel comfortable leaving my things there, with the exception of my winter clothes, for another few weeks. He has also retrieved a few plates and blankets from my house.

My Contour Sheet has been frozen but won't be deleted for the usual five-week period. I put Gray's computer on my lap and get cozy on the sofa with a blanket to catch up on colony news since my death. Notes stream into my Sheet from people who knew me or people who pretended to. "Oh my gosh! She used to sit right next to me! So crazy!" wrote one girl who used to torment me from across the room. But most of the Pulse notes were of the customary, "I'm really going to miss her; life is so short" variety. All of them are liars.

I was famous, apparently. Well, not me. The idea of me is famous amongst many of the Pulse students and some of the Old Colony people who were playing up our association, probably to get some attention for themselves. They write dramatic stories about how I was the president's daughter in the Old Colony. The worst comments are about my mother. "Now they can be together," one Old Colony boy writes as though my mother has died and not been exiled. She is alive, I tell myself. But his words take my breath.

I search the page, looking desperately for any note from Radius. Nothing. The last day before the Sheet is taken down, I check constantly. Nothing. Not one word from Radius. I imagine what he would have written: "She should have been a VL 1,000. I'll miss her so much." And then I imagine pictures he would have put up of me, even some of the more provocative ones. But nothing. He probably didn't even visit my Sheet after I left him.

One girl whom I recognize from the Old Colony posts my last comment. She had a score of 332, so I almost didn't read it. I had seen her at Cherish many times before, but I didn't know her name. "Rebecca was better than this Colony," she wrote. Immediately, I look her up on her Contour Sheet. There she is, hair pulled back in a mousy ponytail, looking more like a mug shot in contrast to the digitally enhanced pictures most of the girls have. It doesn't take long before Pulse students are slamming her. In the twenty-four hours after she posted on my Sheet, her own score has gone down by seventy points. She has committed virtual suicide. But, of course, she probably doesn't care. Maybe she's better than this colony too.

The clock the Colony had put on my own Contour Sheet counts down until the page is deleted. I am a ghost looking in on myself, waiting to see my disappearance. I exhale slowly.

Three, two, one. A message pops up on the screen: Resident Files Deleted. The screen goes white. I am gone. Or, at least the quantitative system to measure my life is gone—same thing, maybe. I know that scattered about the Pulse, pictures of the old me are circulating. Or, the New me, I guess. There are videos too. I cringe at the realization that they'll always be there. Those cannot be killed.

Chapter 19

There are times during the day when I hate Radius. I really hate him. I, like Grayson, have envisioned his destruction. Sometimes it overcomes me and I storm out of the house to throw rocks across the backyard and send the chickens into a panic. There is no one to hear me, and I scream at the top of my lungs. I pace the floor and have imaginary conversations with him, telling him articulately at times what I think of him. Other times, I wildly hurl curse words at him.

But I have my weak moments too, and as soon as Grayson leaves on some mornings I scour Radius's Contour Sheet and sort through pictures of him and the new girls posing with him. His VL has risen to almost nine hundred thanks to the girls surrounding him. One I recognize—a ginger girl with a flat chest and big eyes who looks into the camera seductively. She wasn't from the Old Colony, but she is Ancillary. Of course Radius was probably getting her ready for the covey even before I left. I hate her and pity her at the same time. So, I have been replaced. And perhaps I had also been someone else's replacement. Maybe I was just one in a never-ending string.

Even then in the weak moments between outrages, I fantasize about Radius mourning for me and secretly spending every day in regret. And then guilt rushes in as I think of everything Gray has done for me. He doesn't know that there is a part of me longing for the person he has risked his life to rescue me from.

I type in Lex's name to see how she is faring. She was my first girlfriend here. In spite of the fact that she was also my prison guard, I miss her. We were both imprisoned, really, in spite of the power she had over me. I know the abuse she has endured from Radius, who I'm sure blames her solely for my escape. Of course she is also given credit for recruitment, and so maybe she has redeemed herself by luring in new girls as my replacement.

She was easy to trust, and I followed her directly to him. When I had doubts or suspicions, it was Lex who talked me out of them. It was Lex who pampered me and made me Pulse-beautiful. It was often her voice that I listened to, but it was always Radius's words. He had her trained and leashed just as much as he had any of us—

maybe her even more so. Had I gotten farther in, it could have been me next as a recruiter.

Lex's picture stares back at me from the screen. I can see beyond her painted-on beauty now—she is as broken as I am. It's how Radius picked her, and all of us. I scroll through her pictures, cringing at each one. Even though I'm angry, I want to rescue her, somehow.

I click on a frozen video image of a ballooner ad in the distance to bring it to life. It takes a moment to decipher—someone must have taken this footage from the inside the moving Convoy, I can tell by the way the landscape rushes past. I keep my eyes focused on a ballooner with a moving image of a girl, perhaps the girl I saw crossing the street whom Lex said was a VL-1,000 on my first trip to Dylan's. I wonder if she was one of the lucky few who just floated to the top of our small world. Maybe she was from a long line of 1,000's and was one of the few genetically blessed. What if she spent her whole life knowing that she would ascend, and it was never more than a passing thought as to how she would get there? Or, maybe she had to fight for it. Maybe her perfections were earned with self-loathing that disciplined her into not eating or willed her to endure numerous surgeries. It doesn't matter now, though. She made it, and Lex is convinced that she will too.

Lex must have taken this video. I picture her sitting in the Convoy after a night working in the Pulse, looking up into the sky as she often did to dream of the day when all her work would pay off, and she would float above it all in a ballooner ad as we below looked upon her in worship. But I know now that that false hope was only part of the lies that Radius had woven to tether her to him.

I lean closer to the screen. Someone is standing in the basket; it's almost imperceptible at first. Before the balloon is covered again by quickly passing trees, I see her. The basket is swaying and tilted downward as a girl twitches on the end of a long rope tied to her neck, connecting her to the balloon. She soars high above it all as the VL-1000 bats her lavender eyes.

Grayson won't be home for another three hours. I can't take it anymore. I watch the video of Lex four more times, tears streaming down my face, before I believe that it was her on the end of that swaying rope instead of filming. She was right in saying that Radius would get her there as long as she paid her dues.

I read through the messages left on her sheet, which confirmed her suicide. Who had been doing the filming? Another one of the girls? One of the recruits in the covey? Was it Radius himself? And then the question surfaces that haunts me the most: had she done this because of me?

I sit back in the chair, numb. It's maddening to be here alone with these demons. I grab my coat and go out the front door for the first time in a month. Gray would be furious, but I reason that I will slowly lose my mind if I don't get out.

I walk down the crumbling road that leads to the Pulse. Tree branches stretch silently over the path in graceful arches. The distant winter sun caresses my face. I cut right abruptly to head toward the river. The smell of frozen earth fills my lungs as I take deep breaths. I don't think I have taken this path since Grayson and I were children.

This was also the path that Gray took the night he carried my cuff to throw into the river. I can't imagine running in the dark on this path that has dissolved into the woods since my childhood. As I pass, leafless branches converge on the trail, grasping at my arms and legs with gnarled fingers. Frosted spider webs scintillate like overgrown snowflakes in some mystical land of ice. The rhythmic crunch of my boots as I disrupt the frozen earth is replaced by the gentle thunder of the river as I enter into the clearing where we built our fort. We spent so many days here in our own secret kingdom that belonged to youth and wishes, so far beyond the colony.

A few daffodils, maybe from the same bulbs that gave me the flowers of my childhood, have pushed through the frozen ground. I pick one and twirl it in my fingers. It reminds me of the daffodils Gray would leave outside my window or on the front stoop when he wanted to tell me to meet him in the woods.

To my surprise our dammed pond is still there, much smaller than I remembered, like the rest of the kingdom. Grayson and I had toiled over blocking the current of the river from the natural eddy of water with heavy rocks. It had teemed with the fruits of our hunts—tadpoles, crayfish, minnows—and it had been the sea for vessels of colored blossoms and bowed leaves. Hidden in the shadows, it is frozen solid. I step on it gingerly and gently lay myself down to look up at the branches that sway with a backdrop of the blue gray sky, like Ophelia's hair in the pool. I stay as long as I can, a queen returning to her kingdom to float upon a blossom boat.

"Lex." I speak her name to the trees and sky. For the first time I realize that it might not have even been her real name. Maybe Radius gave it to her as a way of claiming her too. A red bird alights on the branch overhead. "Lex," I whisper again as Gray and I used to speak the names of people we missed from the Messenger Tree to the birds. "I'm sorry," I tell her. Perhaps there's still enough magic left for her to get my message.

I shiver as I make the walk back to Gray's house, but in spite of the cold, I feel invigorated and more peaceful. I haven't been to my house since the night Gray sat with me under the table, and so I decide to make a short visit.

It is as cold inside as it is out. My breath crystallizes in front of me as I walk to my old house. From the corner of my eye, I spot a cluster of yellow on the side of the house. As I get closer I notice more than a dozen daffodils. I turn the corner and discover dozens and dozens of the yellow flowers under my old window—the window I had used to escape to go with Radius each night.

Daffodils—like the ones Grayson used to leave on the step to tell me to meet him in Our Colony.

"Gray," I whisper. Who else would have planted them? I stoop to pick one of the flowers. "Oh, Grayson." He had tried so hard to stop me. I can picture him planting the bulbs, hoping with each one that it would snap me out of the spell Radius had me under, and that I would turn back instead of escaping from my window when I got the call if I saw his flowers. But they had bloomed too late—I had already retreated to the Pulse to live with Radius by the time they had pushed through the frost last spring to give me their message.

I push myself to stand and walk slowly back around the house to let myself in. I haunt each room, lingering in each one and taking it in. Slowly I run my fingers along the wooden furniture in our living room. I kneel by the fireplace that I had seen my mother light so many times. I feel her here—we two forgotten spirits, sitting silently together. Grief consumes me as I embrace the emptiness of our house.

I visit my mother's room last. From my window at Gray's house I have spent so long looking in, half expecting to see her form. I have imagined myself in here so many times, but it is still painful to

184

be around her belongings. I open her closet and run my fingers along her hanging clothes, setting them to motion in a gentle swing. Her shoes are lined neatly at the bottom. Looking at her empty work shoes is almost unbearable.

I start to close the door when I notice a small wooden box next to a pair of her boots. I kneel on the floor and open it slowly. It is filled with papers, letters written to my father that he will never receive. There must be hundreds. I lean back against the wall as I read through them. She has written my father stories of our days and updates on me—an award I had gotten at school, Old Colony members who had come to look for comfort, how tall I was now. I read through each one, absorbing her handwritten notes, wiping my hand across each page that she had touched. Almost every note is full of pride for me. Even in the times when Mom and I were fighting the most, she had written to my father about how beautiful I was becoming, funny things I had said, or an assignment I had done well on. "She has such promise," she wrote in so many of them. She must have believed that we would see my father again one day. Why else would she have recorded this? Each milestone was detailed so that in some way he could experience it one day. My mother brimmed with hope even to the point of foolishness.

I spend almost an hour sifting through letters, and shivering in the cold. As I had as a child, I climb into her bed and hug her pillow tight. It no longer smells like her, but it takes very little for me to conjure up the memory of her scent. I slept with her almost every night when we were first transferred, and I allowed her to comfort me. I close my eyes and feel her hold me, and then I cry until exhaustion overtakes me.

Suddenly, I am awoken. My heart beats wildly before I fully register what is making the sound: a car driving by. I leap from the bed and crouch on the floor. My legs are shaking, and I am still trying to focus my eyes. I strain to hear two car doors slam. I inch under my mother's bed. Has someone been watching me? How could they possibly know that I am here? I shake convulsively from fear rather than the cold. But then, after what seems like several hours, the car doors slam again, and the car pulls away.

I let out a long, slow breath. My mind reels at the possibility of who it could have been. I know Asa has never driven his car out here, and as far as I know he is the only one who knows I am here.

The only colony members who own a car are citizens from the Pulse. I reason that they didn't knock on my door, so maybe they have gone to Gray's. Slowly, I inch my way out from under the bed. I am numb and rub my hands to feel them again. Gray won't be home for maybe another hour, and I freeze with indecision. Should I run? No. I'll stay here until I see evidence of Gray being home. I sit back on my mother's bed.

I can't stay with Gray much longer.

Chapter 20

Gray is shuffling along the road, weighed down by his book bag and two canvas bags pulling his arms straight on either side. Slowly, I open the door to my house and peer out at him. He stiffens as I come into focus and then speeds up his pace.

"Rebecca," he calls. "What do you think you're doing?"

I run to meet him in the road.

"Give this one to me," I say, reaching out for the bag in his left hand. He passes it over reluctantly, and we walk in silence to his house. I can feel him casting me disapproving glances for leaving.

There is just enough light coming from his house to see the note taped to the front door. It has the official colony seal printed on the front.

Grayson groans. "I wasn't expecting them for at least two more weeks," he says, ripping the pale green paper from the door. "Did they see you?"

"No, definitely not." I open the front door and put the bag on the counter. "Who was that?"

"Colony Child Protective Services. They do periodic checks on me, but they haven't come for months. This has been the first drop-in. How long did they stay?"

"Not long. I was under the bed in my house at the time, so I'm pretty sure they didn't know I was here."

The tension in Gray's face fades. "I guess I'm glad you left, then. It would have been hard to explain a dead girl in my house if they looked through the—"

"Gray, did you know about Lex?" I ask abruptly. Gray shifts.

I look at him somberly. "Well, did you?"

"Yes, I knew. It happened several days ago. I was just waiting for the right time to tell you."

"There was no right time, I guess. I saw it on her Contour Sheet today. There was an actual video."

Grayson shakes his head. "I'm sorry, Rebecca. That's a hard way to find out. I should have—"

"It was my fault," I say.

"No. She was in really deep, Bec." Grayson blows out a cloud of frost. "I tried to talk to her, you know. That day she was in such bad shape. I tried to, but she wouldn't listen to me. I was too late or I wasn't the right person to do it, I don't know."

I hung my head and fought tears.

"But his grip was too strong on her. There wasn't anything you could have done, Rebecca," Gray says as if reading my mind.

"Radius will make sure that someone takes her place. I can't stay here knowing that. I'm going crazy, Gray. My mom is out there somewhere while I do nothing. Your whole life is on hold to hide me, and no one is doing anything to stop Radius or any of the hawkers. I can't just stay here in hiding without completely losing my mind. Plus, now people are coming around."

"Just the Protective Services."

"Yeah, just the Protective Services," I say sarcastically. "I don't understand why they're looking in on you anyway. You're eighteen now."

"Yeah, technically. But as long as I'm a student, I'm given a certain stipend until graduation since I don't have a guardian and since I'm not being cared for at Cherish. They have to do periodic checks as long as they're sending me money."

"So then they'll be back."

"They will."

"We've got to figure something out. I can't stay here anymore and you know that."

Gray looks down at the chocolate chips he is taking out of his bag and throws them to me.

"Yeah, I know."

Gray taps his fingers on the counter. "And, I've got a plan. It's not a good plan, mind you, but it's a plan."

Gray brings out the rest of the contents of his bags, one by one. He doesn't seem to be in any hurry to tell me what he has come up with.

"Well . . ." I prompt.

Gray looks up. "You can't stay here any longer, right?"

"Right."

"For one thing, your house could possibly have new tenants in the next few months."

I nod.

"And, you can't stay here because eventually someone's going to find out—either the Colony Child Protective Services before school's out, or someone's going to want to come over or something."

188

"Like friends?" I raise my eyebrows. Gray got along with everyone well—from Ancillary anyway—but he was a loner. I try to remember if he had ever had friends over. Surely he had, but I can't recall any ever coming to the house.

"Maybe. One day, sure. It's a prison for you, especially now that you're stronger. But it's also not like you can stay in the colony." Grayson leans on the counter and pounds his fist on it absentmindedly. The only solution is that you get out."

"As in out of the colony?" I laugh. "Well, when you said it wasn't a good plan, you weren't kidding."

"Nope."

"And how do you propose that I move to another colony? And, why exactly do you think that will be any better? It's not as if I can make any kind of life in another colony. Plus, they'd just trace me back here."

"Right," Gray says soberly. "But I know something you don't." Grayson smiles like he did when he was a little boy. "Your mom told me something before she was exiled."

I sit up straighter.

"There's a group of non-colonists."

I look at him hard and shake my head. "There can't be non-colonists. There's not enough land for any more than a few stragglers and the exiled."

"More like hundreds. Maybe thousands."

I stare at him in disbelief. "I don't believe that, Gray. Where would they live, for one thing? It's too dangerous to live just anywhere. The National Council has determined where we can live safely and *that's* where people live. No one's really dumb enough to live near an earthquake line or land full of sinkholes. Is your solution, then, to move to a place where the earth literally consumes us? No, thanks."

Gray wipes his hair down with his hand. "I saw your mom that day."

"What do you mean?"

"The day she was exiled."

I can feel my heart beating in my ear suddenly.

"She was pretty heavily guarded, and we couldn't have much of a conversation. She told me enough to confirm what I had already learned from Marissa. Before Marissa died, she told me—"

"What, Gray?" I coax. "Something about my mom?"

Gray inhales deeply. "Something about your dad." He looks at me sympathetically. "Marissa said they were lying."

"Who?" I feel anger rising.

Grayson pauses and bites his lip. "I think the National Council fabricated potential land threats."

"As in, he lied about 108's land threat? No," I say flatly. "My dad decided that we all had to get out. He didn't want to make that decision, but he had to. We all got smashed up and sent to different colonies." I stand up and try to stop myself from hitting him. "It ruined families, you know? Where are your parents?" I ask cruelly.

Gray looks wounded but reaches for my hand. I pull it away as though he were a snake. "What are you saying? We could all be at home in the Old Colony if it weren't for him?" I am seething, but Gray remains steady.

"I think your dad did what he had to do. Someone lied to him. I think that the National Council lied to him."

"And the Old Colony is still standing? My room is still there? My house? My damned mailbox is still has the flag up? A whole civilization of families got broken up, but our buildings are still there—safely on top of the ground that *didn't* consume them?"

Gray's face is full of compassion, but I want none of it. "Yeah, I think it's still standing. I don't think that it was ever in immediate danger. And," he paused. "Marissa told me: 'Henry knew it was a lie.'"

The nausea rises. "Marissa was the liar," I say coldly, although I immediately regret my words. Grayson looks at me sympathetically. "I didn't mean that," I mumble.

"That day in the prison, your mom confirmed it," he continues, ignoring my brashness. Grayson leaves the room and returns with several thick envelopes. "There was a guard listening, so she couldn't say much. She asked if I could take care of a few things, the first one being you."

"Yeah." I look down. Mom probably didn't know how big of a request that actually was.

"Then she asked me if I could feed her cat."

"We've never had a—"

"She said that I'd find its food in a container she kept in her closet, but it was tucked under a pair of shoes."

"In a wooden box?"

"Yeah, that's where I found it, along with a lot of other things."

Grayson hands me a brown envelope. I hold it for a moment before pulling out a long list, written in my mother's handwriting, of hundreds of names, ID numbers, and dates. I run my finger down the list.

"Who are these people?" I pause at a name halfway down the first page. "Auden Spence. I know him." My heart quickens as I recall exactly how I know him. There are a few others that sound vaguely familiar and then some names that everyone knows. VL: 1,000's list: Sawyer Milon, Feliz Buchanan, Olivia Maxison, Francesca Peterson. We faded youth had lifted our eyes each morning to see so many of these perfect specimens that were the treasures of our colony: VL 1,000's.

"I don't get it." I shuffle through the pages quickly, reading the names over and over, trying to make sense of it. "She didn't know these people."

Gray shrugs his shoulders. The list goes on for pages.

"She was losing it," I conclude. "She was getting paranoid, writing down people she didn't trust or something."

"No, she wasn't paranoid. She was making records for some reason. Or, keeping records." Gray lowers his voice.

I stare at the list, frozen, trying to take it in. The last few pages include a new set of names.

"Turn to the second-to-last page."

I flip through the thick document. Halfway down—Rebecca Flora. I mouth my name.

"I'm on there too," Grayson says.

"She was keeping records because *why*? You think she was a spy?"

"Maybe."

"Ok, but this doesn't prove anything. Proves *nothing*."

Gray hands me a second envelope, which is carefully labeled "Satellite Views and Maps." "Turn to page twenty-seven," he says. It's an aerial view of the Old Colony followed by matrices of numbers.

"What is this?"

"The proof. This is the data your father had collected for himself. A lot of rumors were spreading that the other colonies being assimilated were based on falsified information. For one thing, it was suspicious that the latest colonies being assimilated were really wealthy in certain resources."

"Like what?"

"Like colony 84, Jenkins's colony."

I remembered Jenkins, a pimple-faced Ancillary from school.

"Eighty-four was rich in coal."

"Ok, rich in coal. But they weren't hoarding it for themselves or anything. All the cells, all the colonies, used those resources."

"But, what if the National Council was using the resources for their own gain while the colony was emptied of people?"

"That's ridiculous. What would they do with all that coal or wind energy, or whatever, with no workers there?"

"Unless they sold it off to someone who has their own workers."

"Like who, exactly?" I shoot.

"Like another country."

"You are out of your mind," I say definitively.

"No. The National Council has been slowly assimilating different colonies. We've been here almost ten years. The Ancillary was almost completely vacant when we arrived, and now there's hardly enough room. More assimilations are happening."

"And so are more disasters," I counter.

"How do you know?"

I stare at him blankly. "Because we've seen it."

"On T.V.," Gray gives a half smile.

"Yes, on T.V.—aerial views that they could have manipulated to look like they were destroyed. They could very well be just fine. That's not proof as far as I'm concerned." I leaf through the sheets. "This doesn't prove it either."

"No, it doesn't. But you don't think it's strange that your mom would have aerial maps of all the colonies? Look at Colony 84." Gray takes the papers from me and quickly finds a shot of a mass of geometric structures pitched on the different altitudes of the mountainous region.

"She's still standing," he says, pointing to Colony 84's structures. "And this is dated two years ago."

"Could have been just as easily fabricated. Or it could be an old picture," I reason.

"Yeah, it could have been. But I don't think it was."

"Why?"

"Something's going on. Marissa and your mom both thought it was made up."

"No, Marissa thought so. What you are telling me is that my dad was given a choice. If he believed that the National Council was trying to take over, why would he have not chosen to stay? These pictures and this list," I say, waving the papers in the air, "don't prove that my mom thought the threat of an earthquake was made up. And besides, she would have told me before you."

Gray purses his lips and looks out the window. "Maybe she tried to. Rebecca, what did your mom tell you when you saw her?"

"Well, she didn't tell me that my dad had destroyed our colony when he didn't have to."

"What did she say?" Gray presses.

I remember my mother's face, how serene she was, how she still sat with a dignity even though her hands and feet were bound. I didn't want to repeat the words my mother had said to me before she was exiled. They were sacred. This wasn't her home. How many times had she said that to me? And she had gone on about how much my father loved me.

"It doesn't matter what she said, Gray. She didn't say she was a spy. She didn't say my dad destroyed our colony. She didn't—"

"She said you know his heart."

I freeze.

"Your mom knew that your father had a choice to assimilate or not. She knew that he had information that meant we weren't at risk." Gray held up the matrixes of numbers. "But he had to do it anyway."

I shake my head in disbelief.

"You know his heart, Rebecca. He is a good man. He had to do it."

I forbid myself from crying.

"I went home immediately and looked for whatever it was that your mom was telling me to find. I found nothing. But then I remembered she had said tucked under a pair of shoes."

"She kept her shoes on the floor."

"Right. They were under the floor. I had to go under the crawl space of the house. I found them in a metal container approximately under her bedroom space."

Everything in me fights against Gray's words. If it is true, if my mom had records that proved the National Council was lying, then why didn't she try to stop my father? If nothing else, I never doubted how much my mother loved him. She would have fought to stay together.

"They were watching her, Rebecca."

"Who was watching her?"

"Colony leadership."

"We had occasional visits from the Assimilation committee," I concede. "Because we had so many Old Colony people visiting. They were overreacting."

"And your house was searched."

"No, it wasn't. Our house was never searched."

"Ok, robbed then."

"We were robbed, not searched. Pulse kids did it just to make life difficult. It's what they do."

"Wasn't Pulse kids." Gray leans in closer. "No one robs Ancillary residents. We don't have anything worth stealing. They— whoever they are, colony powers-that-be—were suspicious."

I sigh. "I'm not buying this. And as a matter of fact, I think you might be losing it. So, my mom has been keeping all these weird maps and names, and no one else has ever said anything about it except for Marissa?"

"No, not true. One other person. I couldn't make sense of the lists and the maps, so I hid them at my house. But I stayed at your house all night waiting for you to come home. You didn't."

I closed my eyes tight at the memory of that night. I had spent it drugged and numb with Radius.

"But someone else did. Nicholas Porter."

"Mr. Porter?"

"He worked with your mom, and he was part of the Old Colony."

"But he died."

"He was shot two days after I saw him."

"Shot? No, you said he died. But—"

"Yes, Rebecca," Gray says apologetically. "I didn't want to tell you that. You were still recovering, and I didn't want the shock to set you back."

My face flushes hot. I'm at least glad that my mother doesn't know. Gray puts an arm around me, and I let him.

"Mr. Porter came in that night and was surprised to see me there," he continues. "He told me there were some things your mother had been holding for him, so I showed him the papers. He said these papers were proof that the National Council had lied ten years ago, and that it wasn't the only copy—your dad had made sure of that."

"What about the names then?"

"Foreigners. People who were placed here."

"You mean assimilated here."

"No. Not from any colony in America. They were plants."

"Who could have been planting them?"

"The National Council. That's all Nicholas told me. They were plants and taking over."

"But how?" I ask. "No one was taking over."

"Weren't they? According to Nicholas, they were. Their VL's were all extremely high. Nicholas and a team were doing data analysis on the VL system. As it turns out, increasing VL was determined only by certain people."

"Not true. My VL went up—"

"Mostly randomly. It went up randomly and intermittently based on only a few stable factors. Only certain people could actually manipulate the numbers in a significant way. They were the ones with the power to determine citizenship. They were the only ones with any kind of control over the system." The rest was illusion.

"Ok, but what's the big deal? Why would the National Council plant people for scores?"

"That's the question. Why were they ranking us?"

"*Why?* I don't know. It helps determine citizenship, and it keeps us on good behavior. Gold star system."

"I have a theory. Your dad didn't assimilate us. He *disseminated* us. Assimilation was the only way to spread us through all of the colonies. There were people like Nicholas and your mom who were working to counteract whatever they were doing. Strange things were happening. Colonies were getting sold. There has been quiet talk about this for years. You've heard it."

And I had, years ago, in whispers over steaming cups that my mother had handed to the homesick in our living room. "Rumors only."

"The last colonies to get assimilated were the ones with the most resources. Colony 554—steel. Colony 92—farm land and water. And then our colony—"

"Natural gas and copper," I say.

Gray nods.

"And then they're putting us on the outskirts of a New Colony and ranking us."

"So, Nicholas didn't say why?"

"He said your mom had a plan for us, that he would be taking care of you, and that he would explain as soon as he felt it was safe to do so. But, he did say because all the resources are being sold off, we're going to hit a threshold soon—not enough resources to support our population. We can't prove it. No one can prove it yet. But, if those people on the list—" Gray taps it hard with his finger. "If the people on that list really are outsiders, they're probably ranking us to see who can be cut."

I shake my head. "Still doesn't make sense. They gave him a *choice*. I was there. I saw him agonizing over the decision. I saw him crying. If he had known, then he would have chosen to have us stay together."

"Our colony wasn't the only one. The National Council was claiming these lands and pushing images of fires and destruction that hadn't happened for more than a hundred years to keep us wary. Suddenly, there had been an influx of assimilations. That's why we got so many new people each year. But we've reached a threshold. Our colony won't be able to support so many people for long."

"And according to Nicholas?"

"We've reached that threshold. And those maps and names are there to prove it."

I hit my head against the wall. "So then, according to your crazy idea, Dad sent us out to figure out who the plants were?"

Grayson exhales. "Maybe. I wanted to talk to Nicholas more, but he was so nervous. He said he'd explain more when he could, to wait until he contacted me first. He said it was better for me to hold onto the papers anyway—I wasn't suspected."

"But he must have been." I thought of all the trouble the colony had given Cherish.

"Right. I think they caught on that he was running analysis of the VL system. They probably took his files."

"Mom had a backup here. Brought to her by whom?"

Gray shrugs. "Maybe there were other analysts."

Suddenly I remembered the influx of homesick Old Colony citizens that came to our house each week to drink tea with my mother and the gifts they had brought her. I recalled once opening a bag of tea only to find a small note included in it with a name.

"Still, the National Council gave my dad the choice. They broadcasted that everywhere."

"I think he did have a choice. If they chose to reveal all the data that showed they could safely stay, they would have shut that down and quickly. People would have rioted."

"Exactly, we stood for freedom. We would have fought, and my dad would have led them. No colony would have been safe. It would have been a revolution," I say.

"And whichever country they were selling resources to would have backed the National Council. Another world war would have started."

"And, what if Dad had not shown them the data. What then? What if he had just said, 'We'll take our chances' and stayed."

"I think they would have still found a way to force him out."

"Then why provide ambivalent data and tell him he had a choice? Why not fabricate really clear data which gives him *no* choice?"

"I don't know, Rebecca. That's what I can't figure out."

My head is throbbing. I can't accommodate any of this. My mother is a record keeper for some underground group? My father is working for Council leadership and Colony 108 is most likely an oil drilling station now, taken over by some other country? No.

"Rebecca," Gray says. "There's nothing you could have done for your mother. She was on their watch list. Having any excuse to exile her was the easiest way to stomp out any potential trouble. They didn't have any proof that she was working as a spy, just suspicions. In the end your confession wouldn't have made any kind of a difference."

I swallow the lump that is rising in my throat.

"*They* did that to her, not you. Nothing could have changed it."

"It was my fault." My voice cracks.

"They seized an opportunity, Rebecca. If she hadn't confessed herself, they would have threatened *your* exile and used it to get information. They would have known that would have been worse for your mother, and she had to have known that. She confessed in front of everyone. There was no way to turn back after a confession, so they just got rid of her and assumed you were not going to be a problem after Radius had you." Gray pauses for a long time. "Think of Mr. Porter. It could have been worse. And actually, exile might have put her exactly where she wanted to be."

"What do you mean?"

Grayson takes out the maps and points to a large green area about five hundred miles from where we are. "That's where they get exiled. It's a low-risk area according to this."

I want to believe it, but by believing these maps I also have to accept that my father had had this information when he decided to assimilate us—or disseminate us. My mom is alive in a safe zone and my father broke apart every family in our colony, *or* my mother might be dead and my father had saved our small world. Neither way is good.

"Ok, so now what?" I ask.

Gray smiles. "We get out. By this." Gray points to an aerial view of all the cells with their colonies—little diverse worlds orchestrated to supply everything that would be needed to survive within its boundaries. "Membrane. We take the Membrane," he says as he outlines the boundary of the cells with his finger. "South. If we want to get out of the colonies, we go there."

"And do what exactly after trekking hundreds of miles through the wilderness?" I ask. "Hand our little paper over to whom? And if we do figure out that piece, what next? Ask them to take out the people on this list whom we suspect might be trying to take over the country? Think they're going to listen to two kids?"

"I don't know. Maybe. All I know is that there's a whole network outside of the colonies, and they're preparing for something."

"How do you *know* that, Gray? Come on. Listen to yourself."

Gray's eyes light up. "Because Nicholas, Marissa, and your mom all said so."

"My mom said so? When?"

"A few times, actually. Remember that one time I saw your mom coming through the woods with Will Skycap? We hid."

"Yeah, that was years ago."

"Well, I did some exploring the next day. There was a whole group of people camping out in the woods. I climbed a tree next to the wall and saw them. I asked Marissa about it. She looked surprised at first, but then she said it was nothing, just the angels watching over the colony. For years I thought that angels *were* watching out for our colony. Marissa even took me out one day to see them. There was a small hole in the wall, just large enough to pass some supplies through—medicines for poison ivy and respiratory illnesses, and salves for their feet."

"Just because some people were living in the woods doesn't mean they were part of some organized group. They were just escapees, and they must have been crazy to live in the woods with the wild animals. Their colonies were probably relieved to be rid of their crazy genes."

"That last day I visited your mother, they let me give her a final hug goodbye. She whispered in my ear: 'Join them in the Membrane and go south.' At the time I had absolutely no clue what she was talking about."

I look at the map until I find a section labeled "Membrane" in printed blue ink. "This?" I ask, outlining the space between the colonies. "This is the Membrane?"

"Yeah. Look at this space between the colonies with certain points' latitude and longitude—it's for GPS."

I nod, turning the map to the side in my hands. "So, it's that easy? We just walk out of the colony and that's it? No walls, no one watching?"

"I don't know. But I think so far fear has been enough of a boundary. No one would go in these areas because they think the earth is going to destroy them if they do."

"Right. Exactly," I say, but Gray ignores me.

"There are already rumors going around that resources are spreading too thin. It's only a matter of time before the National Council has to start skimming the fat. Don't you see? They're going to start getting rid of the extra—we being the extra. Places like Cherish, with everyone in it, are about to get completely wiped out. And I think we have to deliver these names. We have to get them out."

I pace the floor. Could it all be true? I know I can't stay here, and as difficult as it is to accept, some of what Gray says makes sense. What if he's right? "We have to get out," I agree.

Chapter 21

Three more times Child Services knock on Gray's door. After the first visit I remain ever vigilant of their return. Each time, I was able to disappear into the chicken coup before they could see me. It was too close, though. We must go soon.

My mother's instructions on the map are more than clear as to where to get out, down to the geographic coordinates—Latitude: 36.078300, Longitude: 79.005000. It's beautiful. It's the one potential weak point in the wall surrounding the colony—the southwest wall that allows the river to flow under it. That's our exit. If we're able to leave when the waters are lowest, perhaps we can float right under it.

And of course there's the issue of Grayson disappearing. My data has been wiped. It's as though I never existed. We decide that we must do the same for Grayson. We'll have to fake a suicide without leaving a body. It's not going to be easy, but it's the only way we can come up with.

If there is any suspicion at all after Gray's "death," authorities will be able to search his computer for any research he had done. Gray diligently searches for key terms such as "suicide by drowning" and clicks on links that would suggest to anyone curious that he has been planning his death thoroughly and with intentionality.

Once out, we will enter a brand new world the colony has made us fear through images of destruction broadcast on the zeppelins in the sky and lessons in the classrooms. We've pored over the documents that describe the world beyond our colony. It appears there might be a trail, complete with what look like rest stops, that leads about four hundred miles south to our destination. But without our cuffs there will be no way to find it unless we somehow acquire a GPS device. This, we decide, will be one of the biggest risks of the trip. If Gray is traced purchasing a GPS, it will immediately be a red flag after his disappearance.

"I can get it," I tell him. "It's the only way."

Gray refuses. It will mean going back into the Pulse, and that will risk my being identified.

It would be safer for no one to have any information about our plans to leave. But the GPS isn't the only thing we will need. We have to acquire medical supplies in case we get injured, a tent, sleeping bags, fire starters, and water purifiers. Honestly, we don't even know the extent of the necessary supplies. Once again, Asa is the only one we feel is trustworthy, but we hate ourselves for putting him in danger by asking for his help.

"I'll do it," Asa says without hesitation and with an enthusiasm uncharacteristic of him. "I can get you what you need to get out."

Gray and I look at each other. "You understand that if you do this, they could come looking for you," Gray says. "You know what they did to Nicholas Porter. You can say no and we wouldn't fault you for it."

"You've already saved my life once, Asa," I tell him. "You took too big of a risk then."

Asa leans forward and takes my hand but says nothing at first.

"Marissa changed everything for me," he whispers after a few moments. "When she met me, I was in pretty deep here." Asa clears his throat. "She shared a hope for a better world than the one controlled by the Pulse. This isn't my home anymore."

We take every precaution not to be linked to Asa. We decide to not even allow him to come to the house at all from now on. Over the past two months, Asa has met Grayson in different parts of the Pulse in random locations and times so that a pattern can't be detected. In the back rows of movie theaters, stores, coffee shops, and Convoy terminals, Asa whispers instructions on how to prepare for worst-case scenarios and hands Gray handwritten messages on the basics of how to handle things like hemorrhages, broken bones, hypothermia, and snakebites.

When Gray comes home, he and I sit at the kitchen table to frantically review what Asa has told him. Late into the night, we huddle in front of the fire and quiz each other on responses to different scenarios like we are studying for a final exam. But in this case, not having memorized the information, such as later stages of heat stroke or hypothermia, could mean that one or both of us might die.

While Gray attends school, I stay home and memorize chapters from electronic first aid books that Asa was able to steal from the hospital library. Most of it is over my head, but I pore over chapters memorizing how to do CPR or stabilize a broken bone. Turns out learning the New Colony rapid reading method is paying off after all, and I'm even starting to love those red I's and O's.

And somehow it's easier to spend my day imagining scenarios of Gray and me being mortally injured and left to our own incompetence in the middle of nowhere, than being left alone with my own shame. I decide that life-risking purpose is better than hiding.

In addition to memorizing poisonous plants and venomous snakes as well as how to avoid UTI's and bandage burns, I spend my day building back the muscles I had lost during my convalescence. I lean against the wall and sit as though in an invisible chair for as long as my legs will support me. The first day I tried it, I could only withstand about twenty seconds before my legs began to shake violently, and another ten before I'd collapse onto the floor. After a month, I was up to a couple of minutes. Chickens scatter as I run circles in the yard and do lunges along the perimeter of the fence, bobbing up and down like some queen hen. At night I go to sleep with burning legs and a racing mind. I am beginning to feel truly alive again.

Gray and I look around the house to find things we can use as supplies. We have adequate water bottles, and my mother kept a decent first aid kit. I strip old bed sheets to produce a few rags that can be used as tourniquets. Grayson owns a heavy and oversized flashlight, an arsenal of matches, and that's about it. No backpack, except for our school bags. No shelter. Grayson has a pair of boots that he insists will work, but they are heavy and cumbersome. I own one pair of flat-soled neon green running shoes. Between the two of us, we have precisely enough to die after one day away from the colony.

Once again, Asa risks himself to help us. He feigns an interest in camping and researches and purchases several shiny new items that he will transfer to us: tent, canteens, water purifier, backpacks, sleeping bag, pocket knife, and, perhaps most importantly: a GPS.

And then, Asa has to make it look like he has a reason to be making all these purchases. He posts pictures of himself on his Contour Sheet hiking the trails in the southern part of the colony. When he has exhausted those trails, he signs up for a membership at Virtual Fitness and completes their endurance mountain runs in virtual reality rooms. He makes entries on his Contour Sheet about life being too short not to do what you love. A few of his entries include cheesy quotes about the beauty and peace of the outdoors.

To his friends, Asa is undergoing a spiritual transformation. He has even lost ten pounds by hiking and rock climbing at some of the fitness centers. His new buddies at the Colony Outdoors Club embrace him as one of their own. His VL score goes up fifty points during his "awakening," as he calls it. With the help of his new community of "nature freaks," he is able to determine and acquire the best gear—compasses, boots, ropes for rock climbing, first aid gear, and fire-starters. No one suspects that Asa is acquiring and trying out new gear for dead fugitives.

Two months before the Catastrophe Challenge, Asa announces on his Contour Sheet that he will be enrolling as a contestant, a goal he has always had. Colonists compete in replicated natural disasters—earthquakes, floods, and fires—and are granted VL points for their successes. His Contour Sheet boasts that his medical training will put him ahead of the competition in case of injury. When Grayson suggests that Asa actually might be enjoying himself, Asa rolls his eyes. "Those suckers," he says gruffly.

Asa's girlfriend is more in love than ever. The supervising doctors at work have finally started praising his clinical work, as though his outside interests have somehow changed him into a more competent physician. He is invited for dinners out with colleagues for the first time. The women in his department flirt with him over charts. Asa is annoyed with it all. Tired. And spending a fortune.

It takes a couple of months for him to acquire the supplies, but once he does the problem becomes transferring them.

"We'll leave them in a neutral location," Gray reasoned in front of a busy restaurant in the Pulse. "I'll pick them up and bring them back."

"I have two full packs. I can't just drop them at a coffee shop or walk in with them to a theater. I'll take them to you," Asa said in his usual calm tone.

"And then what?" Gray asked. "You take them to us, and if no one is suspicious of that, you suddenly quit on your new outdoors obsession?"

Asa kicked the ground.

"The nature freak community will wonder about that," Gray continued.

"What if I get an injury and am out of the competition?" Asa suggested.

"You still can't come sauntering up to my house to drop them off."

Gray recounts their conversation casually and insists confidently that they'll come up with a better plan. I have my doubts.

"I'll steal the packs," I tell Gray over dinner tonight. He taps his fork on his plate nervously.

"No," he says. "I mean yes, I think we'll have to steal them. But no, you're not doing it."

"Yeah, I'm stealing them because I don't exist anymore. I can't be traced. You can."

My fingerprints and DNA have been erased from the national registry by now. I literally can't leave any evidence that leads anyone back to a real person. One drop of Gray's sweat, and authorities will knock on our door within minutes.

It takes two days for Gray to agree. In the end, Asa convinces him it's the safest way. They create a plan to leave the supplies unlocked in his car trunk. Asa talks to all of his friends about planning a three-day camping trip for some hard-core training with his girlfriend. He bought her a new pair of hiking shoes (in my size) and has them wrapped in the trunk next to their fully stocked packs. He also purchased a dehydrator along with the new shoes and leaves it in the box next to the pack. In all, I will have to carry almost sixty pounds of equipment—two packs out of the Pulse for less than a hundred yards, unnoticed, onto the Convoy and back to our house. More than anything, it will take luck that no one thinks it suspicious that a girl is walking alone at night with two major packs, a box of shoes, and a food dehydrator. Grayson is skeptical, but I assure him that the best way to get past the Pulse is to pass right under their noses.

I need to change my appearance just in case I do run into anyone who might recognize me. My hair reaches below my shoulder blades.

"I'm sorry to do this, Rebecca," Gray says.

"No, I'm ready." Not really.

I take a deep breath as Grayson cuts off at least ten inches to shoulder length. It falls to the ground in thick, dark clumps. Traces of different colors that Dylan put in can still be found when the light hits it. Gray gently pulls my hair back, his fingers sweeping my cheek.

It isn't pretty. My hair is choppy and uneven. It looks even darker than usual without its lighter ends. Radius would have laughed at me in the condescending way he did when he didn't like the outfit I had picked out for a client. "Really?" he'd say, looking me up and down. "This one covers up that belly better. Try this one." And then he'd throw me a low-cut dress with a more cinched waistline. I look down at the clumps of my old life that I had just shed, lying on the floor all around me.

Immediately I start to tear up with shame. I take the scissors from Grayson and try to fix what he has left uneven, but it's no use. I look ridiculous. My scars from the Luminstones are unsightly. I look like I have felt for so long, and it feels like a freely bleeding wound. I brush the hair away from my pale face and tie it back with a band. Gray looks at me in the mirror from behind. "It's not good," I said. "I know—"

"You are so brave." He puts a hand on my shoulder. "You look so brave."

I smile at him weakly and hug him tight. Radius had thrived on keeping me in constant shame. But my shame cannot stand under Gray's gentle gaze.

"Thank you," I tell him.

At 11:00 p.m., Gray walks me down the path that my mother had taken every day through the woods to Cherish. I jump at every rustle and night call in the woods. "Relax, Rebecca," Gray says. "Better get used to this."

The woods are transformed under the blanched glow of the moon. It's nothing like the electric hum of the Pulse.

When we reach the neighborhood that the path empties into, I turn to face Gray. "Don't worry," I say. "I'm going to be so careful and—" Gray grabs me and kisses my forehead.

I walk to the Convoy by myself, knowing that Gray will not move from his post in the woods until I return. The street is completely dead with the exception of a few outside lights that have been left on. I don't have a plan if someone stops me to ask questions—run, I guess. And truly the Ancillary will be the most dangerous place of the night. Ancillaries know their own; outsiders are quickly recognized. I will become invisible in the bustle of the Pulse—unless someone I know happens to recognize me.

I'm alone on the Convoy. Not riding to school this time, Rebecca, I tell myself. Just a quick burglary of camping gear so I can survive in the woods for a few months to find some renegade colony-outsiders. You know, so I can escape from my own colony and die before they realize that I'm not actually dead. No big deal. I throw my head back to laugh at the ridiculousness of this all, and that's when I notice it.

They added cameras. I put my head back down slowly and lean it against the window. No, no, no! I scream inside my head. My heart quickens as I try to reason through this. Those are new. They have to be. Ok, be calm, I command myself. There's no reason for them to review the videos unless they're suspicious of something. But of course they'll be suspicious of something if there's a reported burglary. Can't come back this way on the Convoy. I'll have to walk.

I start to sweat thinking about how far that will be. At least ten miles back once I get there. With two packs. And I'll need to get back before the sun is up, which gives me less than six hours to go in, steal the gear, and walk ten miles. I get off at the next Convoy station, which lands me still more than four miles away from the hospital. But it's worth it not to get off too close to the hospital station, which would be suspicious. And of course there's no way to tell Gray I'll be delayed. I bite my lip hard. He'll be panicked, but there's nothing I can do.

I step off the Convoy near the industrial section. The factories are closed, but a few people still mill about in the parking lot. I pick up my pace but am careful not to walk with my small-stepped, feminine jaunt. I elongate my steps, slump my shoulders, and put my hands in my pockets. I stop breathing as a couple passes my way on the street. They don't appear to even see me. Perhaps I'm a ghost after all. Grayson will be expecting me back in less than twenty minutes. I imagine him watching the minutes creep by as he waits in the woods.

How many times did I walk down this street when I was living in the Pulse? A hundred? I met a few clients in the lounge across the street from the hospital. I keep my gaze in front of me because if I even look at the building I'll lose my nerve. There is no room for panic.

I take a deep breath and talk to myself out loud: "Almost there. Almost there."

Music blares from cars as they pass. It is strange to think of Radius in his apartment with my replacement only a few blocks from here. A wave of nausea sweeps over me. I pick up my pace. The energy of the Pulse has become a mellow sibilation. Maybe it's always been that way, or maybe my own energy has changed. We are out of sync now.

I walk around the edge of the parking lot of the hospital as Asa had instructed so that I will be out of sight of the hospital security cameras. An ambulance screams past me, and I startle. There it is: the red sign that Asa said was where I was to come through the fence.

I look up into the light. The camera is turned down, but Asa has assured me that this camera blew in the winter and hasn't been replaced yet. He made friends with a security officer named Philo who took so much pride in his job that he was more than willing to give the grand tour to anyone who showed even the slightest interest. Security has falsely believed that the mere presence of the camera would be enough to dissuade anyone with intentions of wrongdoing. And on Philo's watch, the hospital can brag incredibly low rates of auto theft. Embezzlement, stolen drugs, and medical supplies going missing internally are a different matter, though.

I count ten cars down to where Asa was supposed to park. Nine, ten. An empty space? I stare at the space and frantically search for the car. Nothing. I turn around slowly to walk back to the fence, my body beginning to feel feverish with anxiety. Maybe I came in through the wrong opening. No, it couldn't have been. Asa's instructions were so clear. Am I on the wrong wing? If I am, then that camera is the wrong camera, and Philo and his buddies could be watching me over their coffee.

He just couldn't find a spot, I tell myself. He was forced to park close, but elsewhere. However, the deck is fairly empty on this side. That couldn't be the case. Maybe something has happened to Asa or he figured out that the camera was actually working, and he bailed.

Maybe I should go back. I consider trying it a different night, getting a better plan where I won't be carrying both packs for more than ten miles. At this moment I know Grayson is pacing back and forth in the woods considering his options in coming to get me or not. I decide to play it safe and go back the way I came.

I walk to the fence and kick it hard. Before I enter through the small opening again, I look both ways. And that's when I see it. Ten *rows* down, not cars down, there in the corner is Asa's old silver car. Thank goodness. I freeze when a metal door opening to the stairs creaks.

An older couple enters the parking deck and looks around. I kneel between the fence and a red car and pray this isn't the one they are coming to. "It's the other side," the woman says irritably. The man grunts something and the door slams shut. Quickly, I walk bent over and pause occasionally at parked cars to listen for anyone else coming. But it is silent.

Finally I reach Asa's car, which is covered in mud. That, too, was probably intentional. He'll have an excuse to hose it down after I steal from it. It will rinse off any trace that I've been there, in the off chance that they have kept any records of me. He'll have no reason to report the theft until two days from now when he is supposed to go camping, and he can claim that he just kept his gear in his trunk.

I stand to open the trunk and close my eyes as I feel the handle. "Please be unlocked," I whisper. I remember to breathe again as it pops open. There are both packs and a wrapped box that must be the shoes that he was to pretend were a gift for his girlfriend. I rip them open and leave the paper in the trunk. I take off my own shoes and put them in the pack while slipping on the new ones. If I'm going to walk ten miles, I might as well do so comfortably. They fit perfectly. Lastly, I slip the dehydrator in one of the packs.

I sit on the edge of the trunk and lean back to fit the straps of the heavier pack on my back. I grunt as I stand. There's no way I can get these both back. I pull the black trash bag from my pocket and put the lighter pack in it. Asa and Gray insisted that two packs would draw attention. But I might pass as one of the many people who live on the streets if I carry one in a trash bag. That means that one of my hands will be carrying at least thirty pounds. I close the trunk quickly and carry the pack with my right hand. It hits my leg awkwardly. I'll only have to carry it out of the Pulse, I reason—only four or five miles. Then I can balance the weight by carrying it on my front when there will be fewer people around.

I close the trunk slowly and look around to make certain that no one is watching. I walk resolutely to the opening in the fence and squeeze out. My heart beats faster as I walk down the sidewalk. Already I have to shift the second bag from my right hand to my left. The burn in my arm helps me focus. A few cars pass, but in spite of my strangeness in carrying such a large load, no one even so much as slows down for a second look.

I hurry across the street and make my way down a series of alleys without looking back. After about a mile I am successfully out of the busiest section of the Pulse. Someone has to have seen me, though. I pass between two long rows of apartment buildings. Several of the lights are on. Music is playing loudly, no matter that it is a Wednesday in the middle of the night. I know this section of the Pulse well. In fact, I have been to a few of the apartments on "errands" for Radius. It is full of some of the white-collar sort who were my clients—a few hospital employees, a banker with a lazy eye, and a colony tech specialist with two grown children.

The panic rises, and so I focus on the pain that pierces my lower back. I fight between screaming and crying maniacally. Just one step after another, I tell myself over and over. A figure moves in front of a window. In spite of how suspicious I look, she won't call the police. In an apartment complex this large she'll expect someone else to call. And the person who sees me in the apartment across from hers will see her light and expect *her* to do the calling. I am safest in the middle of everyone. I could be lying here bleeding and screaming, and they'd still be waiting on the other to make the first move.

I know I'm right. Things got rough with a client who refused to pay, and I did lie here. I waited for almost forty-five minutes for one of the people behind the many lights that came on when they heard my yells to come down to help me. I didn't want the cops to come, but I was in so much pain that I didn't care after a few minutes—I just wanted that sick man to stop beating me. I would have never told the cops anything about Radius anyway. But nothing. Not one person helped me. I was left waiting while the onlookers and gawkers waited stupidly for one another to act.

I keep my head up and walk as fast as I can until I get into the shadows of a parking lot. Already my arms are burning, and the skin of my left hand is getting a blister. I readjust the pack on my back and make my way to a road that leads to the Ancillary. It isn't the fastest route back home, but it is the safest. Radius is only a block from here. I would do anything for a patch right about now— I could float home instead. The cops could pick me up. They could exile me and, with the right patch, I wouldn't care. "Keep going," I say aloud through gritted teeth.

210

I half expect to see Grayson running up to me any moment. Of course that's crazy. He would never find me out here in the shadows between buildings. Grayson doesn't know the Pulse like I do. It had become my prison, and I know the labyrinth of its streets well. What's worse, I know that Gray will be worried that I have run into someone who knows me and that I could be with Radius right now.

I would be lying to say that I don't want that even now—to be lifted up in his light, to forget that it is only his darkness that gleams. Even still, I want Radius to see me for who I am—brave and daring tonight, beautiful in my own way as Gray sees me. I want him to cry and beg at my feet. I want his heart to break for all that he did to me. And I want the new girls to mean nothing to him.

But the new girls are nothing to him, like I was nothing to him. Still, the need to be with him is strong, and it slithers inside me like a snake. I hope it will die before I do. I don't want to live with that piece, that remnant of Radius, still living in me, pushing out all the good that used to be there. It has settled into my spirit, and I don't know how to push it out before it destroys me.

I can feel the intensity of the Pulse at my back as I take the deserted road to the Ancillary. I drop to my knees once I am released from the Pulse, like I have been carried and tossed out by one of its throbbing energy waves. I take the pack out of the trash bag and put it on my front. I'm relieved not to be bearing its weight on my bleeding and throbbing hands, but my back is screaming in pain. My mouth is so dry. I would do anything for some water, but of course Asa hadn't thought to leave any there. This whole operation was only supposed to have taken an hour and a half. One small oversight with the Convoy cameras and the whole night is botched. How exactly are we going to spend weeks in the Membrane again?

I force myself to stand up and keep walking. Faster, I tell myself. The sun will be up in only three hours or so and I still have at least six miles. I can't take the road that leads directly to where Gray waits. It will be safer to go a neighborhood over and circumvent it by taking the woods all the way, just in case there is any suspicion from the video. The road is not well lit, and I stumble several times. Twice I fall outright and skin both hands and bruise my knees.

After about a mile or so I make it to the agriculture section. The moon illuminates outlines of cows sleeping in the field. "Hey," I yell to one of them close to the fence. "Happen to have any water?" My thirst is becoming unbearable. I start to feel a little unstable on my feet and drop down to my knees again.

The road in front of me begins to illuminate. "No!" Immediately I push myself up, throw off the front pack and hurl it over the fence. I leap over after it and lay flat on the ground just as a car quickly makes its way around a bend in the road. I wait for it to slow down, but it only picks up speed on the straightaway. A couple of nearby cows wake and trot closer to their herd. Who would be going to the Ancillary at this time of night? Another hawker picking up a girl? I cringe at the thought.

It's best to continue walking on the inside of the fence in case another car drives by. I continue there as long as I can, but the tall grass slows me down. Then I jump more fences and walk through a series of dry cornfields, newly budding blueberry bushes, and the pen of an angry bull that I woke up. I escape moments before he charges and gasp for breath as I lay on the road.

By the time I reach a more residential section of the Ancillary I am bruised, bleeding, exhausted, dehydrated, and in tears. And I smell strongly of cow manure. As quickly as is possible with my level of exhaustion, I walk past the houses that I know will be waking soon. If I can make it to the woods I will be in the clear. Stray cats that preside over the Ancillary at night dart between houses as the sun comes up.

"Almost there," I tell myself. "One step after another. Come on, Rebecca." In order to get to the woods, I'll have to go through one of the small yards that backs up to them. I choose a house farthest from the street lamp and push into the darkness of the woods. I know if I make my way far enough into the woods I will come into a clearing with the old power lines, and I can follow the billowing land until I find where Grayson is waiting—if he is still waiting, that is.

I jump at the rustle of the nocturnal world in the thick wood as I brush spider webs out of my hair. After almost a quarter mile I reach the clearing and throw my front pack onto the ground. There's a shooting pain down my right leg from its weight, so I decide to switch by carrying it in my left hand. In the clearing the moon is bright, and I can see my path well. I risk falling to save some time by using the momentum of the downward slopes to jog a little. But the uphill climb is torture. My legs and lungs are burning. I make it up one hill and collapse midway. More than fourteen miles I have walked in all, most of the way carrying almost sixty pounds.

Suddenly a figure comes running over the hill. "Rebecca!" Grayson calls.

I raise my hand to him and burst into tears. He slides down the hill beside me and rips off my front pack. "What happened?!" he demands. "I was expecting you *four* hours ago!" he yells.

"I know. I'm sorry," I say weakly. "They put cameras on the Convoy. I couldn't take it back, so I walked."

Gray sits back on the hill. "I don't understand. *Where* did you walk?"

"I got off at the earliest Convoy station and walked to the hospital and then walked back here."

"You mean you walked the entire way carrying these?" he asks, helping me undo my backpack.

I rub my shoulders where the straps had cut into my flesh. "I got them," I say. "We're ready to go." Gray grabs my head with his hands and kisses my forehead gently. He drags the packs to the woods and covers them with some branches. "I'll get them later," he mutters. I push myself to standing and rub my back.

"Come on," he whispers, picking me up. "We're going home."

PART III

Chapter 22

It is quiet. Too quiet. Instinctively, I scan the tops of the thick trees for birds that have suddenly been silenced. A swallow calls out a metallic shriek to issue its warning. It is returned and followed by a legion of birds that have been so well hidden until that point, it appears as though the tree itself has been blown apart like dandelion seeds.

I'm being watched. I strain to hear the danger beyond the pounding in my ears. I crouch lower on the hill that I am descending. It's too open here, and I know that I'm vulnerable. My breath comes faster as I wildly scan the underbrush at the base of the hill.

My body reacts before I actually register what I perceive in the thick underbrush at the base of the hill. I stumble backwards. "Tiger!" I scream. "Gray! Tiger!" I lock eyes with the beast that begins to rise from crouching. "Gray!" I scream again, my voice scaling in panic.

The big cat is about thirty yards below me. I know my pack is too heavy for me to run back up the hill. The tiger is approaching more quickly now. I wave my stick violently. "Hey!" I call to it. "Hey! Get out of here!"

The tiger stops mid-step and growls in a low, irritated way. I take a bold step forward, standing up taller and waving the stick over my head. Suddenly a rock flies past my arm and lands only inches away from the tiger's paw.

"Rebecca! Get back!" Gray instructs. He stumbles twice as he runs down the hill to get to me. "Go away!" His voice is deep and authoritative.

I take another step forward and bend to pick up a rock, my eyes still locked on the beast.

"Take off your pack," Grayson tells me.

I fumble at the straps and let it fall to my side. "Pull out the tent. *Now*," he says calmly, tossing me his pack.

I nod vigorously. We have a plan for this. Gray takes two steps downhill as the tiger begins to pace from side to side, dodging Gray's hurled rocks and insults.

Savagely, I pull the contents from his pack onto the ground—metal cups, canteen, shirt, and packages of food—until I reach the tent that pools around my feet.

"Got it!" I turn my head sideways at the tiger that has now stopped pacing and returned to crouching, waiting for the barrage of rocks that are more of an annoyance than a threat.

Quickly, Gray and I put our walking sticks into the tent to form a loose wall. In the matter of seconds that it takes Gray to take up his stick, the tiger has already moved to standing.

"Now!" I yell.

Gray and I each hold our sticks and run at the tiger with our vinyl wall held high in the air as though we are some amorphous monster attacking. "Ahhh!" we yell in answer to the tiger's deep roar. I can see his tail flick and teeth bare when we are only about fifteen yards away.

"Go away!" I scream.

"We can't go back up the hill." Gray is remarkably composed. "If he attacks, keep going downward and to the side."

I know that if he does attack, though, there's no outrunning him. "Ahh!" I scream again. "Get out!"

The tiger returns to a crouch. We are five yards away.

"Run him over!" Gray commands.

We are upon him. I close my eyes as my legs pound on the earth. The tiger tears through the tent with a powerful swipe of his paw. I turn my stick to deliver a blow to his head, and the stick makes contact with something fleshy I cannot see. There's another growl and I brace myself. My stick has become entangled with the shredded tent, and I thrust it brutally. I strike until I can no longer find him with my stick.

"He's gone, Rebecca," Gray says, hugging me. Gray and I drop to the ground to catch our breath as the cat bounds back into the forest.

I keep my eyes on the woods, scanning for signs that he might return or that some other larger beast is willing to take us on.

"He's not coming back," Gray says between breaths. "It worked." He reaches for the shredded tent.

"That could have been us," I say, pointing to it.

Gray begins to laugh hysterically. "We just defeated a tiger!"

"No, not defeated. Scared away. He's still out there and *that*—" I say, indicating the entrance of the forest, "is the way we have to go." Gray leans back onto the incline of the hill. "We'll camp here," I say. "I'm dehydrated as it is, and I know there will be more cats in there."

There was a time when tigers were a thing of exotic lands and our country kept them in cages. Large cats were the silent mouthpiece for their kind, pacing majestically behind steel bars, proclaiming to the onlookers, who marveled at their savage beauty and destructive prowess, that their kind should be preserved. Conservation programs were created, but the dwindling populations of tigers, lions, cougars, cheetahs, and jaguars, represented by caged advocates, had mostly been wiped out during the catastrophes.

In a strange twist of irony, it was the caged cats that escaped from the largest conservation effort in North America. They bred more quickly once out of captivity, and a small and terrible band now claims this territory. The great-grandparents of these cats were possibly the same caged creatures that my great-grandparents had taunted to make move as they licked their lollipops from the safe side of the steel bars. Now I am their prey.

According to the last safe house, crossbreeds exist and some swear to have seen them—big cats with the body of a lion but with striped fur like a tiger. I prefer to avoid anything with teeth of that size, no matter the stripes, mane, or spots.

It is at least a fifteen-mile hike back to the last safe house—after weeks of hiking, a twenty-mile hike is a day's work for us. But today we had planned on making an entire twenty-two to get to the other side of this thicket before camping.

"I just can't do it," I tell Grayson. "It's hotter than I thought it would be. I can't hike another seven miles and defend against another one of those beasts in this heat."

Grayson puts his hand above his eyes to block the unforgiving sun and look between his fingers. "I'd guess about three o'clock," he says.

"Me too. At the latest."

"I know it's early to camp, but let's get some water and rest to make up the time tomorrow."

Gray and I slip rhythmically into our routines. I collect the firewood while Gray looks for a flat place to set up what is left of our tent. "How about at the top of the hill?" he asks.

"Yes," I agree. "We'll be able to see further and anything coming toward us will be moving uphill, so we'll have the advantage."

I work quickly and quietly at the edge of the woods, always vigilant to hear the potential stirring of the underbrush that might mean another big cat has me in his sights. But the birds have returned, and all I can hear is the shush of the tall grass blowing in the wind, and the birds' improvident chattering,

I dream of turning on the water faucet in my house and filling up a large, cold glass of water. Gray and I determine that it is only a mile walk to the river we have been paralleling now for days.

"We won't be the only ones attracted to the water." Gray is rocking back on his heels nervously.

"I know. We've got to do this quickly."

After emptying both packs, we put all the food into mine—we can't leave even a scrap of food with the cats lurking around. Then we use Gray's empty bag to fill with rocks to throw just in case we happen upon another cat. By the time we finish I am exhausted. I have less than a quarter cup of water in my water bottle. We couldn't have made it very far anyway.

Gray leads the way across the rim of the hill. After about half a mile we go under some long-dead power lines that cross our path. Grayson points to the base of the power lines. "Barbed wire. Go get a big stick."

I peer over the top of the hill at the start of the forest to make sure it is clear of any predators that might have been watching from below. It takes only a few moments before I find a large club that I use to help me clamber back up the hill. Grayson has taken off his shirt to wrap around his hands as protection against the sharp, rusted wire. "If we wrap the wire around the stick, it will make a pretty gruesome weapon, don't you think?"

I nod. "Smart."

We relax a little more on the rest of the trip to the river with our new defense.

I can feel the cool of the river coming off it before we see or even hear it. By the time we reach it, my mouth is completely dry, and it takes considerable restraint not to jump in. I put the end hose of my water filter into the water and pump until my container is completely full. I fall back onto the bank to drink in greedy gulps as Gray does the same. My legs are smeared with dirt and streaked from sweat. And hairy. The travel has made us leaner, lighter for the miles ahead. And pretty disgusting.

Always I think about food—thick beef sandwiches dripping with grease that take two hands to eat, mounds of colorful, shiny fruits, and the rich cream pies my mother used to make each year for my birthday. The map also provided small shelters of food every seventy-five miles or so, but the rations of food we have between each stop are not enough to sustain, and my stomach never lets me forget that my body needs more fuel for the demands I am putting on it. Neither does Gray. For miles at a time he has narrated each step of the elaborate meals he will make for us when we make it to wherever it is we are going.

We'll sleep tonight on the hill and make our way through the big cat territory in the morning. Luckily we see no other animals on our way back from the river and allow our bodies to return to their normal heightened sense of awareness. Gray insists on taking the first watch. Together we build a roaring fire and stack enough wood beside it so that it can be fed throughout the night.

"We're lucky it didn't rain," Gray says as he unrolls his sleeping bag.

"Mmm," I grunt. "If we can keep the fire that big, no cat is going to come near us tonight." I try to sound convincing, but we were warned at the last safe house that night would pose the biggest danger. The cats hunt at night. Sometimes in packs.

It takes me almost two hours to patch our tent. I pull the thread slowly and methodically through the nylon material by the light of the fire and dab water sealant over my work. We'll have to wait until a rain to test how well I did. After patching the tent, I'll patch the bleeding blisters and sores on my feet, another ever-present pain in addition to the agony in my back.

"Here's the plan," Gray says as he stirs our rehydrated dinner of rice, beans, and potatoes—hardly enough to satisfy the ache in my stomach. "We've got around another twenty-two miles until we reach the next safe house. I was hoping we'd make it to the other side of the thicket tonight and hike just eighteen tomorrow, but that's not going to happen. The good news is that it looks like the last five miles before the next safe house are old interstate."

I screw the top back on the sealant and look at him thoughtfully. "Yeah, but it's uphill for the next—"

"Twelve," Gray interrupts. "It's uphill for the next twelve, which means we'll be going downhill for a bit, and the last five will be on a nice paved road. We can do it. I want to put as much distance between us and the cats as we can."

I bite my fingernail and look away as I take in the reality of how far we have left to go. "Plus, we're running low, Rebecca.

We've got to stock up on some more food, properly patch our tent—"

"Hey! This is as good as new," I insist.

Gray looks away and raises his eyebrows. "Yeah, it's perfect," he says.

I throw my boot at him. He pretends to fall backward when it hits him in the stomach. "What do you say?"

"I don't know." I look down at my rust colored bandages and unbind them gingerly. The re-load stations were a good break, but they lacked the security and the hospitality of a safe house, which was a luxury vacation compared to the trials of being on the trail.

"Yeah, let's do it," I agree. I'm desperate for a night in a real bed with a basin to soak my feet. I lean back and remember our stay in the last safe house.

The toothless man's wife at the last one had filled a pan with salts and fresh lavender from her garden. The small basin had turned the color of weak coffee from the miles of dirt and blood when I gingerly lowered my feet into it. The ache had slowly oozed from them, and I had lain back on the cot as tears of relief ran down my cheeks.

The woman spoke very little as she busied herself about her home that had once been a school. Desks had been replaced by cots. I imagined the hundreds of people who had stayed here during the twenty years they had been keeping the home. She heated warm blankets and pressed them against my back, lifting my legs from the water and patting my feet dry.

"We'll get yous washed in the morning," she mumbled. "Right now, you'd probably just drowns in the bath, darlin'."

Gray was put in another room where I expected he'd be receiving the same care. "Thank you," I said sincerely. "I just can't thank you enough." I whispered with my eyes closed.

"Honey, if you are deliverins," she said, lifting my leg to put a warm pillow between my aching knees, "then I'm thanking *you*."

I opened my eyes and watched her curiously. "The names, darlin'. If you are deliverins the names, then I'm to be thankings you." She looked at me suspiciously, waiting for me to confirm or deny, but I closed my eyes again and turned my head as though overcome by fatigue.

I still didn't know to whom I was supposed to be delivering the list. Gray and I had just been following the GPS points to the places indicated on the map, but we knew enough not to speak of the lists that he had converted to data chips that always hung on a chain around our necks.

"My friend has a really bad—"

"Darlin', don't even speaks it," the woman said, raising her hands in the air. "In all my days that is the *worst* poison ivy I've *ever* seen. Mmm. I'm going to sets him right. I've got some steroids that have been waitings for him, that's for sure. Mmm, mmm," she said, shaking her head.

Gray had known almost immediately that it was poison ivy. He had been sitting in it, drinking his water at the base of a tree while he waited for me to come from the tent. Asa had provided an ointment that did little to soothe the red and angry blisters that covered his face and neck and that blazed down his arms in fiery paths. By the third day his eyes began to swell. For three days he had hiked while the blisters baked in the sun. He had rushed headlong into a river to get some relief as the cool water numbed his arms and face. I could hardly look at him without cringing.

"And I've gots something to help with the sleeping," the woman said. "I doubt much he's been able to sleep with that agony on his skin. Mmm, mmm."

Our night at the Greensboro Safe House, as our hosts called it, was the best night we had had since leaving the colony. The Greensboros seemed trustworthy, but we were hesitant to disclose too much of what we knew or even which colony we were from, and they seemed to know not to ask. But the information we learned from these secluded people was more than we had learned in all our time in Colony 215.

I awoke the next morning in the safe house as though rousing after a few days following death. It took me several moments to realize that I was in a safe house. Instinctively, I kicked my leg to nudge Grayson awake before I realized that he wasn't sleeping at his usual post by the tent entrance. I was brought to my senses by the overwhelming smell of strong coffee and something yeasty baking.

I followed the aroma down a dark hallway with flickering lights that were run by an outside generator that roared in the background. I entered what had been a cafeteria where kids my age had once sat with friends of their own grouping in the microcosm of their alive and safe world—flirting with crushes at adjacent tables and bonding with members of their own sex as they pushed around the bland and overcooked food in the compartments of their plates. It was abandoned now. The tables had been pushed to the sides so that only three tables now stood near the kitchen. Grayson was already sitting down, nursing a steaming mug and talking with the man whose real name was Pepper. He smiled as I came in. "Morning, sunshine," he whistled through missing teeth. "Sleeps ok?"

"We can't thank you enough. You have no idea how exhausted we were."

"Wells, I have *somefin'* of an idea. It's clears two o'clock!"

I slumped down in the stool attached to the table next to Grayson and returned Pepper's broad smile.

"Violet's cooking you up something real nice, youngun," Pepper said.

"Smells like it." I inhaled the richness that drifted from the kitchen. I wanted to stay there forever.

Grayson looked at me softly like he hadn't seen me for weeks. "Hi," he said as he took a sip of his coffee. I looked away.

"Hi," I returned curtly.

This was the longest I had been more than thirty yards away from Grayson since we escaped, and I missed him, but he didn't need to know that. Grayson rolled his eyes at me and smiled.

"Mr. Greensboro," he said.

"Name's Pepper. This here used to be Greensboro once upons a time. S'why everyone calls me that. It's *ours* colony now," Pepper said.

"Pepper," Grayson began again. "Sir, I'm not even sure where to start. All we know is that there are these safe houses. But what I don't understand is *how* there are these safe houses. We don't even know *why*, exactly."

Pepper let out a deep laugh, the end of which whistled through his teeth. "Well then, that explains one of *my's* questions," Pepper said, leaning forward. "You twos are fugitives. You're runnings away, I 'spect. Yous two didn't look like no couriers. Too green, I'd say."

Grayson shook his head. "No sir. We are couriers."

I gave Grayson a hard look for not being more discreet, but he ignored it. Pepper nodded soberly. "But we're not exactly sure what it is that we're carrying, or who it's supposed to go to," Grayson continued boldly.

I opened my mouth to protest, but there was really nothing I could say at that point. We were desperate for information, and

Grayson seemed to trust Pepper, so I just had to trust Grayson's instinct.

"We're picking up the job, I guess you could say," I added. "We think my mother was delivering to couriers. But she was, umm . . ." my voice broke off.

"She was exiled," Grayson said gently. "We think she was working with a small group."

"The others were killed," I said with more anger than I had intended. "Plus, we had to get out."

Grayson put his hand on my arm, and I settled under his touch. "Any chance she came through here? Her name is Eleanor."

Pepper shook his head. "No, son. I'm sorry. Haven't seens her nor anyone else for quite some time. But that doesn't mean much, you see. There are other paths leading to Sayon that would be more directs."

Grayson opened his mouth to ask what he meant, but Violet returned from the kitchen with two platters of eggs and bacon, and she balanced a basket on her forearm that was filled with steaming hot biscuits. My eyes welled with tears when I saw them. Pepper returned to the kitchen for some plates as Violet studied us.

"You needs to eat all of it," she said flatly. "There's more where this came from."

"Thank you," Grayson and I said together.

We piled our plates until bacon was arching over the rim onto the table. There was no place to put the biscuit, so I ate it first.

Pepper continued to stare at us gravely. "You's from Colony 215, I'd 'spect then."

Grayson and I stopped mid-bite.

"We haven't hads a courier from there for a whiles. That's a rough one, 215." Pepper looked at his wife, who returned his staid expression.

"Who was the courier before, sir? And you mentioned Sayon?" Grayson asked.

"It was a pairs of them that has been running the route from 215 for that section. Name of Skycap, I believes. His partner came through here, though. They just hikeds together, but the other guys was from another colony. And wells, Sayon is—"

"Wait a minute," Grayson said. "William Skycap?"

Violet shook her head slowly. "Not sure about that. I don't have too many details on the couriers. They prefers it that way, of course. Often use false names. I thought 'Skycap' was justs a play on words."

"Right," I said, making a mental note to try to harness our blabbing, although our reactions had already confirmed Pepper's guess that we were from Colony 215. Grayson cast me a quick look. If it was Will, he had died this past year from a fire.

"And Sayon's where you's heading of course," Pepper said and looked at us expectantly.

We returned blank stares.

"Violet, honeys, I thinks these two have quite a bits to learn," Pepper winked.

Violet looked between Grayson and me with a furrowed brow. "Yeah, I figureds that."

Pepper and Violet explained the courier system as we ate our next three heaping plates of breakfast. It had begun shortly after our colony had been evacuated. Pepper and Violet had both escaped from their New Colonies after their Old Colony here—512—had been evacuated due to sinkholes and earthquakes.

"Used to be a fifteen-story insurance building near about a block over thats way." Violet motioned behind her. "My sister workeds there. Gots eaten up by the ground. Within forty-eight hours we were evacuateds to two different colonies. We's knew we would be," Violet said. "We were too young. Had justs gotten married. I was only twenty-three at the time. This one was twenty-five. Younguns. But you two looks like you're evens younger. Might be the youngest couriers I've ever seen."

Pepper scratched his head. "Things were different back then, so's we heard. We were some of the very first to assimilate. There weren'ts no Decontamination phase, or what have you."

"Although Decontamination probably came about as a direct result of this here colony spreading some *stuff* to the others." Violet laughed and slapped her knee.

"We were ready fors it. Had a plan," Pepper said. "Of course we knew the assimilation process as part of the mandated emergency training. They had been quoting that to us for years. Women and children would be going first. So's when we got married, I got her a gift so we would nevers be separated."

I looked at Grayson. "What was it?" I asked, wide-eyed, assuming he had invented some sort of radio device that could outsmart the metal detectors and the anti-radio buffering system.

Pepper smiled so broadly that I could see he actually had more teeth in the back than I would have assumed.

"Pigeons."

I turned my head to the side.

Grayson slapped the table. "Genius," Gray said.

Pepper rubbed his hands together and winked at Grayson. "Right, son. Homing pigeons. Trained thems for months. Chose my best one."

"Gabriella," Violet interrupted. "Packed her in the one bag I was allowed in a small basket—"

"With a little something I picked up from a vet friend to sedates Gabriella—"

"—and once I got back to the colony I had assimilated to, I just wrotes the name of the New Colony, the directions I was traveling, and how long it took me to gets there. And two words: *south wall.*"

"Gabriella arrived in a records nineteen hours, giving me four hours before my name was called. So much coulds have gone awry, buts it didn't. It was perfect."

"Was a miracle," Violet nodded. "Likes it was meant. I waited for near two years for Pepper to come get me."

Grayson's eyes got bigger.

"Well, it weren't easy," Pepper said. "I knews the direction she had traveled from our Old Colony and the times it took her. Had to do calculations from the directions and times it took me to get to my new colony and pretty much had to makes some guesses on the speed of the aircraft. I had it narrowed down to about a one-hundred-mile general area of where she mights be."

Grayson rolled up on his elbows to lean in.

"And thens of course there was breakings myself out," he said as almost an after-thought.

"How did you do that?" Grayson asked, intrigued.

"They had puts me in the agriculture business of my New Colony. I could have run circles around them New Colony know-nothings. But they didn't want my help since I weren't no citizen. My job was the picking-machine operator—picked tomatoes, apples, cabbage, blueberries, you names it—and then *spray man,*" he said, as though that explained everything.

"Spray man?" I asked.

Pepper put another roll on my plate. "No ones wanted to be the one up in the plane that sprayeds the chemicals on the crops to keeps them bugs off. We hadn't used a system likes that before in the farm I grew up on. But the New Colony was bigger, and they needed more crops—no times for things like crops rotations or going out theres and netting them. No, just spray 'ems," Pepper rolled his eyes. "Seems that the last feller who had been on sprayer duty had suffered such bad asthmas or sickness or somethins that they loaned me the job. Wasn't given moren' I'd say six lessons befores they let me take it up by myself, the dummies. Weren'ts too hard as long as you were just flyings low—push the button just at the rights time and release the spray. Wells, I just kept flying in the direction of my Violet." Pepper looked at his wife, who was smiling smugly.

"I knew he'd get to me. I nevers gave up. He's a stubborn one," she said, taking his hand.

Grayson looked dreamily at our hosts. We had waited for years for our families to return to us. A million times we had concocted ways for them to escape and find us—maybe Grayson's dad had stolen a ballooner and had been searching for years; perhaps my dad had orchestrated a colony coup to bring down the whole system and reunite us all again. In our imaginations they had stolen cars, stolen boats, or just simply followed their heartbeats to the children they loved. Until now, with Pepper and Violet, I had never heard of anyone who had actually found each other. And to look at them, they were also the two least likely. It gave me hope.

"So, I found a bigs lake after about—ohs, I don't know—maybe a hundred miles. Flews low, jumped into the lake, and let the plane burns itself up and half the woods too, if it weren't for them boys from a neighboring colony who puts it out. I watched them from the woods. But me, I gots out with a broken arm and my freedom."

"But how did you find the lake? You must have known it was there," I burst in.

"No, little missy. I didn't. I *hopeds* it would be there and *expecteds* it to be. I knew it was my chance. I'm tellings you. It was meant. All of its was meant. I could feels it in my bones. I just had to keep my eyes open and expects it. I was *expectin'* either a lake, or a giant pillow for me to lands on."

I looked at the old man incredulously. His fate—all the couriers' fate in having a safe house here—hinged on a homesick bird and a well-placed lake.

"He didn't have a things with him, neither," Violet said.

"Exceptin' a compass. I *always* carried a compass with me." Pepper opened his eyes wide as though giving us some wisdom. "I knew I needed to continue exactly two degrees below southeast. Carried that compass with me everywhere, sometimes just to face in the direction of Violet, but always expectins to be given the opportunity to gets out and then I'ds need it for sure. Always I was expectins."

Grayson took a long drink of his coffee. "Sir, we spent weeks trying to get the gear we would need to make it even this far. And weeks dehydrating meals and getting our bodies in shape, and we had a *map*, sir, that we loaded into a *GPS*. Still, we feel like it took just about everything we had to get even this far. There have been a few times I thought we might not make it. I can't even imagine how you were able to get to Violet with nothing but a compass."

Pepper leaned back in his chair and looked at Grayson with a steady, unremitting gaze. "Son, I said I had a compass and the *expectation*. Seems to me that you aren't fully equipped."

I thought of my mother and the letters she had written to my father. "You sound like my mother," I told him.

Violet let out a soft laugh and pushed herself to standing from the table. "I'm making more," she said, taking our plates.

Grayson cleared his throat. "But *how* did you do it, sir? You didn't have a water bottle. You didn't even have a single match."

Pepper shook his head. "Well, you ares right about that. Sure enough. Sure enough. I made use of what I *dids* have. Collecteds dew by wrapping my shirt around my legs and walking throughs morning grass. Just when I thought my mouth was so dry I couldn't stand it anymores, the sky would open up. I'd collect it in what the woods provided—big leaves, bark—or I'd find a stream and risk it. Got sick as a dog a few times from river water, but I mades it. Weren't much to eat—that is true. But, I mades it. Knew what to eats from the bushes and the berries. Coupla times I ates some birds eggs just raws. Had just enoughs to make it to wheres I needed to be."

"You walked right up to her colony?" I asked.

"No, no, no. Uh-uh. Tooks me a solid month. I counted my steps." Pepper turned to me and raised his eyebrows. "Kepts going with the compass, dids my best with calculations, but I reckons I was off by about fifty miles or so. The most beautiful sight I evers did see was the colony dumping ground. Colony drones were dropping things into a sinkhole. Bea-u-ti-ful. I could smells it before I even got there." Pepper slapped his knee. "Then it was simples. Follow the drones."

Grayson shook his head and ran his fingers through his hair. "That's unbelievable."

Pepper shrugged his shoulders. "Took me another week to gets into the colony. Was locked down *tights*. And I was getting weaks. After all that time, it was like a final mountain to climb. From a distance I could sees the main gate at the north wall. It was concrete like the rest of the wall and no ways it would open unless of an emergency. With the drones there was no reason for anyones to be going out. I was so close. I knew my Violet was rights over there. I wanted the earth to shake so violently that they came crashing to the ground. I knew if the walls came down Violet would be standing right there in the dusts with her arms out waitings for me."

Violet came back in carrying another plate of hot biscuits. In spite of how much we had just eaten, Grayson and I both reached for another one.

"So, how did you get in?" Grayson asked.

"I didn'ts," Pepper smiled.

"*I* gots *out*," Violet said.

"But—how did you know he was there?" I asked with my mouth hanging open mid-bite.

"I knews there weren'ts no getting over that wall. That occurreds to me first thing when we cames here. That woulds be the sticking point. I wrote *south wall* on Gabriella's message so he'd know where to be meetins me. Every night at midnights I'd get out of my dormitory that they kept us agriculture workers in, and I'd go to the southernmost parts of the colony, which was a good three miles from where I lived. Rain, snow, it didn'ts matter. I knews I'd have to be there at midnights. Pepper and I had memorized more than a dozen birdcalls. I'd climb as high as I could and sing my heart out."

"My sweets nightingale," Pepper smiled and made the shrill, undulating whistle of the bird.

Violet licked her lips and returned the call and laughed. "When after two years I heards him whistle back, my heart just abouts jumped out of my chest. I knews it was him by the first note."

"So, how dids—er, did you get out?" I asked.

"I didn'ts that night. There weren't no ways out over that wall. Weren't no ways. I'd been thinkings on it for weeks. As soon as I was gone I knew they'd do their best to track me. That had happened to another girl who was transferred just a few years

230

back. Didn't happens much, but when it did, they'd bring yous back quicker than you could blinks your eye." Violet shook her head. "It was miracles enough that Pepper gots out, but I always knews he would. The bests I could do was to throw over some foods and water, blankets, things he'd need—tied them in bundles and tossed thems over with all my might. Drove me crazy that he was just on the others side of that cement wall—alones, hurts, colds. Drove me *crazy.*"

Pepper patted Violet's bony hands, covered in thick veins like vines overtaking the surfaced roots of a tree. "We tooks the risk of her bringing me over," Pepper said, pumping his eyebrows up and down. "Violet stoles a rope and I scurried on over likes a spider."

"I thoughts I would be overjoyed to see him, and I was—part of me was—but he was so changed. Skinny, blistered, covered in rashes and cuts. He was so skinny, mmm," Violet said shaking her head. "Of course he was smilings like that in spite of how bangeds up he looked," she said, thrusting her thumb at Pepper, whose eyes were sparkling above a wide smile like a gaping sinkhole. Violet threw her head back in a low laugh. "We were goings home!"

"But how—how did you get out without them knowing?" Grayson asked.

"Only one way to gets out unless you're exiled, which would have meant Pepper would have had to traipse another few hundred miles to gets me back." Violet looked hard at Grayson. "How did *you* die?" she asked him.

Grayson smiled. "Drowned."

I smiled too, thinking how we had stood on the edge of the river of our old kingdom to make our escape. As children, we had sent small gifts of blossoms and leaf boats down the river to reach those from whom we had been separated after the assimilation. It was finally our turn to be carried away. We wore life vests and floated our packs on small inflatable boats that my mother had brought home from Cherish for me and Grayson to use in the Ancillary swimming pool. We had watched the river carefully and knew when it was at its lowest.

Grayson left a note explaining his macabre reasons for choosing to release himself in the river to end his grieving for me. The sun beat down upon us as we drifted effortlessly in the cool water that flowed under the cement wall. It surprised me that the same sun beat down upon us on the other side of the colony. We had entered a new world altogether that was verdant and unrestrained. It was dangerous, yes, but it seemed we were awakening from a death that we had been unaware of before. We had climbed to the edge of the river and stood in what seemed an endless garden. We were free.

Violet nodded her head. "The only ways to get out is to die. I threw that rope across the cement wall and climbeds on over. Spent a beautiful night in the arms of my Pepper up under a nice littles fort he had made for me out of flowers and fallen limbs. Ohs, it was lovely. Exceptin' for the poison ivy, it was lovely. Made us a bed right out of it. I'm dreadful allergic to it. Course that was on purpose, you sees. I knows poison ivy when I sees it two hundred yards away."

Pepper shook his head. "Hated doin' it to her, but we neededs a distraction."

"Then we scratched me up real goods, ate some berries that made me sicks as a dog, and I dragged my mess of a self outs in front of that big, ugly gate and screamed to be let back in. Those dummies hadn't even figured out I was gone. No one had even gone looking for me."

"You went back in?" I asked incredulously.

"Yeahs, I had to have a fatal disease first, see?"

"Right," I said, though not understanding.

"Well, they finally opened the gate. I tolds them I had lost my mind wanting my husband and had decided to go looking for him, but decided that there was no ways I was evers living out in the woods again like some sort of animal. I was sicks, I said. Sicks, sicks at my stomach. I wouldn't never be trying that again, mercy."

"Damn fools were so embarrassed that they hadn't caught her escaping, they let her go back to her bunk and sleep it off," Pepper laughed.

"The police chief gave me a talkings to, offered some medical care," Violet said. "'What's for?' I asked. 'Just spents me the night under the stars listening to them crickets, fell into a brambles and ate some sour berries. I'm fines now,' I says. 'Just glads to be home.' They all fells for it. Three days later I was covered in a rash from heads to foot of the worst-looking awful poison ivys you ever did see. They figured I'd learned my lesson. About a week later was when the hydrophobias started."

"Huh?" Grayson asked.

"Rabies, son. Rabies." Violet said slowly. "I showed up at my dorm one nights with my skin as on fires as you could ever imagine.

Nice little fever thanks to some infected poison ivy that I'd acquireds from rubbing some cow dung on it. Tolds that citizen boss I just neededs some extra rest—snapped at him real good to leave me alones—I was just fine. The next morning they saw me fighting with one of our milking cows. I had clawed her and was gnawing on her neck when they found me."

"I knews it would work," Pepper said. "She is so dramatics. Only she could have pulleds it off."

"Oh, I gaves them a show." Violet slapped her knee. "Acteds all kinds of crazy. They were scared to death. I was so remorseful for that cow. They put her downs, of course, and had to burn her. Mmm, mmm. I did feels bad for her and was so appreciatives of her sacrifice."

Grayson and I looked at each other with our eyes wide. Grayson shrugged his shoulders and stifled a laugh.

"Weren't nothings could be done about it," Violet continued seriously. "The citizen hospital man kepts asking about holding me downs to see if there was a bite. 'We never saws the bite,' the citizen boss kept saying. 'Must have been when she escaped, the damn fool.' But of course they didn'ts see a bite. I came back covereds in scratches and then a few days later I was covereds in a rash, gets it? All that was a distractions. 'I seen it,' my girlfriend says. 'I seen that bite. She tolds me all about the raccoon.' Wells, I stareds at that girl likes she had lost her minds. I was so gratefuls for her generous imaginations or whatever it were. That was the finals touch on the masterpiece. They weren't going to shoots me, I knew. Just captures me—boy, did I enjoy that fight. Those fellers never looked so scared. Tossed me rights on out the front gate, easy as that. I ran like a madwoman into the woods and straight into the arms of my Pepper."

Grayson and I were in awe. They had made it against all odds and survived. It gave us hope. "We made it back here. *Our* colony. Course it was in shambles. The school was lefts standing, and there was a piece of the land that was parts of our farm. It weren't much. Most of the colony had been destroyed. But it was enough. We had enough seeds and even some stray livestock froms the neighboring farms to make us our own little homestead," Pepper said. "All that didn'ts come together for no reason. We knews we needed to make this a safe haven for anyone who was chosen to escape."

"Chosen?" I asked.

"Sures enough," Violet said. "Weren't a coincidence."

"It was about a year before we hads another passer-through," Violet said. "Young exiled man. Looked awfuls. Was making his way down to the Southern Colony—Sayon. *That's* where your freedom is. *That's* where the couriers are headed."

I tried to look casual. "What do you mean, exactly?"

"Listen, honeys," Violet said. "We both knows you gots no clue what you're doing. You stumbled upon some higher order stuff and you're flyings by the seat of your pants. Yous are about as clueless as they come." I opened my mouth to protest or to at least sound mysterious like we did know, but just didn't want to reveal too much.

"Right," Grayson said. "Anything you could tell us would be helpful." I wanted to slap the back of his head. Instead I rolled my eyes. It was too late now.

"Baby, you is carrying the names of those who are going to be eliminateds and the ones that are doing the eliminations," Pepper whispered.

Grayson and I sat stunned at his plain answer.

"What do you mean 'elimination'?" I asked.

"I means that the powers-that-be have been gettings peoples in place for years so as to do weeding." Pepper nodded solemnly. "When the country started fallings to pieces, if you will, there were some other countries that were scramblings to get what they needed to survive—*us*."

"I don't understand," I said.

"Wells," Pepper began, "At first colonies were put in place as a way to self-protect. We neededs to get where we were on safe land. Our population dwindleds. It was chaos. Colonies were a way of preserving our genes."

"It was desperate, really," Violet interrupted. "Puts us in these little cells that contained all the genetic information neededs for a healthy population. If we had people movings between colonies at their own will—well, for one, we would have peoples fighting over who went where. We couldn't controls the size of the colonies. And those colonies were making just enoughs resources for us to survive. A colony that was too big wouldn't be able to sustains itself. And twos, we'd have a skewed genetic diversities."

I had heard all this before. "The scientists came up with that," I offered. "It's been used for hundreds of years in zoos. Nearly extinct animals were classified based on their genetic makeup. Only certain animals were put in certain zoos based on the genes they needed. Then if they needed breeding they would have access to those genes—they could breed them and voila, the species population was preserved."

"That was the idea behinds it," Violet said. "But we also knew that a divided country would makes for a terribly weaks country, unless of course the zookeeper had some massive weapon to keep them safe."

"Which we did." Pepper interrupted. "We had a giants and powerfuls military that was supposed to protect us. Anyone came ins and tried to takes us over—*Bam!*" Pepper clapped his hands together. "Shots down."

"Weren't two things that the zookeepers were countings on, though," Violet said.

Grayson raised his eyebrows.

Violet lifted her twig finger covered in vines. "Greed." She leaned closer to Gray. "And we could still be taken overs." She raised her second finger. "Infiltrateds."

Gray leaned forward, not blinking. "Infiltrated? You mean—"

Pepper met Grayson's steady gaze. "We means *infiltrateds*, son. It weren't no all-of-a-sudden attack."

"Not the kind of wars they feared," Violet interrupted, tapping her finger on the table.

"*Not* a war." Pepper whispered.

"Not a war. They were readys for that. Colonies were infiltradeds from the *inside*. Other countries were laying their own rights in the middle of our colonies."

Grayson and I looked at each other. "But how could that be?" I asked.

"That's wheres the greed comes in." Violet's eyes became big and knowing.

Grayson ran his fingers through his hair nervously. "These plants were allowed in because they paid their way."

"You gots it," Pepper said. "Top peoples sold them space. Outsiders boughts their way in."

I drew circles on the table with my finger. "Ok, but that doesn't mean they're taking over," I reasoned. "I know that some of the other countries were running out of resources. Our teachers told us that. After the catastrophes other countries came up with their new systems for survival. European countries salvaged what they had and created coalitions. In some places it created a lot of peace. They had to work together to survive."

"That's true. Very true, honeys," Violet said. "But that is not the wholes of it. Those names you's carrying," Violet pointed to Grayson's chest where he had been keeping the chip on a long silver chain under his shirt. "Those names are the directs result of being infiltradeds."

"The eliminated and the eliminators," Grayson said softly.

Pepper nodded and crossed his arms.

"You're saying that people were moving in and then eliminating people? No one is being eliminated," I said defiantly.

"No?" Pepper laughed, looking between the two of us.

"No," I said emphatically.

"Well, honeys, let me ask you a question," Violet said. "What happeneds to your mom?"

I felt a stabbing pain in my chest. I looked away as my face turned red. "That's different. It was complicated."

"Did she commits a crime?" Violet pressed.

"No," I shot back. *I* had committed the crime. It was my fault. My mother wasn't pushed out by some foreign plants. *I* had pushed her out with both hands. Grayson rubbed the small of my back, and I cleared my throat to avoid crying.

"I'm not sure we fully understand what you mean." Grayson kept his hand on my back as he spoke. "We did know people who were exiled. It wasn't talked about much. They were Ancillaries, but it wasn't a large number."

"Wells, it wouldn't be yet," Pepper said. "Not yet. Time weren'ts right. They're waitings, see? Doings it slowly. *Slowly* is the most dangerous."

"People are buying citizenship. I dares say you have their names, some of thems. But if people are moving ins, then someone's going to have to be movings out at some point. Colonies can't support them all."

"Especially with all the new assimilations," Grayson added.

"You gots it," Pepper said, swinging his gnarled fingers through the air. "It's coming to a head and the time to acts will be soon, I fears."

"Now, let's see how clever you twos are. Tell me, how are theys deciding on the eliminated?"

I realize it at once. "VL."

"Clever girl," Violet said soberly.

"But there were some that were data minings the system," Pepper said, looking at us expectantly as though we'd know exactly what he was talking about. We both give him an apologetic look.

Violet clucked her tongue at her husband and shook her head. "They were collecting datas on you, right? Everything—blood type, genetic makeup, works ethic, skill set, perseverance, brains hemisphere dominance, even the plants' personal preferences for you. Gots it all in one big database—*huge* database. Then they were quantifyings those datas and giving you a score. Kept all yous little duckies motivateds and in a line. That's why there haven'ts been the big elimination yet. Just getting rids of the ones that were catching on and waiting to see how the little duckies added up before they decided to get rids of them."

I allowed what Violet had said to wash over me like a cool salve on a burn. They were eliminating the ones that were interfering. My mother was interfering. Maybe Gray was right— were they looking for an excuse to get rid of her? Maybe it wouldn't have mattered what I said or did; she was already on their watch list. Mr. Porter was on the watch list too. The ache wasn't completely gone, but hope crept in where there had only been pain before.

"I don't fully understand how, though," Grayson said. "Data mining? I don't know what you mean."

"Data mining," Violet continued, her eyes wide. "Somes of the little duckies that were catching on started *analyzings* that data— they started *minings* it for patterns that fit together. Somethins weren't right. They started coming ups with these gems."

Violet smiled like a child about to open a present. "Somes of the peoples had high scores. Didn't matter what's they did. *No* matter, ok? Others of them, it stayed low with only minor, randoms variations. If you were in a colony that was low on engineer staffs, say, didn't matters your standardized scores for school. If you weren't showing the aptitudes to be an engineer, didn't matter whats you did—nothing's raising that scores, honeys. Or what's more, if yous had genes that didn't looks like what the high-level scorin' folk wanteds"—Violet shrugged her shoulders—"you gots a low score. Them high-level scorin' folks, they were the plants, see? Theys were makings the rules. Plopped themselves rights down in the middle of the colony and from the insides out they were helping design what they wanteds—who they wanteds, what roles they wanteds filled, and what they wanteds them to look like."

"They was makings their own new colonies to be likes them. That VL system weren't for no keepins people motivateds to do the best with what they had. If they didn't have it, it helped to identify them, *and*"—Violet's eyes got wide and her voice got lower—"it helped to teach them that no matter whats they did, bless their souls, they weren't nevers going to make it. Taughts people to give up. And peoples who have learned that are much easier to control. Easier to get rids of."

I thought of Cherish and the "experiments" the children underwent. My mother and Mr. Porter had done everything they could to keep those kids from learning they were helpless, and they had done so successfully.

As for me, I had eaten up the Pulse's lie. I was all in; the VL system was the rubric for measuring my life's worth. And now I know, the years of trying to make Colony 215 my home were for nothing. I was just a mouse racing in a maze with no exit and no cheese. I didn't have what they needed, so there was nowhere to go. I was disposable. And it had worked too—eventually, that is. I had learned to be helpless. I had bought the Lie, and the Lie had made me want to end it. Until Gray.

I looked at Grayson, who was studying his fingers wrapped around his mug. "They're cowbirds," he said to himself.

"What?" I asked.

"That's how their species survives. Don't you see? We never even recognized them as being any different. But they had all the power. They're taking up the resources and now they're pushing us out of the nest."

238

Chapter 23

Saying goodbye to Pepper and Violet wasn't easy. It felt good to feel safe again after living in hiding for so long and then becoming fugitives. The weeks of hyper-vigilance had worn me down, and for the first time, I really felt it. Not only that, I hadn't spoken to another soul for weeks with the exception of Asa and Grayson. I pushed Gray to let us stay there for a week, let my feet heal, eat some real food, and, for once during the journey, not have an empty belly. But he insisted it was time to move on.

Whatever Violet had put on Grayson's poison ivy rash had taken the itch and the anger out of it almost immediately. Pepper said it was some sort of concoction of his own invention and sent us with a small jar.

It became more and more evident how Pepper had survived as long as he did in the woods. The forest was also a grocery store and pharmacy. He showed us how to boil kudzu stalks and leaves for a tea that could be used for bouts of diarrhea or migraines. Violet had even made kudzu jelly from the blossoms, which we put on our biscuits that evening. Pepper pointed out the hidden medicines along the forest floor—echinacea, ginko, goldenseal, skullcap, and wild indigo. Suddenly, the woods alive with new and serviceable friends.

He drilled us on where to find the herbs and plants and which poisonous plants they could be confused with. Pepper seemed to lose patience with me as I fumbled over pronunciations and kept proudly holding up poisonous berries and blossoms I mistook for medicinal ones.

"Bless her hearts," he mumbled as he stroked his thinning whiskers.

But Grayson was a natural. Pepper slapped him on the back as he detected the most diminutive shoots, pushing forth from the thick forest floor.

"Don't lets the girl be pickings the dinner, son. Be polites, you knows, to a woman who's makings you dinner, see?"

I caught him whispering to Gray in a louder voice than was necessary due to his own slight deafness.

"They's gets all kinds of heated if you's don't say you likes their cookings," he said, shaking his head. *"Alls* sorts of troubles for you's if you say you don't likes their cookings, trust me. But in this case don't be eatings none that she selects, hear?" Pepper raised his eyebrows and nodded his head up and down quickly. Suddenly realizing that I might be within earshot, he gave me a sideways glance.

I rolled my eyes dramatically as Gray started to giggle. "I'll stick with bark," I said curtly.

"Wells now," Pepper said cheerfully, rubbing his hands together. "That woulds not be a bad idea," he trailed off. "Quick, son. Tell her a compliments."

Grayson grunted as Pepper jabbed him in the ribs with a sharp elbow. "Oh, umm," Gray cleared his throat. "You look beautiful today, Rebecca." He grabbed a small bouquet of little white flowers, which he held up delicately. I took a savage bite out of them.

But the most important information Pepper had to share was how to navigate the wild cat territory, and it had saved our lives.

The morning we were to be sent off, Violet put her hand on Grayson's shoulder and whispered, "We don'ts know much, but this here we do knows: them numbers are getting steady."

Grayson had looked at her with wide eyes.

"What it means is that the numbers aren't changing, gets it? They aren't movings the scores much no more. Decisions have been made—weedings is going to be soon, I'd say, if it hasn't happened yet in some places already."

Grayson became somber. "We'll get them there safely."

Violet smiled and patted his shoulder. "And yourselves, son." She sent us off with bags of newly dehydrated food.

"I expects you'll make it just fine," Pepper shouted as we shouldered our packs and rearmed ourselves with disquiet.

I was afraid that opening my mouth for a single word would un-dam a flood of ugly tears and sobs. I thought it might be the same for Grayson, so we walked in silence.

For almost three miles we followed the chasm left by the earthquake that ran through their old colony, until we reached a field of waving grasses that rippled like a golden lake in the wind. Our map showed that we were to veer from the chasm at fifteen degrees southeast and cross the field until we reached the woods, which would eventually lead us into the cat territory.

Grayson and I paused at the edge of the field. "Here we go," I said brightly, trying to push the warmth of Violet and Pepper from my mind and accept how far we would have to go before sundown. Grayson nodded as we waded into the field that seemed to stretch out for miles. The going was slowed by the resistance of the grass. Grayson suddenly wailed as he bent over and grabbed his knee. "Watch out," he said with gritted teeth. "There's a big rock over here."

I moved out to the right as I also kicked something hard. "Yeah, I found another one," I grunted and moved gingerly around it.

A few paces more and Grayson had collided with yet another one. I tried not to laugh as he jumped up and down on one leg awkwardly with his bulky pack.

"What in the world are these things?" I scanned the space in front of me. When the wind blew I could see the top of what looked like gray fish surfacing in the water. "I think they're just weird rocks," I said, walking over to one and pulling back the curtain of tall grass. "It has a name written on it," I yelled back to Grayson.

"This one does too," he returned. "Margaret Donegal, 'Onward to thy glory! Tis always morning somewhere in the world (Horne),'" he read.

"Who is Margaret Donegal?" I asked.

"And who is Eric Frederickson?" I read the worn engraving on the gray stone that had endured years of the elements.

"This one has a date," Grayson called. "2016."

Mine did too—2032. I stepped back. "It's when they died. Someone put a sort of memorial here for them."

"For lots of them," Grayson said. As the wind blew we could see just the tops of smooth stones revealed where the grass bent.

"No," I said, wiping back the grass with my foot to read the rest of the inscription. "'Husband, father—loved and remembered always.' I think he's here. Buried here, I mean." A tingle snaked up my back, and I stepped aside.

Grayson swallowed. "Marissa told me about this once," he said. "They buried people before the colonies outlawed it and mandated cremations. Come on, let's go."

I hurried to his side, wondering how many more beloved family members I might be stepping over.

"Hey, it's ok," he said, offering his hand. "We'll be through it soon enough." Reluctantly I took his rough hand. It steadied me immediately.

We took long, careful steps as we traversed the ground above the sleeping village. Occasionally we would stop to read a poem or calculate the age of the ones resting below. We paused at the really young ones and stood there in reverent silence until we remembered we should keep moving.

The ground sloped up gradually. We lifted our gaze from our careful steps to see a white statue with wings outstretched and hands holding small birds that were soon to take flight. I took in a short breath. For how many years had this creature been guarding the sleepers on the hill? We made our way up to the top of the incline and stood at the base of the statue. I was still holding Grayson's hand in spite of myself.

"Just look at that," Grayson said. From where we were standing we had the viewpoint of the angel. The grass seemed to stretch out forever like an ocean that crashed into the verdancy of the forest. We stood for several minutes catching our breath.

"I *expects* we're going to make it," I said.

Grayson laughed. "Well, now we're fully equipped," he said.

I looked into the newly bearded face of the best friend I had ever known, the one I had tried with all my might to push away. He was the boy who had seen me always as more than I was, who was willing to journey hundreds of miles to deliver the names of people who were at risk of being eliminated.

We had made it almost one hundred miles. One hundred miles away from the New Colony, from Radius. I knew that to my back balloners were out at that time of day. Radius had probably been making plans for his new girl while I was in the Membrane with everything I owned on my back. I did the math in my head as we walked—more than a million steps away and farther still with every second.

"It's like Pepper said." I squeezed his hand. "It was meant."

The next two days of the journey after the burial field had been slow going in spite of the fact that there was somewhat of a trail that made things easier. Both of us had been concerned about the section that Pepper and Violet had warned us might be the most perilous of the journey—cat territory. And, of course, they were right. I can't think what would have happened if we hadn't been warned. We were prepared for the attack, and even still, it was a close call.

And here I am now—tired, sore, hungry, but alive. After we returned from the river, we were relieved to find our campsite untouched by cats or any other animal that might have been curious about these strange creatures traversing their territory. Grayson and I took turns keeping watch throughout the night, just in case. I had sat in the dark thinking about Pepper and Violet and the last hundred miles and worrying about what might lay ahead. I jumped at every rustle in the dark that could mean the cat had returned—with its pack.

Grayson and I decide to take the club with the barbed wire when we wake up, in spite of the added weight. I insist on bringing a torch of some sort, but, try as we might, we can't keep it aflame.

"This thing isn't going to last ten miles," Grayson says, holding up a smoking stick. "Let's just go quickly."

And we do.

We walk in silence and jump at every forest sound. Although Grayson and I typically allow a bit of space between us when we hike, we walk side by side, our arms brushing one another. "What's that?" Grayson asks every five hundred feet or so. We turn in circles and strain our eyes expecting to find them looking back at us, ready to pounce, but we never see another. I know they're out there. And I know that the reason Grayson is so on edge is for my sake. He wants to protect me. In a moment, in a single strike from behind, we could both be taken down by a beast. One or both of us could die—and if one, then it is only a matter of time before the other will go down.

Still, a heavy peace falls upon me. It isn't as though I don't care. The desperation that I once felt to be out of this world is gone. In its place is an aliveness and purpose that I have never known. Perhaps this is what my mother felt, why she was able to accept her transfer to the New Colony, and even her exile, with such dignity. She had purpose and perhaps with it comes this inexplicable peace. Or maybe it was how Pepper and Violet had said that it was "meant." Maybe they too had been blanketed in the calm during the storm.

I laugh out loud. Grayson turns sharply as though it's a tiger growl. "What could possibly be funny?" he whispers.

"We're walking in lion and tiger territory." I smile.

"And why exactly do you find that funny?" Grayson asks indignantly.

"Because we just keep walking." I say. "We must be crazy. We're still walking."

Grayson looks at me as though I might have lost my mind. "Come on," he says, taking my hand. "You're turning as wild as they are."

The woods become thinner, and in the distance we can see the open ribbon of a wide and cracked road.

"We're out," Grayson says. I can hear the relief in his voice. "I don't think they're going to bother us anymore."

I turn behind me. "Maybe not, but I'll still feel better once we make it to the next safe house. What if they're following us?"

Grayson shimmies off his pack and looks up and down the road. "At least it's more open."

"Hotter," I add, blocking the light with my hand. Grayson takes his water bottle from his pack and shakes it.

"I'm going to look at the map," he says, taking out the GPS. "I think we have another mile or so before we hit water. Looks like we have to ford it."

"Great," I say as I take a swig from my water bottle. "Think it's a river or just a creek?"

"Looks more like a river. That's probably the official end of the cat territory."

I wipe my brow. "Let's do it."

We walk for another twenty minutes. My feet are killing me and the heat emanating from the dark road isn't helping. Every minute or so Grayson and I look down the long road that stretches out like a discarded streamer. It led somewhere once. Maybe even two hundred years ago cars buzzed down this highway to visit family, or perhaps for the frivolous privilege of visiting another part of a unified nation. What I wouldn't give for the Convoy with some air conditioning and a lemonade overflowing with ice.

We can hear the water before we see it. Grayson turns back one last time as though a cat has been waiting for us to reach the water before pouncing. "Whoa," I say as we get closer. "Not a creek." We stand on the edge of what is actually a roaring river. In the middle, small whirlpools form. Grayson runs his fingers through his hair, which will surely be falling out soon if he keeps up that nervous habit.

"Maybe it's higher than usual," I suggest.

Grayson shakes his head. "It hasn't rained in days. But people have been crossing it. There has to be a way."

244

I take off my pack and rifle through it to get out my water filter. Even lowering the filter in, I can feel the current's force.

"We can't cross here," I say after taking a drink of water. "I can't swim that. Not with a pack."

"But people have been crossing it. It has to be possible. I wonder if maybe it's farther up." Grayson looks up and down the water that flows and gurgles like it is alive. "Looks deep out there in the middle."

I nod. "Get the map. There has to be a bridge. This was a highway after all."

"Yeah, but it's not as though this river was here when the highway was being used." Grayson studies the map carefully. "I think this must have be a chasm from the earthquake. No telling how deep."

I let out a low, guttural moan. "No." I point across the river. "There was a bridge." From the distance we can see the end of a hanging bridge being tossed mercilessly in the current and dangling its attachment on the other side. Grayson has gone pale, but he pulls out the map and looks again. "It just goes on forever," he says, following his finger upward on the map."

"Well, we can't stay here. There's got to be a way across."

"Let's follow it upstream and see what we can find." Grayson looks back again behind his shoulder and sighs. "We were so close."

"We're still close."

We walk another mile at the edge of the water and look longingly at the other side. It seems we could jump across in some parts. A few times Grayson tosses rocks that land safely on the other side. "We need a balloon," I say.

"Or a boat."

"Or a miracle. I'm surprised that Pepper and Violet didn't mention how serious this water is," Grayson says.

"Well, they didn't know the bridge was out. And besides, they were probably more focused on the cat problem."

Grayson looks at the map again. "Got to keep going then," he says. "At the first place where we think we have a shot, I'll go first."

I swallow hard. I'm more scared now than I have been during the entire trip, and Grayson can see it. I don't want to be standing helpless and stranded on the edge.

"Hey, come here," he says, and puts his arm around my shoulder.

"Only if I approve of the place, Grayson," I tell him, pushing away.

"All right."

"You can't take that risk."

Grayson takes his arm from my shoulder and scratches the back of his neck.

"Bugs here are horrible." I look down at my hairy legs that are covered in bites.

"Ugh," Gray says, running his hands at the base of his neck and looking off to the ground as though he's concentrating really hard. "There's something in my hair. Little round things."

I slide my pack off and pull him down to where I can see the back of his neck. "Nothing there," I say, looking at his neck that is dark from sun exposure and dirt. "You're just filthy is all. You probably have some small animal living in your hair."

Grayson parts his hair in the back. "Anything there?"

Oh, my gosh. Disgusting. "Yeah, little black round things. Like a half dozen of them or so," I say, gingerly pulling his hair apart and trying not sound as grossed out as I am. "Ticks. And they look like they're about to burst."

"Great," Grayson says. "I don't know how I didn't notice them before."

"I do," I laugh. "You were more concerned about getting maimed. I'd bet you've had them since we walked through that tall grass. Think I have them too?" I look nervously at my arms and brush the back of my neck. Suddenly I am itching all over.

"Ok, here's the plan," Gray says. "We get across. And the upside to falling in is that they'll drown."

"No way. We'll drown before they do. They'll still be sucking your blood happily under water."

"Let's just get across and then we'll deal with it, ok?"

"Fine. But just so you know, it's disgusting."

Grayson bumps me with his pack. We walk another two miles. Twice he stops where the chasm seems only slightly more narrow.

"Not happening," I tell him each time. "No way."

The woods get thicker as we go. Gradually, we begin to see more debris in the water—floating sticks, leaves. The water seems to turn to an almost thirty degree angle and there it is, what we've been waiting for—a tree that has fallen over to the other side. Not a large tree, but the closest thing we've seen for several miles and may hope to see again. In places, the water rushes over it menacingly. We stop to look at it and smile at one another.

"It's pitiful. It might even be rotting. But it's something. What do you say?" Grayson looks at me nervously.

"I changed my mind," I say. "I'm going first."

Grayson crosses his arms in front of his chest.

I stand up taller. "If it's not safe—which, I mean, look at it—and I fall in, you at least have a shot of pulling me out. If big old you crosses and falls in, you are in so much trouble. No way I can get you out." Grayson still doesn't look convinced. "Then I'm stranded and out here all alone."

Grayson relaxes his arms; he knows I'm right. "I don't like this."

We have a rope, but it's not much—certainly not long enough to stretch across the width of the water. We've used it before when fording to tie us together.

Grayson takes my pack off and ties the rope around my waist. He looks troubled. I twist from side to side as he pulls the rope to make the knot.

"Hey!" I complain loudly.

He looks surprised that I'm standing there before him.

"You're not tying it to a rock. Be more gentle. That hurts."

"I'm so sorry," he mumbles. "I think we're going to have to both go across.

"No," I say assertively. "The log will break."

"But then that means that I'm going to—"

"Right, you'll have to let go. I'd say it will be about three-quarters, maybe half of the way across."

I can't tell if Grayson is angry or just really focused. He stands studying me for several moments, his expression like the night he carried me to the chicken coop to hide from Radius. "I could just inch out behind you. It could be tied to me. That way—"

"If it's rotting, we're both going under."

Grayson nods his head in defeat. "Loosen your pack just in case you need to cast it off." Grayson holds up my pack for me to put back on. I loosen the shoulder straps just a bit and don't attach the chest or waist straps. Grayson jerks on the rope suddenly, and I almost fall over.

"Watch it!" I yell.

"Sorry, sorry. Just checking it."

"It's fine. Sheesh."

Grayson ties the end of the rope to a tree by the edge. "Untie me from the tree when it gets too short," I tell him. "I'll reel your end in and tie it to the log so that I'm only without a tether for a matter of seconds." Gray looks slightly assuaged. "When I get across, I'll untie myself and tie my end to a tree. So one end will be on the opposite bank, and one end will still be tied to the log.

And then when it's your turn and you get that far across, untie it from the log and tie it to yourself. Until then you won't be tethered, so you'll have to be really careful. Once you reach the rope, tie it to yourself and then if you fall in, you'll be anchored to the tree on the other side. If you're going to fall, just fall *after* you get the rope around you. Sound good?"

"Bridge sounds better. Hey, you take the map." Grayson rummages in his pack and removes a waterproof bag with the paper map. "Put it in your shirt," he says, although it's also saved in the GPS. "And this." He hands me the list of names and slips the data chip hanging from the chain on his neck and puts it around mine. "Now you're set."

I stare at the rushing water as I stand on the edge of the bank. The log seems solid enough, although bark is coming down in strips, which makes footing more difficult. I decide that the best strategy is to crawl on my hands and knees. "Just go slow," Grayson calls.

"Slow is good. It feels solid."

The tree must not have fallen that long ago. It's obviously dead, with no foliage, but the branches are still intact up ahead. They will make it somewhat easier to have something to grasp when I get up a bit further.

"You ok?" Grayson yells to me.

"Doing fine."

"You have plenty of rope. Looking good. You're doing great."

The rush of the water below me is dizzying and the pack is so loose that it makes balancing that much harder as it shifts.

"Hey, Grayson," I yell without looking back. "There's a cat behind you!"

"Har, har," Grayson says a moment later. I don't have to turn around to know that he looked.

Slow and steady does it. The other side is close. "How much more rope?" I yell.

"You have five more feet."

I stumble and grab hold of the log until my fingers blanch and my heart returns to a normal rhythm before I begin my slow crawl again. I can't tell if Grayson has let out a deep growl or it's the rush of the water, but I know I've just made him panicked.

Finally, I reach a thick branch where I can hold on with one hand. I desperately want to take off my pack, which has shifted to the left and is causing muscle spasms in my neck, but I'm worried to try it. Where my feet were hurting before, now my knees are screaming at me to relieve them. It's like kneeling with all my weight on grains of rice.

The rope is taut.

"Want me to untie it now so you can reel it in?" Gray yells above the rush below.

I slide one leg down over the log and then the other like I'm riding a horse.

"What are you doing?" Grayson yells nervously.

"Trust me, this is better," I shout back. "Ok, ready!" I feel a tug as Grayson works to untie his end from the tree so I can reel it in.

"It's ready for you, Bec! Just be careful!"

Slowly and without looking, I pull the rope to me as the river pulls against it. A few times it catches on branches and I grip the log with my legs even tighter until pain shoots up my back.

"Almost there!" Grayson encourages from behind me.

"Got it!"

Now I just have to tie it on, which means I'll have to get it around the log first. I drop several feet of it into the water and allow the current to wash it under the log. To the left I can see it streaming out the other side. I kick wildly with my leg to try to wrap it around my foot, but it's clear that I'm not going to reach.

"You ok?" Grayson asks nervously.

"I can't get it. I'm going to try a branch." I get back on my hands and knees and inch forward until I reach a branch that I think can be easily broken off.

"Whoa, what are you doing?" Grayson yells. "The rope's not tied to anything!"

I choose to ignore him and settle down again as though I'm riding in a saddle.

The branch is dry, but it takes serious effort to break if off. I fall backward when it snaps but right myself by gripping the log with my legs.

"Rebecca, forget it!" Grayson shouts, but I can hardly hear him with the roar of the river. "Just go over. You're almost there."

I get back on my knees, gripping the cumbersome branch in one hand as I inch backward. "Rebecca, no! Just go forward." I shake my head again at Grayson who I know is panicking. I'm glad my back is to him so that he can't see the fear that I'm sure is evident in my face. Managing the branch is making things so much more difficult. I can't see behind me and I have to keep lifting the branch to accommodate more branches that are sticking out. A couple of times it gets tangled, and I falter trying to extricate it. Finally I'm back to the end of the rope, tied onto a knobby branch. I ease myself back down to sitting and use the long branch I have taken off as a fishing pole of sorts.

"Almost!" Grayson is yelling now.

It takes me several blind scoops, but I am finally able to lift the other end of the rope and pull it in to tie it around the log with a tight knot.

I can hear Grayson laughing from the edge. "This is going to work!" he shouts. "Almost there, so just be careful!"

If I fall in now, at least I will be dangling from the log. Of course, I'll have to lose my pack and probably my shoes too, so either way my chance of survival goes down—but with the rope at least death won't be quite so imminent.

"Hey!" I yell from over my shoulder. "If we do drown, then we didn't actually lie to the colony."

"Shut up, Rebecca, and just get to the other side, will you?"

Of course, if I fall now, I know that Grayson will hurry over and try to pull me out. Then he could get pulled in, and I could just dangle here until I die. I decide not to think about it.

With the rope tied to the log, I have to keep moving it out of the way of branches to make any progress forward. It keeps getting caught, and so I have to reach behind me and drag it forward. The last quarter of the log is much easier, with the exception of one space where the branches get much thicker. I have to move from my hands and knees to standing and then turn to the side to push forward while holding up the rope so it doesn't get tangled again. "This part's tricky!" I yell.

"What?" Grayson calls back.

"Tricky!" I yell louder. "Be careful on this part!"

I make it to the shore and collapse into the dirt and pebbles. Grayson is cheering from the other side. I raise my hand and wave in victory after throwing my pack off and rolling over onto my back to take a breath. I did it. I actually did it. I untie the rope without looking at it and laboriously push myself to standing. There is a warm trickle running down my leg. My left knee is badly scraped. The adrenaline was rushing so much while I was out on the log that I didn't even feel it, but now that I'm safe, it's a throbbing, stabbing pain. I'll take care of that later.

I cup both hands around my mouth. "Your turn!" I yell twice before he can hear me.

I tie my end of the rope to a tree. When Grayson gets to the knot I tied in the middle, he can tie it around his waist. At least he'll have some security at that point, but I worry about him having to make it almost halfway across without anything to tether him.

I watch from the other side as Grayson loosens his pack and then, like me, inches forward on his hands and knees. Grayson is much bigger and longer than I am. He looks awkward moving across the log, like a bear. In spite of his gracelessness, he makes good time and is at the tied rope quickly. He unknots it from the tree and ties it securely around his waist without issue.

"Nice!" I call to him and let out a breath I didn't know I was holding. "Now take the last part slower. The branches make it trickier."

He's close enough now that I can see the beads of perspiration rolling down his face. "Almost there, almost," I say to myself.

Only a matter of miles and we will be in a safe house tonight, eating non-dehydrated food and sleeping on something other than the ground. We're making it.

"This is the tricky part!" I call as he reaches the section where the branches get so thick that he has to stand. He uses one of the branches to steady himself. He leans forward slowly, slowly.

"Grayson!" I scream as he falls through the branches and lands contortedly, pack first, into the river. "Grayson!" I scream over and over, but he doesn't surface.

The rope has pulled taut. I run my hand along it and kneel by the rushing water. I pull on the strained rope, but it's like lifting a thousand pounds. No, no, no. This cannot be happening. I close my eyes and pull with all my might until I am screaming from the exertion. "Come on!" I yell with gritted teeth.

Suddenly I can feel him moving on the other end of the line like a fish fighting to get away. "Grayson!" The tears come.

I pull harder on the rope. All of a sudden, Grayson breaks the surface and gasps for air.

"Gray! Gray!" I shout hysterically. I work to push down the panic. "It's going to be ok!" I call to him.

He brings a hand above the water to wave to me. He looks exhausted.

"It's all right, Gray. It's all going to be all right," I say more to myself than to him. I can see that he has lost the pack. "Can you pull yourself back up with the rope?"

The current is pitching him side to side. Occasionally he goes under again. Each time he does I hold my breath as though I'm also being submerged. "Don't give up, Gray!" I yell.

Already I can tell that he is tired. He's going to die, I think. This is it.

"Pull, Gray!" He goes under again. When he surfaces he is closer to the log, but completely out of breath. "Closer!" I shout. "Come on!"

For what seems like hours Grayson goes under, and then gets closer as he pulls himself with the rope. Over and over, he goes under and then gets closer an inch at a time. My hands are shaking. Finally he's within feet of the log and then the riverbank.

"I'm ok, Rebecca," he says weakly and raises a hand. "Stay there!" he commands.

I pace the edge of the river nervously. With what sounds like a roar, Grayson pulls himself the last few feet toward the edge.

"You're here. Almost! Almost! Come on!" I lay down on the ground with my hands outstretched for him.

With a final burst of effort Grayson reaches the bank and is able to get his footing on the rock. I grab the back of his shirt and heave him in with all my might.

I tackle him and kiss every inch of his head. "Thank God," I say between kisses. "Grayson, thank God."

Grayson puts a strong arm around me. "I'm ok, sweetheart."

I cry and laugh at the same time and collapse into his heaving chest.

"It's ok. I'm ok," he whispers breathlessly.

"I love you," I hear myself say impulsively. "Thank God, thank God. I love you so much." I sit back on the bank and cry with his arms around me until there is nothing left.

Grayson has lost his pack and both boots. His hands are completely raw and bleeding, and he has a large purple bruise around his waist like a belt where the rope had tightened around him. One of his ribs is so sore and swollen I fear it might be broken. I have the first aid kit in my bag, fortunately, so I tend his large, rough hands as though they are the delicate ones of a small child. Then I turn him onto his side and remove the ticks that have decidedly *not* died in his hair.

"We didn't get eaten by a cat," Gray smiles.

"No, we didn't."

"I can't believe I lost it all. It was so stupid."

"You didn't lose it all. *You* got out."

Grayson squeezes my hand. "And you said you love me."

Slowly, he props himself on one elbow to look at me. I look back at him seriously. It has always been true and I know it now. It's hard to feel the truth when you're so broken. I'm healing now, and I know without a doubt that I love him.

"How could I not, Gray?"

"Then we had a bridge after all."

Chapter 24

I ignore Grayson's insistence that we keep going and build a fire to cook the last dehydrated food. Grayson takes off a layer of his clothes so that I can dry them. I spread out my sleeping bag, the only one we have between us now, and prop him up on his side with the uninjured rib. Almost immediately, he is asleep.

I take the opportunity to inventory what we have left. We still have the names, which were around my neck, and the paper map, but the GPS is gone. We have the water filter and one water bottle between us, which means that our water intake will be cut by half, or we'll have to refill more frequently. I also have the first aid kit, tent repair kit, one pot, our bowls, sporks, the fire starter, my sleeping bag, two large bags of dehydrated food, some spare clothes, and of course the rope. Grayson had been carrying the heavier items. He had another pot, three bags of food, and the tent in addition to a spare bag of clothes, a spare water filter, water purifying tablets, flashlights, and the knife—all of them gone now. I pound my fist on the ground in frustration.

Judging by the map, it looks like we would have had four more miles if we had crossed the river where the bridge had gone out. But now we'll have to follow the river back downstream for at least two miles to get back to where we should have crossed. There's no way Grayson can do the six-mile trek at this point. He's exhausted, and I'm concerned with how much water he might have inhaled. Plus he has no shoes.

I sigh. My feet are blistered and tender; his are the same. The terrain on the side of the river is filled with roots, sticks, and small rocks. Once we get back to the road, we'll be walking on the hot pavement. Without boots, he's in trouble. I figure I can bandage his feet with some of my spare clothes and wrap them with tape from the tent repair kit, which otherwise is completely useless now that we have no tent. If we can just make it to the safe house, maybe we'll be able to replenish our supplies.

I lay on my back next to Grayson, who is beginning to snore. I press my cheek against his back and hear his heart beating. "Thank God," I say. Somehow he seems more real now. I notice everything about him as though I'm taking him in for the first time. The fullness of his bottom lip, the gentle slope of his forehead that leads to soft but discerning eyes, the small flecks of gold in his dark hair, and the way he makes me feel that I no longer try to suppress. I know now that nothing I can ever do will repay him for the sacrifices he has made for me. I am found, and I want nothing more than for him to allow me to love him. Hope rushes into my broken places, and I think of my mother. She is out there somewhere. Maybe she, like the other exiles who were able to make it back down to the southern colony, is on her way. I will find her.

The sun is still up when I begin to nod off, safe with Grayson beside me. We're going to make it. We are.

Grayson is dangling his feet in the water when I wake. The fire is roaring back to life and Grayson is rehydrating something in the pot. "We're going to have a weird breakfast," he says. "You got all the dinner meals. I think I had most of the breakfast ones. So now the fish are eating our breakfast. How does pork, rice, and beans sound before the sun comes up?"

"Sounds incredible, actually."

"Good, because I think that will be our lunch as well."

"I was thinking that we probably need to get going fairly early. That road is going to get hot about midday."

"Agreed."

"Yesterday was exhausting. Everything aches."

"It should, I guess. Look what you were fighting against," I say, pointing to the roaring river. "I don't know how you did that."

"It wasn't what I was fighting against, it was what I was fighting for."

I turn from the water to look at Grayson, who is smiling.

"It'll take more than that river to hold us back, won't it, Rebecca?"

The two miles to get back to the road take us more than an hour. Grayson wants to carry my pack, but I won't let him. "You need as little weight as possible on those feet," I tell him.

It can't be past 8:00 a.m., and already the air is thick with humidity and getting warmer by the minute.

"How you doing?" I ask.

"I'm fine," he lies.

"Are you? You don't look well."

"I'm ok. Just tired. And achy."

I study Grayson's face. He looks pale, and I notice he is shivering. "Your stomach feel all right?"

"Yeah."

"You didn't eat much for breakfast."

Grayson shrugs. "Maybe I ate some fish or something while I was under there. Wasn't too hungry."

I smirk at Grayson. "Well, you need to drink this whole bottle before we go." I lean by the edge to pump water into the filter.

Grayson rests by a tree and falls asleep for a moment or two.

"Can you drink this?" I whisper.

He opens his eyes weakly and takes the bottle. When he has finished it I return to refill the bottle, and I drink the same amount. Grayson returns to dozing by the tree. I pump the filter one more time to fill the bottle all the way to the top. I look at it and swallow hard. This will have to last us both eight miles in the heat, and by the looks of Grayson he will need every drop.

I kneel beside Gray while he sleeps and carefully wrap his feet with my old t-shirt, which was easily torn into strips. I think of how he bandaged my feet the night I ran from Radius. I had sworn then that I would make it up to him, and that I would do whatever it took to do so. I no longer feel the weight of that debt. All I want now is to walk this road with him by my side as a courier of names, with the knowledge that our names are on that list too. Every step I take now is because of love. That, I decide, is freedom. It's an abundance of it.

"Hey." I nudge him gently, but it takes me shaking his shoulders to wake him up. "You ready? Sorry. We just need to get going before the pavement gets too hot."

Grayson is shaking from being roused from his much-needed sleep.

"How's your rib?"

"It's sore, I guess—but then everything is."

I stand and offer my hand to help him up. "I'd carry you if I could." I flex the muscles in my other arm.

Grayson smiles. "Nah, I'm just kinda worn down today. Seriously, I can take a turn at carrying the pack."

"We'll see."

I take our map back out to check the route one more time. No more rivers. No mountains. Nothing but a flat expanse of winding road leading us straight to the safe house. Typically, Grayson is the one out in front. Though he never complains about my short stride, his one step usually equals two of mine, and I know I slow him down. But today I slow my pace for him. "Want to tell me what you'd cook for dinner?" I offer, needing to break the silence.

Grayson shrugs. "I'm ok, Rebecca. Don't worry about me. A near-drowning is exhausting, that's all."

"Watching one is too."

After several minutes of silence, Grayson interrupts, "Maybe this is crazy, but when we get to the southern colony, I have this hope that I can't shake."

"That they'll be waiting for us?"

"Yes."

I sigh and re-adjust my pack. "I know. I have that hope too. It's a bit maddening, isn't it?"

"It is because, honestly, what are the odds? Part of me even expects to see Marissa there."

I take Grayson's hand and give it a squeeze. "I know. Odds aren't good, maybe, but I have this feeling that my mother is still alive."

"She was so peaceful."

"She hadn't given up. It wasn't a peace from resignation. It was like she knew what she was moving toward."

Grayson asks for the water bottle and takes a long swig from it. "Feeling better?" I ask.

"Yeah," he lies again. Already the bandages on his feet are coming off.

"Do you think she knew just how dangerous it was to keep the data? Her friends were murdered."

"Yes, I think she did," Grayson says after several moments. "I think that's why she had that gun."

"She got that gun because of me."

"You're right that she had it because of you. But I don't think she thought that Radius was the first threat against you. She and Marissa both must have known what they were stirring up."

"Maybe," I concede.

Grayson pauses for a long time. "I don't think Marissa died of a natural cause."

I turn to face him. "She had a brain tumor, Gray," I say gently.

Grayson is so pale. Maybe he is only speaking out of exhaustion. "I don't know. Something about it didn't feel right."

"Someone can't just give you a brain tumor."

"Can't they?"

"No, they can't."

"All the same, Marissa told me once about some research the cancer center was doing in the colony. Studies in which animals were being injected with cancer cells in saliva to see if it would take in another organism. There was a 'contagious cancer' already identified in dogs before colony formation, she said. But another colony was recently undergoing high rates of a resistant and pervasive form of cancer. Our colony was tasked with helping to find a cure and to test the possibility that they were being transmitted, rather than being genetic."

"I don't know, Gray. That doesn't mean she was injected. She would have noticed that, right?"

"Right. Maybe she just didn't bring it up to me. It was like she knew a while before she got sick, is all. I don't know, Rebecca. Maybe I'm getting paranoid."

"Maybe I should have been a little *more* paranoid. Anything is possible at this point."

"And maybe that's good too." Grayson smiles. He seems smaller, worn. Every now and then he winces in pain.

"Hey, let's take a break for a bit."

"They knew from the very beginning," Gray says, ignoring me.

"What do you mean the very beginning? Like, the *very* beginning?"

"Yes, I do. I think they knew the first step they took onto New Colony soil. I think they knew even before that."

I stop in the road. "Before they even got to the New Colony?"

"Yes, I do. I think they were sent with a job."

"Grayson, don't start the whole 'they were disseminated, not assimilated' thing."

"Yes, I think they were equipped—or at least some of them were prepared and knew exactly what they were doing. They were sent."

"Like Mr. Porter?"

"Yes, like Mr. Porter. Your mom, Marissa, Will Skycap. I think there might have been more."

"Sent by whom?"

Grayson lifts his chin and keeps walking.

"Who sent them, Grayson?" I ask irritably, walking quickly to catch up. "Stop, what are you saying? You really do think my dad *knew* about *all* this?"

Grayson puts his arm around me, but I shrug it off.

"We've been through this before. My dad didn't know anything. He was just trying to get us to safety. That's why we were assimilated. Please don't start this again."

"Ok, Rebecca," Grayson says calmly. "Your dad is a great man. I think he did what he had to."

"Right," I agree under my breath. "He sent us to safety. He didn't know."

My father would have died rather than risk getting my mother exiled or having Mr. Porter and others murdered. And here I am, trudging through the middle of the woods without my father. I watched Grayson fight a tiger, almost drown, and now he is walking without shoes through the Membrane. That wasn't my dad's plan. "You think my dad sent us out to be spies in another colony, collect some data, and risk our lives transporting it?"

"Hey, let's not talk about it right now, how about it?" Grayson asks and takes another swig of the water.

"No," I insist. "I want to talk about it now."

"Ok," Grayson says softly.

"You think my father wanted certain people in the other colonies to work as spies, is that right?"

"Maybe," Grayson says.

"No. That all happened after. They started working together *after* they were assimilated."

"I don't know. Maybe he did what he had to."

"He did do what he had to! Maybe he did *disseminate* us and not assimilate us. That's just how he conceptualized it or something. But he had to. He couldn't have done it if he'd known that his daughter would be risking her life in the Membrane to carry on his work. He had to make the choice of thousands of people dying in a catastrophe or sending us to safety, and he chose safety. If he thought we were already safe and he was sending us out to rescue others, then he *sacrificed* us. He sacrificed *you, me, my mother, everyone.* And we're still on that list for elimination. There had to be another way. The other colonies could have taken care of it themselves."

Grayson takes a step back to give me some space. Even in the middle of nowhere on an abandoned highway there isn't enough room for my anger.

"You know his heart," Grayson says, repeating my mother's words.

260

"No."

I take off running down the road until I outrun my tears. How could this, any of this, be for my own good? And all the while, he's out there somewhere, not looking for my mother. He doesn't know where I am. He doesn't care. He never turned around. Still his back is to us.

My back spasms from the pack. I slide it onto the ground and kneel beside it until Grayson catches up. I feel guilty for leaving him on the road when I know he's not well, but after only a few moments Grayson kneels beside me. I want to collapse into his arms. Instead I pick at the scab that has formed on my knee.

"Look, Rebecca," he says. "All I know is that we're exactly where we are supposed to be. There's a lot that I don't know. But what I do know is that we've got to keep taking this road. Something's changing. And we're part of it."

Something in me deeply rebels against my father. Maybe there's even a place that hates him. But there is also a part that does know his heart. And I know my mother's. She trusted him so profoundly, and even though they were so far apart, somehow she still knew him intimately. I trust her faith where mine runs out.

"I don't know why all of this," I say, gesturing to the thick woods that surround the road. "But I do know him. And one day when I see him he'll tell me why." Grayson pulls me onto his lap, and I let him rock me until the pain subsides.

The last few miles on the road take close to four hours to walk. We stop almost every mile so that I can re-bandage Grayson's feet, which are cut in some places. He's getting more and more pale and in spite of the sun, which is excruciatingly warm by almost midday, he begins to shiver.

"Take some water," I insist. My throat is completely dry, but I tell Grayson that I drank so much at the river that I'm still full. "You're sick," I tell him. "Do you think you swallowed too much contaminated water? Is your stomach hurting?"

"I feel a little nauseated. I'm ok."

He isn't.

"I'm guessing two more miles," I tell him after looking at the map. Just straight on this way. Can you make it?"

"Think we could sit down for a minute?" Grayson asks.

"Of course."

Grayson makes it to the side of the road and kneels down slowly, like every muscle is hurting. I try to think of what medicinal plants Pepper recommended, but kudzu was the only one I was very good at identifying, and it won't work for fever. Before I even touch Grayson's forehead, I know it will be hot to the touch. He shivers by the side of the road and almost immediately falls asleep with his head on my pack.

"Grayson?" I whisper after several minutes. "I'm going to get help."

He opens his eyes. "I'll go with you," he says distantly but doesn't make any effort to get up.

"We're so close, maybe two miles. I can run it and come back with some help." Grayson opens glassy eyes.

"I'm coming," he says and props himself up on one arm.

"No, it will make it worse. You need to just stay here."

Grayson sits up with his head between his legs.

"Are you dizzy?" I ask.

He nods.

"Look, just lay back and rest for a minute, ok?" He nods again and eases himself back onto his good side. "I'm leaving my pack and the water."

"Be careful."

I take off at a full sprint, partly to ease tearing myself away from Grayson, and partly because the panic is fueling my energy now. I'm terrified to be leaving him in the heat with how sick he looks. I calculate how long it will take me to arrive at the safe house—less than twenty-five minutes normally, but the heat is getting to me, and I've not had anything to drink for at least six miles. I run until I think I might vomit and then slow to a walk. Once I catch my breath, I take off at a sprint and continue until I feel like I might vomit again.

The safe house has to be close. I take out the map and check the mileage. If I had the GPS, I could check the latitude and longitude to get a better estimate. I just haven't gone far enough, I tell myself. The map had shown the safe house immediately to the right of the road. I scan the thick underbrush for any sign of life but find nothing. Again, I take off at a run.

After several minutes of sprinting and walking I start to wonder if I've passed it. The road seems to just keep going endlessly without any signs of the safe house. I thought that surely it would be easy to see. Although Pepper and Violet's house wasn't exactly obvious, we had the advantage of the GPS and followed it directly to their doorstep. I decide I must have passed it. It wouldn't be a safe house if it were too exposed anyway. I retrace my steps on the road. The heel of my right foot is becoming very wet and I know that I'm probably developing deep blisters in addition to the other healing sores on my feet. I start to feel the pain when I slow to a walk. I strain my eyes to see through the thick underbrush. Nothing.

"It has to be here!" I yell to the trees that have been silently watching my mad search. Is it possible I didn't go far enough? I take out the map, running my finger along the curve of the road I just took. This has to be right, I think as I look back at the road. I recognize a hollowed out tree that I passed soon after leaving Grayson. I'm almost back to where I started now. The woods around me begin to spin. I haven't had any water since early this morning and the sun is almost directly overhead. Dehydration is making me weak. I decide to make one pass, slower this time to make sure I don't miss it.

I think of Violet's warm biscuits. Maybe there will be another sweet old woman who wants nothing more than to feed me, and who has an entire shelf of medicinal plants she's collected that will cure Grayson. I think of the possibility of a bath and not sleeping on the ground. Somewhere in the woods is a safe house, and I'm going to find it. My throat is too dry to swallow now, so I spit instead.

There it is, a roofline that blends in with the trees. I tear through the thick underbrush, pushing spider webs from my face. A large cabin stands in front of me, but there is no hint of life. No warm yeasty smells emanating from its windows. No toothless smiles to beckon us in. No clothes hanging out back. Something isn't right. I take a step back to retreat to the road. Maybe this isn't the right house. There might be lots of random, abandoned houses out here in the middle of nowhere. Come on, Rebecca. I return to look in the windows. Perhaps the owners are out hunting or tending a garden they have somewhere that is chock full of medicinal herbs. The door is slightly ajar.

"Hello," I say softly. "Anyone here, please?" A squirrel rustles the leaves behind me, but otherwise it's silent. The cabin looks to be in good shape with the exception of some clinging vines that creep to the roofline. I push the door open with my foot and peer inside a completely vacant house. No cots. No kitchen. Light streams in through a dusty window enough to show three words written on the wall: "We see you."

I stumble backward and fall through the threshold and scan the woods looking for eyes. Grayson. I've left him on the road. As quietly as I can I push through the woods, looking back periodically to see if I am being followed. Once I make it to the road, I take off and don't turn back. My heart is pounding so wildly that I feel like I might pass out. *Who* is watching? I feel dark and penetrating eyes, more menacing that the big cats', upon me.

I try to come up with a plan as I run, but it's hard to think clearly. All I know is that we have to get out of here, and fast. Our only known water source is six miles back, and Grayson is almost delirious with his rising fever. We can't cross back over the river. We have no food. And no GPS. I pick up my pace as I round the bend to where I have left Grayson.

A man stands over him as he sleeps.

Chapter 25

I do my best to silence my heavy breathing as I freeze in the road. Suddenly every muscle fiber in my body comes to life, and I am ready to attack this stranger if he makes even the slightest motion to suggest he will hurt Gray. I move to the side of the road and crouch near the underbrush. It occurs to me that he might not be alone. I scrutinize the road, expecting someone to jump me from behind. I can still see Grayson moving almost imperceptibly, shivering in the heat. The man is wearing long, dark green pants and a shirt with the sleeves cut out. He has a bulge in his back pocket that I have to assume is a gun, but he makes no motion to reach for it.

Suddenly I feel very calm. I know exactly what Grayson would do. I slip the list and the data chip from around my neck. Without a sound, I dig a shallow hole with my hands in the dirt and place the items in it. Then I cover them with a large rock and some underbrush. I look up. It is next to a distinct tree with flowering blossoms. I will know where to return to get it if I need to.

The man kneels and looks at Grayson's feet. "Hey," the man says, nudging Grayson with the toe of his boot.

I cover my hand with my mouth to stifle a rising scream. Still the man does not reach for his pocket. Grayson opens his eyes slowly and squints at the man but doesn't seem to register him.

"You a courier?" the man asks.

Even in his feverish delirium Grayson has the sense to shake his head no.

"I asked you if you are a courier? Or are you part of the Coalition?" he asks accusingly.

Grayson puts his hands up and rolls onto his back. "I'm a sick man is what I am. No threat. Making my way back after being exiled."

"Like hell you are. Look like a courier. But sick, sure enough. And young." The man takes a step back. "How in the world did you make it across the river? Bridge is out."

"I'm aware," Grayson smirks. He looks to the side and catches my eye but turns back quickly.

The man doesn't seem to have noticed. "Well then, how did you cross it? You didn't do it by yourself. That's sure enough." The man stands up and begins to turn toward me to look down the road.

I crouch as low as I can and steady my breath.

"I swam it alone. I'm a good swimmer," Grayson says, trying to distract him, but the man ignores him.

"Like hell. They'd just leave you here, or are they looking for some hel—" He sees me.

I crouch lower and turn my head, but I can feel the pierce of his stare on my neck. "Hey kid, come on out here!" he bellows.

I curse under my breath I as stand and walk to the road. Grayson's eyes are huge as he pushes himself to an unbalanced standing.

"Leave him alone!" I scream.

Grayson is almost a head taller than the man, but if he has a gun, he'll be no match. Plus Grayson looks like he doesn't have the strength to stand much longer.

"He's sick. We're just making our way south. We don't mean any trouble."

The man takes a step toward me, and I fight the urge to take a step back. Is this who is watching us as the sign said? How many other couriers have been stopped this way? Even if I run, there will be no survival out here. And I can't leave Gray.

"Who are *you*?" I yell back.

"Depends on who you are, I'd say. We're either on the same side or we aren't. So we're either best friends now, or we're enemies." The man looks me up and down.

I feel my heart pounding as though another panic attack is coming on.

"But by the looks of you—and you really look like hell—I'd say we're on the same side. Can't be sure, though." The man reaches into his pocket and pulls out the gun. It gleams in the sunshine.

I freeze as he points it at Grayson. "No!" I plead. "We aren't here to cause any trouble."

The man strokes his wiry black beard and lets out a deep laugh. "Then maybe we aren't on the same team after all."

I swallow hard.

"Tell me," the man says. "You looking for a safe house?"

"Maybe," I say, not knowing how to avoid being this guy's enemy.

"Not an answer," he says, cocking the gun. I decide that either way I had better just tell him the truth. If I avoid his questions, he'll shoot us and raid our bodies to find the list he thinks we are carrying. At least there's a chance of survival if I answer the questions.

"Yes, we were looking for a safe house."

The man doesn't take his eyes off me. I look at Grayson to get some direction. He nods.

"Not sure if I believe that," the man says. The woods begin to spin again. Muscles are starting to spasm in my right leg. "If that's true, you'll know another safe house."

Grayson nods again behind him, encouraging me to speak. I'm worried, though, that in his feverish state his instinct for judging people is off.

"Yes," I say, my voice cracking.

"Name one."

I look at him hard. There's no way I'm going to rat out Violet and Pepper. The man waves his gun at Grayson, and I hold my breath.

"You *can't* name one, or you're worried about getting them in trouble?"

I shift my weight and look at Grayson, who just stares back at me. "Pepper and Violet," I blurt out, but torture could not get their location out of me.

The man lowers his gun and sucks on his teeth. "Yeah, I knew you were couriers. Young, green, pathetic couriers," he mumbles as he puts the gun in his pocket, "but couriers nonetheless. Same side."

I exhale and fall to the ground.

"So we're best friends then," Grayson says weakly.

"Looks that way. That's good for you. I shoot Coalition jokers," the man says gruffly.

Grayson seems to relax.

"Well, who are *you*? How do we know we can trust you?" I ask with venom.

The man gives a deep laugh and raises his eyebrows. "Well, little miss, you don't have much choice. I owned that safe house before the Coalition boys came through. Pepper and Violet have been sending me folks for years." His voice is lighter now.

I get up and go to help steady Grayson, who is beginning to sway. It feels good to be near him and safe, at least for now. But I'm worried by how much he's shaking. His clothes are soaked through. He kisses the top of my head. "I'm ok," he tells me.

The man studies me. "Never seen a boyfriend and girlfriend couriering together. You might be the first." He scratches his head thoughtfully. "And you look straight out of playschool. Boy, you two are green."

I give him a hard look. "Well, we've made it this far, haven't we?"

"I'd say so, sure enough, though you look terrible. How in the world did you cross that river?"

Suddenly I feel as though I can't stand much longer. The adrenaline is wearing off. "I think he took in too much water. He's sick. Really sick. We were hoping to make it to the safe house tonight. We lost half our things in the river."

"Did you lose the names?" the man asks anxiously.

Neither Grayson nor I make any indication that we will answer his question. "Look," he says, rolling his eyes. "I won't ask you where they are. I won't even ask you to see them. I just want to make sure they're safe."

"We might have them," I whisper, feeling suddenly like I might vomit.

"Stop messing around, girl. The time is coming. You have the names or not?"

"Yes," Grayson says. "We have them."

The man seems to relax his shoulders and takes in such a deep breath it's as though he has just come up for air after being under water.

"The name is Gabe."

"I'm Grayson. This is Rebecca. Colony 215," Grayson says soberly.

"We thought you weren't coming. You're the last. Numbers are stabilizing. Now's the time, son."

Grayson and I nod as though we know exactly what he's talking about.

"Come on, go get the names," Gabe says to me. I stare back at him. "You look green, but not completely stupid. If you do have them, you hid them where you were crouching over there. Go get them so we can go home, and I can feed you two," he says as though we are three years old.

I scowl at him and return to my hiding spot. Grayson hands me the rest of the water bottle, which has less than a half cup left. I down it as I walk to where I hid the names.

"It's about three miles from here. You going to make it?" Gabe calls to me.

I turn to look at Grayson, who looks like he is about to fall to the ground any moment.

"Maybe," I mumble under my breath. But then again, this is better than being shot.

The three miles turns out to be all through the woods, and there's not much of a trail to follow. Gabe ends up supporting Grayson and helping him walk. It takes us almost three hours to get to the clearing that is the new safe house—or safe shack, rather. A middle-aged woman, who I assume is Gabe's wife, opens the wooden door when she sees us. A young girl follows behind.

"What in the world are you bringing in here, Gabe?" she calls. "Bless their hearts. Come on in, child. Come on." She beckons for me to follow her.

I throw my pack off before entering the structure that looks like the start of a log cabin, but with a tarp for a roof. It's even hotter inside, and I'm guessing there won't be any biscuits.

"My friend is sick," I tell her. "Could we have some water?"

"Anna," the woman says to a young blond girl with wide set eyes. The girl immediately runs outside and returns with a large bucket of water. The woman dips two metal cups into it and hands them to Grayson and me. We drink in large, careless gulps, letting the water spill out over our clothes. Again and again she refills our cups until we cannot drink anymore for fear of getting sick.

"Try this," she says, handing Grayson and me some dried meat. "The salt will help too. And then you're going to lie back for a long nap." Four pallets with tattered blankets rest on the dirt floor. No lavender water to soak our feet, but the beds look wonderful, makeshift though they may be. I stand to help Gray. His clothes are soaked through.

"Can I have a rag to sponge him off?" I ask.

The young girl is already busy getting strips of cloth and dipping them into the bucket. "We'll cook up something for you two." The girl's voice is high and light as you might expect from a child, but her tone is serious and authoritative. "Won't take Cassie long. I'm going to get something from the smoke house. Once she gets the fire going, Cassie will come back in with some sort of ointment for those feet."

"Thank you," I say sincerely. When she leaves, I ask Grayson, "Think we can trust him?"

"I feel good about it," he says.

"We have to." I sigh. Grayson's skin looks translucent and his breathing is becoming more rapid. "You just need some rest is all," I tell him. "Sleep," I insist as I stroke his head with the damp cloths. Grayson smiles and within moments he is soundly sleeping. I unwrap tattered rags from his feet.

"What's your name, girl?" Cassie asks when she returns.

"Rebecca," I whisper.

"Well, Rebecca. Tell me what happened to that boy of yours."

I explain about the river and fight back tears when I describe how often he went under. "Too much water intake," I say.

Cassie leans her head near Grayson's chest and listens to his breathing. She sits back on her heels and chews on her lip. "When did the fever start?"

"This morning."

"Vomiting? Diarrhea?"

"No, not at all. He wouldn't eat much this morning, but he never vomited."

"Well, it wasn't the water that did it. And his lungs sound clear." She pauses and looks at him like she's deep in concentration. "Maybe it's just a virus, but I'm going to give him something for bacteria just in case. Time will have to tell."

I lie back on the mat next to Grayson. He takes in sharp staccato breaths. I breathe more slowly, trying to will him to become in sync with me and push out the fever that is threatening him. Everything in my body is hurting, my feet and back especially, but I'm too tired to tend them. I reach for Grayson's warm hand. Sleep takes over.

The sun is beginning to set when I wake. Immediately I turn to Grayson, who looks troubled in his sleep as though having a bad dream—still pale, still breathing rapidly.

Anna is kneeling beside him. "Good evening," she says with the seriousness of a surgeon explaining a life-saving procedure. "Your friend is going to be all right. I've been watching over him and giving him water every hour."

"Thank you," I tell her sincerely.

I notice that Grayson's feet are bound in clean cloths and the covers are tucked neatly around him.

"Cassie gave him some medicine."

"He doesn't look much better." I brush the hair from his eyes.

"We'll know in a couple of days," she says, stroking one of her long, blond pigtails.

"May I have some water?"

Anna turns behind her to hand me a flask.

I drink it savagely. "Ugh," I say, wiping my mouth with the back of my hand.

"Has the medicine in it." Anna smiles a bit coyly. "Just in case. Cassie says you're supposed to drink the whole thing."

"Could have warned me," I mumble as I force the rest of the bitter water down.

Anna returns to her serious expression. "I'm going to get you some dinner."

"That would be wonderful, thank you so much."

"Then you can take a bath and we'll get you some fresh clothes."

Anna comes back quickly from outside with a steaming metal bowl of some sort of stew. I eat until I am scraping the bottom. Without being asked, Anna takes my empty bowl and returns it full again.

"What happened here?" I ask her.

The young girl raises her brows in a woman's expression and says in her child's voice, "Gabe said you found the old safe house."

"Yes."

"It was raided. By the Coalition. They were here almost six months back."

"Who is the Coalition?" I'm embarrassed to ask.

Anna is incredulous and a bit put out. "The ones who are buying up the colonies, of course. The ones causing all the trouble."

"I'm sorry," I tell her. "I don't understand."

"You're a courier, right?"

"Of a sort." The sort that has no idea what she's doing.

"Well then, they're the ones you're guarding the names from. They're the ones who have been making the selections."

"But *who* are they? Violet and Pepper didn't say anything about a Coalition."

"Pepper and Violet call them the eliminators. Not everyone is agreed that it's an actual Coalition. But Cassie and Gabe sure are. After what we've seen, there's no way they can be working alone.

Pepper and Violet didn't see what happened around here last winter."

I nod, still not quite making sense of it. "And who do Cassie and Gabe think that the Coalition is?"

"It's the countries that we've been doing trade with all this time. They're getting bigger, building back up. And while we got weaker—richer maybe, but weaker—other countries started getting jealous, see? They teamed up. Put their money together and *together* they were strong. They got in somehow and now they are weeding us out."

Well, that did sound like Pepper and Violet.

"And Cassie and Gabe think it's a group of them? Do they know who?"

"We think we might have somewhat of an idea."

"Do Pepper and Violet?"

"Probably not. We haven't had communication with them for some time. Been a little tied up."

"So, what did happen here?" I ask.

Grayson rolls onto his good side and groans.

"Hey," I whisper to him. "You feeling any better?"

"Time for some water," Anna says. "And how about some broth?" Grayson opens his eyes to slits and looks back and forth at both of us as though he's trying to piece together where he is.

"We're at the safe house," I remind him. "They've given you some medicine, and you're going to be fine."

Anna hurries to get him some water and hands me a rag to wipe his forehead.

"He's still burning," I tell her.

Grayson sips the water, which judging by the face he makes, also has some of the medicine in it. Within moments he is sleeping again.

"They didn't know we were a safe house," Anna continues. "They're idiots, the lot of them. And we were ready."

Anna hands me the broth and a wooden spoon to feed Gray. I help prop him up on my pillow and attempt a few spoonfuls that he sips in his half-sleeping state. "Three of them. Men who saw our smoke when they were gutting the colony."

"What colony?"

"Not too far from here. Nothing to it anymore. They came after the assimilation."

I suddenly make the connection. "Wait. Colony—"

"2220," Anna confirms.

"There was a girl in my class from there."

"Yep. They were the most recent to assimilate. And, they'll be the last too."

"How do you know?"

"Because the numbers are stabilizing, that's how. The names— you know," she says slowly. "The names that you're carrying. Every year couriers have been bringing them down to the Southern Colony—Sayon. Only now, the names aren't changing. They've made their decisions, so it seems."

"We're the last couriers."

"Dead last. We were expecting something from Colony 215 for some time. His partner came through here, though. Glover was his name. Said that Skycap never showed at their regular meeting place, but he had to keep on."

"Pepper and Violet said that too."

"We were all hoping that he was just delayed. Gabe had completely lost hope. Cassie kept saying that we just needed to hang on, there'd been a holdup somewhere."

"Why do you call them Gabe and Cassie? Aren't they your parents?" I ask, trying to change the subject before Anna starts wondering what the holdup had been.

"No, they aren't." A shadow falls over her small, porcelain face.

Immediately I am sorry that I asked.

"My parents were trained to be couriers before our assimilation. They were able to sneak me out to Gabe and Cassie before—"

"Wait a minute. What do you mean they were trained to be couriers?"

"I mean that the colony was training them for when they were assimilated," she says slowly.

"Couriers know *before* they get to their new colonies?"

So Gray was right. My heart starts to pound.

"Yes. It was a high honor to be selected." Anna smiles proudly.

My mother must have known what her role was to be before the assimilation. Grayson was right. She knew all along. My father knew. Marissa knew. Mr. Porter knew. They were even trained, but by whom? Still, this doesn't prove my father was behind it.

"There's a lot of information sent through the Membrane." Anna smiles like a schoolteacher talking to a young child.

"So do you ever see your parents at the safe house?"

"Yes. I get to see both of them when they come through each year. Once on the way down and once on the way back. Mom and Dad are hiking partners. They were assimilated into different colonies, but they're able to meet up and travel together, like Glover and Skycap," Anna says. She brushes strands of her smooth blond hair that have fallen out of its braid away from her face. "They've made it down to the Southern Colony by now. I've been expecting them back for some time."

"And who were they delivering to?" I ask.

"To the rebels who are going to end it."

"And who are they?"

Anna looks at me disapprovingly. "*You're* one of the rebels."

"Right." I allow this to sink in. "I'm one of the rebels," I say, trying to sound confident.

"And Grayson," Anna gestures toward Gray, who is shivering in his sleep. Anna looks between the two of us and shakes her head.

Cassie runs a tight ship. Before the sun is up, she starts the fire to make us breakfast and hauls water from the river to boil. For living out in the woods she looks remarkably put together. Whereas Gabe looks rough and unkempt, Cassie has an air of sophistication and elegance. Her dark hair is pulled back neatly into a tight bun and her emerald green blouse and long, light colored skirt don't have a single stain in spite of the messy work she tends. Every muscle is taut beneath delicate skin. Her face is kindness and knowledge.

Cassie directs orders to Anna and Gabe, who jump at her commands. About a quarter mile through the woods, Gabe is preparing a new safe house. Perhaps there won't be any more couriers to come through this way, but he's building it all the same.

Cassie suggests that I help Gabe with hauling some of the logs for the new house. I watch as Gabe rhythmically and patiently swings his axe at the base of small trees. Then I help him roll them into place. It's hard work, and Anna flits back and forth between the two of us, offering water.

"What happened when they found the safe house?" I ask Gabe as he swings his axe in graceful, regular strokes to take off the limbs of a tree.

"Idiot Coalition boys found it," he says without breaking cadence. "Thought they'd scared us real good. We made it out into

274

the woods, and they were thinking that would take care of us, so they didn't pursue. What they didn't know was that we had been expecting it for some time. Cassie and I had hidden supplies in different locations all over the woods—like squirrels hiding nuts for the winter. They found some things in the cabin, but it wasn't all we had. Of course they took that and wrote their cute little message on the wall. We decided to leave it in case they came back."

"How did you know they were coming, though?"

"The colony had just been assimilated. We knew they'd be coming to gut it."

"What do you mean?" I ask, using the smaller saw he'd given me to take care of some of the weaker branches.

"They were coming to get their prize. They raided most everything like they usually do—copper, extra food, livestock, you name it. But what they were really coming for was the phosphate rock."

"I don't understand."

"They needed it. The colony had it. So, the Coalition came in and took it—*gutted* the colony after everyone had assimilated," Gabe explains slowly.

"They're like vultures coming in after the colony has been emptied of life. They scavenge," I say disgustedly.

"You could say that, in a way maybe. Some people think they're the ones *causing* the assimilations, though."

I pause and think of what Grayson said about my father knowing about the assimilation before it happened. Was he a part of the Coalition? "Can't be," I tell him with a little too much force.

"Just a theory," Gabe shrugs.

"They're vultures," I say definitively.

"They were *ugly*, I'll give you that." Gabe swings his ax high into the air and plants it firmly into the log. "Tell you what, Miss Greenie. Let's go take a look. A rebel ought to at least know what she's rebelling against."

Without warning, Gabe takes off into the woods. I scramble to follow. Anna stands up from where she has been making pictures in the dirt with a stick and falls in behind me. We walk for about forty-five minutes, Gabe making sharp turns as though following some invisible trail.

We arrive at a thick wall rising high into the air. Anna crosses her arms as we follow the wall up with our eyes. "Gabe says *I* can have the colony now. So it's mine," she says and runs along the perimeter of the wall until we can't see her anymore.

Gabe takes long strides, and I struggle to keep up. When we find Anna, she is more than three-quarters of the way up a rope ladder and moving quickly.

"You next," Gabe says. I wait until Anna is all the way over and then mount the ladder that swings and creaks as it becomes taut.

"After finally breaking out, I'm breaking back in to a colony." By the time we make it over, Anna has already disappeared.

"Come on." Gabe motions for me to follow.

We walk through tightly packed, abandoned houses, many of them with toys in the backyard or rocking chairs on the front porch that move by themselves in the wind—they look like ghosts are sitting in them. Gabe walks up to one of the porch steps and takes a seat. "Don't stay long," he says, stretching out his thick legs.

I pause.

"Go on now," Gabe says sharply.

I shudder as a chill runs down my spine. It is as though everyone is asleep in the colony. I expect any moment for a car to pass me on the street, or a drone delivering packages to fly overhead. I squeal as a bird flies from the bush when I pass.

From the road I can see inside a small blue house with white shutters. I open the gate to get a closer look. On the front porch, two pairs of muddy children's boots sit by the welcome mat. Inside, dinner plates have been laid on a simple pine table. The chairs have been pulled out. Light streams obliquely into the kitchen. At first I think I see the silhouette of a woman, but it is only a mop propped on a door next to a bucket, transformed by the play of shadows.

I back out quickly and continue down the road. A door is open from one of the houses down the way. Curiosity drives me and I decide to go in. I sit down in a wide armchair next to a piano. The chair faces a table where I imagine a TV once stood. Perhaps this is where a girl who lived here first heard the news that they were going to be assimilated as her parents held each other.

I jump and cover my mouth to stop myself from screaming when I hear a faint pattering sound upstairs. It's just a cat or a bird caught up in one of the rooms, I tell myself. The Coalition is gone. No need to panic. But then I hear it again, this time with a muffled verbalization. Slowly and silently, I get up to leave. With trembling hands, I pick up a very solid-looking metal vase on the entrance table in case I need something to hit an attacker. Just as I cross the threshold, there are footsteps at the top of the stairs.

"Rebecca!" Anna cries happily.

I scream and drop my vase, which clatters loudly. "Anna!" I clutch my chest as I gasp for breath.

She looks at me disapprovingly. "You are the jumpiest courier I've ever met."

"I'm a sub," I remind her indignantly.

"Come see my room." Anna turns on her heel.

I roll my eyes and follow her to a light pink room at the top of the steps. Anna practically skips to a small dollhouse and resumes her play. I sit on the side of a quilted comforter.

"I like this room," I tell her.

"Me too. One day I'll have a room like this. My mom and dad will be downstairs, and I'll invite the little girl who lives next door to come play with me."

Anna seems too old in spirit to still be playing with dolls, but I guess she's never had a chance to do so before. Nor does she have friends her age. I sit down next to her and take one of the dolls to make her go up the steps and sit in a small chair.

"So have you explored the whole colony?"

"Yes. I play a game as I walk through it."

"What's that?" I ask.

"I see it as it will be. If you think of it as it was, it's too much. You can almost feel the people who were here. It's like walking with ghosts."

"You're right."

"And you can't think of it as it is *now*. You'll lose your mind. You have to walk down the road and see beyond it. These houses are just waiting. The New Kingdom is coming."

"The New Kingdom?"

"Yes, it's already been started. We just have to wait for it to invade here, you know? We have to be patient."

I sigh. "I'm familiar with the New—"

"No," Anna says abruptly. "No, that was a new colony just trying to be better than an old one. That was a new cage. I'm talking about a Kingdom that doesn't have an end. My mom and dad say we're going to be free one day. And I can feel it already creeping in. Can't you feel it, Rebecca?"

Anna's face seems to glow. It's like the New Kingdom she's describing is pouring out of her.

"Yeah," I smile. "It must be getting close."

Grayson's fever rages. I wait by his side, feeding him, helping him to the latrine outside, sponging him off, talking to him softly while I give him the bitter water that Cassie prepares for him four times a day. Today is the morning of the second day and I notice that his feet have small, rosy spots. The same spots cover his hands and wrists.

I shake Grayson gently. "Do your hands and feet itch at all?" I ask. Maybe he has another case of poison ivy, though the bumps looks less fluid-filled. Grayson shakes his head.

I call for Cassie, who studies the bumps as though deciphering a code. She pulls up his shirt and eyes his torso accusingly. His chest and stomach are flushed from the fever, and his hurt rib is now varying shades of green, black, and yellow, but it contains no spots.

"Mountain fever," Anna says from behind her.

Cassie nods in agreement. "I was right to give him the medicine I did. I suspected it."

My eyes dart between the two of them. "Mountain fever?" I ask nervously.

"Rocky Mountain spotted fever," she confirms.

Anna turns to go get more water and a damp rag, avoiding eye contact.

My eyes begin to fill up with tears. I clear my throat, afraid to ask. "Could he . . ."

"People have before," she says gently. "But he won't. I gave him the right medicine on a hunch, but I do wish I could have given it to him earlier."

"Thank you," I whisper gratefully. I can't allow my mind to think what would have happened if we were stuck on the trail with him this sick and no tent or food.

"The worst ticks are the smallest ones," Anna interjects. "He might not have even known he had it for a couple days."

"He got this from a *tick*?" I ask incredulously.

"Yep. Nasty things. Something in common with the Coalition boys." She smiles, twirling a braid.

"You're telling me that we just went through cat territory and survived, but he picked up a tiny little demon bug, and it did *this* to him?"

Cassie smiles. "That little blood sucker might have picked it up from one of the cats, actually. If it makes you feel any better, the cats might have contributed. Deadly beasts, ticks. It's the creatures that sneak up on you and you don't even know they're there that are the most dangerous. You can't really fight ticks like you would a big cat. You have to *detect* them, not fight them. In my experience, detecting evil is always the harder of the two."

I can't decide if I want to laugh or cry. As bad as Grayson is, he is going to be all right thanks to Cassie's thorough care in giving him the medicine on a hunch.

I'm itching to get back on the trail. It seems that the time is upon us for whatever is going to happen, and I want to deliver our names. But Grayson's sickness might slow us down considerably.

As if Cassie could read my mind, she says, "He's not close to over it yet with this thing. And we still don't know if he's going to have any issues after it passes." Cassie sighs. "It might be another week before it lets go of him."

A week here, doing nothing. Do we have a week?

"He's losing muscle too," Cassie notes. "He'll be weak when the bacteria does surrender his body," she says in a low voice as though the massive implication of her words will do less damage if spoken softly.

"We were doing ten miles a day at a minimum," I tell her soberly. "Some days twenty."

Cassie shakes her head sympathetically. "And you're late."

I've been sitting in the woods now for more than two hours, trying to allow the weight of our situation to settle in. I want desperately for Grayson to come with me. But it's risking too much. Even if he's able to make a full recovery without any further issues, he'll be weak. Already he has lost weight, even more than he had lost from weeks on the trail. His cheeks are sunken behind his beard. And I can't pack extra food to help him make up the weight he has lost. He risks injury again if he's not fit for the trip, and if we're in the middle of nowhere, I can't do much to help him. It would put us both in danger. We need to make up time at this point, not move slower.

Everything points to the same conclusion: I must continue on without him. But my mind fights, throwing in grand excuses that I know are only weak, illogical reasons to stay. I put my head between my knees and sob. I want to feel Grayson's arms around me. If I tell him I'm leaving, he will do everything he can to stop me. I know that with certainty. He'd walk with no shoes and no pack in a feverish delirium to try to keep me safe, which of course, he can't. It's utter madness, but I won't be able to talk him out of it.

I pound my fists into the dry leaves of the forest floor and cry silently as hot tears streak my cheeks. I cry until I can't catch my breath. There are more than a hundred miles to go. What if another bridge is out, or I fall and get an injury? What if I get mountain fever too? I'm completely on my own now for the first time. The list of names around my neck feels even heavier, and I know it's not a choice. More than a thousand names—people, *children*—are on that list. *Grayson's* name is on that list. I will have to leave before Gray is well enough to understand that I am abandoning him.

When I return to the camp, Cassie is sitting on a stump and slowly stirring a pot. She holds her chin a little higher when she sees me. She knows. The night before I leave, I wrap my arm around Grayson and watch him sleep, his chest rising in steady breaths. I lie awake longer than I sleep. Before the sun rises, I gently kiss Grayson on the lips to say goodbye.

Immediately he opens his eyes. "What's going on?"

"Nothing," I say as casually as I can. "You need to go back to sleep is all. It's still early. Cassie and Gabe will have breakfast soon, and you need to get some strength back."

Grayson closes his eyes, but furrows his brow. "Something's not right."

"Maybe you had a bad dream when the fever came. It's lingering. Sleep now."

I wait for him to close his eyes before I slowly step to the door and take my pack. It takes all my strength to force myself to do so. Cassie and Gabe already know I'm leaving. No one stirs to see me off for fear of alerting Grayson. I slowly open the door and step out into the cool air of the morning. I make it to the edge of the woods before I hear Grayson call for me from the doorway.

"Rebecca," he calls weakly. "Don't do this."

I know he is trying to run after me now. I do not pause as I walk determinedly to the woods and then break into a run. I can hear the faint sound of Gabe pleading with Grayson. He's probably restraining him.

"*Rebecca!*" he calls one last time as the foliage of the woods envelops me.

I want to run back and hold onto him until he gives me permission to leave, but I know he would only insist he come. There is nothing more in the world that I want than for him to walk by my side. But this is no longer a choice.

In this moment, I forgive my father. For the first time, I understand why he didn't turn around.

Chapter 26

I run until my legs are numb and I can be sure that he's no longer following me. Gray will be coming up with a plan as soon as he can to come find me. But I have the map now, and Gabe promised me that he would not let Grayson leave his sight.

I still feel the tearing feeling in my chest as though part of me is attached to Grayson and the farther I go, the more intense the pull. It takes every ounce of willpower I can muster to keep going in the opposite direction. Constantly my thoughts are on Gray. Several times I turn abruptly, expecting him to be right behind me. But the woods are empty.

Don't think, just walk, I tell myself. Every step is becoming more painful for my feet, which are now covered in new blisters where the old ones have healed. I welcome the sharp pain as it takes the edge off the ache in my chest.

Cassie filled my pack with dehydrated foods—mostly meat killed by Gabe and seasoned with roots and small, fragrant leaves. I also have Cassie's fruits, grown in the sunny clearings surrounding the camp. Gabe was able to restock my needed supplies. I now have an extra water bottle, some medicinal leaves in waterproof pouches that have been sewn closed, and the best prize of all—a GPS and extra batteries. Not as good as the one that Asa had given us, but it will help me locate water sources and find the next safe house with some assurance that I won't get lost. What I don't have, though, is a tent. The best Gabe could offer was a tarp, which I took gratefully. I was worried at first about sleeping outside without some sort of covering, but now I am glad to not have the extra weight.

The mosquitoes feast on every inch of my exposed skin. This is the worst they have been so far, but they too help with getting my mind off Gray. What would once have been torture is a welcomed distraction from the unbearable pain and guilt.

I down my first water bottle before noon and decide to turn on the GPS to find a water source, which must be close based on the prevalence of mosquitoes. It looks as though a creek is located less than a mile through the thicket. I decide to refill my bottle. It will have to be an emergency backup. I promised myself to never let it go empty. Now that I'm on my own, I must take every precaution. Grayson and I usually fall asleep well before the sun sets. But I can't stand the thought of sleeping out here by myself, and I push for several more miles before it's almost dark and I'm forced to stop. I camp just off the road, which I can't imagine is the safest choice, but it's the only option that requires minimal energy—all I have left.

I force myself to build a small fire to rehydrate a meat stew that Cassie has packed so that I'll have enough energy for the next day. I eat it unenthusiastically. My stomach churns.

I don't bother to set up the tarp—I just lay it flat on the ground after removing some rocks. I unfurl my sleeping bag and toss my shoes by my pack. The exhaustion and the pain in my back and feet dull my loneliness, and I sleep.

Birdcalls wake me before the rain can. It begins as a thin mist that covers my bag and skin in glass beads. Before I'm able to attempt a fire to boil water for breakfast, it is coming down in thick drops that soak my clothes within minutes. I yell curse words at my tarp that is completely dry inside my pack. Five minutes it would have taken me to set it up. Five. I decide to eat the dried berries as I walk and stop for a more substantial meal once the rain stops.

But it doesn't stop. By noon my stomach is aching and my feet slosh inside my shoes. "I have no tent!" I scream at the sky, which only releases more rain into my face. For the first time since leaving the New Colony, I am cold. You will not get sick, I command myself. Should I take some of the medicines that Cassie has packed? No, I'm overreacting—how long can it rain?

I walk with my water bottle out to catch droplets. It's full after only a couple of hours. "Enough!" I yell at the dark clouds. "Somehow this is the Coalition's fault," I mumble.

All day it rains and shows no signs of letting up. In the weeks we have traveled, never has it rained this much or for this long. At least Anna will be pleased that Cassie won't be fussing at her to hurry with carrying water for her blueberry and blackberry bushes inconveniently located several hundred yards away from the river.

I tell myself that it will be over soon, before nightfall, and that I will be able to find a flat place to lay down my tarp. No problem. In the morning, the sun will come out—surely. Thank goodness Grayson isn't here. It's at least a comfort to think of him dry and well fed. He's in the very capable care of Gabe, Cassie, and of course Anna, who is probably fussing over his broth and timing his next dose of medicine this very moment. I pick up my pace as I descend the sloping road.

Suddenly the water rushes on the right side of the road. I pause in disbelief, trying to figure out what is happening. *No.* The creek is flooding. Within moments the water is upon me. In spite of the fact that it is only to my knees, it knocks me down, and I fall backwards and to the side, pulled by the weight of my pack. It carries me several feet before I'm able to right myself and attempt to stand again. Instinctively, I grab for the names hanging on my neck. They're still there.

Again, the water pulls me down and drags me back more than a dozen feet. I grab frantically at my waist belt ready to cast off the backpack. The weight is dragging me down, and I try desperately to lose it in my panic. No. If I lose my pack, I'm as good as dead. I struggle to keep my head above water, sometimes going under for a few seconds at a time before I can gasp above the rushing surface.

The water rises. "Don't panic," I tell myself as the woods are suddenly illuminated by a burst of lightning followed almost immediately by thunder, which roars threateningly.

I'm able to get my bearings enough to stand. The water is now as high as my waist, and I know I won't be able to walk through it. I surrender and allow it to thrust me unmercifully into the trunk of a tree. My pack buffers the impact, but I ricochet off the tree and am pushed into a thick web of underbrush that grabs at me with searching fingers. My pack continues to pull me down, but I fight the panic that makes me struggle against its weight. In spite of everything in me that is telling me to throw it off, I keep my head back and take in breaths of thick air before being pulled down.

Just when I think I can no longer stay above it, and I resolve to cast off the pack, the water pushes me into an overturned tree with its tangled roots grasping pathetically into the air like it too is trying to avoid drowning. I grab at the roots wildly. I use them as a handle and cling desperately to the wall of the knotted and twisted roots while I catch my breath. "Enough!" I scream.

I remain pressed to the wall of roots for several moments, my hands numb from gripping them so hard. The water continues to rise for several inches but then seems to level off after about a half hour or so. Every muscle in my arms begs me to let go. My back is beginning to spasm from the awkward position and the weight of my waterlogged pack. I can't hold on much longer.

I will have to get on top of the log before my strength gives out. Again, the lightning comes followed shortly after by thunder. I need to be at high ground to avoid drowning and low ground to avoid the lightning. I'm stuck.

I allow the water to push me to the side, making careful decisions about the next roots to hold onto in case they should break off, and I am thrust under the tree. Gradually I am able to maneuver my hands so that I am in position to push up with my enormous weight and onto the top of the log. I cry out in pain as I do. "Come on!" I yell at myself. I am finally able to throw a leg over the top and hoist myself up. Only about six feet of the trunk that slopes to the forest floor is not submerged in the water, which rushes beside it. My only hope is that the water doesn't rise higher.

I sit on the trunk with the weight of the pack against the roots and secure myself by gripping the thick tree with my legs. I'm able to take off the pack. With a trembling hand, I hold it securely and unzip it with my teeth to retrieve the rope, which I risk grasping with the other hand that has been holding me steady. I tie the pack to the tree with thick, messy knots, but they seem to hold.

As the sun goes down completely, I'm able to see the woods in quick glimpses as the lightning illuminates ghost trees reaching wretchedly toward an angry sky that shows no signs of yielding. The flashes bring me back to the camera of the photographer in Radius's apartment. I jump each time, more unsettled by being thrust back into Radius's apartment than by the imminent danger of electrocution.

After an hour, the rain stops, and the moon looks down on me kindly. I shiver under its silver bloom, but allow the relief to set in. I'm able to get wet jerky from my pack, which I eat with trembling hands. My sleeping bag is completely soaked through and useless. I lie back on my pack and shift uncomfortably on the curvature of the tree.

"Just you and me," I tell the moon.

I wake in a whimsical, new world. The trees above are alive with the tuning orchestra of bird songs and the scampering of squirrels who seem un-vexed by the new river that has claimed their wood. A calm has settled. Light dapples the water, which dances in its morning brilliance. A snake swims by in undulating grace. Small fish swirl around the base of the log-island that saved my life. The water has only subsided a matter of inches, but it has worn itself out and is peaceful after the storm.

I take out my water filter and plunge it into the water by crouching on the lower part of the log. In front of me, something is floating, speckled like a rock. I jerk my filter back from the water when I realize that it's an animal. It takes some time for me to make sense of its awkward orientation. Under the water I see a small cloven hoof and realize that I am looking at a drowned deer fawn that is tangled in the branches.

There's no use waiting for the water to subside. I must be in some sort of natural bowl; I've traveled downhill for so long. Plus the earth must have been so dry from so long without rain that it absorbed little water. It might take days for it to subside, and I can't afford the time. I untie my pack and slip it on my shoulders. The water now comes up just below my waist, and it's possible for me to wade through it slowly. The trek is made more difficult by the fact that the forest floor is muddy, and my feet get stuck in it easily. I'm cautious about my step in case more floating animals are trapped below the murky water.

When I make it back to the road, which is slightly higher than the woods around it, the water only comes up mid-calf and wading through it is much easier. I refill my bottle and then adjust the pack back onto my shoulders for an entire mile. The hill begins to slant upward, and the water comes to my ankle. Finally I'm on dry land. I throw my pack savagely from my shoulders, which are now rubbed raw from the damp material chafing for so long.

Sleep last night was sporadic. The exhaustion settles in again with its full weight. I consider building a fire to make some breakfast and dry my sleeping bag, but it will take too long with the wood so wet. Instead I eat the last of the dried, though now soggy, berries and a strip of meat. I take the sleeping bag out and wrap it around myself in a sort of bulbous cape so that it can at least partially dry in the sun.

At some point I will need to check to see what has gotten wet and what has survived. I put my hope in the waterproof bag that the medicine, the GPS, and the matches were in. I can't deal with the frustration right now if they are wet. I just need to walk—walk and not think for as long as I can.

When the sun is mid-sky, I check the map. It looks as though I only need to follow this road for another eleven miles before I make it to the safe house. Eleven miles before sunset—with a waterlogged pack, blistered shoulders, blistered feet, and blistered spirit. But the promise of a roof over my head is so alluring that I tell myself I can push through. Hot food is surely waiting. My stomach moans its insistence that I press on.

Several miles later I'm getting drier, but my pack seems all the heavier. I throw it off in the middle of the road and lay the sleeping bag out like a picnic blanket. I eat the last two strips of jerky. At this point, I have to either find a safe house or build a fire to heat water to rehydrate the meals. I chew on the meat and kick my shoes off so that my feet can throb in the sunshine. My left heel is bleeding and sheets of skin are coming off on the balls of my feet. The nail of my right big toe looks like it might also come off. I do my best to tend them with the first aid kit, but the tape is damp, and I don't expect it to stay on for long.

I lay back in the sun. Everything throbs. Everything. For a few moments when I close my eyes, I see Grayson. I can almost feel him lying beside me. "Keep going," I tell myself.

He must have heard the storm and looked in the direction of it, knowing that I was somewhere out in the lonely land without a tent. It must have tortured him.

I have to keep walking.

I check the map again when the sun dips below the trees. Miraculously, the GPS is still working. I throw my hands up into the air in victory when it blinks to life. Four more miles, it looks like. Just four. With my current speed I should be there shortly after sunset.

My legs are beginning to cramp and every step becomes agony. I dip into my emergency water, hoping that the hydration will give me some energy. Twice I stumble on the road; the second time leaves my knees bleeding and my hands aching. I crawl for a few feet as I try to stand. I'm too weak to get back up with my pack on, so I push it off and put it back on once I'm upright. "Get it together, Rebecca," I tell myself aloud.

I walk with my eyes closing shut every few steps. "Wake up," I say. I stop to check my GPS again. A quarter mile and I will be there. It occurs to me that it could be like the last safe house, which wasn't visible from the road. The thought that the Coalition might have found the house sobers me. The flashlight was in Grayson's pack, so I'm wandering in the dark. "Never mind. Just keep going." After a few more minutes, I take out the GPS and follow it until I am within fourteen feet of the house. There it is! A soft light is in the small window. I want to cry as I stand in front of the door and throw off my pack.

Twice I knock. There are verbalizations inside, a face appears at the window, and the door is thrown open. An older man and a young girl my age stand framed in the threshold.

The girl looks me up and down. "Welcome," she says.

I collapse at her feet.

Chapter 27

For as long as I live, I will never again enjoy a bed as warm and soft as this bed. I lean back on clean pillows as the man brings me bowl after bowl of warm, rich soup while the girl immediately goes into action taking things out of my pack and laying them out by the fire.

"Tomorrow you'll tell us what's been going on, 215. Tonight you need to sleep and refuel," the man says.

I nod my appreciation.

"I want to check your feet," the girl tells me. "Your shoes look terrible." She bends down to untie them for me and brings me a basin of warm water that she fills from a pot on the fire. "Take them off," she insists.

I kick off my boots with great effort and rip the tape that has bunched into a tight cord around my ankle. I exhale slowly as I submerge them in the water. The man and the girl speak in soft whispers as they take thinned blankets from a cabinet by the fireplace.

"She's by herself," the girl says.

The man gives her a hard look. "We'll understand more tomorrow," he says under his breath as if I can't hear him. "Do you have a name, 215?" he asks more loudly from across the room.

"Rebecca."

"Well, Rebecca, you've been through quite a lot, that's clear. We haven't had a courier for some time. Get some rest now, and we'll figure out what needs to be figured in the morning. Sound good?"

"Sounds wonderful. Thank you." To my surprise tears begin to roll down my face. "Thank you so much."

The girl gave me something to drink "to help me sleep and dull the pain," she said, and I was grateful for it. I make it through a dreamless night but wake with every muscle in my body on fire and throbbing. The girl takes me outside to a large tub and helps me soak away the grime that has accumulated for so many miles. When I wince lifting my arms to wash my hair, she takes over scrubbing it herself with a soap she says her father made. She rubs my head as though it weren't attached to my body and then parts my hair methodically to search for "passengers," as she calls them.

Somehow, a girl I have just met searching for parasites on my head is less embarrassing than the treatment I got from Dylan. I picture Dylan finding a tick or some lice in my hair and falling to the floor of the beauty salon in shock. It's a satisfying image.

The girl returns with new, fresh clothes that she says must have just been waiting for me. They fit perfectly. Then she wraps me in a large quilt that smells like the clothes—like the earth just after a rain—and walks me back into the house so she can tend the blisters on my feet and shoulders. She gives me a thick salve that she insists I apply to the blisters on my face.

"What blisters?" I ask.

She grunts and assures me that I am cardinal red and that the blisters will be popping up before the end of the day if I don't put on the thick mixture, so just do it already.

Her father left before the sun was up to hunt and has promised to return with our lunch. Though the thought of my lunch frolicking in the woods would have repulsed me in my former life, I hope he'll find a deer or perhaps a fat rabbit. I can almost taste it.

The girl changes the sheets from my bed, which was filthy from my sleeping on them the night before. "Lay down," she orders gently and then busies herself in the kitchen.

I obey.

She returns with a plate of baked apples, a mug of mush, wild blueberries, and duck meat. I realize while eating a second helping that I do not know this girl's name and that we have hardly spoken at all.

"Thank you so much for everything. I can't tell you just how badly I needed this," I say between bites.

"My father was a courier. He gave me a pretty good idea about how difficult it is." She smiles such a broad smile that it seems to glow from her dark skin.

"Your father was a courier?"

"Yes, he was. Before he was replaced. He's retired, you might say."

"I'm sorry, I don't know your name."

"Jamie. My dad's name is Tom, but everyone calls him Bear." She pauses and looks at me imploringly. "We had almost given up hope on Colony 215," she leads, but I'm not ready to divulge too much information.

Saying either my mother or Grayson's name aloud will unhinge me. "I'm a sub, you might say."

"Well, the couriers haven't returned from their trip south. Dad thinks this is the year."

"And I'm late. I need to get down there."

Jamie smiles. "You need to take a day off. You're moving like you're rusting."

Bear enters the house with a heavy load of wood on his back and a goose slung over his shoulder. The head from its long neck swings pathetically. "Think we'll have a feast tonight," his voice booms. Sounds perfect. "You taking care of our friend here?" he asks his daughter.

"Absolutely," I assure him. "I'm so grateful, sir."

"Well, we are too, honey. We've been waiting for you long enough."

I look away. "I was telling Jamie that I'm a sub. I understand that you were a courier for some time."

"That I was. Sounds like we have some things to discuss."

I nod hesitantly.

Bear smiles a broad, glowing smile that makes him look like his daughter. "Jamie, I'd like you to prepare some leg wraps for Miss Rebecca. Mix some honey with that water. She needs to drink it regularly. And small meals every couple of hours, ok?"

"Yes sir." Jamie jumps up and immediately sets to work.

"Did you check her pack for repairs?" Bear asks like he's an officer drilling a soldier.

"I did. A few holes in the pack, and I've already sewed them up."

"Waterproofed them?"

"Yes sir."

"Boots?"

"Terrible condition. I've done the best I can with them, but she needs new ones."

Bear grunts. "Hundred more miles to go. We'll just have to make repairs as best we can."

I watch the two go back and forth as though I'm not even here. It's clear where Bear got his nickname. He stands at least a head and a half above his petite daughter.

"How about resupply?"

"She'll need more food. Looks like a lot of it got ruined in the rain. No tent. No flashlight. No gun."

Gun?

"Nor matches. Some shoddy medical supplies. No knife, sunblock, extra clothes, or bug repellent."

"Hmm." Bear raises his eyebrows. "And no partner."

I shift uncomfortably. "No," I confirm. "I did have one. I mean, I have one still, but he's waiting on me at the last safe house. Mountain fever."

Bear strokes his coarse, dark beard with his free hand after tossing the flaccid bird onto the table. "Had that once myself. You were right to leave him. Cassie and Gabe will take good care of him." Bear looks at me with concern. "You realize that there are one *hundred* miles to go and no safe houses left? Just one resupply station. This is one of the most grueling stretches of the trek, and you're doing it with not enough equipment and no backup."

"Yes sir," I say. "I don't have much of a choice about that."

Bear smiles again and his whole presence seems to soften. "You look pretty tough. I think you'll make it."

Jamie pushes a mug of warm, sweet water into my hand, which I drink obediently. "You'll leave tomorrow. Today your job is to recover," she says.

I want to stay in the cozy, tidy haven of hewn walls and soft light. It smells of rich foods and healing. I wish that Grayson could have made it at least this far. "My friend," I say to Jamie. "There's a chance he'll make it down this way if he recovers."

"Well, we'll be here."

"Please tell him," I clear my throat to thwart the tears that are threatening to come.

"He'll know," Jamie says as she binds my legs with warm rags. "He'll know, but I'll tell him anyway."

Just as Bear promised, dinner is nothing short of a feast—the goose, wild berries, cornbread, fish stew, boiled carrots, roasted potatoes, dark greens, and baked apples with wild honey for dessert. I eat until I am sure I can no longer fit another bite into my stomach.

After dinner Jamie and Bear tell riotous stories of other couriers who have stayed with them. Bear recounts one couple who got so frustrated with each other after the husband had gotten

294

them lost that the wife had made him sleep outside when they finally did arrive at the house. I laugh, in spite of myself, as he does an impression of the furious wife, hands on hips. Bear howls with laughter as he tells the story of a first-time courier who had mistakenly used poison oak leaves after a bout of diarrhea. He gets up to show me the wide-legged and hunched-over way he had walked into the house. Jamie almost falls out of her chair from laughing.

And Jamie and Bear tell the heroic stories of the men and women who have risked it all to carry the names to Sayon to be counted. Not one name has been lost in spite of tornadoes, sickness, bleeding feet, cracked ribs, and animal attacks. They listen intently as I tell my own story of surviving the flash flood. I am part of the great movement now. I am a rebel. Had Grayson seen this in me so many years before? Had he known I had it in me to come hundreds of miles and survive the earth that was bent on destruction? Or, perhaps it was because he had believed in me so much that I was able to come this far.

"Tell me, sir," I ask Bear. "How did you become a courier?"

"Well, same as you, I figure."

I shake my head. "It's a long story, but I guess you could say I stumbled onto the job. It was a bit of an accident."

Bear leans forward and looks me straight in the eye. "It was no accident. You were called just like I was, only under different circumstances."

I smile back at him with pride.

Bear leans forward and speaks slowly. "The movement has been around for years. When the nation got divided there was a group of people who had serious concerns. Those concerns fell on the deaf ears of scientists who had insisted that this was the only secure method for preservation. And they were backed by the military. Unity was the foundation of the country's success. That was the way for preservation. In the end, however, the men and women who favored the colony system won, and our country got divided. The nation was reincarnated in a sense. It had experienced a death and then went back to its infancy—colonies—but this time it was set on staying that way."

Jamie clears the table and sets a hot pot of coffee from the fire onto the table next to her dad. He looks at me seriously. "The people who were against colonies pleaded. They made the case that we would be unchecked and susceptible to corruption. And as it turns out, they were quite right. But they were overruled. They couldn't get enough support. So, before the birth of colonies, a group was formed—the League, they called themselves. They decided to set up lines of communication between the colonies, but of course colony supporters had already thought of that and set up methods to block technical communication between colonies. So, the group left to form their own colony of a kind, a headquarters. It's the Southern Colony, or Sayon as most call it, and it's under the protection of the British and Mexican alliance that moved into the southern part of what had once been the *United* States."

"And you've been there?" I ask in wonder, as though he is talking of some magical land.

"Many times. I was one of the very first couriers to actually carry names. Before then, we just carried data on the condition of the colony and possible corruption—were they dividing resources fairly? Was everyone receiving the same medical care? Were there significantly more exiles coming from one colony? Were colony officials for the National Council elections free and fair, et cetera? The League was able to compare colonies and determine if there truly was equity."

"And was there?"

Bear leans back and rubs his stomach as he thinks. "For the most part they were fair, actually. And when they weren't, the League was able to send information back to the colony members who were allegiant to the League, which helped the people regulate themselves. But of course you've heard of the War for Freedom."

"Yes of course, that war was led by Colony 108."

"My grandfather fought in that war," Bear tells me.

"So you were from Colony 108?" I ask excitedly.

"I was. And very proud to be."

"I was from there too. That was my colony before I got assimilated—and my hiking partner's too."

"You have a lot to be proud of, then. You come from a noble colony."

I consider divulging the fact my father is President Flora, but think better of it.

Bear continues soberly, "And it was Colony 108 that was instrumental in determining that the Coalition was moving in. It had been waiting to make its move. Actually, the Coalition had attacked a few times in the last fifty years, but we shot them down

296

every time. Colonists didn't even know they were being threatened. The Coalition had to come up with a more effective way of takeover."

"With plants and the VL system," I answer.

"Exactly. Colony 108 was significant in making sure that we are able to finish the work of eliminating the Coalition as a threat."

"How is that?" I ask, my stomach beginning to turn.

"Well, I have a theory."

Jamie leans back and crosses her arms. "Brace yourself, Rebecca. It's quite the theory, and most of the couriers who come through here don't believe—"

"The theory is," Bear continues, "that the colony assimilated as a sacrifice."

I freeze in my chair. "How could it do that?" I ask, trying to stay calm.

"Several of the couriers from the League had been running short. We were losing our backups and partners were dropping like flies. We had holes in the data from several of the colonies— 215 being one of them. It was like there was a shift. We needed new, well-trained people in there. Colony 108 was able to supply just those people, but the only way they would be able to get in there was if they assimilated in."

"That doesn't mean it was on purpose," I say more defensively than I'd like.

"No, it doesn't. But the timing of it sure was perfect."

"There was an earthquake."

"Yes, there was. I think they caused it."

"That's absurd!" I yell.

"I told you," Jamie says, shaking her head. "It's a crazy theory."

"Enough dynamite right outside the colony in the Membrane would have been enough to set off the measuring devices. It would have been enough for them to claim they were experiencing an earthquake and ask to be assimilated."

"President Flora didn't ask for assimilation. He wouldn't have."

"He might have if it meant he could then go to the powers that be and request an assimilation for a *trade*."

"I don't get it. A trade for what, exactly?" I ask derisively.

"A trade for a position and power. The theory is that Flora traded his colony for a spot in the national government."

"You mean we were *sold*."

"I mean that now former President Flora is part of the national government. He's working at the top," Bear smiles. "He's right where he needs to be to save us."

My head begins to spin and I feel like I might throw up. We were sold. We were sold. I put my head in my hands to steady myself.

"I'm sorry," Bear says, looking remorseful. "It's a lot to take in. Shouldn't have broken it like that."

"Are you ok?" Jamie asks. "You don't look well."

I put my hand up to show her that I'm fine. "All those families," I spit. "Sacrificed?"

"Yes and no. You were in clear danger anyway. If some other country we were trading with wanted Colony 108, which they probably did, then they would have found a way to take the colony eventually—by force or by fabricating a natural disaster threat themselves. Flora might have saved 108 from a more violent takeover by beating them to the punch if he engineered an earthquake reading and forced an assimilation. And it might have been the only way to save *all* of the colonies. One colony wouldn't have been able to fight the military. The other colonies weren't willing to unite. It might have been the only way."

"But it's been years now. A lot can change in that time. What if Flora doesn't save us? What if he's become corrupt too?"

Bear leans back in his chair and rubs his chin with thick fingers. "Then we're lost."

In spite of the medicine that Jamie gives me to help me sleep, I toss and turn throughout the night. The little sleep I do get is riddled with nightmares of my mother and father. I desperately want Grayson. Several times I talk myself out of going back to find him. But surely he's better now. There's a chance that he could hike with me. I can't do this alone.

I wake before sunrise and feel almost worse than I did when I arrived. My head is pounding and every muscle in my body is protesting against what it knows I will ask of it today—twenty miles. My goal is to make it to Sayon in five days. Bear assures me that this is an unwise idea. It's uphill for part of the way, and from here I detour from the road and hike wooded and rocky regions. This part of the trek is riddled with sinkholes that I must be vigilant to avoid. The temperatures are now in the nineties by

298

midday. It would be reckless to push too hard, too quickly. But I am ready to be unwise and reckless. I need a hundred miles of rugged terrain to abate the storm that is now brewing inside me.

Jamie helps me with my pack. "I've restocked you. You should be set. Make sure you put on the sunblock. You're going to need it the next few days, trust me."

"Thank you," I tell her.

"Couldn't get you a tent," Jamie says apologetically. She throws her arms around me. "You're a hero, Rebecca. You're going to make it."

I don't want to be a hero. I want to stay here with the only real girl friend I've had since Liza in the Old Colony. I realize that I'm the first girl she's probably seen in months. She must be lonely here too.

"You're the real hero, Jamie. What you do for the couriers—"

"It's a pleasure," she interrupts. "You've got to get going."

I'm afraid she's close to tears, which will incite my own, so I turn quickly.

Bear is splitting logs when I walk outside. "Thank you," I tell him. "You all were so good to me."

Bear lays his axe down. "Be careful out there now," he says. "The next part's tricky."

"That's what I hear." I smile weakly. "I'll be very careful."

"My little girl did a wonderful job on those shoes of yours. Worked a miracle."

"Yes sir," I say, tapping them in the dirt. "She does a good patch job."

Bear's smile transforms him. "Listen, Rebecca, honey," he says, shifting. "Your dad did what he had to do."

I swallow hard trying not to let my shock show.

"He knows what he gave up. And he knows why. All of this is in his control from where he sits in the Executive Colony. It's always been the plan."

"I'm sure I don't understand."

"Secret's safe with me, Rebecca. But it wasn't too hard to put together with you turning white as a sheet at dinner and then talking in your sleep like you did." Bear's smile turns mischievous.

I look at him hard. I can't decide if I want to curse him or thank him. "He did what he had to," he repeats more slowly, as if I didn't understand him the first time.

"There had to have been a different way," I insist. "You don't know what we've been through."

Bear looks off into the woods as the sun comes up, as though he's searching for something. "I don't know what you've been through. But I know where you are now. And I know that your name is on that list hanging around your neck."

I nod solemnly.

"And I know your dad. Or I did, which might be the same thing." Bear smiles. "You're one of those tough ones. Truth is, I knew you because you've got your daddy in you."

Bear brings me into his tight embrace. "You know, girl, you just might be the last courier. That's what we've been praying for. This is all about to end. Last courier. Last hundred miles, and every step brings you closer to freedom."

"Yes sir," I tell him. "Yes sir. But the last one hundred were my freedom. The next hundred are just to make sure everyone else gets it too."

Bear laughs a deep, rumbling laugh. "You got it. Take 'em home."

Chapter 28

Jamie was right about the sun-block. I might literally be baking. She had refilled both my water bottles and generously added a third. I don't mind their extra weight. By midday I have drunk two of them and am halfway through the third before I am able to find a water source. The heat blurs my thinking and dulls my senses, but I'm grateful for it. Being too clear-headed makes my memories all the more painful.

I spend the first night on the edge of a small lake on my tarp. The mosquitoes are unbearable, but I find that, after digging a little farther in my pack, Jamie has also supplied me with a net that I'm able to rig up on a tree like a drooping tent that keeps out most of the swarm. She has also packed some of the herbs that she gave me to help me sleep while I was in the safe house. I mix them with my water and drink them gratefully.

The country here is more open. Most of the journey before was through parts of the Membrane that are more wooded, more protected with the exception of the field of graves. Here, I am exposed to the wide sky, and my loneliness fills the empty landscape. I know from the map that I have a serious elevation increase ahead. My consolation is that at least the temperature will drop slightly.

I tick the miles off quickly now. When Grayson and I started, we celebrated each mile and couldn't believe it when we were actually making eight miles a day up a mountain. Now I am able to push more than twenty miles a day, at least. My feet are more sure, and I tell myself that I'm walking toward Grayson with every step even though he is behind me. That alone is enough to keep me going.

I left Jamie and Bear's house two days ago and am feeling strong. I cross a field of open grass, watching my step for stones or snakes. I make a note to check every inch of myself for ticks tonight.

"How do you like me now, Radius?" I yell to the sky. "How's my style, babe?" I throw my arms out wide. "Well, Panel? How's this? Could the colony use a girl with hairy legs and blistered skin? Brushing hair isn't really my thing now, you know. What's that?

Why yes, I do stink. You think I'd make a perfect ballooner ad? That's what I was thinking too. It makes a difference now, doesn't it? Now that I have the safe list hanging around my neck and your names are definitely *not* on—" I stop short.

For the first time it occurs to me that I'm carrying thousands of names to safety, but I don't know what it will mean for those on the other list. Destruction? In saving these, am I sending others to their doom? I grasp the metal chain around my neck. The others had a choice. They were willing to push out those who didn't become one of them or support them. But it didn't have to be this way.

I think of Radius, who used me for his own gain, whose lies pushed out truth so that I was almost nonexistent—lies that whispered to me that I was someone's to be owned and that my purpose was to be for someone else's pleasure. But where did he learn that? How did he become the Lie? I remember the time I tried to video him as he held the bird, and his panic of something that had happened in his past. Was there a time when he was someone different, a time before the Lie took him over as well?

Still now, as I walk, I know that another girl is living in my old prison. My heart breaks for her, whoever she is. That young girl might be on this list—and now I'm walking her and me both to safety. I think of all the clients who took advantage of the young girl who would one day climb mountains and survive a flood, but cowered under their sick demands.

And I think of Lex, who lured me in and made me believe I had a friend, and the people who exiled my mother and forced my father to carry an unbearable burden. They had all surrounded themselves with so much shimmering light that I couldn't see how truly dark they were. But was there some pain that caused them to become that way?

Suddenly, a roar fills the sky. I hit the ground as it trembles. That's not thunder. I scan a clear sky. The sound gets closer, coming from the east. A plane, not a drone. A *plane*. Perhaps there has been another assimilation? International trades are done in the neutral zones in the ocean and wouldn't be down this far south or west. I don't recognize this kind of craft. Is it the Coalition? If so, Colony Military Intelligence will have already detected it. If it has gotten this far, it's either allowed or going to be blown up in a matter of seconds. I cover my head so that I cannot be detected, and also because the roar is so loud that it makes my eardrums feel like they might burst.

It fades as it passes behind me. I lay where I am for several minutes in case more are to follow, but the earth returns to the peace that it had before. I stand, still shaking. There are sixty more miles, but suddenly it feels like a thousand. I pick up my pace.

Today I made my longest distance yet—twenty-seven miles. It's dark before I stop to set up camp, although there isn't much to set up without a tent, and I'm too shaken by the plane to start a fire. I decide to skip cooking and unfurl my sleeping bag beneath a tree. I drape my net over it by hanging it from a low branch. It's dried fish and cold water mixed with corn meal for dinner tonight. By the light of my new flashlight I re-bandage my feet.

I'm worried about getting into too deep of a sleep tonight in case I need to get up quickly, so I skip the sleeping medicine. I know the pain will keep me in a light sleep at best, but it's necessary to stay alert. I wish Grayson were here so we could take turns. If another plane comes, surely they won't be able to see me. All the same, I jump at every nocturnal creature's rustle.

My sleep is fitful. I assume every night noise is the Coalition coming to find me after receiving a suspicious report from one of their aircraft. They were flying low, but still I know I'm being more paranoid than is reasonable. What worries me even more is that Grayson is out there. Did he hear the same plane? Or a different one maybe? Perhaps more are coming. I wish he were here with me more than anything now.

"Almost there, Rebecca," I tell myself after I wake sometime in the night. "Just take it easy. Deliver the names and go back for Grayson."

I calculate the time it will take me to return. If I don't get caught in a flood, and I'm able to restock the right supplies, I figure I should be able to come back fourteen days from now. One day to rest and restock in Sayon, five days back to Bear's and Jamie's house, one day to rest, and the final stretch of quick hiking. With new boots and a little better gear I could go quicker, maybe. Total, I will have only left him for eighteen days.

"Please just stay there, Gray," I say to the northeast. By the time I come back Grayson will have completely recovered. He will have helped put the bridge back up and maybe even built Cassie and

Gabe's house. I fall asleep to sweet thoughts of him holding me, and letting his peace envelop me.

What seems like just moments later I wake to a deafening boom that shakes the ground. Without hesitation I grab my pack, tear down my net, ripping it in the process, and move deeper into the woods. I coil under a tree with my sleeping bag over my head before I realize that the sound has stopped. It wasn't a plane. Explosives? Again, the sky booms, and I put my hands over my mouth to stop myself from screaming.

Not far in the distance I see what looks like an electric claw reaching down to the earth forebodingly. "Storm," I whisper. "It's thunder. Just thunder." I laugh into my sleeping bag. "Boom!" I yell excitedly when it rolls again.

I count the seconds between the lightning and the sound. It's just less than two miles away, but with any luck it will move just north of me. All the same, I check my GPS to look for any water sources so I don't get caught in another flood. The creek where I refilled my water earlier is two miles away. "Go to sleep, Rebecca," I tell myself coarsely. "You only have to hike twenty miles tomorrow. Just a couple of hours of sleep will do."

I resort to resting instead and give up on any kind of sleep between the thunder rolls that come more frequently. An hour or so later the eastern sky is illuminated with morning's glow, competing with the staccato light symphony in the northwest. Across the meadow, lightning strikes a tree that looks to be stranded from its herd. Within seconds it is consumed in flames.

I scan the dry grass around it. I've got to move to lower ground and quick. As fast as I can, I shove everything into my pack, grateful for once that I don't have a tent. I run between trees, keeping my eyes on the west and turning often to keep the burning tree in my sight. The rain begins, much to my relief, and although the tree shows more smoke than flames now, it's clearly still on fire and could spread. It's burning from the inside out, but already a couple of the branches are falling onto the grass. I run low and quickly through the sparse trees. Lightning touches down again not far from me and again a few minutes later somewhere behind me. I yell against the thunder.

For several minutes, I outrun the storm and the threat of a forest fire. Several times I slip in the downpour that makes the rocks beneath my feet untrustworthy. I know I am bleeding, but I get up and run harder. And then it rains harder; we are in a

304

competition, the rain and I. Frantically, I search for a low spot, a ditch, something, anything away from these trees. Ahead I see a low outcrop of rocks where the land slopes downward. I race to it, throwing my pack under the overhang of rock.

I burrow under it as fast as I can, clutching my pack to my chest, and cry out as though it's on fire when I remember that the pack has a metal frame. I dump everything out as quickly as I can and wildly throw my pots and the pack as far away from me as possible.

I watch in silence as the sky asserts itself on the earth with powerful, dynamic fingers that testify to its authority. Birds fly haphazardly to other trees in a desperate search for safety. All around me the lightning strikes and the thunder hovers above.

I didn't survive assimilation, Radius, and almost four hundred miles under this sky for it to claim me now. I may have walked the last hundred miles without a partner, but I am not alone. There is authority behind that sky—the sky itself is not the power. Heavy peace embraces me. All of this is merely a show, a display, a performance just for me. I sit back and see its beauty in the silhouettes of the trees and the silver of the illuminated earth. Each bolt has been commanded where to strike for my pleasure if I allow it, not to incite fear. I lay back and linger in the certainty of my safety as the sun rises and the storm begins to pass.

I get up and collect my pack. "Twenty more miles," I tell it.

Twenty more miles on a path that was laid just for me.

The next two days are steady. Sayon pulls me in like a magnet. I push through the pain and tick the miles off quickly. Food's low, but there will be feasts once I arrive. Fresh fruit, thick, juicy meats, and baked pies like my mother used to make. They will have it all. Dozens of people will be there to usher me in. "We'd almost given up hope!" they'll say as they clap me on the back. "But you did it! You've made it!" I'll enter Sayon a hero. And that night—a bed, a real bed. Without a mosquito in sight. I can almost feel the warm water dripping down my body from a real shower. Maybe I'll even shave my legs. Or maybe not.

Wild blackberry bushes line the trail. Their fruit is bitter but satisfying and reminds me of the unripe berries Gray and I sucked in the Messenger Tree. I'm foraging in a small bed on a hill when I hear it—the thick rustle of a bush. My first thought is that it is a big cat, and I freeze in my tracks. Quickly, I get off the trail and hide behind a tree that has overturned with its roots up, just in time.

A man with white blond hair is bent low with a large pack as he makes his way up the gradually sloping hill. He is moving quickly. I get as low as I can behind the upturned tree and close my eyes when I know he is passing right beside me. He must be only a few feet away and I can hear the rhythmic thud of his boots.

I crouch there, holding my breath, until I can no longer hear him. Slowly, I rise up to see the trail again. Couriers usually work in pairs. That couldn't have been a courier. But then again, I'm hiking alone. I wait for more than thirty minutes before emerging from my hiding place. Maybe another courier is following along at a slower pace. If he were part of the Coalition, then he's probably armed. It's not worth the risk. Rebel or Coalition, either way I can't prove who I am and getting shot is a real possibility.

I make my way through the woods instead of the trail for a few miles so that I can easily hide if there are more of whoever that guy was. By sunset, I get back on the trail and run. The sooner I get to Sayon, the better.

The last two days of the trek are treacherous. A mountain stands in my way. Just one lousy mountain to go. "Couldn't they have put the headquarters on this side of you?" I ask my mountain. "Move out of the way!"

By mid-afternoon I have summited. It's almost barren up here. A few sparse trees and I look out over the abandoned land. Once, in the time before assimilations, families probably sat here, perhaps ate a picnic, and looked out over their glittering and secure world. I close my eyes and picture the scene they must have looked out on—thick foliage dotted here and there with the evidence of human life, and buildings rising in the distance of nearby cities, bustling with life.

It has gone silent now. The landscape I see is scarred with deep pockets from sinkholes and disfigured from the ripping of earthquakes. We once were the masters of this land until it shook us off and we were forced to move north to safer areas. We scrambled to continue our civilization until we could be masters once again.

Down there, somewhere to the southwest, is the hope for thousands of people, and I have only to walk to it. I stand and look back at how far I've come, but even looking back along the horizon from where I walked, I see the land that reshaped me. The earth and I have this in common. We both abide.

I can't sleep the night before I reach Sayon. I haven't heard another plane since that day. It isn't fear that keeps me awake, it is pain—every muscle is lit aflame. My back pain is excruciating. I take some of the medicine that Jamie gave me, which allows me a few hours of sleep. The earth is still except for the thin evergreens that yield to the breeze's gentle persuasion. The night orchestra of the woods—small frogs, chirping and buzzing insects, and the hunting owl—play their inharmonious lullaby and for a few moments I escape from the pain and am able to sleep.

I dream of my mother, sleeping somewhere far away on the ravaged earth, under the fickle sky. We lay there together, in my dream, looking up. My mother turns her head to me and smiles.

"I'm sorry," I tell her. "I'm so sorry for everything." I want her to know how far I carried the list and all that I've been through. I part my lips to speak, but she holds her finger up to her mouth to silence me.

"Shh," she whispers, but when she does her face begins to fall away as sinkholes open in her skin. Her smile and then her body crumble as though an earthquake has been unleashed inside her.

"Mom!" I scream into the night until I wake myself.

I splash water onto my face from my bottle. The pain in my back and in my feet is almost unbearable. "First, I'll get Grayson, and then I'll get you. I promise, Mom. Somehow."

I pull out the map from my pack to preserve the GPS battery and read it by flashlight, which I secure with my mouth. I groan as I lift my arms over my head to read the map. Eleven more miles. That's it. Downhill. Straight to headquarters. "I'm going now," I mumble with the flashlight still in my teeth.

Never before did I think it possible for me to go on so little food and sleep. Everything hurts—intensely. I want to cry as I put my pack on my back. My spine is crumbling beneath its weight. But I want to get out as soon as possible in case I run into another person. Seeing that guy has unnerved me. Within minutes I am back on the trail. I figure the sun will be up in about three hours and I should arrive just after daybreak.

My flashlight casts a surprising amount of light for its small size. "No problem," I tell the moon. I stumble several times on thick roots, but I get up quickly, thinking that this will be the last of my falls before I make it. "Almost," I say each time I get up.

After two hours I have gone through a water bottle and a half. The falls might be more frequent, but traveling without the glaring sun overhead is worth it. "I should have done this long before now," I tell my companion, the moon. "No more oven hiking for me. I'm nocturnal from now on."

I stop briefly to get some jerky and a handful of dried fruits from my pack. The night sounds begin to fade and I can just see the hint of morning light in a faint haze to the east. The trees become more pronounced.

I take the opportunity to empty my bladder next to a small tree. I unbutton my shorts and lean down, still with my pack on, next to the tree that is covered with gnarled roots. I stumble a bit as I squat and right myself with my hand.

"Ahhh!" I scream into the darkness as I feel flesh under the weight of my hand and the sharp stab of whatever has just pierced my arm. I jump up and fall over, grabbing my flashlight in time to see one of the roots curling in on itself. I stumble backward and flash the light, trembling from my unsteady hands, over the ground in case there are more of them. In the light I see small eyes reflected back from a triangular head.

"No," I whisper. This cannot be happening. "No!" I scream as the reality sets in.

I turn quickly to the trail and shine the light on my arm, which is throbbing from the stab.

Suddenly it seems as though there are snakes everywhere. I scan the trail with the light while still trying to walk quickly. "That's a root," I say as I make an exaggerated step over a serpentine figure in front of me. "Stay calm, Rebecca. Just stay calm."

I remember to hold my arm up to keep the swelling down, but that's all that I can remember. What was it that Pepper said about some four-leafed plant that—? No, that was for headache. Maybe he didn't say anything. I pound my fist against my head.

The east continues to get lighter but not quickly enough. "Come on," I growl. "I need some light!" Stay calm. That's the plan. It's only another seven miles to get there. Seven, after hundreds of miles. Seven. I can do anything for seven miles, right?

Asa's instructions come back to me. I can see his written directions for snakebite in my mind. *Do not cut, or attempt to remove the poison.* Ok, no problem. *Clean the wound, try to identify the snake, and get to medical treatment as quickly as possible. Do not overexert as this will cause the poison to flow more quickly though your system. Apply ice.* No, wait. *Don't apply ice?* That's a sprain. No, snake bite. I can't recall. What happens if you get a snake bite on a sprained ankle? Stay focused, Rebecca!

No problem, I'll just prop it up on some pillows and take a picture of the snake that just bit me, so I can show it to the paramedics once the ambulance arrives to bring me ice. Or not. Seven miles with a thirty-pound pack isn't overexertion, right?

I stop by the side of the trail and take a long drink of water. "Get it together." I take deep breaths until my hands stop shaking, and I can feel my heart, which is quickly pumping poison throughout my body, return to a normal pace. I pour some water on the bite, which is already beginning to swell. Two small puncture holes erupt thick blood that glows bright crimson in the beam of the flashlight. I rip open my pack and dig through it with one hand to find the first aid kit. I liberally pour a small bottle of disinfectant on it and grit my teeth beneath the burn as I gingerly dab the wound with some clean cotton.

All I had to do was sleep through the night and get up in the morning. "What were you thinking?" I scream at myself as I wrap gauze around the arm that is throbbing now from the disinfectant. I use the rope around my arm and neck to make a sling so that it can remain elevated.

Getting my pack back on isn't easy with one arm. I crouch down and get one strap over my right shoulder and then pull the left strap on with my good arm. It takes me almost five minutes to get the buckles connected. The rope presses into my back painfully. Seven miles. Nice and slow so I don't pump poison to all my organs. They probably have gallons of anti-venom just lying around in Sayon. Just seven miles, and everything will be fine. I'll take the medicine while I eat hamburgers and fresh pies.

The sun rises steadily and my arm is swelling rapidly. I have to loosen the ropes after less than a mile to accommodate the inflammation.

"Ahh!" I yell in frustration at my own stupidity. I could have just now been getting up, eating some breakfast, and then hitting the trail again. In the light—where I could *see* things like, you know, venomous snakes for example. I flush at the thought of explaining my recklessness to Grayson.

Whether it's the pain or my nerves, my heart begins to beat rapidly. I unscrew the cap to my water bottle with one hand and drink it slowly to help me calm down. Moments later I vomit and my stomach begins to cramp.

"Ok, Rebecca. Pick up the pace, just a little," I whisper once I recover.

It's a race now—me against the venom. I know I need to get to Sayon as soon as possible to outrun the poison and receive the anti-venom. But the faster I go, the more quickly the venom can spread. I decide to move as quickly as possible without being able to feel my heart pounding. It's a balance, interrupted by the sudden and staccato rhythm of my heart that precedes another vomiting episode.

I don't know what kind of snake bit me. It was too dark to get a clear view, but even if I had, I wouldn't be able to identify it, necessarily. Many times on the trail Grayson had spotted slithering creatures that I would have walked right past. He seemed to have a knack for picking them out from the underbrush, where I would have assumed they *were* the underbrush.

Grayson would run his fingers through his hair and determine which species we were looking at. "This one's a king snake. No problem." Or, "See that red guy? He's a corn snake." Almost always they were non-venomous, he claimed. But we stayed clear all the same. Grayson might have thrown out names, but there was no one to validate his claims. Surely, real couriers received this in training. But I was no real courier. The only venomous snake that I can successfully identify is a rattlesnake, and only if it were to shake its big ugly tail in my face. It hadn't done that, so I successfully ruled out one snake from among hundreds of possibilities.

After a couple of hours hiking downhill, the dappled trail in front of me begins to blur. I shake my head and strain my eyes trying to sharpen my vision. It's fully light now, glaringly so, and it makes my head pound. I can't be far, perhaps another two miles or so. I trip on a rock and fall hard on the path onto my hurt arm, the full weight of the pack on top of me. The stabbing pain that was shooting up to my shoulder now feels like fire pulsing up to my neck. Hot tears come to my eyes, blurring my vision even more. "Get up!" I command myself.

The temperature is rising, and I know I need more water intake after vomiting. I sip carefully, hoping to keep it down. My stomach begins to cramp painfully again, and I crouch, using my good hand to balance until it passes. Exhaustion, pain, and poison overtake me. I lean against a tree, fighting to stay conscious.

It takes me some time to figure out what exactly I am looking at. I moan. A river, I determine by the sound of it ahead. I have to ford a river. My face begins to get numb. "No problem," I tell it. I can't determine how deep it is, but it looks more like a creek than a river.

I step in it boldly. The cool of the water rouses me a bit, and I trudge through it with stiff legs. I fall into it during a wave of abdominal cramps, but push myself back up. I scream through gritted teeth. "Almost there! *Come on*, Rebecca!"

The pain now is unbearable. I look into the sky as I walk and breathe deep, slow breaths. This last mile is the longest one of my life. Ahead the woods disappear into what looks to be gray, dilapidated buildings, their windows winking in the sunlight. I'm not entirely certain that I'm not hallucinating. But either way, I begin to run toward them with the last energy I have left.

"Hey!" I yell, waving my good arm. "I made it."

I enter the colony with wide eyes. It's hard to focus on any one thing. My eyes dart to the beams of a bridge that once stood and billboards with their advertisements, now grayed and faded, flapping in the wind like flags. It is silent. There is no bustle. No verdant landscape or colorfully dressed welcome committee to hail me a hero. No parade. No pies.

An abandoned kingdom stretches out before me. I walk crumbling streets, convincing myself that this is a hallucination. The poison has won the race, and I will have to give it its reward until it releases me from its grip, or I am able to at least crawl the remaining miles to the glittering colony that has been my hope for four hundred miles.

I allow my eyes to climb the soaring building that seems to touch the sky. It has been completely taken over with kudzu.

I begin to feel lightheaded. My thoughts become slow and cumbersome. "Well, I'll be." I gawk at the verdant building, wondering if it is real or hallucination. "Kudzu. Now *that* one I recognize." My head pounds and my stomach cramps. "Silver lining," I tell the kudzu. "I *finally* have the right symptoms for you."

I decide to gather a few leaves to test if this is real. I take a step toward the vine-covered building, but I can't tell if the building is swaying or I am.

"Hey!" a man calls from behind me.

"Hey, yourself," I call over my shoulder to the man I'm hallucinating without taking my eyes off the climbing plant. "I could just boil this up and it would be great for treating a migraine or diarrhea—so it will mitigate my symptoms as I die. How do you like that, Pepper? See, I'm good at this," I mumble as I reach to pick some of the plant.

"Girl! Who are you?"

I hear heavy footsteps behind me. A large hand grasps my left shoulder, and I cry out in pain.

Not a hallucination.

I turn to see a man, his face blurred. His words seem to be coming faster than his mouth, which is moving in slow motion.

"I asked, who are you?" he repeats roughly.

"Rebecca, Colony 215. Courier . . . sort of."

Chapter 29

Pain rouses me. A steady beeping sounds in my ears, intensifying my headache. I open my eyes expecting to see the woods surrounding me, but instead my vision comes into focus on a bag of fluids hanging from a metal pole.

"Rebecca?" A woman's voice whispers beside me.

I turn to see a gentle face, but it takes a moment for it to come into focus. I study each feature: the small lines around concerned eyes, the flush of her cheeks, the delicate gray along the hairline. I feel the warmth of her hand on my face. I smell earth and citrus. It is the venom playing tricks.

"Mom?"

The woman nods. I close my eyes, waiting to wake up.

"It's me, sweetheart."

Another woman and a man who are hovering above me speak to each other in hushed tones. "Severe dehydration. Two bags of fluids."

The man asks, "Dilaudid? The morphine could suppress respiration, correct?"

"Correct, she's not out of the woods yet."

"Look at the level of the necrosis. Do we conclude it was a viper?"

"Yes. Administer the anti-venom."

I try to sit up without opening my eyes. "No," I groan. "I'm almost there." I swing my arm to get the woman away, but find that somehow it is caught in wires. The pain in my left arm sends shocks through my body.

"Charles, the midazolam."

I dream of Grayson. We're walking in the field with the winged woman who watches over the sleepers below ground. Grayson takes my hand as we approach her. She turns her stone head to me and looks at me with white eyes. Air rushes over me with each wave of her powerful wings. "Wake up," she says. "Rebecca. Wake up."

The window is dark when I open my eyes. "You did well, darling. Very well."

I jump at the woman's voice. "I'm home? Did I make it?" The woman comes into focus. "Mom?"

"Yes, sweetheart. It's me." She laughs and cries as she kisses my cheek.

I shake my head back and forth. "Am I home, Mom?" I ask her over and over. "It's not you."

"Yes," she soothes, wrapping her arms around me. "I've got you. I've got you," she repeats until I know it's true. I cry until I can't breathe.

A young woman rushes into the room as the beeping increases.

"It's ok," my mother tells her. "She's just getting a little overexcited."

The woman nods and checks my arm, which has been newly bandaged and is suspended in a sling. "The anti-venom is working," she says.

I take in every detail of my mother's face again. She has been resurrected.

"Mom, I'm so sorry," I sob into her hair.

Shame, more powerful than the venom, courses through every inch of me and sets me on fire. I suddenly feel the scars burning in my neck where the stones once were.

"Rebecca, it wasn't your fault. You have to let that in, do you understand?" I close my eyes while more tears escape.

"But you don't know what I've done. After you were exiled I—"

"Shh. I know. I am so sorry I couldn't protect you." She strokes the scars along my neck and collarbone.

My mother holds me in her arms until I stop crying, and I allow her words to comfort me. I know there will be a day when I can allow the full truth in. But not yet.

"I was going to come for you," I tell her.

My mother sighs heavily. "There's also an underground system for the exiled who know about it. I made it back here not too long ago." My mother looks thinner, paler. Her journey here had likely been just as difficult as mine.

"Rebecca, honey, is Grayson—"

"He's ok, Mom," I tell her quickly.

She presses her hand against her chest and exhales slowly as though a heavy weight has finally been lifted.

"He got mountain fever. He was too sick to go on. He's still at a safe house about a hundred and fifty miles back. I felt like I had to keep going." I reach for the chain around my neck, but it is missing, and I sit bolt upright.

My mother puts her hand on my shoulder. "We turned it in. You were right to go when you did, though I thought Will Skycap would have been the one bringing you here." Her face darkens. "Will was supposed to—but then I expect the New Colony had lots of suspicions they needed to tend to."

I look away and confirm her fears.

"Will was a good man," Mom says. "His hiking partner, Richard Glover, said he waited three days for him to show. He had to keep going." My mother suddenly looks very tired. "But you made it here, Rebecca—thank God you're away from there and that man. And you made just in time. The reckoning could be any day now. Colony 215 was the missing piece."

"What's going to happen?"

My mother smiles. It's like being home again, sitting across from her at our breakfast table. "For more than ten years we've been getting ready for this. No more colonies. And the people on that list that you carried, my darling, will be taken to safety."

"And those who aren't on the safe list?"

Her face darkens. "Let's talk about it when you're feeling better. In fact, we have a lot more to catch up on," she says, glancing at my scars. She looks like she might cry. "You've been through—"

"Tell me now. Please. I want to know. I've earned it."

My mother looks away and turns back to me resolutely with the poise of a first lady. "The colonists who could work were going to be sold to other countries. The ones who couldn't were going to be eliminated. We have enough evidence of that now to prove to the United Nations, and we have the names of those who were issuing the takeover. We'll see that they are brought to justice, and that the innocent people who were being pushed out are safe."

I lean back onto my pillow. "I had wanted to be a part of the New. I would have done anything, but they were so cruel."

"Yes. And you and Grayson were a big part in ending it. Families will be reunited and innocent people will be saved because you were willing to carry their names."

"I wouldn't have made it without Grayson."

"I felt confident that you both would make your way here. The *plan* was that you were to stay at Cherish for a year and then leave this spring with Will and Gray. I expected you a couple of months ago. When Glover said that Will hadn't met him, we hoped you all were just delayed. My mind went to the worst, though, and we sent someone to go find you as well as bring back the safe house hosts in case we evacuate. I was hoping against hope that you were somewhere in the Membrane and that you hadn't been"—my mother clears her throat—"Well, that you hadn't gone back to . . ."

I look away as her voice trails off. I'm afraid she might cry. "Mom, it wasn't your fault."

Mom hugs me tightly.

It suddenly dawns on me. "I think I saw the person you sent. But I hid."

"Good. He'll get word at the next safe house and go to find Grayson, I'm sure. He'll bring him back."

Tears of relief begin to fall again. I wanted to be the one to get him, but now he'll be here even before I could get to him.

"Hey," my mother says, squeezing my good arm. "Right now, you need to rest."

"I don't know what kind of snake it was. Cream spots. Slithery—I don't know."

My mother purses her lips. "They could tell by the necrosis and the bruising and by how much it was bleeding that it was some sort of viper, most likely a copperhead in these parts. They gave you anti-venom. You started responding to it within a few hours. You're the big talk around here, you know, but everyone's been given instructions to give you some space until you recover fully. Let's not worry about anything, *anything* until you recover. Everything else can wait."

I spend the next twenty-four hours in the simple room of the infirmary. My mother never leaves my side. In addition to the anti-venom, I also receive several bags of IV fluids. My feet are bandaged, my blistered skin tended, and x-rays are taken of my back, revealing two small stress fractures in the lower vertebrate. The doctor inserts a small needle into my spine and fills the fractures with some sort of bone cementing agent. I am given anti-inflammatory and pain medications and instructions to rest and gain weight. My mother brings calorie-rich meals and stuffs me full of vitamins. For the first time in weeks I spend a night without pain due to the powerful medicine that drips through my IVs.

But it does nothing for the ache in my chest. Sitting in this room is maddening, especially after being in the wild expanse of the Membrane. I am suffocating without the open spaces and choking on my worry over Gray.

"Dr. Ottosen said that had you been bitten the day before, you might have lost the use of your hand."

I watch the IV drip slowly. "There were so many other times I could have been harmed but was spared somehow."

My mother smiles. "Thank goodness."

From my window I can see the ruins that are Sayon, a far cry from the glittering kingdom I thought it would be. In the distance I see the mountain that I stood atop days before. I want to hike. I want to run back to Grayson and hike that final stretch together as it should have been.

The doctor, a pretty blond woman with a kind face, gives my mother instructions for caring for me in our dormitory. I dress quickly into a pair of rough cargo pants and a navy tank top. We step out of the hospital onto the crumbling road.

"I thought Sayon would be different," I tell her.

"There are very few of us here. It's a pit stop of sorts. Just forty miles from here is a port where ships come to pick up the exiled to take them to South America. It's where we'll be going soon. Technically, Sayon was purchased by the Latin American Mission Board. We are under their protection. The colonies don't know that we've been using it for our operations."

"What happened here?"

"Earthquake. This was one of the first areas hit. At one time half a million people lived here."

I look around at the skeletons of empty and decaying buildings that stretch into the air, still noble in spite of their blight. I try to picture this as a thriving city—people zipping their bikes between traffic, men and women in suits talking on their phones as they hurry to their next appointments, children pulling at their mothers' hands as they cross the street. It rings with silence now.

"Thousands died in the series of earthquakes. The terrorist organization, the Syndicate Ten, also known around here as the Coalition, is composed of ten governments that have been trying to take over for some time. It was a beast that emerged from the sea—first it set up a naval force in the Atlantic to get closer, and then it launched biological warfare initiatives. After the earthquakes, hundreds of thousands died from a deadly virus that was sprayed from drones. By the time the US discovered what was happening and launched a counterattack, it was too late."

It is no wonder that the colony system was adopted. The generation alive during the destruction must have been forced to learn survival over attachment. I pictured the chaos that ensued after the earthquakes—thousands trapped under toppled buildings and crumbled bridges. And through the thick air, the scrambling few who tried to rescue their buried friends began contorting as their skin made contact with raining viruses. I thought of an anthill that Gray had discovered in Our Colony. We had watched with fascination as the creatures, like these people, had erupted in confusion as we hurled rocks onto their small city, and washed them away in a deluge from our water bottle.

"The city was abandoned in a mass exodus," my mother continues as she leads me down a wide street lined with what were probably once thriving shops. "This land was sold to the Latin American Mission Board, which had fared much better in the destruction. Our country needed the funds to focus on colony reconstruction. We have been working with the Latin American Mission for years now. This abandoned colony has been used as our headquarters. Currently, there are fewer than one thousand people here. We have a well-staffed infirmary, intelligence base, and housing for the couriers and the exiled."

"So how do the Colonies not suspect anything?"

"Many of the colonists use research as a cover. Marissa did. She was one of the analysts."

"She was one of the data miners? She was analyzing the VL system? So you think that they suspected, and that's why . . ."

My mother sighs. "Can't be proved. It was risky. We've been using secret codes to send information to other colonies through research papers for years. As well as Morse code with ballooner ads—eye blinking, that is."

"You're kidding me."

"No. And it's the same with Sayon. Our front is research as well. We have a station just outside the city to watch for meteorites and asteroids. One thing the Colony system lacks is a sophisticated program to watch the skies for meteorite and asteroid activity like they once had before the coastlines were washed away. We keep them informed with reports; they open trade for us and waive taxes."

"Sounds like a good deal."

"It's working for us. The earth crumbling around them has made colonists pretty paranoid, which keeps them motivated. We've been able to take advantage of their hyper-vigilance by providing them with information about one area they are unequipped to keep their finger on—the sky. They feel pretty in control of what's beneath them but don't have the resources to keep watch above. We've provided some fabricated data that suggests we've had some near misses with asteroids. They feel safer knowing we're watching out for them, and that keeps us valuable to them. What they don't know is that we have essentially been a watchdog operation for the UN for the last ten years."

"Smart," I say.

"And Cherish, as you know, has been training couriers. Nicholas has been heading up that program since the beginning. It's why I sent you there, for your training, of course."

No, I hadn't known they were training other couriers. Mom might know that I spent some time with Radius, but she doesn't know the extent or the fact that I only stayed at Cherish for a day. Nor does she know about Mr. Porter. And I'm not sure she's ready to hear about either. "Mom, about Cherish —"

"But we are limited here in what we can do. The colonies have made it nearly impossible to get any sort of information due to the sophistication of their surveillance protection. For ten years we have relied heavily on couriers to do our work. It was the least risky system for being detected. But it was also the most primitive. Maybe that's why they never suspected. For *ten* years it worked. We've had some pretty roughed up couriers, but few causalities."

"Until they started catching on."

"Yes," my mother says sadly.

"They caught on to Nicholas." I say gently. "He was killed not long after you were exiled."

My mom's eyes get wide.

"And I didn't stay at Cherish for long—not even long enough to receive proper training." I rub my hand along the scars on my neck. "Actually Will didn't train me at all."

My mother's shock is clear. "I see," she says flatly. "You're telling me that you and Grayson—"

"Gray kept me in hiding for months when I escaped from the Pulse a year later. The colony must have thought I had disappeared into the Pulse. I was never suspected, or they thought I was in too deep, under the care of a hawker. Gray found your documents and a Pulse citizen, one of Marissa's friends, provided supplies."

My mother covers her mouth and stifles a sob. "I'm so sorry," she whispers.

"It wasn't your fault. It could have been even worse if they had discovered I was undergoing training from Mr. Porter or Will, maybe."

My mother wraps her arms around me and holds me for what feels like minutes. "It's a miracle you made it."

"There are more girls there, like me."

My mother takes my hand. I can feel her trembling.

"I'm ok, Mom," I tell her confidently, though shame overtakes me. "Mom, I'm so sorry. I did terrible things. I said terrible . . . If you knew everything about that year you might not forgive me."

I cry so hard I gasp for breath.

"Shh," she soothes, rocking me in her arms. "There is nothing you could ever do that would stop me from loving you. Rebecca, it wasn't your fault." She pulls me away and looks me in the eye. "It's how you finish, not how you begin. You are finishing a conqueror." She looks at me fiercely. "It's how you *finish*."

I straighten. She is right. Like a fever breaking, my shame lifts from me. Radius will always be a part of my story, but this isn't the end.

I wipe my eyes. "It's how you finish," I repeat.

We spend as long as my dwindling strength will allow me to walk around Sayon. I play Anna's game that she played as she walked in Colony 2020, of not thinking about what it was, or what it is, but what it *will* be. One day it will be the glittering colony I saw in my mind before I came here. I play the game on myself too—I don't see myself as I was, or as I am now, exhausted and in pain from the journey. I see myself as healed and whole, walking these streets with Grayson.

My mother turns from me and opens brass doors into a large building with faded but luxurious décor—painted murals now chipping on the walls, mosaic tiles, and sparkling, heavy chandeliers.

"This place was spared somehow. It was once a theater," she says absentmindedly. From the lobby we move into the theater house where an audience sat years ago. It's been stripped now and filled with rows of cots. "We'll stay here if it's ok with you."

I pick out a bed under a balcony and lay down upon it. "I could make this work." It's better than sleeping on rocks under a mosquito net.

A few other people mill about and occasionally whisper something to each other in our direction. "Are they couriers too?" I ask.

My mother nods. "Not that one," she says, pointing to a young boy about my age. "He's part of the transport crew that helps the exiled get back here. He was my guide here. And that woman there, she's a part of the stock crew for the reload stations."

"Mom, you didn't tell me how they're planning on getting the people out."

My mother sits down on the cot next to me and sighs. "There's going to be a war," she says soberly. "They won't go without a fight. And it will be deadly—they are well stocked with sophisticated weaponry. The retaliation will be swift." My mother puts her arm around me and squeezes me tight as though she's trying to shield me from the reality. "They will not go down without a fight."

Now more than ever I want Grayson by my side.

"Your father—"

I cringe.

"He's been working at the National Council in the Executive Colony for almost ten years."

"I know," I tell her, my words acid in my mouth. "I know what he did. He forced us out so that he could move into a position at the top."

"That's true," my mother confirms. "The greatest amount of evidence has been what he leaks to us. He was working with Sayon long before the VL system was introduced."

"Mom, he sold us," I say bitterly. "He planted explosives and made it look like an earthquake—"

"Yes," my mother says serenely. "There were four earthquakes actually, or what felt like earthquakes rather, all relatively mild."

"But how could he do that to us?"

"We needed an opportunity, so we had to make it." My mother takes my hand, but I can't look her in the eye. "Your dad didn't believe the assimilations were legitimate. He thought that people

321

were being pushed out. He had had connections with Southern Colony—Sayon—intelligence for years, and we had already been training our own intelligence and potential couriers for the event of our assimilation, which was going to come one way or another.

"Your father had been given maps of areas of high risk based on data that scientists here had collected. These differed from the National Council's data, which was rigged to make it look like certain colonies were at great risk. But we knew that with our colony having large natural deposits of copper and an abundance of natural gas, assimilation would be inevitable. Your father knew it, I knew it, and our trained intelligence was ready. The earthquake we created provided the opportunity for us to do it on our terms."

I watch my mother dumbfounded. It was a choice. My father had made a choice that had created a domino effect and resulted in ten years of suffering.

"Your father and I were very dedicated to ending the injustices of the colony systems and this was the only way. They had their eye on us anyway, Rebecca," she says solemnly. "It was inevitable. Either we would go on our own terms or we would be forced out. Your father had already spoken to the National Council representatives a full year before our assimilation. He explained to the Council that he had reason to believe, and reports from our own scientific investigations, that showed that the neighboring assimilations were based upon fabrication, that they were the Council's method of obtaining the colonies to sell resources to the highest bidder. Your father simply gave them an option—he, as a respected leader, would convince the people that this 'earthquake' put us at risk, and that he had decided as colony president that assimilation was the safest option for our viability. And in exchange, he would be allowed a position in the Executive Colony. Or—" my mother sits up straighter, "or he would out the Council. And we would have war."

"But why not then?" I ask feverishly. "Why not just out them? We would have fought."

"Yes, they would have fought. Some would have fought anyway, but not everyone—some would have been forced to fight. And if we had won, even some of the people who had fought would eventually have been corrupted and we might have found ourselves in the same position a generation later. We needed a way to determine what the colonists were made of—down deep did they have it in them to oppress, or give up everything for freedom?"

I nod. It was a test, then. Perhaps 108 had members whose hearts were willing to enslave others, and my father wanted them gone.

"And, at any rate, we were in no position to engage in a war—not that kind of war any way. Your father was bluffing. And probably the Council knew that," she says sighing.

"But regardless, no one wanted that on their hands; the National Council certainly didn't want that kind of war. For one thing," her face turns to disgust, "an outright war like that would have resulted in a genetic loss to the Council. It would have been a waste to the Council to be forced to kill the rebels whose genes could have been valuable, or whose expertise would have been needed to make them money. Make no mistake," she says raising her eyebrows, "they didn't mind killing us. They just wanted to make sure they had a pick in whom they murdered. They preferred the surgical removal that the VL system allowed rather than haphazard ablation."

I rub my hands together and clear my throat as it all comes together. My father was beating the Coalition at its own game. The National Council and the Coalition were using the VL system to determine who was valuable for making them money. At the same time, my father was using the VL system to turn their kingdom upside down and determine who he believed worthy to be saved.

"So your father took the blame so that we would not die—so that we would have a chance," she pauses. "Or at least a *choice*. And your father's request was granted. He successfully convinced them that he was selling his colony for power. They believed it, of course, because they had become so corrupted themselves that sacrifice seemed a foreign concept. And so your father was allowed a spot on the Executive Colony, and from there he gathered intelligence for the Latin American Mission Board."

I lie back on the cot and allow all this to settle in. "So Dad was in complete control all along. When we assimilated, everyone was then given a choice whether they wanted to gain citizenship to their new colonies."

"Exactly. And he would never take that choice away. He didn't want to force 108 to fight and he didn't want to force them to stay under his leadership if they didn't want to. And he couldn't allow the people who were already citizens to remain so without having a chance to know a different way."

I thought of Asa, a Pulse citizen who did not consider 215 his home after his friendship with Marissa.

My mother strokes my hair. "The only way for 108 to get to them was for us to join them and help be a presence that stood against Coalition values. That was the work we did at Cherish."

"And assimilation of 108 was inevitable unless we had an outright war?" I still can't fully let this fact in, but if it's true, we might have all been wiped out.

"It was a certainty."

My head spins.

I remember the pain on my father's face, the agony he must have gone through in taking the weight of the blame on himself. He drank from a cup that I would not have had the strength to sip.

"He did what he had to do to be in a position to help us one day," Mom says, "no matter how long it would take. And from where he was positioned in the Executive Colony, he has been able to be in control. He's been waiting for the right time for the Latin American Mission Board to step in. That time is coming soon. The Coalition and the colony members who have become loyal to them have made their own beds."

I cover my face with my good arm. I wasn't abandoned, I tell myself. He didn't do the pushing out, the corruption of the National Council did. My father just had the good sense to recognize it.

My father loves me.

My mother rubs me softly on my good arm. "It was almost unbearable for him, Rebecca. But he knew that thousands of people were relying on him."

My father is a hero. I know that, but it doesn't end the hurt.

"He's coming back, Rebecca. I know him. He will stop at nothing."

Representatives from Sayon left yesterday to present evidence of violation of international ethical standards in the attempted sale of persons. We wait anxiously to find out if we will have international backing to perform a rescue mission to deliver those whose names are on the list and bring the suspected plants, who are attempting a takeover, to justice.

If we are able to gain international support, there will be a standoff. The Colonies' military is strong, very strong. And they will have the support of the Coalition as well. Of course it's in the best interest of the international community to thwart any efforts for the Coalition to expand to North America. Though its expansion has been a gradual takeover, it would threaten the world economy and trade relations, and their combined military power could mean world domination. Surely the UN will vote to fight them.

On the other hand, my mother insists that it won't be quite so simple. Because the Colonies' military is so strong, countries might fear stepping into something that doesn't directly involve them. If that's the case, the Colonies and Coalition will continue to grow and thousands of people will be eliminated one way or another. Will the rest of the world really stand by to watch? My mother says maybe.

Sayon is no longer safe, either way. There's too much risk of a leak. Ships are already being prepared for our evacuation. Still, Grayson is not back. One of the best and swiftest couriers has been sent for the safe house hosts, although I'm worried about Pepper and Violet making the trek, and they have the farthest to go.

My arm and back continue to heal. Perhaps too much, as it is tempting to pack up and return to Grayson. A hundred times today I have considered how I will be able to sneak out to make the journey and bring him back. But I don't have the map anymore. All I can do is wait. And hope.

My mother allows me a hike to the top of the mountain in the cool of the morning. I stand on it and look toward where I hope Grayson is steadily making his way here. I climb a tree as I used to in our Our Colony by the river.

"Tell him I'm waiting for him," I whisper to the birds as I did in our Messenger Tree. I sit for an hour in the tree looking back over the landscape that unfolds to meet him. I do the same for the next four mornings. Still, he doesn't come. Nor is there word from the representatives, which buys me time.

We eat each night in the downstairs of what used to be the theater. It isn't the feast that I anticipated, but it isn't cold cornmeal mush and dried fish either.

"You aren't gaining back as much weight as I'd like," my mother tells me. "You aren't eating enough."

"It's been nine days and no word from Grayson. I'm worried that there might have been complications from the illness, and that's why it's taking so long. Or what if something else happened?"

My mother puts her fork of stewed tomatoes down and wipes her mouth. "Waiting is hard, Rebecca, but what can we do—"

"None of them have come back yet, Mom. I'm not even sure that Pepper and Violet can get back. The bridge was out. Grayson and I were lucky to have gotten across. Something doesn't feel right. There was an aircraft that flew over not too far from here."

"Yes, there have been several sightings. At first we thought it was a craft carrying trade goods. But those interactions are usually done over neutral waters at designated bases. Now the consensus is that those are more Coalition members getting ready to move into the colonies. The couriers have all been given orders to stay in Sayon. It's the longest they've ever been away and their colonies will be wondering where they are before too long."

"And what if they happen to see Grayson or any of the other safe house hosts?"

Mom takes my hand. "They're there to transport—not to search. They aren't military aircraft and likely don't have any expertise in identifying someone on the ground. Besides, it would be almost impossible for them to see anything on the ground during the summer. They'll be hidden by thick trees, even if they do fly directly overhead of one of the safe houses."

All the same, I don't like it. I have nightmares about masked men being lowered from the craft into Gabe and Cassie's camp. Secretly, I begin stashing food. I've made up my mind. If word comes back that we are to evacuate before Gray returns, then I'm not getting on that ship, even if that means hiking all the way back to find him.

This afternoon Jamie and Bear stagger wearily into camp. Leif, the courier they had sent to retrieve Grayson and me, met up with them at the safe house and sent them back. I run to give Jamie a hug. Now I have the opportunity to return her hospitality. I set up her bunk and bring salves back from the infirmary to tend her feet and sore muscles. Jamie has never hiked this far and had little time to prepare for it. In spite of her obvious exhaustion, she is all smiles. Of course I'm not the only courier she has served, and she is met by a small crowd, ready to spoil her.

"I'm sorry, Rebecca," Jamie says, shaking her head once I have a turn to talk to her. "He didn't come through before we left. Dad and I made sure there was plenty stocked in the house, though, for when he does."

"Thank you," I tell her sincerely.

Now that I have been given enough time to rest, the other couriers come to visit the girl who made it to Sayon with no training. It seems I am famous, though I know my presence here also reminds them of their friend Will Skycap's absence. Richard Glover, Will's hiking partner, is the first to introduce himself. He looks like a darker version of Will; they could have been brothers.

Richard shakes my hand and sits beside me on my cot. "Will would have been proud of you for continuing the race for him," he says in a soft voice that contrasts with his chiseled appearance. "Do you know what happened to . . ." He trails off and clears his throat before looking me in the eye. "How did they do it?" he asks more forcefully after collecting himself.

I hesitate. He deserves to know the truth. "They set his house on fire," I tell him as gently as I can, though it doesn't soften the blow by much.

Richard looks off as though he's searching the distance from the top of a mountain. He nods like a soldier receiving orders and rubs his hands on his knees before standing quickly to leave.

I have seen him several times since we met. Richard sits by himself, sober and focused. He looks like he's calculating how he will singlehandedly take down the Coalition. My mother says he is.

I am struck by the stark differences between each of my visitors. Michelle, a pretty petite brunette woman in her thirties, introduces herself over breakfast as one of the original trainers and immediately begins by asking for a detailed account of what I chose to carry in my pack. Michelle is all business and has the reputation of being the most skilled technical climber, although she looks more like one of the Threes teachers at Cherish. She was the only solo hiker—that is until me, of course. She furrows her brow in concentration and nods as I describe my pack's contents. "Could have been eliminated," she says periodically, each time I mentioned an item that she thought was too heavy to earn a place in my pack.

Billy looks like he should be a banker; maybe he was when he lived in the colony. His hiking partner, Toad, is thin and wiry, with long hair and a soft brown beard.

Each time I see him he slaps me on the back. "Snakes!" he booms. "How ya been, Snakes?" Then he laughs as though he's made a hilarious joke and throws his arm around my shoulders.

Billy always looks annoyed with Toad. "Could you kindly keep it down?" he asks dryly.

I don't know how they were able to hike hundreds of miles together. But apparently they've been partners for the past six years.

And there's the double-woman team—Eloise and Margaret, two women in their forties. Both were exiled and forced to leave behind young children whom they haven't seen for more than fourteen years. Of the lot, these two look the most gentle. Eloise is tall, with dirty blond hair streaked with silver. She's graceful in her movements and smiles warmly while Margaret, the more gregarious of the two, talks for both of them.

Margaret waves her arms wildly as she recounts the stories of near misses with hypothermia and sinkholes, and Eloise's two-week bout of diarrhea after their water filter broke. When I ask them why they chose to become couriers, Eloise darkens. "They took our kids," she says. Margaret nods as though that's the only explanation needed.

Zall and Frederick are in their sixties, though according to the other couriers, they are the fastest team. Both dabbled in cartography while they were part of colony life and were instrumental in creating the trail as well as the map leading to Sayon. They look like two serious professors, wiry and slightly hunched. It's difficult to tell them apart at first.

And then there's the husband and wife team. I meet them in the storage room when my mother, who has not stopped moving since she got here, insists that I help with taking inventory and prepping supplies in case we are evacuated.

"Hi," I say to the woman who is folding linens. "You're Anna's mom, aren't you?" She has the same serious look, wide set eyes, and pixie face as her daughter.

"Yes," she smiles warmly. "And I know you, you're Rebecca. I'm Lucille. My husband is over there—Michael."

"Anna took really good care of us—me and my hiking partner, Grayson. She nursed Grayson through mountain fever. Never left his side. It was easier leaving him, knowing that she would be there to take care of him."

Lucille beams with pride. "She's a good girl. Cassie and Gabe are pretty good folk too. They've certainly been angels to our Anna. Grayson is in good hands." Lucille returns to folding. "Rebecca," she says without looking at me. "They need to come back here to be safe. They sent someone to look for you and bring the safe house hosts back, but I have a bad feeling. The time is too close."

"I know. I'm concerned. I've even considered going to get him." I say it lightly to test what Lucille will say in response.

Lucille turns to me and raises her chin. "We're not evacuating without Anna. They could get caught in the crossfire if there's retaliation. We'll be leaving soon to get her." She speaks in a low voice and does not break her rhythm in folding.

"Then I'll go with you."

Lucille sighs. "I'll have to talk to Michael—"

"No, I'm going. With or without you."

"No offense, Rebecca, what you did was heroic, but there was a lot of luck involved. Michael and I have done this now for more than eight years. You're still inexperienced—lucky, but inexperienced—and now you're injured. It will be faster if we go it alone."

I meet her eyes. "With or without you."

Lucille studies me intently. "I'll talk to Michael. No promises."

At breakfast the next morning, Lucille sits with me on the bench and takes a bite of her apple. "We're leaving tomorrow morning. Waited long enough," she says with her mouth full.

"So, is this an invitation?"

"You have to keep up. If you can't, we still have to keep our pace." She stands up quickly. "Oh," she says, turning to me. "Michael stole you a pack."

I have to tell my mother. My heart pounds. This is it. Never again will I do to her what I did to her in the New Colony. I won't ever deceive her again. I know too that she will stop at nothing to find me if she thinks I could be in trouble. Surely then, I tell myself, she will understand why I have to go back for Grayson.

I find her in the infirmary packing boxes for the evacuation.

"Mom," I say, my voice cracking.

Each time I see her now, her face brightens as though I've come back from the dead and she's seeing me for the first time. She puts her arms around me and holds me in a tight embrace. I squeeze her and take in the scent that immediately delivers me home.

"I know," she whispers.

I pull away. "What do you mean, you know?"

"You're leaving."

I can tell there is hurt in her eyes, but there is pride too.

"I want you to understand. I have to, Mom. After everything he's done for me I cannot—I will not leave him behind if we evacuate."

My mother brushes my hair away from my eyes. "Of course you won't. You have so much of your father in you."

I hug her until the tears come. "I'm going to be ok," I say for myself as much as her.

"I know you will. That's why I convinced Michael and Lucille to take you." My mother smiles coyly.

Chapter 30

The pack Michael stole was completely stocked with the very best of equipment—fire starters, lightweight but better shoes, an assortment of supplies to tend our feet, and bags of water with a long tube to drink from instead of the clunky water bottles. The weight is more balanced and my back is not screaming out in agony as it was before.

"I could have hiked it twice if I had all these things," I tell Lucille, who has become a fast friend.

"Huh, that's funny," she says. "There's no copperhead repellant in here with the toilet paper." I blush. Michael snickers and walks ahead quickly.

We make good time—twenty miles a day. Even with my arm and back still sore, we are able to make it to Bear and Jamie's house within five short days. The pull I felt as I walked away from Grayson is now even stronger in drawing me back. It's the same for Lucille.

"We were able to see her twice a year—on the way down and again on the way back from Sayon," she tells me once we hit the road. "My baby girl. We were lucky, you know. Most people haven't seen their children since their assimilations."

"Like Eloise and Margaret."

"Right," she says. "Best four days of the year. Those days fuel hundreds of miles—reminds me why we signed up for this crazy thing."

"Well, the day is coming when it will be permanent. You'll have Anna all the time."

Lucille covers her face and shakes her head up and down. "The day is coming!" she yells to the road.

Lucille and Michael slip into steady routine as they set up camp. There is very little that is spoken, or needs to be spoken, between them as they set up the tent, prepare dinner, and build a fire. At night we sit around the flames, so tired that the only energy we have left is to stir our rehydrated food.

Bear and Jamie's house is very well stocked. It feels strange to enter their home without them—it doesn't even feel like the same house. "Should be only another two and a half days until we're there," I say.

"I think we could make it in even less time," Michael speaks in a deep, faraway voice.

"Maybe." Lucille looks worried. "We want to get there safely though, Michael. It's bothering me that they haven't come back yet. Leif was sent more than two weeks ago. He should have made it there days ago. Either something happened to them coming down, or he didn't make it up."

Goosebumps travel down my back. The powerful waters of the flash flood invade my mind, but I push the thought out quickly.

"They're fine," I insist. "There's been a hang-up is all, but that's why we're going there, right? We're going to bring them home."

Lucille smiles uncertainly. "In less than a week, we'll all be here in this house together."

Michael takes her hand. "That's right," he says. But I hear the anxiety in his voice.

The next two days of hiking are brutal. Though Lucille and I typically pass the miles by talking, both of us are becoming increasingly on edge, although neither one of us speaks it. Even with better supplies and food, the twenty miles a day are taking a toll. At night I notice how badly Michael's feet are faring. He's lost two toenails already. Lucille has been stopping more frequently than usual and rubbing her back. She cried out in pain once when she took a small stumble. Something is hurting her, and badly, but she doesn't mention it.

"How does it work being a courier?" I ask her. "I mean, where do you live when you aren't transporting messages?"

"In our colonies."

"They don't know you're missing?"

"Nope." Lucille smiles. "The suckers."

"But how in the world do you manage that?"

"Simple enough. I'm a teacher. Summers are off for me. Another one of the rebels takes over my Contour Sheet. She makes me look like a recluse for three months and manages my house to make it look like I'm home. I make it my job, because it is my job actually, not to have many friends—stick to myself, don't get too close to anyone. Every colony is different, but mine had a tunnel out. It's amazing what you can put past people so long as you do it right under their noses."

"And Michael?"

"Same thing. Teaching position at the college. He does 'research' over the summer. One of the rebels there writes and submits papers for him. But he's in a different colony than I am. We have to be extremely careful about our timing to meet up since we don't have any communication otherwise. Yeah, summer vacation is my favorite."

"So you bring the data from two different colonies?"

"Yep."

"And the other couriers?"

"Some do as we do. Not many of them though are as lucky. Michael and I were perfect candidates. We were chosen because it would be easier for us to get out for enough time each year to make the journey. As a result, we're the second-fastest courier team—but Michael is even faster. His colony is farther north. He has almost fifty miles before he meets me, and he does it in a day and a half. Runs part of it. We have to get back before classes start in the fall."

Lucille and Michael are both lean and muscular. They look like they're built for speed. For them, it's a race. "We aren't faster than Zall and Frederick, mind you. Those guys are machines. They live in the Membrane throughout the rest of the year, maintaining the trails and leading the team that stocks the resupply stations. Like them, some of the others faked their deaths and now live out in the Membrane or Sayon."

Michael, who must be a quarter mile or more ahead on the road, turns to us and begins waving his arms. As we walk I hear the deep roar of aircraft. Michael's yelling something, but I can't make out what.

"Rebecca!" Lucille yells and grabs me by my pack to pull me off the road. "Get down! Now!"

I dive for the underbrush and cover my head as it passes. I can't tell if the earth is trembling from the thunder of the aircraft, or if I'm just shaking.

"It's traveling low," Lucille remarks from somewhere down by my feet.

Michael is out of breath when he reaches us. "I don't like it," he says with his hands on his knees.

"My mother said it was the Coalition sending in more citizens. Just another sign of the takeover. She wasn't worried," I tell them, also trying not to sound worried.

"It didn't look military," Lucille adds.

Michael looks off into the distance, following the streak the plane left in the sky. "Still, I don't like it," he murmurs. "We're too exposed on the road."

We walk the rest of the day in complete silence. Michael drops back to walk with us. Lucille and I try to pick up speed to keep with Michael's swift pace, but it's more like a run for our short legs.

Some time after noon, Michael stops abruptly. Lucille and I instinctively make our way to the side of the road, ready to dive for cover. But no matter how hard we strain, we can't hear anything.

"Michael?" Lucille whispers to her husband. "What's the deal?"

He points his arm out toward a bend in the road.

"There's nothing there," she says. I strain my eyes looking for a wild animal.

Michael throws down his pack and begins to run toward it. "What are you doing?" Lucille calls after him. Then I see it—a booted foot sticking out from the underbrush.

Leif is the second dead man I've ever seen, but he is almost unrecognizable as a person. He must have been dead now for well over a week, and his face is distorted, bloated, and covered with flies. He has been shot through the torso multiple times, but it looks like animals have also been working on him. I cover my mouth and gag.

"From above, I would guess. They shot him from above." Michael wipes his face with a hand thoughtfully as he searches the clear sky.

Lucille crosses her arms and stands on the road. "We need to get there. *Now*," she says, her voice quavering.

We hike our longest day so far—a full thirty miles. I'm exhausted, and even without taking my boots off to check, I know my heels are bleeding. My back is in agony, and I wonder if it's the old stress fractures, or if I've developed new ones. It's well past sunset when Michael announces wearily that we have a few miles remaining. "Right through here," he says. "And watch your step. Especially you, Rebecca."

The last time I had been frantically searching for the safe house. Now that we're this close, I'm anxious for what I might find. None of us has said it aloud, but finding Leif has made us all wary of what we will find once we do arrive at the safe house. I can hear Lucille sniffing as she pushes through the labyrinth of thick underbrush. Michael mutters curse words under his breath as he walks. I'm numb and push on steadily.

Suddenly a gunshot rings out in a deafening crack. "Stop *right* there," a man calls from a far distance into the night.

We shine our flashlights wildly but can't tell where the voice is coming from. I put my hands up.

"We don't mean any harm," Michael calls back, but I notice he has a gun drawn as well.

"I'm not the only one pointing a gun at you right now. I'd put mine down, if I were you," the voice calls from the dark.

Michael stands his ground. My heart pounds. I consider turning off my flashlight. Surely from the distance he won't be able to see me. That there is more than one gun pointed at us could be a bluff. We stand in silence for some time without moving. All I can think of is Grayson. This man has Grayson.

"What did you do with the people here?" I yell angrily.

"Rebecca?" It's a woman's voice.

"*Cassie*? Cassie, is that you?"

"Well for goodness' sake, Gabe," she says.

I can hear Lucille let out a ragged breath beside me. "It's Michael and Lucille! Rebecca's with us!" she yells.

"Mommy!" Anna's sweet voice pierces the darkness.

Lucille and Michael scan their flashlights wildly until they land upon the small golden girl running toward their silhouettes in the moonlight. Michael and Cassie follow behind.

I throw my pack off and move quickly through the underbrush until I can see the clearing of the camp.

"Grayson!" I call his name several times without answer. I scan my flashlight over the shelter, the water bucket, and the smokehouse. Nothing. "Grayson?" I whisper.

What if he's not here? What if . . .? There by the woodpile, I can scarcely make out a form. I drop my flashlight and throw my arms around Grayson, who is kneeling on the ground.

"I'm home, Grayson," I say.

Grayson stands slowly and wraps strong arms around me, putting a large hand behind my head. He holds me so tight that it's hard to catch my breath. His face is damp as he buries it into my neck. "Thank you, God." His voice breaks.

I kiss his broad shoulders and every inch of his head.

I am home.

In the distance I can hear Anna and her parents laughing and crying as they make their way back to the shelter. Grayson takes my face in his hands and kisses me gently on the mouth.

Chapter 31

Though the effects of the fever are subtle, they are still there. Gray's face has become more chiseled from the weight loss, making him appear slightly older, as though time has sped up in the Membrane. He moves almost imperceptibly slower than he used to, and he runs his fingers through his hair more frequently—like he does when he's deep in thought or nervous. Maybe it was the fever that changed him. Or maybe I changed him. We have not spoken about the morning I left. I still see hurt in his eyes, but I see forgiveness as well, and that's all I can ask.

He strokes my hair in the dark outside the shelter as I tell him about the flood, Jamie and Bear, and the last stretch of the journey.

His brow furrows when I explain the snakebite. "Copperhead?" he asks anxiously after I recount the description of the snake that bit me. He looks even more worn after my story. Grayson covers his eyes with his hands and exhales in a long, slow breath. "I should have been there," he tells the darkness.

"I'm not going anywhere without you from here on out," I promise.

I tell Grayson every detail about Sayon and how he will be hailed a hero there. He looks off like he's picturing it in his mind and making the necessary adjustments to his own imagination's concept of it based on my description. And I tell him everything my mother had said about the Coalition, my father, and the time being near.

"And your mother's all right?" he asks.

"Made it back safe, yes. She's the one who made it possible for me to come back here for you. She was so relieved that you were ok." I explain to Gray about the network to get the exiled back as well.

Grayson closes his eyes. "Any chance that—"

"Your parents weren't there, Gray. But we'll find them. The borders between colonies will be coming down soon."

To my surprise, Pepper and Violet are also here. In stark contrast to Grayson's pensiveness, Pepper is as jovial as ever. "Well, it certainly took you's long enough," he says, slapping me on the back.

"How did you get here?" I ask, hugging him warmly and laughing.

Violet takes my face into her weathered hands and kisses me on the cheek. "We could feels it in our bones," she says. "Something weren't right. Nevers before. *Nevers* have we waited that long for the couriers to come back, especially not Michael and Lucille."

"It's time," Michael says soberly with his arm around his daughter's shoulders.

"We knews it," Pepper nods. "In our bones."

Cassie hurries about the shelter, bringing us water and steaming bowls of soup. Michael, Lucille, and I practically collapse on the floor when we get into the shelter. I lean against Grayson as I eat, grateful for how peaceful I feel for the first time in so long.

"Truth is, so many planes went overhead that we were preparing for the worst," Gabe says. I can see in the candlelight how serious he has become. "We waited for word, but nothing. Planned on leaving the day after tomorrow if we didn't hear anything by then. We were getting our supplies ready."

"They weres worried about me and this young spry lady," Pepper says, rolling his eyes. "How do you thinks I made it all the ways here?" Pepper holds up both of his feet and makes marching motions in the air as he lies on his back. "They're workings just fine. We're ups for it, aren't we, Violet?"

"Oh, hush up," Violet snaps. Pepper purses his lips at his wife.

"You all did well," Gabe says curtly. "That was a dangerous trip you made. We were making plans to come and get you, but it took us longer than we anticipated to repair the bridge. Less time than it would have, thanks to Grayson here." Grayson drops his eyes to the ground and smiles.

"A messenger was sent for you more than a week ago—he was coming to escort you to Sayon," Michael says soberly. "We're evacuating as soon as we get word from the UN. For all we know, it's already happened."

"No messengers arrived." Cassie shoots Lucille a troubled look. "Who did they send?"

"Leif," Lucille returns sadly. "He was able to reach Jamie and Bear, who made it back safely. But we found him on the side of the road not too far from here—shot dead."

Anna covers her mouth and buries her head in her father's shoulder.

Pepper nods solemnly. "He was a goods one."

"I don't know that we can go back that way." Lucille scrapes her bowl with the wooden spoon. "It's too open. I think someone is watching."

"Four days ago they came. You're right, they're looking out," Cassie says. "And we've been watching them. They're resurrecting the colony they gutted. They'll be watching this area from now on."

"So then, what can we do if we can't get back that way?" I ask.

Pepper raises his eyebrows up and down. "We finds anther way."

Planes continue flying over throughout the night. The sound is different, though. It isn't the deep roar that we heard before. It's a shot—like a missile being fired through deep waters.

"*That's* military," Violet says from her pallet on the floor. Grayson and I sleep head to head. He reaches back to put a hand on my cheek reassuringly.

"But whose military?" Cassie asks. "The rebels'?"

"Let's hopes so," Pepper says. "If it's not, it means they've gottens wind of what we're up to."

"Either way, the evacuation might have already happened. If not, then Sayon is trapped," Cassie says.

"Let's hope the evacuation has already happened," I whisper.

"Then *we're* trapped," Gabe points out. "Sayon has been ready for years. There's a whole underground fall-out shelter that will last for months. They'll be pretty snug in the case of a bombing."

"Hey," Cassie says, looking at Anna, whose eyes are wide in the dim light of the lantern she is holding. "Tomorrow will be a long day, and we all need to be prepared for whatever it may bring."

I ease back down into my sleeping bag.

"Shh," Grayson says, stroking my hair. "She's safe."

"I know," I lie.

We are awakened the next morning, before the sun rises, by the distant sound of thunder. Cassie is already laying out breakfast—flat bread, dried meat, and some fresh berries. "Eat quickly," she instructs.

"There's going to be a storm," I tell her. "Do you hear that?"

"Ain'ts no storm like *you's* thinking," Pepper says. "Those are explosions. It's abouts time to go."

"*Eat*," Cassie says, ignoring Pepper. "Don't know when we'll get much of a chance later."

In spite of a sleepless night and the exhaustion from the day before, everyone is up and ready within minutes. We eat without tasting.

"Make sure your water bottles are filled to the top," Gabe instructs.

"Where are we going?" I ask. "Where *is* there to go? We can't stay here if Leif was already sighted. We can't take the south road if the Coalition has caught wind of anything. And I'm not really willing to head back toward the sound of those bombs."

Plus, I'm not sure how much distance we can make with Grayson, who doesn't look completely restored to health. Neither he nor Gabe or Cassie are used to hiking these distances. And then of course there are Violet, Pepper, and Anna—too old and too young to keep up very well.

"We're goings east, past the gutted colony. They're already swarmings it according to Gabe here. That's onlys a matter of miles away," Violet says.

"We'll have to make good time for that—" Lucille begins nervously. She must be thinking the same thing I am.

"Oh, we's will indeed," Violet laughs and slaps her knee.

I'm so exhausted today that I can't imagine going one more mile. I throw my hands in the air. "Perfect. So you have a jet we can take or maybe a—"

"Boat," Gabe interjects.

Anna glows with excitement. "Cassie and I stole it from the colony after the Coalition left and added it to our emergency supplies," she gushes.

Less than an hour later we're all standing on the side of the river holding a yellow inflatable raft. I have my doubts but few options.

"Everyone in," Gabe says, pointing his thick finger at the craft. Grayson and Michael hold it steady while we climb in carefully.

"Tie your things down as well as yourself," Cassie yells as she tosses us ropes that we loop through the nylon handles on the rubber seats. More bombs go off in the distance.

"Are they closer than this morning?" Anna asks. Her mother shakes her head, but Grayson gives me a troubled look and nods subtly.

Grayson, Gabe, Lucille, and Michael each take a paddle.

"I'll trade out," I tell Lucille.

"Won't be much to it right now," she says. "Current is doing most of the work. Your job is to cover us with this in case anyone spots us, got it?" Lucille hands me a dark green tarp. "We're bright yellow out here—might as well have flashing lights. This will helps at least a little."

Ironically, the water that almost took Grayson's life and prevented us from going any further now provides an escape route for us. We drift along silently, each of us scanning the bank for signs we are being watched. But only silent trees look back.

Anna sits upright as we glide down the river. How different her life has been. She has had no other children to play with. No wonder she's so serious. I hope that once this is over, she will be able to have a small world with other little girls, and her mother and father to go home to. I smile. Maybe that's what I want too. What will any of our lives be like after this is over?

"Get down!" Pepper yells.

Faintly in the distance I can hear the hum of a plane. I fumble to cover us with the tarp, made more difficult by the wind. The four paddlers each grab an end, and we huddle under it.

"It's ok," I reassure Anna.

The plane passes quickly.

"Military," she mouths to me.

What a remarkably brave little girl.

"Gone now," I smile.

The river bends and curves like a giant snake. We ride it throughout the day, too seasick to eat much and too hot to talk. We run our hands in the river to splash water on our faces, but it must be well over one hundred degrees today, and it doesn't help much. Cassie had the forethought to bring a basin for relieving ourselves, and we take our turns crouching in the back of the boat and then washing it out in the river. Although most of us have been able to hold off on using it any more than twice during the day, Pepper visits the basin almost hourly, crawling over the rubber seats to get to it.

"How abouts you just sit back now?" Violet asks irritably on his fifth break. "You're liable to falls out and you're tanglings me with your danged rope!"

Lucille and I take turns manning the paddles, and Cassie steps in for Grayson when he looks too fatigued to keep steering. More than a half dozen times I cover us with the tarp as military craft soar overhead.

Pepper peeks out from the edge of it. "Can't tell whose sides they're on," he says.

Above the roar of the river, we hear more explosions in the distance.

We ride into the night. Cassie and I sit at the head to shine our flashlights in front. Michael and Gabe must be exhausted, but they continue on without complaint. It's almost midnight when Gabe says he can't take it anymore. He's got to get some sleep. We decide to have two paddlers, mostly to steer in two-hour increments while the other paddlers rest. Lucille and I volunteer to go first. Almost immediately Gabe and Michael are asleep, curled up in the foot of the boat.

Grayson keeps his hand on me as I row. "I'm taking over in a little while," he says.

"I'm fine, I promise," I tell him. Grayson still looks weak. He moves slower, and I'm worried that this trip will cause him to relapse with his sickness. I'm tired, but alert. Overall I'm in much better shape than Grayson. A new energy courses through me like the river itself. It will soon be over. One way or another, it will soon be over and something new will begin.

The full moon is out, casting a warm glow upon the dark waters. I have no idea where we are going or what we will find, but somehow I feel that everything is as it should be.

Lucille and I fight to keep our eyes open during our last few minutes of our shift. "What do you suppose we'll find when we get to where we're going, wherever that is?" I ask her.

"A new kingdom," she says without looking up. "The world will be new when we make it through this." She sounds like her daughter.

"How can you be sure?" I ask.

Lucille smiles and looks up into the sky as she paddles. "For the last ten years my life has been divided into two parts—walking toward my daughter and walking away from her, which is more than most any of the other people can say in the colonies. But always I've been moving toward this new kingdom. I've never lost sight of it, and that is what has kept me going. I can't see anything else."

Lucille puts her paddle in her lap as we approach a straightaway in the river. "You know, Rebecca, your father saw it too, as clearly as if he were on top of a mountain looking out while the rest of us were still in the valley. None of this will be new for him, though it will be for everyone else. He saw it years ago and knew what he had to do. None of this would have been possible if it weren't for your father."

I look up at the moon winking back at me through the trees. "Do you think my dad's life is divided into moving toward me and moving away?"

Lucille puts her paddle back in the water. "No, I think *your* life is divided into moving away from and toward *him*."

Grayson wakes me up for my paddling shift as the sun rises the next morning. Cassie looks like she is still asleep as she tosses us more flat bread and dried meat.

"When do we stop?" Anna asks.

"Soon enough," her father soothes.

"Do you smell that?" she asks.

"Yes, mores dried duck. My favorite," Pepper says sarcastically.

"No, it smells like smoke." Anna's voice is thin.

I tilt my head back and take in a deep breath through my nose. "Maybe," I say. "But just faintly."

By midmorning, it is undeniable. Violet is the first to point out the smoke billowing in thick, ominous clouds in the distance.

"Do you think we have to go through there?" Cassie asks Gabe, who doesn't answer.

By lunchtime, the ash begins to collect upon the boat, turning it speckled. By midafternoon, it is a certainty that we are heading toward the fire.

"We've got to get around it," I tell Grayson.

He shakes his head. "We're safest here in the water."

As we turn a bend in the river, we see not just a fire, but a conflagration, consuming trees and underbrush. The air is thick with ash, and it burns our lungs with each toxic breath we take. I can feel the heat on either side, but the air is so thick with smoke that I cannot see more than a couple feet in front of me. Violet puts her hands in the river to cup out handfuls of water to douse a pale and trembling Anna. "Keep yours head down, sweetie," she tells her. "We don't want a sparks coming this way."

"Row faster!" Michael calls, and the crew picks up speed. Through the haze I can see the paddlers attacking the water with rhythmic thrusts. A fox swims past, his head bobbing in and out of the water. The fire roars on either side of us. "Steady now!" Michael yells over his shoulder before breaking into a coughing fit.

It can't be much farther, but there's no sign of a clearing. The wind blows in from the west, and we wipe our eyes against the sting of the ashes. Anna begins to cry at the bottom of the boat.

"Ho!" Cassie yells to Gabe. "A tree! In the water, Michael, look!" Cassie points wildly at a dark, diagonal log ahead.

I blink my eyes hard and squint to make it come into focus.

"Right! Right! Right!" Michael and Gabe yell together.

Grayson and Michael grunt from the left side of the boat as they paddle harder to move the craft to the right. Gabe and Cassie move over to the left side as well and thrust their paddles into the water.

"Pepper! Rebecca! Violet! Shift to the right side to balance us out!" Cassie orders.

I obey and lay flat against the side.

"Harder!" Grayson yells to the paddlers. The tree is aflame where it is above water, and the rest of it lurks dangerously below the surface with branches ready to slice through our rubber boat.

Violet tears off a piece of her skirt, dips it into the river and tells Anna to put it over her mouth.

"Come on!" Lucille and I call to the paddlers. "*Harder!*"

They paddle furiously. I hold my breath in apprehension as another tree on the left side of the boat falls near the bank, just missing the water. Grayson and Gabe grunt from the strain.

"Harder!" Lucille yells. Anna whimpers in her arms.

We miss the tree by a matter of feet. Cassie and Gabe slide back to the right side and Lucille and I take their paddles to relieve them.

"You ok?" I call to Grayson and Michael.

As best I can tell, they nod.

We row for perhaps another mile, coughing and shaking and wiping our bloodshot eyes. The smoke begins to clear and we pass the charred remains of trees pointing upward to the dark sky. Cassie and Gabe take over for Michael and Grayson, who collapse onto the floor of the boat.

"You dids good," Pepper says, handing them some water.

The bottle shakes as Gray drinks. He leaves behind a red handprint where he held it with raw and bleeding hands.

We ride into the second night putting as much distance as possible between the fire and us. Again, Lucille and I take the first watch. My stomach aches miserably, but I don't ask for more food.

Cassie has taken care of rationing, but it's not enough calories to sustain us for long. Just stay the course until dawn, I tell myself. Just stay steady.

After two days on the raft we are sore and stiff from our positioning. We take turns stretching out. Luckily, Cassie also had the forethought to bring some sunblock, but I can feel my skin bubbling on the back of my neck where I must have missed a spot. I run my tongue against brittle lips. My back is burning as though it has also been ignited. I stomp my left foot as numbness sets in.

By the morning light we can see that the river has opened to a broader ribbon. There are more rolling hills here, and it is more open than before. The water begins to rush even faster.

We know we're more vulnerable. No one speaks. Several more planes pass over, and I'm quick with the tarp. Bombs go off more frequently in the distance.

"It's coming from the northwest," Pepper says. "We were rights to get out when we did."

Cassie hands us our ration for the morning meal. I notice Lucille and Michael discreetly hand Anna a small bit of theirs in addition to her own. Grayson attempts to do the same for me.

"You need your strength to row," I whisper to him.

But he forces the extra food into my hands. "I feel good," he lies.

"The river's pickings up speed," Violet says, pointing a gnarled finger in front of us. "Somethings don't feel right."

Michael stares intently at the water up ahead. The rowers lift their oars and watch as debris in the water bobs up and down in the white caps.

"Somethings don't feel right to me neither," Pepper says. "I think we've gots to stop here."

"How can we stop?" Grayson asks as he leans to the side, scrutinizing the rushing force of the water.

"Do it now," Violet commands in a stable, firm voice. "Times to get off."

Though her words are calm, they spur the rowers to action.

"Pull right!" Gabe yells from the back right corner. He plants his oar down into the water as if it is a pick into rock. He growls as he fights the waters by rowing backward. Cassie also rows backward on her side while Grayson and Michael paddle furiously on the left. The boat shifts right but is picking up speed quickly.

"Harder!" Gabe yells.

What didn't feel right in Violet and Pepper's bones is now before us.

"What's that?" Anna asks nervously.

"Waterfall." I see Lucille's mouth shape the words, but they are drowned out by the roar.

"Straight ahead!" Violet points to a thick tree growing out of the side of the bank. "Lucille, Rebecca—you two catch it as we pass," she tells us calmly.

"We're not going to make it," I tell her. I feel the panic rising deep inside me, restrained only by my complete exhaustion.

"Quickly!" Lucille yells, taking my arm and dragging me to the front of the boat. Violet and Pepper move to sit with Anna, who is crying now. They hold her down to brace against the impact.

The rowers continue to grunt and yell against the force of the current. "You've got to turn it more!" I scream. The tree approaches more and more quickly. I shake my head. It's too far. It's too far.

"Ready!" Lucille yells in a deep voice.

We are twenty feet away.

Now ten.

"To the side!" Lucille points to a branch for me to hold onto, and I ready myself.

We collide into the tree. Lucille and I grunt as the trunk takes our breath when it hits us in the chest. I grab wildly at the branches that tear my face. Cassie throws her paddle into the boat and grabs onto the branches as well. "Pull!" she commands. Lucille, Cassie, and I are tangled in the tree, but it has stopped our boat.

"My feet are coming out from under me!" I start to panic. Pepper throws himself over the seat and grabs my legs.

We are a matter of ten feet from the edge of the bank. The boat lifts up in front, dangerously close to turning over.

Michael and Grayson throw their paddles into the boat as well and move to help us, but it offsets the balance, and I think for sure we are going to capsize.

"Sits down!" Violet shouts. "No ones move. Rebecca, Lucille, Cassie, you's have to pull us in."

We strain to ease ourselves over to the bank by inching our hands along the trunk of the tree. Michael and Grayson row backward, turning the boat sideways so that Gabe can then grab onto the tree. We are now within four feet of the bank.

"Harders!" Violet yells.

Two feet.

346

"Anna, darlings. Time for a leap."

Anna crawls to the back of the boat and waits, her face set.

When we are one foot away Violet nudges her. "Now, girls!"

Anna jumps gracefully to the land.

"Unties yourself," Violet tells her. "Now you's, Grayson."

The boat rocks as Grayson makes his way to the back and then jumps to the shore.

"Grayson pulls the rope that had tied him onto the boat and reties it around the tree. Next, Gabe and then Michael jump to the shore

"We're going to pull you all in now!" Grayson yells to the rest of us as the three men begin to pull against the rope.

Slowly, we loosen our grasp on the tree as we feel the boat being dragged against the current.

"Now, sit back!" Gray commands.

We ease down. I almost trip over Pepper. There is a bump, and the pull of the water is replaced by the rough of the ground. Grayson runs to take me out, and I can feel him shaking from exhaustion as well. My arms are so weak I can barely hold onto him. We fall onto the ground and gasp for more air.

Gabe lets out a loud whoop. "That's right!" he cheers.

I lay my head on Grayson's shoulder. I can't tell if I'm going to laugh or cry from the relief. I do both. Grayson kisses me softly on my forehead. He leaves bloodstains on my cheek from his blistered hands, and I notice I am also bleeding where the branches ripped at my arms.

Gabe stands at the water's edge and looks out to the impending waterfall. "Pepper and Violet," he says. "Sure am glad we brought you along."

For almost an hour we lie on the bank of the river and tend each other's wounds and blisters. My back is hurting from sitting for so long almost as much as it does from a day of hiking.

"What now?" Grayson asks.

But no one answers because no one knows. The bombing seems to be farther in the distance, and it doesn't seem to be moving any closer. Pepper calculates we have traveled more than one hundred and fifty miles southeast in just two days. For the moment, we are far away from the threat of bombs and biological warfare. We are safe, though I fear for the colonists who are so close to the fighting.

We refill our bottles and decide to build a camp for the night under the protection of the trees. Violet and Pepper give the orders. Grayson and I are assigned to rigging up a fort of some sort. We use the tarp as a cover and turn the raft upside down for a soft bed for Anna, Lucille, Pepper, and Violet. The rest of us will be sleeping on the ground on top of blankets. Pepper and Gabe go deeper into the forest to hunt. Michael and Cassie try their hand at fishing with the pole that Cassie had the forethought to bring.

Grayson and I go to explore the river farther down past the waterfall. One look at the cascade of water and I know that we never would have survived the almost ninety-foot drop. We stand in awe as the water crashes down. Grayson pulls me into his arms and holds me close. He kisses me softly on my forehead and runs his thick hands across my hair. "Tell me again," he whispers.

"I love you," I reply. With every fiber of my being it is true.

He kisses my mouth, my cheeks, my hair.

"Grayson, I'm sorry I left."

He pulls me in closer.

"It was the hardest thing I've ever done. I knew I had to—"

"Shh. You did what you had to. I know that."

I kiss him back softly and taste the salt on his skin.

"You did it, Rebecca."

I smile. "Yeah, I guess I surprised myself."

"Not me, Rebecca Flora," he replies.

"I'm told I have my dad in me."

Grayson and I hold each other close. Both of us broken. Both worn, hungry, exhausted, and in pain, but somehow whole at the same time. Suddenly Grayson pulls away.

"What's that?" He turns his head as though trying to decipher a sound.

"I don't hear anything. Just the water," I say, straining to listen.

"*That*," he says, and suddenly I hear the low hum too.

"Another plane?" I ask.

"Some sort of craft. Come on, let's head back and tell the others." Grayson jogs up the hill to where the camp is in sight. "Put the fire out!" Grayson yells. "Put it out!"

But already the others are scrambling to douse it with water and smother it with dirt.

The sound is getting louder, though we still can't tell where it's coming from. Suddenly, it is almost deafening. There, parallel to the waterfall, out over the river rises a helicopter. Grayson grabs my arm and runs with me into the woods.

"They've seen us!" I scream.

"Everyone scatter out!" Cassie yells. She and Michael help carry Violet into the thicker part of the woods. "Anna!" Lucille screams to her daughter. She grabs her by the arm and pulls her in the opposite direction. They disappear quickly into the woods as well.

Grayson and I run with the river to our back. We cut through the thick branches, which tear at our faces. I fall and catch myself with my hands and cry out in pain from a stab in my wrist.

Grayson turns to help pick me up. "We've got to keep going," he says gently.

We run until I feel like I might vomit.

"Over here, " Grayson says, pulling me behind an outcrop of rock.

We've got to be more than a mile away. I bury my face in his chest. By now we can no longer hear the whir of the helicopter blades.

"The others," I whisper anxiously.

"Everything's going to be ok. We're going to wait it out. We're not worth their time."

I exhale a ragged breath. "They'll give up looking for us. We're not worth their time," I repeat shakily.

Grayson covers my head and strokes my hair. "Shh," he soothes.

"This is wrong," I say. "We shouldn't have left Anna. We've got to go back!"

"No, it was better for us to split up. They saw *us*, but I doubt they even saw Anna and Lucille. Give it just a minute. We're going to hear the helicopter fly back over any minute." Grayson kisses my head absentmindedly as we both watch the sky expectantly.

After twenty minutes or so of hearing nothing, I can take it no longer. "Something's wrong," I whisper. "I'm going back." I try to stand up, but Grayson pulls me to him again.

"Down," he says sharply. "Quiet. What is that?"

I strain to hear. Grayson puts a finger up to his mouth to tell me to be quiet. His eyes are wide. I hear it now too—footsteps on the brittle leaves. Grayson pulls my head to his chest. I hear his heart beating rapidly.

The footsteps get louder.

"Rebecca!" a man calls in a low voice.

I turn to look at Grayson in complete disbelief.

"Rebecca!" he calls again.

I can feel the blood draining from my face.

"We know you're close, Rebecca. Come on out."

Grayson moves to cover me with his body. The man is almost upon us. Grayson whispers in my ear, "Who is he?"

I shake my head with eyes wide. "He called my name," I say so quietly that I almost mouth the words. Fear snakes through my insides.

"You run. I'll fight him." Grayson picks up a loose rock.

"Rebecca!" the man calls again.

Grayson mouths, "One. Two—"

"Rebecca Flora. We picked up your tracking signal."

I gasp and push Grayson to the side.

"My tracking device"—I run my finger behind my neck and stand up—"from before the assimilation . . ."

Grayson pulls me by the arm, but I'm already in sight of the man.

The man is dressed in a green jumpsuit. He has thick stubble and scratches on his face where he has also been scraped by the thick branches. He nearly falls over when he sees me.

"Rebecca Flora?" he asks.

"Yes."

"Rebecca, we've been searching for you."

Grayson steps in front of me protectively. "Who are you?"

"I was sent to retrieve Rebecca Flora."

"*Who* sent you?" Grayson's fingers blanche where he grasps the rock.

"My father," I whisper.

Chapter 32

As we ascend, the river becomes a silver ribbon fallen from the hair of some young girl. It twists carelessly, silently through the wood, and it appears so delicate that it might again be blown away in the wind as the girl plays, curling and lengthening in great wisps before it is released.

Grayson wraps his arms around me and holds me tight. We look back over the landscape, the earth that shook off a civilization only to be rebuilt in a strange and ultimately more destructive way. It's a remarkable thing, this world that remains, in spite of us and our corruption. The miles sprawl out seemingly forever. I picture myself walking over it. I am but a speck down there, but somehow it seems that all of this was created just for us. It's an unspeakable freedom that gives me significance and makes me feel infinitesimally small both at once.

Pepper and Violet hold hands in the seats in front of us and look at one another while the rest of us peer out the window. Occasionally Lucille covers her mouth and allows the tears held in for so many years to finally fall.

"Some of you are couriers?" the man asks loudly.

"Yes sir," Grayson says. "Michael and Lucille are—were. Rebecca, too."

The man's face breaks into a broad smile, and he looks me in the eye. "A courier, you say. No kidding." He shakes his head and looks out the window. "Well, I'll be damned. His daughter was a courier."

I smile humbly at him. "I was a sub."

"And the rest of you?" he asks.

"Safe house hosts, sir. Without them the couriers wouldn't have survived," Lucille says.

The man appraises each of us. "None of it would have been possible without all of you. Your data was taken from Sayon to our headquarters in Belize. We evacuated Sayon forty-eight hours ago. All of your friends are waiting in safety."

Grayson squeezes my hand. Mom is safe.

"Well, what's next?" Violet asks.

"The world was ready for this. We've been watching the Coalition for some time now. In Europe the Coalition had already been making military advancements in other countries. Their involvement in the colonies had been suspected, but thus far unproven—until this year, that is. The United Nations was not ready to risk a war unless we had clear and convincing evidence that their takeover was inevitable. This summer proved that it was. We now have proof of their plans, down to the names of the individuals they had chosen for elimination. We also have documentation of multiple evacuated colonies that we believe they were planning to use as a death camp as well as factory labor to feed resources back into the other colonies."

"We knew something wasn't right more than a year ago," Gabe says. "I sent word down with the couriers."

The man nods. "We were able to confirm. In fact, one colony had already sent more than two hundred people to the gutted colony. They have all since been retrieved. It seems the plan was to annihilate those who could not work, and force those who could into slave labor. We also have documented proof that contracts had been set up with certain trade countries for the sale of citizens. Some of the people whose names were on the lists you carried would have been sold to other countries as a commodity for the same purpose."

I pictured the children from Cherish being shipped to the colony the Coalition had gutted. Would they have been told they were being re-assimilated and hope to reunite with their families?

"Coalition citizens would then slowly move into the colonies once space had been made," he continued.

"So then, are we at war?" Grayson asks.

The man laughs. "Son, we've *been* at war for more than a decade. It's been going on right under everyone's noses in the colonies. But in Europe, there has been fighting for some time. Fear of a complete Coalition takeover was enough to unite the rest of the world to swift action." The man rubs his hands together. "Boy, were we ready. We hit them hard in the motherland. And thanks to your father, Rebecca," the man says, turning to me solemnly, "we knew exactly where every single weapon of war lay in the colonies. We knew their military size, strength, and positioning. To be honest, their power wasn't as significant as was widely believed. We were able to take them out with minimal casualties. As we speak, rebel forces are inside the colonies establishing a New

Order. Every person on that list will be accounted for. And every Coalition plant will be brought to justice."

"Just like that?" Pepper asks.

The man shook his head. "No sir. Believe me, it's ugly. Coalition plants aren't going down without a fight. It will take years to sort out and for the New Order to be established, but it's safe to say that the colony system will be abolished. Already the citizens have taken to breaking down their own walls."

Grayson puts his head in his hands. I wrap my arms around him as he shakes. "I'm going to see them again," he says between sobs.

"Rebecca," the man says softly. "The Executive Colony was the first to be attacked. It wasn't easy getting him out. Your father insisted that he be taken to Colony 215 to get his daughter, but records there showed that you had died."

"I did," I tell him.

The man laughs. "Your father sent us out to retrieve you. He assured us that you were very much alive. We've been searching for days now. It took some time for us to get close enough to pick up the tracker."

"Where is my dad now?"

"He's on his way."

The last time I passed over the colony I was being assimilated. I was a child and the city was a dazzling gem thrust into the faded nest of the Ancillary. Beautiful, celestial beings floated by on balloons, and the world below was one of promise and intrigue. The gem has been thrust out now, and the suspended, beautiful creatures now lay upon the ground. There is glimmer in the dust here. Hundreds of military uniforms line the streets to enforce the redemption that is finally coming to the non-citizens of the formerly sparkling colony. The rebels of my Old Colony knew this day was coming. Some of them gave their lives as they waited for it to come. And now that day has finally arrived.

Once, Colony 215 was my home. So much pain it caused, and yet as we circle over it at this height, it seems that all the troubles of the world below have become strangely dim in the hope for what I know it will become.

We land atop a high building.

"Rebecca?" a woman calls from the door.

My legs tremble beneath me.

"Yes!" Grayson yells above the hum of the helicopter when I cannot seem to find any words. "Yes, this is his daughter, Rebecca," he says.

The woman motions for me to follow her into a doorway. Grayson squeezes my hand and nudges me in her direction. "Go on," he prods.

I follow her down two flights of stairs to a silver door. "Right in here," she says. My heart pounds as I step into the room.

There by the window is a man leaning against the glass, his silhouette illuminated by the sun. As far as I've come, I cannot seem to make myself walk across the room. "Daddy?" I whisper.

He appears even larger than he did when I was a child. His hair has grayed, but his face still has the softness and strength that I have never forgotten.

"Rebecca." He calls me the name that he himself gave.

I'm so overwhelmed that I can no longer stand, and I fall to my knees in respect, in surrender, in love for this man. My father kneels beside me and wraps me in strong arms, as he did when I was a child.

"Daddy, I've come home."

"Well done," he says. "Well done."

Acknowledgements

I hope that in at least some way, this work will glorify my Lord Jesus. I daily drown in his grace, am transformed by his love, delight in his freedom, and conquer in his name. I owe him all, but he gives freely. One sweet day I long to hear him say to me, "Well done," as Rebecca's father said to her.

My most sincere gratitude to my high school sweetheart and husband, Tommy. Like Grayson, Tommy saw me for more than I was. He saw me as an author when I was too timid to write, and his confidence gave me the tenacity to write this book. Grayson's sweet spirit, protectiveness, determination, servanthood, intuition, and unconditional love were so easy for me to write because I have the gift of witnessing them in Tommy. Being his wife is one of the greatest privileges of my life.

Thank you to our four beautiful children for their patience as I balanced being Mommy and author. Grace, who inspired the character Anna, Benjamin, Jack, and Isabelle are my heroes. (The attentive reader will find each of the children written in as minor characters.) The messages of this book were largely written for them. May they always know their true worth and fight for a greater kingdom than the world can provide.

Thank you to my mother, Janet Lewis, who has always been my greatest encourager, taught me unconditional love, and has supported me through thirty-three years of crazy ideas and projects in addition to this one.

I am so grateful for the people who took the time to edit this work to make it what it is. Each of my editors is also a character in the book. My dad, Bruce Lewis, went above and beyond in helping improve the text. When I was a teenager he taught me about data mining, a topic he teaches as a business professor. I never expected that discussion to later be used as a cornerstone in a dystopian novel I would write more than a decade later. Glad I tuned in for that one, Dad, and now I'm wondering what other business discussions I should have paid more attention to . . .

Thank you to Stephanie Norton, my youth pastor from almost twenty years ago, who is still taking care of me by editing my book. Stephanie's insight transformed several sections of the book and helped breathe life into the characters. And much appreciation to

Robin Sartain, a friend on whose honesty I can always rely. I am so grateful for her beautiful gift of encouragement.

Thank you to my best friend, Michelle Pugh, whose adventurous spirit inspired Part III of this book. As an author herself (*Love at First Hike*), she provided incredibly helpful feedback to improve *A War Against the Cowbird*. But mostly I am grateful to Michelle for her rock solid friendship. As is fitting, Michelle is a courier and a trainer of couriers in the book.

And thank you to Anna Ottosen, an incredibly talented editor. I am so very thankful for her services in formatting and doing the very final edit.

I am so grateful for the work of Transforming Hope Ministries, an anti-domestic human trafficking non-profit in Durham, North Carolina, and for all the fellow warriors against human trafficking, especially Abbi Tenaglia, who believe in investing in our youth. I am humbled by the courage of all those affected by trafficking and for those who take a stand in ending it. And I am thankful for you, the reader. My hope is that in some small way *A War Against the Cowbird* inspires you, and that you will join in the war to end human trafficking.